ISLAND

ALSO BY ANNA-LOU WEATHERLEY

Vengeful Wives (published as 'Chelsea Wives' in the UK)
Guilty Wives

Pleasure ISLAND

ANNA-LOU WEATHERLEY

bookouture

Published by Bookouture

An imprint of StoryFire Ltd.
23 Sussex Road, Ickenham, UB10 8PN
United Kingdom

www.bookouture.com

ISBN: 978-1-910751-30-5
eBook ISBN: 978-1-910751-29-9

For Mum and Lisa

ACKNOWLEDGEMENTS

I wrote Pleasure Island during a personally difficult time in my life and it saved me in a way; it's for this reason it will always be a special book to me and why I'm proud of it.

I would like to thank my lovely editor at Bookouture, Claire Bord, for doing such an amazing job on the cover and for all her helpful comments, suggestions, guidance, belief and support – and to all the Bookouture family, Oliver Rhodes and the wonderful and prolific Kim Nash for all her help and hard work with publicity – proud to be part of such a great team.

Thanks also to my agent, Madeleine Milburn and Cara Simpson at the Madeleine Milburn agency.

Big love to my boys, Louie and Felix (mummy promises to write a book about you soon!) and to my amazing and supportive friends, LM, Sue Traveller (a keeper!), Kelly, Susie Rabbit, Andie, Michelle and Kringe in the 'Dam, and my new friend Erica - love you all. Also thanks to LDB.

In particular I would like to thank my beautiful sister, Lisa, who has been here for me in so many ways, her love and kindness is testament to the wonderful, strong woman she is. Ditto my amazing mum; I would not have got through the last year without your love, help and support and all your wise words. So, Mum and Sis, this one's yours.

'Pleasure and pain, though directly opposite are contrived to be constant companions.' Pierre Charron.

PROLOGUE

A hush instantly befell the room as Martin McKenzie made his entrance, his very presence enough to ensure it.

'Gentlemen ... and lady –' he spoke addressing them in a low, authoritative tone that could easily be mistaken for menacing '– so glad you could all make it, especially given our respective hectic schedules.'

Eight pairs of unfamiliar eyes watched him intently as he made his way across the non-descript room: plain, blue carpet; a large, oval meeting desk; and nine matching swivel chairs. An oscillating fan lightly churned and squeaked above them, the unforgiving strip-lighting making the faces of his eight guests appear slightly harsher than they usually might. Nine bottles of Evian water with accompanying glasses sat in the centre of the table. There were no other points of reference – no art on the bare walls, no soft furnishings – just a plain, cheap-looking white plastic blind covering the modestly sized window.

None of the eight guests had any idea where they were, or indeed exactly how they had got thereIt had been an operation of the highest subterfuge; picked up in darkness and flown in via private jet from an unspecified location, then collected by unmarked cars with blacked-out windows where they had been taken to another undisclosed destination. That was all they knew – all they were *allowed* to know.

'You'll forgive me for the lack of finesse,' McKenzie said, gesturing around him with what appeared to be genuine apology, 'but as we have all agreed, the less we know the less there will be to remember.'

The room remained silent save for the fan.

'Let me be perfectly clear on what that means exactly.' McKenzie pulled his trousers up from the knee as he finally took a seat at the head of the table, a slightly effeminate gesture that belied his large frame and foreboding presence.

McKenzie had worn the same suit for twenty five years without exception; bespoke made, Italian, black wool crepe, single-breasted, three buttons which he matched with a collection of coloured, plain, cotton shirts, in this instance, white. Aside from having little sartorial truck, McKenzie had more important things to be concerned with than fashion, despite the fact that the world's most prominent and successful designers were clamouring to dress him and thus put themselves on the map.

By default however, the suits – he owned at least one hundred, all of them identical – had become something of a trademark themselves, making him an unlikely fashion icon in the process, an idea that both amused and bemused him simultaneously.

The silence in the room was deafening but McKenzie was in no rush to amend it, savouring every moment of power it afforded him. Finally, a thought broke the surface of his mind and he held it there for a split second before addressing the group.

'We are all aware of the purpose of today's meeting,' he began, beginning to take in the faces of the strangers in front of him. Not that they meant anything to him; he had zero interest in what these people looked like and would never see them again after today. Like most evil, this meeting was simply a necessary one.

'There shall be no reference to what is spoken about in this room today to anyone else other than who is present; of this we must all be clear.'

The response came in a varied sequence of nods and low muttered agreement, which seemed to satisfy him.

'Good. First on the agenda ...' McKenzie shuffled a collection of marked A4 envelopes in his large, thick fingers, passing them to the woman – the only woman – on his left to distribute, which she duly obliged.

The woman interested him the most, and had done so from the beginning. She had been quite proactive, a key-player in getting the ball rolling for this little 'enterprise' of his. He glanced at her quickly, his astute eyes absorbing everything about her from her neat shiny brunette bob to her smart, navy, fitted skirt suit, the slightest hint of cleavage flesh, a flash of her lace underwear beneath. She was young, British by account of her accent, and in her 30s, though he suspected her slightly hardened features gave the impression of a more advancing age.

The rest of the Super Eight, as he referred to them, were as he suspected: a Japanese man; two Americans; a Frenchman; a German; and two Englishmen – all largely fat, balding and bespectacled, not forgetting rich, though financially he easily usurped them all put together ten times over.

McKenzie was the seventh wealthiest man in the world, his personal fortune outnumbering royalty, governments, oligarchs, Saudi princes and shipping magnates across the globe.

The undisputed 'King of Media', he had been widely credited for the birth of reality television and talent shows and had put some of the world's biggest superstars on the map. 'Making ordinary people extraordinary' was how he liked to put it – not to mention making himself beyond rich in the process.

The public had a fascination with him, ensuring he was both revered and reviled in equal measures, his unashamed epicurean lifestyle becoming something of an obsession to the press. McKenzie accepted this with good grace, however. He understood the game only too well; after all, he had practically created it.

'Second on the agenda ...' McKenzie cleared his throat. It had been a little on the tight side ever since the face-lift, leaving not only his skin taught, but his eyelids too. The surgeon had assured him this was temporary but six months down the line there had been little improvement. His wife, Elaine, had been complaining that it was creeping her out at night, him sleeping with his eyes half open. Her discomfort contrarily amused him, enough for him to be tardy in seeking some sort of correction.

'All guests have confirmed, as you can see. The plane leaves next week, as per the script.' McKenzie looked up. 'I trust we are all on the same page, yes?'

The sound of copy paper shuffling filled the small room.

'Let me continue ... please help yourself to Evian,' he nodded in the direction of the bottles on the table. As yet no one had touched them but following his comment a few tentative hands came forward. He noticed the woman's didn't.

'The pilot and crew have all been briefed ... and the casting for the staff completed. Please, read the script at your leisure, we've plenty of time for any questions at the end.'

At that point, a small grey-haired woman with a beehive hairstyle entered the room suddenly and unannounced. She was carrying a tray of pastries, apricot, Pain au chocolat, croissants and Danish rolls.

'Ah –' he said as he beckoned her forward,'– everyone, this is my wife, Elaine. Say hello, darling.'

'Your wife?' the woman expressed a degree of surprise, more than she'd have liked to.

While it was public knowledge that McKenzie had been married to the same woman for twenty-seven years, her identity had remained fiercely guarded. In all their years of marriage Martin and Elaine McKenzie had never been publically photographed together, a deliberate ploy that was all part of McKenzie's carefully constructed enigmatic persona; a wife people knew existed whose face they had rarely, if ever, seen.

The media had often suggested that she didn't actually exist at all and that McKenzie had simply concocted her in a bid to appear mysterious, which was half true. It had become something of an urban myth that anyone who managed to get a shot of them together was in line for one hell of a payday – £10million if legend was to be believed.

Elaine McKenzie was something of a surprise in the flesh, perhaps even a shock. Far from being the glamorous wife of one of the world's richest men, she was a dour-looking, wizened little thing, dressed as she was in a black trouser suit and white shirt – almost identical to that of her husband's – and her face, while obviously worked upon, was pinched and expressionless, her thin lips forming a grim line. She was diminutive; five foot one at best, and seemed to disappear further still in her husband's presence.

Elaine smiled in silent acknowledgement, though it did not reach her grey watery eyes as she carefully placed the selection of pastries down onto the table and left the room as abruptly as she'd entered.

'Was it wise, allowing your wife to be able to identify us?' the Japanese man spoke in a nasal accent.

The guests looked over at him, then at each other.

McKenzie allowed a small smile to creep across his doughy lips.

'I could ask you the same question in reverse,' he responded, his tone suggesting there was no need for further discussion. The Japanese man was duly silenced.

It was the woman's turn to speak. 'Act five,' she said in a clipped British accent. 'I think there needs to be more ... more tension ...'

McKenzie unscrewed a bottle of Evian and discarded the lid onto the table, taking a large, audible swig before deciding to address her. The woman held his gaze, seemingly unperturbed by his thinly veiled psychological games; after all, she played them too. She knew who McKenzie was: a despotic power-freak of the misogynistic kind, *the worst kind*. She had caught his fleeting glance upon arrival and had read a thousand assumptions into it. But she was the client here, *she* was paying *him* for the privilege of being part of this experiment and if she had questions she would damn well ask them.

'You would like it re-written?' He glanced at her smiling, turning his head slowly, his eyes following a few seconds later.

'Well,' she replied, unsmiling, 'I feel it could use a little more ... drama ... more action ... more ...'

'... more what? Sex? Blood? Violence? More *suffering*?' he held her in his gaze intently for a moment, his dark eyes almost black, burning through her small, fragile looking skull. 'Ah, I see,' he said, with an understanding nod, '*suffering*.'

The woman's eyebrow lightly twitched, her eyes glassy as marbles.

'And the rest of you?' McKenzie swiftly abandoned her gaze.

The Frenchman spoke. 'The guests ... they are an obscure collection, no?'

I assure you I have been meticulous about my selection,' McKenzie interjected.

This was partly true; McKenzie *had* hand-selected the guests himself, though he was not about to disclose his reasons just yet and spoil all the fun. All would be revealed in good time.

A balding gentleman wearing a shabby, brown, V-necked pullover coughed by way of announcing himself.

'And they have signed the disclaimer?'

He sounded nervous though McKenzie knew this not to be so. He recognised the man's voice, had spoken to him many times over the years thanks to their 'shared interests', and despite his lack of sartorial finesse, McKenzie knew him to be one of the most pernicious, and financially secure, of the Super Eight Club.

'There can be no comeback, McKenzie, none whatsoever, because I think we all know – and forgive me if I speak for everyone around this table – what the outcome for all of us would be if there was. We're playing with people's lives here.'

McKenzie had expected this, yet the challenge made him want to wrap his hands around the man's throat and squeeze it until he turned blue.

'Every eventuality has been accounted for on Pleasure Island,' he responded evenly. 'There won't be any "comeback" as you put it. Rest assured you have my word on this.'

'Yes, but –'

McKenzie cut him off gently but abruptly. 'In all the years we've being doing business have I ever failed you?'

One of the Americans, bald, fat, ill-fitting shiny suit, unadvisedly cut in. 'The man has a right to ask.'

McKenzie felt his blood pressure rise but tempered it with steady breathing.

'Indeed he does,' he agreed disingenuously.

'This is serious stuff, McKenzie. I mean, looking at it in the cold light of day it's ... well, it's ...'

The room focussed on the American and he suddenly felt very self-conscious.

As the newest member of the club he was still wet behind the ears but now he felt way out of his depth and it was giving him the freakin' shits. Jesus, fucking Christ, who *were* these people? He'd only joined for a bit of fun, though arguably it was not your average interpretation of the word.

McKenzie wholly objected to being questioned and equally being referred to by his surname. It was basic bad manners. And he detested bad manners. He made a mental note of this and allowed it to pass. For now.

'It's a-a-ambitious to say the least,' the American stammered, wishing his mouth would engage with his brain.

'Ah yes, ambition!' McKenzie stood abruptly, arms outstretched, a preacher addressing his flock. 'The last infirmity of noble minds!'

The American was struck by an urgent need to leave the room. This was too real for him. *Way too freakin' fucked up, man.* Admittedly he enjoyed the fantasy from the comfort of his own home, but this ... this really was going to the next level and, as a relative novice, was not something he felt entirely comfortable with or ready for.

'Does the gentleman have a problem?' McKenzie enquired with a wry smile that seemed so genuine it was sinister. 'Does the gentleman not trust me?'

The American shook his head, tiny cold beads of sweat prickling his temples. *Jesus, it was hot in here.*

McKenzie didn't wait for an answer.

'Any more questions?' his eyes swept the table like laser beams. 'Good, in which case, gentlemen – and lady –' he glanced fleetingly in the woman's direction 'let the games commence.'

The woman began to clap and a couple of the others followed suit.

'All business transactions must be paid in full before commencement commences, then the rest is pay-per-view as discussed,' McKenzie instructed, the mention of money causing his tone to switch into cold, hard business. 'This fee will cover all expenses as stated on the agreement, the breakdown of which can be perused on page eight of the document before you. And of course, it buys you the right to change the script at any given point, in fact, I actively encourage this – all input will be considered as previously discussed.'

'All?' The woman raised a thin, black brow.

McKenzie turned to her, and felt the heat of her from where she sat, her fragrance lightly reaching his nostrils.

'*All*,' he said, matching her smirk with his own. 'So,' he continued, 'if everyone is happy?'

The men in the room exchanged brief looks at one another, each in the hope that the other would instantly forget their faces.

'Good. The plane leaves next Tuesday. Access will be via the usual method. Your individual pin codes will be delivered personally to your door via Fed Ex. I suggest, if I may, that you memorise them and then destroy them.' He rose from the table. 'Your cars, gentlemen, are waiting for you outside. I trust you will have a safe return journey to your respective destinations. I do hope we don't meet again. And above all –' McKenzie paused for dramatic effect '– enjoy!'

The men began to stand but the woman stayed seated, watching as they made their solemn leave one by one until it was just herself and McKenzie in the room.

As the door closed behind the final guest, the woman stood to face him, unfazed by his imposing bulk. McKenzie stared into her eyes, catching a flicker of recognition in them as he undid the zipper on his trousers. *Kindred spirits.*

'It's been a pleasure doing business with you, madam,' he said as she silently dropped to her knees and looked up at him, her red lips parting slightly, dark eyes ablaze. He saw his own reflection in them and smiled as she reached inside his trousers and took him in her red manicured hand.

'The *pleasure*, sir,' she said, as she bared her teeth and let out a small primeval growl, 'is all mine.'

CHAPTER ONE

The sound of the post hitting the doormat caused Angelika Deyton to momentarily look up from her newspaper.

'What time are you due in court?' she asked her husband, watching as he made himself busy with their new Gusto coffee maker, his gown flapping as he attempted to make sense of it.

'You should know,' he immediately retorted, growing impatient with the machine, 'you lot seem to think you know everything about this case.'

She ignored the comment and reached for another piece of French toast.

'You need to fill the water up to the marker level. And it would probably help if you plugged it in first.' She flashed him a little smile, one he translated as a smirk.

'You really do know everything, don't you, Angelika?' he snapped irritably. He glanced around, looking for their housekeeper. 'Where's Miriam today anyway? She usually takes care of all of this.'

'She's on holiday. Remember I told you? She's gone away with her husband and kids, you know, like normal people do.' She shot him a condescending look.

'I'm in court at eleven,' he said, finally answering her question.

'Kirkbride wants me to file copy before 5pm,' she said, 'to make tomorrow's headlines. Do you think you'll have made your closing speech by then?'

He gave her a glance that told her she should know better than to ask such a question.

She bit the bullet. 'Do you think he did it, Rupert? Do you think he's guilty?'

Rupert Deyton sighed. 'You know we're not supposed to discuss it, Angelika. He's my client.'

'And I'm your wife. Come on, off the record.'

'Nothing is ever off the record with you lot,' he smarted. 'You have it your way and the poor man would be hung drawn and quartered before he'd even been to trial.'

'It's a rape case, Rupert. No one likes a rapist, especially a famous one.'

'The girl was falling down drunk,' he fired back. 'She'd been all "up on him" as the kids say these days, just another groupie, a tart wanting her five minutes of fame. She'll sell her sordid little story for a six-figure sum once I get him off, you just bloody watch ... little tramp.'

She raised an eyebrow. 'A little tramp who said "no".'

'Get the post, will you,' he said roughly, refusing to rise to the bait. 'I'm expecting a postcard from Malaysia. Serg should be there by now.'

Angelika inwardly sighed. She was used to being spoken to in this manner by her husband. These days they rarely had a normal conversation; it was just a series of snide snipes littered with the odd bit of need-to-know information. It depressed her but she couldn't seem to do anything to change it. Any sort of civility between them was always a conscious effort and painfully short-lived. They had both tried, but it was never too long before they reverted to type. Being at each other's throats and point scoring was par for the course with them now. It had become habitual.

Deliberately scraping her chair across the marble floor of their perfectly designed country-style kitchen just to grate on her husband's nerves, Angelika schlepped from the room in her cotton pyjamas to collect the post. Plain, comfy and functional, she only wished they were indicative of her marriage. She would have settled for that now.

The Deytons had been such a dynamic couple once upon a time: him the brilliant barrister in the making – her the rising young journalist with star potential – young, fabulous and in love.

And they had gone on to achieve such dizzying heights together; Rupert was now a high-profile celebrity barrister, one of the Bar's most dynamic and charismatic, and she was at the pinnacle of her journalistic career – a household name whose opinion counted.

On paper they had it all: the Mayfair town house complete with AGA, designer furniture and housekeeper, a couple of four-by-fours in the driveway, a holiday home in Tuscany and platinum membership to the Hurlingham Club. Hell, they even hobnobbed with royalty and celebrities.

However, the love they had once felt for each other – that mutual appreciation, respect and admiration that had been the underpinning of their relationship at the start – had somehow diluted along the way, replaced instead by a need to compete.

Their marriage was now little more than a game of one-upmanship, a game in which they were equally complicit, and equally matched.

'No postcard from Serg,' she said almost gleefully, tossing her long, caramel-blonde hair over her shoulder as she shuffled through the post. 'Perhaps he's having too great a time to remember his old dad. Now ooh, this looks interesting,' she remarked, coming across the gold-leaf envelope. 'An invitation. The polo perhaps?'

Rupert took this to be a dig, just as he took everything his wife said to be a dig. He was an avid polo player and felt that she resented the small enjoyment it afforded him.

'Or maybe there's a sale on at net-a-porter.com,' he reposted with a grimace. 'Or one of those high street surgeries ... buy a new pair of tits and get a facelift for free. You should think about booking yourself in, dear, now that 40's knocking on the door.'

'Oh, shut up, Rupert,' she said, unamused by his lame attempt at humour as she opened the envelope and began to read. 'Actually, it's neither.'

'Oh?' his interest was pricked by her expression. 'Well...?'

'It's from Martin McKenzie.'

'*The* Martin McKenzie?'

'How many Martin McKenzie's do you know?'

He rolled his eyes. 'And …?'

She straightened her back. 'And it says we've been invited – actually it says, '*exclusively chosen*' – as two of six – oh my God – just *six* guests to attend the opening of his latest state-of-the-art venture into the world of luxury holiday destinations.' She looked up at him, mouth open.

'Really?' Rupert pulled his chin to his chest. 'And why the hell would he invite us?'

'I have no idea,' she said, staring at the exclusive hologrammed invitation that had been embossed in gold-leaf calligraphic ink. 'Perhaps I made a lasting impression when I interviewed him that time,' she joked.

'Or perhaps more likely he wants to thank you in person for it. What was the headline again, "Media whore is 64..."?'

'Well, I was instructed to write a controversial piece on him. Not that it was a stretch, mind.'

Angelika had not warmed to McKenzie in person and as such the subsequent article she had been commissioned to write had been a less-than-flattering portrait. She wondered if perhaps McKenzie saw this as a chance to set the record straight – that or revenge for ever having written it in the first place.

Either way she suspected it had 'ulterior motive' written all over it because that's how men like McKenzie rolled. She'd neither liked the man nor trusted him on sight but her inquisitiveness as to why he had picked them for such an auspicious invitation was enough of a reason for her to want to agree to it.

Whatever McKenzie's true agenda behind selecting them was, she recognised it as being a once-in-a-lifetime opportunity. At the very least she would get a fabulous holiday, not to mention story, out of it – a win-win situation as far as she was concerned.

'It's a marketing ploy, Angelica,' Rupert said dismissively, already moving on to the next envelope on the pile.

'No,' she said, her tone suddenly serious, 'no, it's really not. This is a bona fide invite, Ru. We've been invited as one of six hand-selected guests to fly in his private jet to, and I quote, "the most exclusive island in the world; a homage to state-of-the art five-star luxury and beyond". A place called Pleasure Island.'

'Pleasure Island? How original,' he snorted. 'Bloody hell; let me see that.' He dropped the rest of the mail and attempted to snatch it from his wife's clutches.

Martin McKenzie was one of the most powerful – not to mention richest – businessmen on the planet. The self-styled 'King of Media', he was the brains behind the most successful reality TV and game shows in the world, and was well known as an bon vivant of the highest order, famous for his excessive lifestyle as much as his body of impressive work. The media were obsessed with him and his strange-looking elusive wife, Elaine, who, rarely photographed, seemed content to remain in the shadows of her husband's planet-sized ego.

'"The ultimate in hedonistic luxury", it says here.' She raised an eyebrow. '"State of the art accommodation in private and secluded surroundings on one of the most beautiful unspoilt islands in the world ... the finest haute cuisine and the most spectacular entertainment on earth." Wow, that's some statement!'

'Unspoilt island?' Rupert scoffed. 'Who does the man think he is, Christopher bloody Columbus?'

'The plane leaves next Tuesday. They're sending a limo to take us to the airport.'

'Next Tuesday? I promised Lucian I'd take part in the polo next week, and stand in for Boris while his ankle heals.'

'Are you kidding?' Angelika glared at him. 'This is Martin McKenzie we're talking about here. He's invited six people, *just six* people, of which, Lord only knows how, we are two. Two weeks of unadulterated luxury of the like we've never see before and are never likely to again, and you'd rather play bloody polo. Are you insane? Can you even begin to imagine what it's going to be like?'

Reluctantly he conceded she did have a point.

'What's the bloody catch?' he grumbled, 'aside from very short notice?'

Angelika wasn't sure how to answer him, though she also suspected there was one.

'You can get the time off.' She was suddenly excited, her sharp journalistic brain sensing that regardless of motive, this was not something to be turned down. 'The case will be over then and you're due a holiday. We were planning a Tuscan trip anyway.'

He sighed. He'd been thinking of how to get out of that one too.

'Yes, but I think we ought to at least know who the other guests are going to be. I mean, you and I have both upset a few folk in our time. Frankly you'd be fucked if Nancy Dell'Olio turned up after that piece you wrote last week.'

'Oh, come on, Rupert, it's only a couple of weeks. Let's do it; let's say yes!' Perhaps it would also be an opportunity for her and her husband to spend a little quality time together. It was a long shot but maybe a fortnight spent in abject luxury was just what they needed to begin to bridge the gulf between them, a gulf that had become so wide you could launch a thousand ships in it.

'What does the small print say?' he asked.

'Formalities, by the looks of it,' she said, ignoring her sharp intuton, her mind already made up thanks to her intrigue. 'It says here it just needs one of us to sign a disclaimer.'

'A disclaimer? Ha! See, I told you it was a bloody marketing ploy. Well, I'll have a proper look at it when I'm back from court, and then we'll decide.'

He was standing now, making his leave, the coffee he'd spent so long making only half drunk.

'See you in court, Angelika,' he said, turning to leave without so much as a goodbye kiss.

'Good luck getting the famous rapist off,' she goaded, as he left the room, the sound of the front door slamming behind him.'

Angelika Deyton looked at the invitation once more.

'*Pleasure Island*,' she said aloud, biting her lip nervously as she hastily signed the accompanying RSVP form. She felt sure that McKenzie had something big in store for them. And she wanted to know exactly what that something was.

CHAPTER TWO

'I'm afraid it's not *bwilliant* news, sugar.'

Lennard Bailey looked up at his client from his desk as she flounced into his plush New York office, swishing her long curtain of jet-black hair from her thin, delicate face and depositing a waft of her trademark Shalimar fragrance around her, a fragrance that seemed to linger inside his nostrils for days, forcibly reminding him of her presence – which, he assumed, was the whole point.

'OK, Bailey, hit me with it.' Mia Manhattan flopped into the leather chair opposite him and lit a cigarette. She already had a look of disappointment on her face which he vehemently resented. Damn woman hadn't even heard everything he had to say yet.

'Well?' she prompted him with a raised eyebrow.

Mia Manhattan was one of Bailey's oldest long-standing clients. She had been huge once upon a time, a proper star, not like these fly-by-night flash-in-the-pan charlatans he was forced to represent today. Mia had been 'The Tiny Girl with the Big Voice' who'd sung with them all: Barbara, Whitney (God rest her soul), Aretha, Shirley, Stevie, Cliff, Tom, Rod, The Bee Gees … she was a quintessential child of Studio 54, which, sadly for her, was now defunct and largely irrelevant by today's standards.

'Can't you hook me up with that Guetta DJ chap, or how about Adele … now she's right up my boulevard, darling,' she'd announced with astonishing self-entitlement. *Like it was that easy.*

Bailey had welcomed the comeback conversation with Mia like an unexpected visit from the IRS, but he had expected it regardless. He suspected that the recently divorced Mia's sudden burning demand for another shot at the limelight was largely fuelled by revenge as opposed to revenue. After all, her marriage had been purported to be one of the strongest in the industry, not least for its twenty-five-year longevity. It can't have been easy being ruthlessly cast aside for the stereotypical younger model. A woman with the kind of ego Mia possessed simply wouldn't be able to rest.

Mia blew smoke in Bailey's direction in a deliberate bid to commence with the conversation. Surely the old bastard had something for her. He was still on a hefty retainer, after all.

Bailey had been her agent for more years than she cared to recall and their relationship had always been tempestuous at best, but he was one of a very select few people Mia actually trusted and had been surprisingly sympathetic during her recent divorce from Richard. *Richard Adams*, a name that was so familiar to her but now sounded like a stranger's.

Mia felt the familiar ache in her chest begin to burn as she thought the man to whom she had given the very best years of her life, a man she had trusted so implicitly and loved so unconditionally. His betrayal had decimated her, not least because it had been so unexpected.

Well, she had certainly had a lesson in humility, make no goddamn mistake about that. That treacherous bastard had been her life, and moreover he was one of the only people who knew her past. *Her real past.*

Bailey cleared his throat and wondered if it might be too early for a nip of Cognac. A meeting with Mia practically demanded it.

'How's Josh?' he asked. 'Still busy battling it out on the pub circuit with his little pals, turning it all the way up to eleven?' Joshua was Mia's latest in a long line of revenge fucks, the prerequisite being the younger the better. Still, he regretted the words as soon as he'd spoken them. He needed her on side today, especially after what he was about to put to her. His fat ass depended on it.

Mia's arched brow twitched. 'You may mock, Bailey –' she crossed her legs, a defiant swing of tanned skin '– but actually Josh-*ua* has had a recent breakthrough career-wise.'

She sounded smug. She was. After all, what woman wouldn't be? Joshua Jones, or JJ as his adoring legion of young female fans called him, had just signed a rather lucrative record deal, or rather his band, *The Dopamines*, had. He was young and talented with the face of an angel and the kind of body that had made women want to drop to their knees, even at her age. *Two can play at that game, Dickie darling.*

'Sony has given him a two-album deal.' She flashed him an sickly smile. 'He'll be a star in no time, mark my words.'

'Good for him.' Bailey was unable to fully disguise the surprise in his voice. From what he'd seen of Josh-*ua*, that useless layabout would be lucky to get a kite off the ground in gale force winds.

'Isn't it?' came her rhetorical response. Joshua Jones was just another walking dick as far as Mia was concerned, another way of trying to fill the bottomless black void inside her. Still, as far as revenge fucks went he was certainly above average: terribly young, terribly energetic, and terribly eager to please.

Her mind flashed back to that morning as she had looked down at him between her open thighs, his curtain of soft, wavy, blond hair – so very *rock star* – gently brushing against her pelvis …

'You've done this before,' she'd smiled between gasps, his breath warm against her delicate skin, 'many times.' He'd glanced up at her and grinned, wet lips glistening. So what if he was young enough for her to have given birth to him (and brought him up), she was Mia Manhattan, for fuck's sake, and he was an aspiring rock star who she could introduce to people. It was a mutually advantageous arrangement, for now at least.

Bailey flashed a warm smile that belied his true feelings. Silly old bint, flashing her clout to men young enough to be her second son, she was making a fool of herself with this conveyor belt of virtual teenagers keeping her four-poster-bed warm, the latest being the most wet behind the ears, and the most cerebrally challenged. When the lad spoke, the word lobotomy sprang to mind.

Mia looked past Bailey and out onto the spectacular midtown-Manhattan skyline displayed like a postcard behind him in the floor-to-ceiling office window. The Empire State, Chrysler and Rockefeller buildings in all their art-deco inspired splendour, spires standing erect and proud in a one-fingered salute to the world. God, she loved New York. New York, New York, so damned good they named it twice. She'd never tired of it in the decades she'd been coming here. What was it Liberace once said … 'too much of a good thing is … wonderful.'

'This is the thing, sugar.' Bailey had no choice but to give it to her straight. She was too long in the bloody tooth to bullshit; besides, he needed to play this one very cool indeed. A lot was riding on it, his neck for one. He adjusted the collar of his stripy, ill-fitting shirt. 'What can I tell you? No one's *weally* biting …'

Mia winced. When Bailey was imparting bad news, his speech impediment became almost intolerable.

'OK, forget about a bloody comeback,' she snapped. 'What about a Vegas tour? It worked for Manilow and Celine.'

Bailey audibly exhaled. 'We've been over this a million times, Mia.'

'I don't know, Bailey,' she sing-songed, then took a deep sigh. 'You must be losing that magic touch of yours.' She lit another Vogue cigarette, her jewelled Manolo's tapping anxiously against the polished, wooden flooring. 'I've been in this business for nigh on forty years – *forty fucking years* – and not one bastard wants to throw me a lifeline?'

Bailey jumped up from his desk, his crumpled shirt sticking to his ever-expanding waistline with perspiration. He stood by the huge glass wall and looked out onto the skyline –

a view that continually provided him comfort no matter how often he looked at it – and he paused for a moment, preparing to play his final card.

'Well, actually, there is *one* thing ...'

'Oh?' Mia's eyes widened, a flicker of interest reigniting, momentarily softening her obstinate expression. She watched as Bailey opened the drawer to his antique desk: Victorian, very Sherlock Holmes, shipped over from London, no doubt. Bailey slid the envelope across the desk towards her.

'And what is this?'

He took a cigarette from her discarded pack on the desk. He'd spent the past six weeks on those damn patches in a futile attempt to quit but ten minutes with Mia was enough to have him reaching for his Dunhill lighter.

'It's an invitation,' he said, biting the tip between his yellowing veneers as he flicked the flint with his thumb.

'To what?'

Baily snorted, smoke escaping his nostrils like steam from a raging bull's.

'Well, read it and you'll see.' He was careful to keep the impatience from his voice, watching her carefully as she began to read. There was a moment's silence before she finally spoke.

'I take it this is a joke?' She looked up at him with dark eyes, her lips thinning into a grim line.

'Do you see me laughing, sugar?'

Mia threw the envelope back at him across the desk as if she'd touched poison.

'Forget it, Bailey.' Her tone was sharp as a blade.

'It's a free holiday, Mia,' he quickly added as part of his pre-rehearsed sales pitch. 'Think about it: two weeks of unadulterated luxury on this new place of his ...'

'But *McKenzie*...' Her voice was tight as a trampoline.

Bailey took a breath and softened his tone. 'Look, you want a comeback right? Well, if anyone can give you what you want it's McKenzie.'

'That *bastard* has nothing I want,' Mia fired back, her hands visibly shaking as she extinguished her cigarette.

Bailey felt the panic swell inside his guts like rising dough. He'd made McKenzie a promise he'd get her to agree to this somehow – anyhow – though frankly that goddamn blackmailing motherfucker had given him little choice.

Bailey watched his client carefully for clues as to her state of mind. He'd always been intrigued by Mia's hatred of McKenzie. Clearly she had her reasons.

'As your agent I would advise you to think about it,' he said, with as much professional clout as his conscience would allow. 'Personal opinions aside, you know he could turn things *wround* for you in a heartbeat.' He paused. 'And imagine Dickie's face when he sees you back in the spotlight, eh? Think about it, cherie, hmm?'

Mia stood bolt upright, and Bailey's spirits instantly lifted.

'Who else has been invited?' she enquired with a sideways glance.

'Ah, well, regrettably that's P 'n' C, apparently.'

Mia struggled to supress a burgeoning sense of intrigue. She had to concede that Bailey had a point. Regrettably that evil bastard McKenzie could put her back on the map as fast as he could stick a pin in it, should he be so inclined. And Dickie would no doubt get wind of it: an idea that pleased her more than was necessarily healthy.

She tentatively picked the envelope up from the desk once more, and tapped it against her Rouge Noir lips.

'I guarantee that with the *wight pwress* exposure my cell will be on fire by the time you return.' Bailey cocked his large, shiny, balding head to one side. He was selling her out and he knew it, but McKenzie had given him little choice. Hell, he'd given him *none*.

Mia chewed her bottom lip for a moment.

'OK, Bailey,' she eventually said, with a deep sigh, 'make the goddamn phone call.'

CHAPTER THREE

Miami was hot. Smokin' hot, in fact. At least it was when Billie-Jo Simmons was in residence. As far as she was concerned she turned the heat up to a hundred degrees wherever she went.

'What's the face for?' she addressed her husband accusingly as she clicked-clacked across the marbled floor towards him on the balcony of their penthouse suite, straddling him with her long, tanned legs, the Asian-inspired, raffia sunlounger creaking in objection with their dual weight.

Nate peered at her from underneath his Ray-Bans, his heart dropping like a brick in a pond. She had disturbed what had been a rare peaceful moment of solitary reflection.

'The face?' he replied, with a forced smile. He didn't want to set her off. Not this early. 'Sorry, Bee, it's the only one I got.'

Billie-Jo sniffed loudly, the remnants of her nostrils audibly making their way down her oesophagus. Depressingly, her coke habit was squaring up to rival her shopping one; and her desire for fame and attention weren't too tardy up the rear either.

'I haven't got long.' She bit her lip, running her small, mani-cured hands up her husband's tanned, toned chest, her long, pointed fingernails leaving imprints on his oily skin. 'That pho-tographer is bang on my case – minute I slip off for a marlie light he's right up my arse.'

Billie-Jo had spent the morning shooting her first-ever swim-wear calendar on Miami Beach, and was buzzing from all the excitement and attention, not to mention the Grade-A powder the kooky stylist chick had supplied.

'Mmm, I'll bet he is.' Nate raised an amused eyebrow as he squeezed his wife's firm buttocks with both hands, but there were no pangs of jealousy. He only wished there were.

Billie-Jo: gold-digger; fame-hunter; wannabe model; coke-head. *His wife*. Whatever she was, Nate couldn't deny that she was a sight for sore eyes; he only had to look at her sometimes and he was hard. If only the inside matched the outside then he'd be onto a winner. He glanced past her at the spacious, private balcony of the Delano South Beach penthouse suite and surveyed the oasis of calm before him. The view was un-paralleled: the sun-dappled ocean stretched out before him like Persian blue carpet, still and tranquil. He felt a sense of discomfort as she mounted him without emotion or affection, mesmerised by the rays dancing upon it like scatter crystal decorations, the silence he had been enjoying shattered by her amplified vocals.

'You're such a prude,' she mocked him, sensing his discom-fort. 'Who cares if anyone hears us?' She tossed her hair back from her neck, the idea obviously turning her on. 'Perhaps the paparazzi are spying on us!'

Nate could think of nothing worse but his fixed smile re-mained as his wife continued to bounce on top of him. It's what was required of him and he knew it. Keeping Billie-Jo happy was a full-time career in itself. Still, he only had himself to blame for that one. Nate had assumed that the night they had met at Nik-ki Beach in Marbella some five years previously, sampling Billie-Jo's charms – and admittedly there were plenty – would simply be a one-time occurrence – a hi-and-goodbye fuck – something he had made a depressing habit of since his premiership-footballing days. But he had quickly learned that Billie-Jo had had bigger plans for the pair of them...colossal, in fact.

Billie-Jo King, or Bee as he called her, was from humble beginnings, though she would rather be seen without make-up than ever confess as much. She had completely re-written her history to suit the persona she had created and make herself sound more interesting, when in truth her provenance made his own look like he'd been brought up in Buckingham fucking Palace. Despite growing up on a rough sink estate without educational or fiscal advantage, the ambitious Billie-Jo had soon discovered how to use her best assets to her advantage. Nate supposed he admired her for it in a small way; after all, he understood what it was to drag yourself from the gutter, a place that was far easier to fall into than it was to pull yourself from. He knew she was damaged; he was sucker for that, wanting to fill up the spaces she lacked. Yet still he wasn't sure exactly how he'd ended up marrying a girl like Billie-Jo. She had a knack of making everything feel like a good idea at the time, and could be persuasive to the point of manipulative while simultaneously making you believe it was all your own idea. The girl had skills.

Nate supposed he had been flattered by her relentless pursuit of him in the beginning Her attentiveness had been intoxicating; what man's ego could resist? She certainly wasn't lacking in charm either, especially when she wanted something, i.e. him. As an unrepentant hedonist, Billie-Jo had brought out the less serious side of his naturally sedate nature, something he was grateful for he supposed, and she could be loving, even sweet when the mood took her. Yet Billie-Jo was the proverbial paradox – sunshine and showers – and as a result you were never quite sure whether you were going to get soaked or sunburned.

'So, do you think you could marry me, Nate Simmons?' she had probed one night, following one of their marathon sex sessions.

'Keep doing what you're doing, and I'll marry you tomorrow,' he'd said, high on post-coital endorphins. Billie-Jo, however, had taken this brief discussion just three months into their relationship as a solid declaration of intent. The pressure she had subsequently gone on to methodically apply had been, in hindsight, subtle but solid, especially once she had begun to inform family and friends of her suspicions that he was about to propose to her. What was he supposed to do? As pathetic as Nate now felt about it, he realised he'd been backed into a corner, obligated, his conscience unable to let him speak up. And so he supposed he'd just gone along with it, telling himself that perhaps they would've ended up marrying at some point anyway, and that he could do a hell of a lot worse. This way at least he could make her happy, even if he wasn't one hundred per cent happy himself. As it was, though, somewhere deep inside of him he knew that Billie-Jo King was not great marriage material and that it was a mistake to tie himself to her for better or worse, the latter of which he suspected would usurp the former. But what Billie-Jo wanted she inevitably got. She was nothing if not single-mindedly ambitious.

'Have you thought any more about the invitation, sweetie?' Billie-Jo grinned down at him, forcing him to squint up at her in the unforgiving Miami sun. Martin McKenzie's invitation to this luxury island had been playing on her mind incessantly to the point of obsession ever since it had arrived, not least because of Nate's outright rejection of it.

'I don't like that unscrupulous fucker,' he'd said, and had discarded the gold-leaf embossed envelope in the bin where she had promptly retrieved it, horrified. 'There's something dodgy about him. He gives me the willies.'

Yeah, well, McKenzie could give *her* the willies any day of the week. *Martin fucking McKenzie*, no less – the don of the celebrity world, a multi-multi-billionaire business man who made careers at the click of his manicured fingers – had invited them as guests on his private island and that lamp she was married to was dismissing it! Was he off his fucking cake? This was a dude who took nobodies off the streets and turned them into serious A-listers overnight. He made millionaires like other people made a mess. But Billie-Jo understood her husband well enough to know that an argument was unwise at that point. Nate could be a stubborn, bloody-minded little fucker when he dug his heels in, but she would get her way eventually. *Hells, would she.* The fact that McKenzie had chosen them, *them*, as guests on this new paradise island of his gave her an even bigger buzz than a mountain of that shit she stuck up her hooter like Columbia had gone out of business.

Her husband may well have been content to retreat into obscurity since the accident that had cut his glittering career short but she sure as shit wasn't. *Nut-ah!* The Golden Bolt, as Nate was referred to in the press, was her Golden Goose and she wasn't about to let him rest on his laurels any longer than necessary.

Recently she'd won a small victory by managing to cajole him into starring in a reality TV show called 'Couples', a truly dire concept that had sat somewhere between *Take Me Out* and *Wife Swap*, highlighting the very best of neither. The whole experience had been nothing but a humiliating nightmare for Nate, one which he'd sooner forget, but Billie-Jo was convinced that as a result McKenzie had spotted her star potential and was about to make her his next protégée.

As such there was not a chance on God's green earth that she was going to let such an opportunity slip past her nail extensions. Still, she wasn't unduly concerned yet. She could be very persuasive when the stakes were this high. By the time she'd worked her magic on her husband he'd promise her a sex change if she asked for one.

'Jesus, Bee,' Nate moaned as she slid off of him and worked her way down his taught belly with her tongue, saliva trails glistening on his skin.

Billie-Jo could tell her husband was getting close and calculatingly climbed back on top of him. Perhaps it was time she got herself up the stick anyway, and secure her future just in case he royally fucked it all up for them both with his recent reclusive leanings. Besides, a kid had the potential to bring in all manner of opportunities: magazine spreads; product endorsements; maybe even her own little range of baby accessories. She could always have lipo afterwards, and follow it up with a fitness video. Then she'd hire an ugly nanny to take care of the sprog while she concentrated on her career. Job done and quids in. She had it all figured out.

Nate could feel his mechanical orgasm rushing to the surface and did nothing to will it back. It was best to let his wife do what she wanted, get it over with.

'*Bay-beeee*, I really want us to go to Pleasure Island … to McKenzie's place. Please say that you'll think about it some more … *please* …' she begged between mouthfuls of him, running her hands through her hair as she arched her back. The camera crew could be heard re-grouping on the beach below them now and the exhibitionist within her hoped they might catch a glimpse of them, give them all something to think about while they were screwing their ugly wives and girlfriends when they got home.

'C'mon baby … this is *Martin McKenzie* we're talking about. That man makes Elton John look like he shops at Primark. Say yes, baby … for me, *pleeease* …'

Nate willed her to shut up. She was totally killing his hard-on.

'And think about the press interest … it'll be good for me … it'll be good for *us*.'

Nate closed his eyes and tried to concentrate on the task at hand. She was right about one thing, though: McKenzie was known as an unparalleled host who was a big fan of the very grand gesture.

But there was something about the whole thing that had given him a nagging sense of unease from the off. Why them, for starters? These days he was practically a nobody: an aging, former pro-footballer, injured out of the game; and Bee was little more than a fame-hungry, glamour model who would go to the opening of a packet of crisps if there was a photographer present. Besides, he was hardly on good terms with the press, and he wanted to avoid dealing with those bastards at any cost, especially in light of recent events.

Thanks to them, six weeks ago Nate had discovered very publically – very painfully – that he'd been adopted. Those bastards hadn't even afforded him the usual twenty-four hour notification period, which was protocol in such sensational stories. Instead it had been splashed across the headlines without warning, causing his phone to buzz like a porn star's dildo until he'd been forced to buy a copy of the filthy rag and discover the truth, or lack thereof, for himself.

Those unscrupulous fuckers didn't care how it decimated his whole life – how he had learned so brutally that the man he had called 'Dad' his entire life until his death the previous year was not his true blood. And his 'mother' – a woman who had died when he was just two years old and had no recollection of – was nothing more than a virtual stranger.

The shock of it alone had sent him spiralling into a black abyss of depression that so far no amount of expensive therapy had been able to drag him from.

And Billie-Jo? Well, she seemed tickled pink. Viewed the whole feeding frenzy as nothing less than a photo opportunity, a chance to promote herself off the back of his misfortune, impervious to his shattered emotions.

Nate had always been suspicious of the press; even at the pinnacle of his career he had somehow felt they were out to get him, waiting for him to screw up. They had practically destroyed him following the accident, almost relished the fact that it had put paid to his glittering career.

Now, however, he loathed them with an intensity that was not entirely healthy, or so his therapist seemed to think. Easy for her to say, Nate had thought bitterly; she wasn't the one who had discovered her entire life had been a lie, leaving him with a catalogue of unanswered questions, the most critical being, *who the fuck am I?*

Billie-Jo had planted herself on top of him again and her ecstatic caterwauling was reaching a crescendo. He could never be sure she wasn't faking it for the invisible cameras she seemed to believe were following her every move.

'Ohh, *bay-beee*, yes … fuck me baby … ah, ah, yesss, that's it, yeah, ooh, yeah, you bad boy!' She looked down at him and his blue eyes met with her dark, heavily made-up pair. 'Say yes, baby … say we can go to Pleasure Island … oh, please, baby … please say yes … ah, ahh, oooh yeah …'

Nate inwardly cringed at his wife's theatrics. Sex with Billie-Jo was akin to starring in a third-rate skin flick that no one wanted to watch. It was all so … contrived, the opposite of intimate.

'Jesus Christ, Bee.' He felt his erection flounder inside her. 'Whatever, ok?'

'Is that a yes?' she squealed, mouth slightly open, eyes wide. She reminded him of a blow-up doll.

'Yeah, yeah,' he answered, irritation replacing his resolve. It was fruitless to fight her. These days he lacked the energy.

Billie-Jo squealed loudly again, her eyes sparkling, pupils dilating wildly. She would celebrate immediately with a fat, victory line up her left one.

'Hey, BJ!' A gruff American voice rose up to meet them on the balcony from one of the camera crew on the beach below. 'Quit screwing around and get that pretty little ass down here pronto, *capisce*? We're shooting in five.'

Billie-Jo leant forward and kissed her husband on the lips for the first time that day.

'I'm coming!' she called out to the voice below as her cries reached fever pitch.

And in this particular case, she wasn't lying.

CHAPTER FOUR

'Bit bloody cloak and dagger this, isn't it?' Rupert Deyton re-marked, unimpressed, as he reclined into the back seat of the un-marked limousine next to his wife. 'Why send a car at silly o'clock in the middle of the night anyway? Couldn't he have organised an afternoon flight instead … why all the ridiculous subterfuge?'

Angelika shrugged. She could feel the irritation coming off of her husband in waves.

'You missed your vocation in life, Rupert; you should've been a journalist, all those questions … perhaps he wants us on the island first thing. Maybe this was the only slot he could get in airspace or the pilot needs to be somewhere else by midday. Or maybe there's absolutely no reason whatsoever.'

'This is Martin McKenzie we're talking about,' Rupert snort-ed, flicking his dark, salt-and-pepper hair from his face. These days it was more salt than pepper, something he would've liked to have rectified before this infernal trip had come around, but the State vs the well-known actor, Peter Cheshunt, had gone on far longer than was good for anyone, least of all Cheshunt him-self. 'Believe me, that man has a reason for everything he does.'

'Perhaps it's to add a bit of drama to the occasion.' Angelika's eyes widened and she squeezed his arm for effect. He automati-cally recoiled from her.

'Aren't you even a little bit excited, you miserable old sod?' She pulled away from him, though was careful to keep her tone light and playful. There was still time for him to change his mind after all. 'I mean, it's not every day you're flown via private jet to a paradise Island *gratis* by one of the world's richest, most powerful men is it?' The Deyton's weren't exactly on the bread-line but they weren't in McKenzie's league, not many people were, and Rupert had always grumbled about shelling out for expensive holidays, preferring to spend his hard earned cash on property and cars, 'things that hold value and don't just become memories' as he stoically put it.

Rupert shook his head. 'There's no such thing as "gratis" where men like McKenzie are concerned, trust me. We'll end up paying for it somehow, mark my words, and less of the old, Angelika.'

Angelika exhaled. She wished she could just have a normal conversation with her husband, one that didn't automatically degenerate into a series of sarcastic barbs, subtle snipes and asides. It was all so futile, so … exhausting.

'Don't pretend you're not as intrigued as I am about the whole thing,' she sniffed. 'You wouldn't have agreed to it other-wise, and you damn well know it.'

She was right, not that he would ever admit it. In fact he was more than just a little intrigued by McKenzie's latest venture – and by the man himself, truth be known. Yet his natural cyni-cism told him that this was not simply going to be two weeks of unadulterated luxury like his ever-optimistic, and frankly naïve, wife seemed so convinced of.

'Didn't have a choice really, did I dear?' he mused, looking out of the blackened window in a futile bid to try and fathom where the hell they were headed. 'It was either that or stare at your miserable face for all eternity.' He pretended to be more annoyed than he actually was by his wife's blatant stitch-up. Cross as he'd been to learn of her agreeing to this on his behalf, he was also admittedly as intrigued by it as she was. Not that he was about to let Angelika know that.

Angelika instantly thought of a caustic comeback but stopped herself short.

'I hope I packed the right things,' she said, changing the subject. She chewed her bottom lip. 'The invitation didn't specify a particular dress code … I mean, will it be formal evening wear, round the captain's table, that sort of thing, or do you think it's going to be bit more of a chic, bohemian, Ibiza vibe?' She sighed once more, realising the futility of asking him such questions. Rupert's idea of dressing for dinner amounted to throwing on a bow-tie. 'And of course we don't know who else has been invited do we? No doubt a supermodel or two … just to make me feel better.'

'With a stroke of luck,' he muttered, though frankly he wasn't in the least bit interested. 'At least the view will be half decent, even if the conversation isn't.'

Angelika ignored him. She was excited about this trip and wasn't about to let the joyless shit she'd married spoilt it for her. Her sharp journalist instincts told her something momentous was about to happen. Something she wanted to be part of.

'Aren't you even a little intrigued as to who the other guests are going to be? After all, McKenzie's seriously well-connected. We could even find ourselves spending the next fortnight in the company of royalty.'

'Yes,' Rupert agreed, his wife's zealousness beginning to grate on him, 'which begs the obvious bloody question as to why he's invited the likes of us comparative no-marks?'

'I guess we're going to find out soon enough.' Angelika's blue eyes were alight in the darkness as the car came to a slow halt.

'Looks like we're here,' she said, clasping her hands together, her heart beating a song inside her chest.

'Wherever here is,' Rupert continued to mutter underneath his breath, a habit she found infuriating, as the chauffeur opened the car door.

Angelika exited first and after a few seconds stopped dead before turning to look at her husband, her expression giving him immediate cause for concern.

'Holy shit, Ru,' she said, eyes wide, her mouth forming an ominous 'O' shape as her heart dropped to her wedge-heeled sandals, 'you're not going to like this … not going to like it at all.'

'Call my agent now!' Mia Manhattan was practically destroying her Jimmy Choos as she stomped up and down the tarmac. 'Get that fucker Bailey on the phone,' she commanded to the young, hapless Asian woman wearing a red and black uniform to match her hair and lipstick. 'I don't give a flying rat's fucking arsehole if it's the middle of the shitting bastard night; I want that treacherous cunt on the phone this instant!'

Joshua Jones stood behind Mia and tried to refrain from laughing. Boy, did this broad have a dirty mouth on her!

'I'm afraid that's impossible, mam,' the young woman advised her gently. If she'd been offended by Mia's choice language she certainly didn't seem it.

'Impossible?' Mia visibly recoiled, her head retracting into her neck, veins protruding, fat with blood.

'I'm afraid I don't have your agent's number,' she replied with the slightest raised brow.

Mia let out an incredulous laugh. She'd been so used to having people jump through hoops for her that sometimes she was inclined to forget small details – such as the facts.

'Well, if you think I'm getting on that plane with *him* –' she pointed a manicured burgundy nail in Rupert and Angelika's direction '– then you've got a long wait ahead of you. I'd rather eat a shit sandwich than spend the next two weeks with that incompetent Eaton-educated arsewipe.'

JJ laughed out loud, he couldn't help it. This was a side of Mia Manhattan he hadn't seen before, though arguably he'd only really seen her on her back. They'd not exactly done much talking since they'd met. But then that suited him fine. During the few occasions they'd actually had dinner together, she had regaled some 'back in the day' type tales that had meant nothing to him about people he knew shit about. Way before his time, man. But the woman was still a legend and was kinda hot for an older broad. Besides, the paps had gone fucking ape for them ever since they'd hooked up, giving him some serious exposure which was A-OK with him. He couldn't be sure that she'd had any sway in the fact that his band had just been signed to Sony in the UK, but it sure as shit hadn't done him no harm that was for certain. So what if the dudes in the band had ribbed him about fucking Grandma's pussy. He'd do that shit all day long if it meant his mug shot made the dailies. Joshua Jones had waited for his fifteen minutes all his goddamn life and was prepared to go to any lengths to get them. Screwing a famous woman old enough to be his mother ... hell, maybe even Grandmother, was a no fucking brainer. Besides, that cougar was using him just as much as he was using her. He read the papers; she wanted to get back at that old man of hers for boning some young chick behind her back and frankly he was stoked to be of assistance. Anyway, at least she wasn't giving him bullshit like the chicks his own age did with all their possessive crap, wanting to tie him down and get all exclusive on his ass.

'Jesus, do I have to do everything myself?' Turning her back on the woman, Mia reached inside her tote for her phone and pressed her agent on speed dial. 'This had better be fucking good, Bailey,' she hissed as it began to ring, 'fucking good indeed.'

CHAPTER FIVE

'Good morning, ladies and gentlemen, and welcome on board Mr McKenzie's G650 private, business jet. My name is Aki. I am your flight attendant and I will be serving you for the duration of your flight. Your captain today is Hiro: a very experienced pilot, and Mr McKenzie's personal favourite.'

The young woman spoke with authority and a radiant smile as she gestured towards a red, velvet curtain where a pilot with a small, pinched face and severe, slicked-back black hair sat, unsmiling. He saluted the six guests formally, silently, before closing the curtain.

'I'm afraid I am unable to tell you our exact destination due to strict instructions from Mr McKenzie,' she explained, 'but what I *can* tell you is that you will not be disappointed.' She paused. 'First things first, if I may take your watches and mobile phones please. The G650 is as sensitive as she is powerful. This is simply for flight security, you understand,' she quickly explained, 'they will be returned as soon as we are airborne.'

She made her way through the small but palatial cabin with a soft, black, cloth bag.

'Why can't we just switch them to airplane mode like usual?' Billie-Jo enquired, panic settling in her flat stomach. She wasn't enamoured by the idea of relinquishing her beloved Samsung, nor the diamond Rolex that Nate had gifted her on their wedding day. It was the most expensive thing she owned.

'I'm afraid I must insist on having both your phone and watch, madam; the plane cannot take off until I have them all in my possession.' Aki's pasted-on smile remained in perfect tact as she spoke.

'Bit drastic, isn't it?' Rupert chipped in, though he duly obliged, throwing his iPhone in the bag as he undid his Breitling.

'Just a safety precaution, sir, at Mr McKenzie's request, you understand.'

'What is this, the Third Reich?' Rupert muttered under his breath, snatching Angelika's phone from the small, drop-down table, and tossing it inside the bag after his own. 'My wife doesn't wear a watch, do you, darling? Doesn't like anything too tight around the wrist,' he whispered loudly, 'she was a convict in a previous life.'

Aki's smile remained unchanged as Angelika bristled. Rupert liked to make jokes at her expense, subtle putdowns that he passed off as humour. She supposed it was harmless to an outsider's ear, little more than a husband's banter, but over the years it had become damaging.

'I don't wear a watch either,' Joshua remarked as if imparting such knowledge would somehow be of benefit or indeed interest to anyone. 'I've met some awesome people through asking them the time.'

He grinned and Angelika smiled at him. She'd read about Joshua Jones and his band, The Dope-a-somethings or the other. They had just secured a record deal with Sony and were set to become the next big thing. He looked much younger in the flesh than all those paps shots she'd seen of him and Mia together. His fair skin was smooth as a baby's and his wide, green eyes had an innocence about them that belied the whole rock-star image. It was little wonder the press had dubbed Mia a cradle snatcher. Jesus, he looked about twelve years old.

Belongings collected, Aki turned to the seated guests.

'I trust you will have a comfortable flight. I am here to fulfil your every request as best I can, so please do let me know if here is anything I can get you should you so wish.'

'Yes, I wish you could get me off this fucking plane right now!' Mia piped up from her seat. She was absolutely fuming, shaking she was so incensed. Thanks to that treacherous old bastard Bailey, she was now sharing confined space with a man who had helped practically destroy her life and career. And that was even before she got to McKenzie. Moreover, according to Bailey, there was absolutely bollock-all she could do about it.

'You signed the contract, Mia,' her agent had advised during the tense phone call that had just taken place between them, finally managing to squeeze a word through her high pitched shrieking. 'It clearly states that you're obliged to go or else pay a forfeit of one million dollars.' It had been enough to silence her almost immediately.

'Did you know about this?' she had asked, her voice a low growl through clenched teeth? 'Were you aware that Rupert Deyton would be here. Because if I find out …'

'I swear to you,' Bailey had cut in, wondering which fate would be worse, Mia discovering the truth or disobeying McKenzie's orders. Talk about rocks and hard places, 'I had no idea who the other guests would be.'

Mia chose to cut him off without so much as a goodbye. She would deal with Bailey when she got back. First things first she would need to tackle Deyton.

'Well, well, well, if it isn't my learned friend,' Mia had said as she'd come face to face with him on the concourse.

'Mia,' Rupert Deyton had reluctantly acknowledged her. She'd looked at him with such contempt that it had practically altered her entire appearance. 'What an … unexpected surprise, I take it you're also one of … one of McKenzie's special guests.'

'Unparalleled levels of deduction, Sherlock.' The sarcasm had dripped from Mia's voice like poison. 'That education of yours really did pay off, didn't it?'

Rupert had managed a small, thin smile, though inwardly he was supressing a diabolical mix of outrage and despair. Mia Manhattan being a fellow island guest had been his worst nightmare realised. He had history with this woman – unpleasant history.

During the early 90s, when Mia had been at the tail end of the height of her career and he had been a young, up-and-coming barrister, Rupert had been bequeathed the misfortune of representing her in a lawsuit that her then-record company, Polyright Records, had taken out against her for having failed to deliver an album on time and in accordance with her contract. Rupert had been brought in by her attorneys, Clinton Smyth and Jameson's, to take care of business.

He hadn't truly expected it to become the long, bitter and acrimonious battle that had dragged on for almost half a decade, practically bankrupting her in the process and undoubtedly damaging her – until then – unblemished career. Mia had hardly worked a day since, largely citing her 'inept legal representation' as the main reason, something which Rupert was vehemently resentful about to this day. She still brought it up in interviews, dragging his good name through the gutter.

However, Mia's attempted decimation of him in the eyes of the media had been bittersweet; arguably, and somewhat ironically, it had actually helped raise his profile, but it had also given rise for future clients to be suspicious of his abilities, giving him a dubious reputation before he'd even had the chance to prove himself. Even today, over a decade and a half later, his name was still associated with that damn vengeful woman's case.

Similarly, the whole business had all but broken Mia, leaving her finances and career in ruins, not to mention her professional reputation. If the press had been unkind to him they had completely annihilated her, painted her as a stereotypical difficult diva who viewed herself above the need to deliver on her promises, not too far off the money as far as Rupert Deyton was concerned.

This was the flipside of fame; every miserable bastard she'd ever had a cross word with in her life had come crawling out of the woodwork like lice, eager to jump on the bandwagon of haters, stick the knife in, in exchange for a few bucks. Her career had never fully recovered from it. Neither in truth had Mia herself.

It was common knowledge that following the trial's less-than-favourable outcome, she had suffered a complete mental and physical breakdown and for the most part of five years had been strung out on medication that had rendered her a reclusive zombie. It was only thanks to her then husband's continuing love and support throughout that she hadn't gone on to top herself.

Mia momentarily closed her eyes, the memories of that ghastly period in time too painful for her to revisit. It had been undoubtedly the second-worst experience of her entire life, the only saving grace being that somehow the press had never discovered the truth about the first.

CHAPTER SIX

Put quite simply, the Gulfstream G650 business jet was *the* platinum standard in private business aviation. Outclassing any other business jet, it boasted extreme, superior comfort as well as being the fastest and safest way to travel via airspace. Martin McKenzie owned five of them in his vast collection of luxury aircraft.

'I'm gonna have a plane like this one day,' Billie-Jo announced with such breath-taking self-entitlement that Nate was in no doubt she meant it. 'Look at it, it's fucking awesome,' she said, running her neon-pink false nails along the jet's pristine white-leather interior, while simultaneously wondering if 3am was too early for champagne plus a cheeky livener to get the show on the road. *Fuck it, they were on holiday, right?*

'Hmm.' Nate was busying himself with the Gulfstream's handbook. 'It says here that the G650 comes equipped with powerful Rolls-Royce engines and can cover shorter distances at a speed of Mach 0.925 … apparently no other traditional business jet will take you closer to the speed of sound.'

'Fascinating, babe.' Billie-Jo flicked her new, blonde, hair extensions from her face and buckled up next to her husband. She was seriously impressed by today's mode of transport and equally as unimpressed by the calibre of her fellow guests: a couple of nobodies by the names Rupert and Angelika or something – hardly Brad and Angelina – and some old cougar she'd never even heard of with a toy-boy wannabe rock star in tow, though admittedly her eyes *had* lit up somewhat when Joshua Jones had introduced himself.

'Pleasure,' he'd said in a nasal New York accent that had caused her to twitch a little, his gaze lingering upon her a few seconds longer than was strictly necessary, though nonetheless welcome.

'Good of you to bring your mum,' Billie-Jo had remarked sweetly as she'd shook his heavily tattooed hand, the outline of his lithe, toned abdomen faintly visible through his tight V-neck T-shirt. *Tres rock star.* Lack of A-list aside, at least there was no other real female competition to give her cause for concern. That Angela bird, or whoever she was, was pretty enough but she had to be pushing thirty-five, and as for the singer, at least that's what Nate had said she was, though undeniably glamorous and clearly minted – Billie-Jo's hawk eyes had already clocked the Jimmy Choos, this season's, and the rare Cartier timepiece – she was old enough to have birthed her, and her boyfriend too by the looks of it.

'Wonder what the beef is between the old woman and that posh twat,' Billie-Jo whispered in her husband's ear hotly, intrigued by the frosty exchange she'd witnessed between Rupert and Mia. 'Do you reckon she's shagged him?'

'You have a very vivid imagination, Bee,' Nate commented without taking his eyes from the handbook. 'And that *old* woman is Mia Manhattan, a very famous soul singer.' He didn't know why he was even bothering to try and educate her. If it wasn't Calvin Harris or Nicki Minaj it didn't register in his wife's head. Frankly, unless it was pink, shiny and expensive, he wasn't entirely convinced that anything did.

Angelika glanced sideways at her husband. He had a serious *noir* look on his face. She opened her mouth to speak.

'Just don't, Angelika, OK?' he snapped. 'Don't say a goddamn word.' Rupert lunged forward. 'Excuse me, miss!' He clicked his fingers as the hostess made her way past them.

'Yes, sir,' Aki stopped short and turned to him with a fixed, wide grin. 'Can I get you something?'

Rupert leaned over across his wife.

'Look, I'm terribly sorry,' he apologised, 'but I think there's been some kind of mistake. Not your fault, of course,' he added sagely, 'but my wife and I, we need to disembark … immediately.' There wasn't a chance in hell that Rupert was prepared to spend a second longer in Mia Manhattan's company, let alone the next fourteen days. Being stuck on a desert bloody island with one harridan was enough, but Mia Manhattan harboured a deeply personal grudge against him, one that was completely unwarranted in his opinion. He'd done his best for the woman all those years ago, and in return she had done everything in her power to discredit him, making no bones whatsoever of her abject dislike of him. Well, the feeling was bloody well mutual as far as he was concerned.

Aki nodded but did not respond. She was still smiling.

'I'm sorry,' Rupert apologised disingenuously at her lack of response, 'perhaps I'm not making myself clear. Look, er –' he fought to recall her name '– Aki, is it? What I'm saying is my wife and I, we're leaving … getting off the plane, so if we could just collect our luggage …' Aki's unwavering smile was beginning to irritate the hell out of him.

'I'm afraid that's impossible, sir,' she replied with such joviality that it momentarily disarmed him.

'Impossible!' Rupert shot back. 'Bullshit! Get our bloody bags. Come on, Angelika.' He practically hoisted her up by her forearm. 'We're getting off this goddamn plane right now!'

'Ru!' Angelika hissed as she struggled to free herself from his grip. Her husband was being obnoxious, not to mention embarrassing.

'It is as I explained to Ms Manhattan, sir –' Aki's robotic smile remained, making him want to wipe it clean off her flat face with his spare fist '– the contract states that once you have boarded the fight you cannot disembark.'

'Contract? What bloody contract?' Rupert's face contorted with indignation and confusion. 'I didn't sign any contract. I'm a barrister, for goodness sake's, woman … it's my fucking job to read the small print.'

Billie-Jo watched from her seat, enthralled. She hadn't expected things to kick off so soon in the proceedings and was loving every second of the drama. Posh people fighting; hell, this was even better than an episode of *Made in Chelsea*.

'Yes, sir – the contract you signed, sir.' Aki's polite smile looked pasted on. 'It states clearly that once all parties have boarded the aircraft and the doors have closed, then no one is entitled to leave.'

'Entitled?' Rupert had unbuckled himself now and was standing. 'I'm *entitled*, lady, to do whatever I damn-well choose.'

'Rupert!' Angelika placed a hand on his arm.

'Show me this contract I supposedly signed. I demand to see it!'

He turned to Angelika. 'Jesus, this is a set-up, that's what this is – a set-up!'

Angelika shot her husband a sheepish look.

'*Angelika* …?' Rupert glared at his wife, his voice a low growl. 'Oh, Angelika … tell me you didn't sign anything.'

'Only the disclaimer I told you about!' she answered quickly, defensively. 'Look, let's just calm down, shall we?' She pulled her husband back down into his seat. 'Jesus, Rupert, you're making such a scene,' she hissed at him. 'Look, we're about to take off … I wasn't to know that Mia bloody Manhattan was going to be here, did I? I know she's not your biggest fan but –'

'– Nor I hers!' he cut her off.

'OK, OK, but it was a long time ago now … can't you just stay out of each other's way? I'm sure the island will be big enough. Besides,' she added, her voice softening in a desperate bid to placate him, 'maybe it will be the perfect opportunity for you to bury the hatchet.'

Rupert looked at his wife with such disdain that for a split second she genuinely thought he might strike her.

'Yes,' he agreed, 'in the back of her fucking head.'

CHAPTER SEVEN

The G650 had been cruising at 35,000 feet for approximately two and half hours and with the chilled Ruinart flowing and a breakfast menu of eggs Florentine, smoked salmon, beluga caviar and Bellinis served, the six guests, appetites stated, were beginning to relax – no one more so than Billie-Jo.

'Do you think they'll be shops at this place?' she asked Nate as she wiped the remains of her eggs Florentine from her plate with a Bellini, the idea of spending his money ever appealing.

'We're going to a paradise island, Bee,' Nate said, 'I highly doubt it … besides, haven't you brought enough stuff with you already?' Billie-Jo's five Louis Vuitton suitcases had taken two drivers to put them in the hold. She didn't exactly travel light.

'Just because it's an island doesn't mean there won't be shops,' she sniffed indignantly, gulping back champagne between her glossy, collagen-filled lips. 'Dubai has shops.'

'Dubai is a country, Bee.'

'Well, all right then, smartarse. Britain has shops and correct me if I'm wrong but that's an island, too...isn't it?'

Nate smiled at her in surprise as much as anything.

'Well, yes, it is...'

'See, not just a pretty face, eh?' Billie-Jo grinned, wondering if it was safe to slip off to the restroom for another livener without her husband growing suspicious. She didn't want Nate to know how out of hand her coke habit had become lately. In fact, she didn't want him to know about it *per se*. Her greatest concern was that he might cut her monthly allowance if he found out just how much of his cash she was shovelling up her nose. Their conversation was suddenly interrupted.

Angelika, smiling, was approaching them with an out-stretched hand. 'Hi, I'm Angelika, Angelika Deyton. Really nice to meet you both. Well, this is all pretty exciting, isn't it? Did you enjoy breakfast? Fabulous, wasn't it?'

'It was great, yeah,' Nate agreed, smiling at her friendly ef-fervescence, 'Nate, by the way. Nate Simmons.'

Angelika accepted his hand and was pleased when it gripped her own with some purchase. 'Yes, I know who you are.'

'And this is Billie-Jo.'

'His *wife*,' Billie-Jo added, her heckles raised for reasons she didn't fully understand.

'Pleasure to meet you both; this is my husband, Rupert,' she cocked her head behind her. Rupert raised a hand of ac-knowledgement from his seat without so much as turning to face them.

'Please excuse him, he's sulking,' she said, unsubtly poking him in the back of the neck with an apologetic smile. For some-one as educated and intelligent as her husband was, he could be so socially inept.

'I saw him arguing with the woman earlier,' Billie-Jo said, fishing for the low-down.

Nate nudged her in the ribs.

Angelika smiled and Nate noticed how it seemed to light up her entire face. He tried to place an age on her, something he wasn't particularly good at with women, but he figured she fell somewhere around the early-thirties mark like himself. Her skin was smooth and clear, her face fresh. Yeah, thirty-two at a push.

'Yes,' she explained, the apology evident in her voice, 'I'm afraid they have a little … how can I put it … *history*.'

'Were they once an item or something?'

Nate elbowed Billie-Jo in the ribs once more, sharply this time.

'What?' Billie-Jo shrieked in response. 'I'm only asking!'

'No, really, it's OK.' Angelika's smile remained. 'It goes back a long way. No doubt he will bore you all to death with it once we're on the island –'

'I heard that, Angelika!' Rupert called from his seat. Angelika bit her lip and crossed her eyes humorously. Nate found himself smiling broadly.

'So, how come you've been invited to Pleasure Island?' Billie-Jo continued with her less-than-subtle line of questioning, making it sound like Angelika had no right to be there.

'I'm a journalist,' she explained, 'for the *Daily Voice*. I have a column.'

Nate felt a jolt of disappointment from his solar plexus. She was a hack, *great*.

and he'd kind of liked her as well. She had a soft face: sweet and feminine, naturally pretty without being over-done. For a fleeting moment he found himself picturing what she might look like in the morning with bed hair and cute, sleepy eyes.

'You don't look like a hack,' he said without thinking.

'If you mean I don't have a snout …' Her smile was broad and genuine, her teeth neat and perfect except for one of the incisors on the left which turned slightly inwards. He liked it; it gave her face character.

'He hates the press, don't you, babe?' Billie-Jo explained. 'They've been proper bastards to him ever since the accident, and then there was all that adoption business. That paper you work for proper done him up like a right kipper.'

'Bee, please.' Nate wished to God that she would just keep that gaping hole in the middle of her face shut sometimes.

'I wouldn't worry,' Angelika said as if reading his thoughts, 'I'm not here to spy on anyone. I'm simply a guest like you. In it for the free holiday!' she giggled, not wanting to expose her true motives. 'Anyway, if it's any consolation, I'm sorry about the story – can't have been easy for you.' She felt a little guilty about her profession at times, this being one of them.

Nate averted his gaze and gave a brief nod. He didn't really want to get into a conversation about it right now. Besides, he couldn't be sure she wasn't fishing for a follow-up story, like the fact that he had appointed a PI to track down his real parents. She'd be on the phone to her editor faster than Usain Bolt through a finish line if she got wind of that little piece of info. He would have to remind that wife of his to keep her trap shut on that count.

Joshua Jones glanced sideways at Mia who was almost reclined in her white-leather seat, a black silk mask covering her eyes, her face still as stone, mouth a grim, thin line. He figured she was probably sleeping. Glancing over at the woman standing chatting to two of the other guests, he made to get up and go over, ostensibly to check out the foxy little blonde married to the footballer dude. He'd already given himself a lazy hard-on just thinking about watching her strut around near naked in a bikini for the next fourteen days. So what if the girl was married. He could still look, hell, judging by the look she'd given him on introduction, he could probably touch as well. JJ instinctively knew just by looking at a girl if she was the type to give the green light from the get-go. Billie-Jo was *definitely* one of those girls.

'Just off to the restroom,' he said, adjusting his skin-tight black jeans as he stood, 'Need to pee.'

Mia silently watched him from the gap beneath her eye mask.

'Hey guys, you all cool?' JJ said as he made his way through the cabin.

'Hi!' Angelika said brightly. 'You're Joshua, right? I was just about to ask these guys where they thought we might be headed to today. It's all a bit secretive, don't you think? We were thinking about taking out a wager, maybe. My money's on the Bahamas somewhere.'

Rupert smirked from his seat. *I was just about to ask these guys ...*' His wife sounded like a bad children's TV show host. She was pushing forty, for God's sake.

'Who knows, dude,' JJ said, shrugging with deliberate rockstar insouciance, though in reality he was just as intrigued as everyone else was about their intended destination. 'I'm just enjoying the free champagne!' *And the view.*

Billie-Jo raised her glass, eyeing him flirtatiously. 'I'll drink to that.'

'You'll drink to anything,' Nate remarked, though he made sure to laugh as he said it.

'Let's have a toast, shall we?' Angelika suggested, caught up in the moment of bonding with her fellow guests. She poked her husband. 'Rupert ... and we mustn't forget Mia. Mia!' Angelika called over to her.

'Bloody hell, Angelika,' Rupert complained. Did she have to do this; it was damned awkward enough as it was being stuck on a bloody plane with his nemesis without his damned wife trying to recreate a scene from the Fucking *Partridge Family*.

'After all, we're all in this adventure together aren't we?' she smiled, determined to drag him from his moribund mood.

Mia reluctantly removed her eye mask and looked over at them. If that silly bint who had the misfortune to have married Rupert Deyton thought she was going to toast to their shared experience she had another thing coming. Snowmen would survive hell before she would chink glasses with that arsehole. Mia felt utterly depressed, not to mention still furious. It wasn't enough that she'd agreed to have anything to do with Martin McKenzie in the first place, a man she despised even more than she did Rupert Deyton. It was as if someone was playing a sick joke on her, a very sick joke indeed.

'Excuse me, Aki,' Angelika called out to the flight attendant who was busy clearing away the remains of the breakfast they'd not long ago enjoyed. 'Would it be possible to bring more champagne ... we'd like to make a toast.' She was feeling a little light-headed already, something she put down to the early morning rise and champagne combined, though she hadn't even had half a glass. The plane juddered a little, causing her to momentarily grip the edge of the seat in a bid to steady herself.

'Absolutely, madam,' Aki nodded obligingly. 'Right away.'

The diminutive woman disappeared behind the red curtain, reappearing a few moments later carrying a magnum of vintage Krug.

'Only the best stuff for Mr McKenzie, right?' Angelika noted, watching as she teetered towards them. The plane was juddering ever so slightly harder now, enough for Angelika's grin to settle into a smile.

'Must've hit a bit of turbulence,' she said, nerves beginning to flutter gently on her stomach.

'You should sit down,' Nate suggested, 'wait for it to pass.'

Angelika agreed, taking her seat next to her husband and buckling up.

Aki began to distribute the champagne into the cut crystal flutes, seemingly impervious to the fact that she was spilling half of it onto the pristine black carpet in the process.

'It's just a little turbulence,' she assured them as the glasses tinkled.

Billie-Jo swiped her glass of fizz.

'I hate turbulence,' she said gulping back the Krug, wishing she'd had that little livener to accompany it now. 'It gives me the shits.'

'It's nothing,' Nate placated her, making sure he'd said it loud enough for Angelika to hear too. He noticed she'd turned a little pale and felt the odd need to reassure her too.

The plane suddenly lurched sharply to the right.

'Fucking shit!' The magnum of champagne hit the floor and exploded with a bang and hiss. Billie-Jo's glass followed suit.

'For God's sake, Angelika!' Rupert snapped irritably as his wife dug her nails into his arm in a bid to stop herself form falling backwards.

'What in God's name …!' Mia Manhattan was practically hanging over the edge of her reclined seat, her belt the only thing preventing her from having been thrown to the floor.

The force of the sharp lurch had forced JJ onto one knee.

'Fuck man, that was heavy,' he said, a little lightheaded from the violent rush of adrenaline that had mainlined through his system like a line of coke. He scrambled to his feet as the plane seemed to momentarily adjust itself. 'You OK, Mia?' He helped her back up into a seated position. She was too stunned to reply. She felt woozy with stress and just wanted to sleep. Perhaps then she would wake up and realise it was all just a dreadful nightmare.

'Ladies and gentlemen, if you could all remain seated with your belts on.' Aki's voice was authoritative. 'We're experiencing some extreme turbulence but it is nothing to be concerned about, I assure you nothing to be...' but she was suddenly drowned out by a diabolical high pitched whining sound followed in quick succession by a loud explosion similar to that of a car backfiring. The plane began to shake and roll...the sound of glass smashing causing Billie-Jo to scream in terror.

'It's OK, Bee.' Nate instinctively put a hand on her leg as they veered violently to the right once more. The plane was rolling now, careening from side to side. He was aware of objects falling, but couldn't locate where they were coming from. An acrid smell of burning machinery quickly contaminated the cabin.

'Shitting hell on earth …' Mia attempted to pull herself upright but the g-force prevented her from moving. She was pinned to her right, her forehead impacting with JJ's knee.

'What the fuck's happening, man?' JJ's voice crackled with fear. 'This gotta be some fucking turbulence …'

'One of the goddamn engines must've blown.' Rupert scrambled to reach for the safety card he'd spied in the front-seat pocket earlier. 'Where are the fucking exits on this plane?' he shouted, panic evident in his voice. 'Where are the goddamn exits?'

Angelika struggled to breathe; it was getting unbearably hot inside the cabin and the acrid stench felt as if it was going straight to her lungs.

'I can't breathe, Ru,' she spluttered. Everything was happening so quickly.

'If one of the engines has blown it's OK … we'll make it with just one.' Rupert was struggling, his shaking fingers finally making contact with the safety card, snatching it into his grasp.

'Are we gonna crash?' Billie-Jo started to cry, fat black tears escaping from her heavily made up face. 'I don't wanna die … I'm too fucking young! I don't wanna die!'

'Bee, Bee, it's OK, just stay still … hold my hand.' Nate attempted to calm her but as usual Billie-Jo was following her own agenda.

Angelika turned round to her with an outstretched hand.

'It's OK, honey,' she said, taking Billie-Jo's fingers in her own. 'It's going to be fine. OK, just relax, yes?'

'What in God's name is going on?' Rupert unbuckled his belt and attempted to stand as the plane once again appeared to steady itself. 'Where's that bloody Jap gone … excuse me! Aki … hello … can someone tell us what the hell is happening here? Is there a problem with the engine … the Hydraulics?'

Rupert glanced over in Mia's direction. She appeared to be praying.

'Dear God,' she said as she frantically rubbed the small Graff diamond cross necklace she was wearing between her fingers, 'don't let me die like this...not like this...'

She felt tears stinging the backs of her eyes. She supposed in a way it would somehow be befitting: 'former superstar dies in luxury jet crash'. Admittedly it had certain cache. Besides, many of the greats had gone the same way, like poor old John Denver. She'd sung with him once upon a time when she'd been a slip of a girl and the memory caused a small cry to catch in the back of her throat. She glanced over at Joshua. He looked pale and scared and so terribly young that she suddenly felt ashamed of herself. What a stupid, selfish woman she was inviting him to accompany her on this godforsaken, ridiculous trip. He would die too now, long before his time without even having made his mark on the world.

The plane suddenly dropped violently like a rollercoaster and Angelika felt her stomach lurch and rise up into her diaphragm.

'Is this it, Ru?' her voice was low and shaky, her mind desperately struggling to come to terms with the gravity of the situation. 'Are we going to crash?'

Rupert didn't answer her, he was scan-reading the safety card, forced to squint without his glasses.

'I know we don't always see eye to eye,' she said, 'but I do lo –'

Ladies and gentlemen.' Aki's voice sounded different, lower, as it rang out through the intercom system. 'The captain has informed me that he has lost control of the aircraft. Please remain seated and adopt the brace position. I said remain seated and adopt the brace position!'

'Oh, fucking shit. …oh, Jesus fucking holy fucking Christ!' Billie-Jo's piercing screams filled the cabin as she crossed her arms in front of her chest. 'We're gonna fucking die,' she wailed, 'we're all gonna fucking die!'

'Where are the oxygen masks?' Rupert frantically ran his hands on the ceiling above him. He looked at Angelika as he gave up and buckled himself in his seat, engulfed by a terrible sense of *fait accompli.* 'God, Ange,' he said, his voice despairing, 'there aren't any oxygen masks.' He hadn't called her Ange in years.

Helpless, he looked out of the window but saw only darkness.

'Are we above the sea?' Angelika enquired. 'Should we look for life jackets?'

'Somebody help us!' Billie-Jo wailed in despair. 'We'll be eaten alive by sharks … no … no … God make it stop … get me off this plane … Nate … please … get me off … I don't wanna die.'

'For goodness sakes, shut her up, will you? I'm trying to concentrate here,' Rupert shouted as Nate attempted to console his wife's burgeoning hysterics.

'Can't you see she's terrified?' Angelika said just as the lights in the aircraft failed, plunging them all into total darkness.

The plane lunged with such brute force that it violently threw them all forward. Billie-Jo's face impacted with the seat in front of her, silencing her immediately. Instinctively she brought her hand up to her face, it felt wet but she was still alive. Oh thank god, *thank God.*

Suspended from her seat, practically upside down, Mia groaned. This was it. Her time was up. Her number called. She thought about Richard, her darling Dickie. How she'd loved that man, how she still did. At least she would have her revenge this way; dying a brutal death befitting of a world-famous singer. He would mourn her, she felt sure of it, weep over her grave while begging her forgiveness for ever having deserted her, for trading in all those precious years in exchange for a young bit of strange. In that moment Mia fleetingly forgave her husband's betrayal, wanting only to feel his arms around her one last time. An eerie calm had descended upon the cabin now, a dark silence of the condemned. She hoped she would be forgiven for her sins when she met her maker; more than anything she hoped Richard would forgive her for her futile attempts at making him jealous, for being too self-absorbed to realise her marriage was disintegrating around her, but above all, she wanted to be forgiven by *him*.

'Forgive me, baby,' Mia said as she felt the tears, or perhaps it was blood, drip from her face. 'Wherever you are, please forgive me.'

The final explosion, when it came, was louder and sounded more alien than anything any of the cabin's occupants had ever heard before. The diabolical crunch of metal ripping, the smell of burning, of fire, and the shrieks and cries of human pain and terror, felt as if they had gone on for eternity.

After that … silence.

`

CHAPTER EIGHT

'Angelika! Angelika!'

Rupert Deyton had come to with such a start that he'd audibly gasped, a sound he so rarely emanated that he couldn't be sure it had come from him. Once he'd established that he was both alive and relatively unscathed, he quickly took stock, his sharp, logical mind beginning to assess. He was on a beach, at least of sorts, the sun dappled sea stretched out in front of him, calm and almost perfectly still. He was filthy, covered in sand and debris, his hands black with a soot-like substance. Remarkably, aside from a small gash on his left shin, he was unhurt. He saw the wreckage.

The plane, what was left of it, was situated on what looked like sand dunes … where in God's name were they? The front nose was completely missing, torn off like the top of a tin can displaying the inside of the once magnificent Lear jet. The outsides were black; smoke-stained from the explosion he assumed must've taken place on impact. The jagged edges where the nose had ripped off looked like teeth, the wing of the plane reminiscent of a fin, a beached shark come to rest by the water, thin delicate waves gently creeping underneath in a stealth-like bid to drag it into its deep; ugly chunks of metal and plastic debris, incongruous somehow with the flora and fauna that surrounded it, wires and metal exposed to the elements, an alien exploded. He spotted one of the expensive-looking white leather plane seats to his left, discordant on its side where it had been jettisoned from the aircraft and other unidentifiable objects: red plastic – a drinks tray, perhaps; torn fabric that clung to tufts of dry grass on the sand dunes, bright like flags fluttering in the gentle but steady sea breeze.

Rupert involuntarily shuddered; the sight he was witnessing was as sickening and disturbing as it was alien, the eye unable to fully comprehend it, the brain struggling to process. *Where in God's name were they?* Blinking, bewildered he forcibly pulled Angelika up into a seated position. She *would* regain full consciousness.

'Angelika, wake up!' he commanded in a voice similar to the one he used whenever she overslept. 'I need you to wake up!'

He glanced at the boy next to her. The bone of his forearm was sticking clean out of his skin, just below the elbow, the repugnant smell of flesh filling his nostrils as he drew closer to inspect it.

'The boy's going to lose his arm.' He announced the fact without emotion as he removed his shirt and began ripping strips of fabric from it in a bid to make a tourniquet, and stem the bleeding. 'He needs our help fast … Angelika! Angelika, wake up!'

Angelika was groggy but awake, slipping and sliding in and out of consciousness, struggling to keep her eyes open, seconds lost as her body fluctuated between the two.

'I'm here, Ru,' she whispered. 'Darling, I'm here.' She was sitting upright without assistance now, which was enough for Rupert to begin focussing his attention elsewhere.

Mia Manhattan's dress had been torn from her body as she lay half naked and exposed on the sand. Her face was bloody and messy but instinctively Rupert knew her injuries were superficial. She was spreadeagled, legs and arms wide in an undignified star shape, her expensive underwear, what remained of it, barely covering what little modesty she had left.

Rupert crouched over her, his mouth almost touching hers as he listened for breath. He was too scared to touch her initially but soon overcame his apprehension and put his hand on her naked chest. A heartbeat. She was alive, for now at least.

'Is she...?' Angelika croaked through the foggy haze inside her head.

'Alive …' . Secretly he was relieved and they both knew it. He may not have liked the blasted woman but he didn't want her dead. Not like this.

A figure approached.

'Nate …' Angelika said, her voice cracking like the embers of a bonfire, hoarse and dry.

He stumbled towards them, a dishevelled human mess, shirt ripped and black with debris and smoke, his smart jeans torn and gaping open at the knee, a diabolical fashion statement that seemed somehow almost contrived. And there was blood – a deep burgundy stain – on his once-pristine white shirt, though the source of its origin was not yet obvious.

'Oh, thank God.' He sunk to his knees before he reached them, tears making visible white tracks down his ashen face. 'Thank God,' he repeated, sobbing and struggling to contain raw emotion and relief.

'Are you OK? Are you hurt? … Your wife?' Angelika stood, a bruising pain sweeping through her hip like fire. She forced herself to make her way to him, her feet disappearing into the sand beneath her with every painful step. It was only then she realised her dress had been torn off from the waist down, exposing her underwear, a thought that registered with her mind but bore little significance. Now was not the time for modesty. 'Billie-Jo …? Is she OK?' She fell into Nate's arms on the sand. His body felt strong as she held him, a moment of comfort with a virtual stranger, survival instinct usurping any form of social convention, embarrassment or etiquette.

Nate nodded.

'Yes,' was all he could manage; it was enough.

Nate looked down at Joshua; he was unconscious. 'Oh, Jesus Christ ...'

Angelika was crying now though she wasn't aware of it.

'We need help,' she said desperately, turning to look up at Rupert. 'We have to find help ...'

Rupert ignored her. He was trying to think, to focus. Did they have water? They needed water, the boy especially. He would check the wreckage...

'Get your act together,' he addressed Nate calmly but with an efficiency that made him look up. 'This man here will die unless we get water and find help fast. Looking at the wound it seems like a pretty clean cut...he hasn't severed a femoral artery, thank God. I've applied a tourniquet but he needs emergency medical attention. He'll bleed out in an hour tops, if the hypovolemic shock doesn't kill him first, that is. And frankly I don't fancy burying his body. Do you?'

Nate composed himself. He nodded. He was strong and fit; they could make it.

'The phones,' he said, suddenly remembering, 'the woman took the phones ...'

Rupert's spirits instantly lifted. Of course.

'We need to find them. Search the plane.'

'The pilot?' Angelika suddenly thought, 'and the girl ... the Japanese girl. Ari ... Annie ...Aki? What happened to them?'

'Don't touch him, Angelika!' Rupert screamed at her as she gasped, covering her mouth to stifle the horror that swept through her like a backdraught. The pilot was slumped onto the control panel of the cockpit, his small body mounting the desk, eyes wide open in horror, a line of blood trickled from his mouth.

'But he might still be …' She didn't finish the sentence; it was pointless and she knew it.

'And the girl?' Nate asked. He tried to avert his eyes away from the horror that confronted him but they remained fixed upon it. He would remember this sight until his last breath. In that moment it was the only thing he was sure of.

'No sign of her,' Rupert said, his attentions had already shifted. There was nothing to be done here. The man was clearly dead. Right now it was survival plain and simple. Fight or flight. As cold as it seemed, there was no choice. There was nowhere to run.

CHAPTER NINE

The American's disposition generally hovered somewhere between mildly sociopathic and borderline narcissistic. Sometimes, even during his professional life as a highly respected psychotherapist, he liked to consciously make a morally dubious decision just to see what the outcome would be, for nothing more than his own personal amusement. Now, however, he was having an unusual attack of conscience.

The line on the conference call crackled loudly causing him to grimace and move the receiver away from his ear.

'So far so good?' McKenzie enquired.

'No complaints from me,' the woman responded, 'The arm was a sublime surprise. And the pyrotechnics ... wow ...'

'I knew *you* would approve,' he responded, 'although I have to say, I can't take full credit for the arm because it wasn't entirely intentional –'

'The arm,' the American interjected, 'was unexpected and ... frankly ... well ... we agreed no one would be *physically* hurt. This was supposed to be a purely psychological experiment after all.' They both knew how ridiculous this statement sounded, that he was using supposed professional interests as a smokescreen for his own personal perversions.

'I realise it had to be authentic, but I agree, it was perhaps a little too much.'

Another of the gentleman spoke, though McKenzie wasn't sure which one: 'What were you thinking, McKenzie? We weren't consulted on this; I don't see it anywhere in the script.'

McKenzie cleared his throat. What these schmucks failed to understand was that he was calling the shots in this game; they were merely enablers and voyeurs, paying guests at his party. This was history in the making and frankly they should consider themselves lucky enough to be part of such a pioneering moment.

'You disapprove?'

'As a matter of fact, yes, I do; breaking his arm was gruesome and unnecessary, but what I object to the most is the fact that we weren't consulted on it.'

McKenzie stifled an incredulous laugh; the words horse, door and bolted springing to mind.

'Well, I loved it,' the woman cut in, 'such beautiful … *suffering*. And the reaction … the horror, the fear on their faces, especially the young Barbie doll, though I wouldn't be too fooled by the bimbo act; something tells me there's more to her than she's letting on.'

'I agree,' a male voice interjected, 'she's intriguing, and so is her husband, or at least the dynamic between them is; I would like to see what their marriage is really made of.'

'And you will,' McKenzie cut in. 'I assure you I have chosen these delegates carefully, and soon you will understand why.'

'Well, I'm guessing we know why you chose the journo,' one of the men said, 'after that expose she wrote on you I'm surprised you didn't have her bumped off. She was hardly complimentary after all.' The caller chuckled.

Martin McKenzie loosened the collar of his pristine, white, Tom Ford shirt, one of the identical hundreds that he owned with a growing sense of irritation.

The gentleman was indeed correct in his assumption as to why he had selected Angelika Deyton as one of his guests. Six or so months ago she had come to interview him, ostensibly to discuss the global domination of his most-recent reality TV creation, '*Sing When you're Winning*', a hybrid mix of part-talent, part-game show. He had been rather taken with her, in all honesty. She was attractive and wore her intellect like a badge; he'd been impressed by her sharp wit and direct, fearless style of questioning– a breath of fresh air from all the other sycophantic idiots with their predictable, inane questions. As such he had rather enjoyed sparring with her. In retrospect, however, he realised she had duped him; she had come with the intention of doing a hatchet job, her friendly-yet-challenging approach merely a cunning ruse to lull him into a false sense of security, thereby dropping his guard a fraction more than he would normally allow. Martin McKenzie considered himself to be infinitely smarter than anyone he knew, not least some household hack with a pretty face and nice ass, and because of this he chose to conduct all interviews *sans* representatives. He didn't need some simpering PA to veto any questions put to him, and certainly the answers he chose to give in response. He didn't play the game; he'd *invented* the game. And yet this little tart with a degree had somehow managed to get the better of him. The subsequent first-person feature she had written for that filthy rag she worked for had been detrimental both professionally and personally, both of which McKenzie could handle without question; one didn't rise to such stratospheric heights without expecting some criticism along the way, even he understood this. But he'd felt tricked into such candour by Angelika Deyton, like she'd outsmarted him, something he simply could not allow to pass.

"McKenzie crushes hopes and dreams like the rest of us crush an empty crisp packet – and then discards it with as much contempt and consideration for its onward journey … .he displays a frighteningly diminished interest in the psychological well-being of his contestants … his narcissistic leanings suggest he conducts himself without reproach, or conscience … I imagine he shouts out his own name at the point of orgasm …"

Publically, McKenzie had dismissed the writer's rhetoric as 'amusing'; privately, however, it had been a different story, culminating in a rage that had seen him destroy his office and sack his press officer, a loyal member of his team for over a decade.

'All will be revealed in good time, I assure you,' McKenzie stated, Angelika's written words resonating like poison inside his mind. She had been rather *laize faire* with the word 'sociopath' in her description of him. Now she would discover first-hand what this truly meant.

'It's the hack's husband; the barrister's the biggest problem,' the Japanese man said. 'He's a little bullish, hot-headed, certainly very intelligent and more than a touch arrogant, which will be his ultimate downfall, of course.'

'Of course,' McKenzie agreed.

'Have you noticed that there's a spark of something in the footballer's eyes whenever he looks at her … the journalist, I mean,' the woman interjected, 'I'd like to explore this.'

'All in good time, my dear. All in good time.'

The American stared at his computer screen, at the chaos ensuing in real time, panic and fear etched upon shocked and horrified faces. He had muted the sound of the live stream so that he could make the telephone call; frankly he found all the histrionics more distasteful than he'd thought he would, though admittedly the stunt had had been impressively executed, right down to the last detail, even the way the footballer's jeans had been deliberately ripped and the skirts torn from the women. Very authentic indeed.

'We agreed this would be a purely social experiment, McKenzie,' the American reiterated his fellow voyeur's earlier sentiment, 'a calculated insight allowing us to study the human condition.' His nasal voice was whiney. 'We're paying a premium and this kinda shit ain't really my bag, you know.' A super-intelligent forty-five-year-old somewhat-sexually-deviant professor of psychology he may be, but he wasn't a complete sadist, at least not generally speaking. 'I didn't sign up for a Goddamn horror show. Now we got a situation on our hands. There's a man, hell, he's practically a boy, down there in agony, probably bleeding to death. Lucky that the barrister had the good sense to apply a half decent tourniquet and stem the flow.'

'Yes,' a new voice interjected, a British one, 'we can't let him die. Look, I don't give a rat's arse about the odd deviation from the script, unforeseen or otherwise. I mean, that's the whole premise, right? And unlike my American friend here, I don't have a stick up my arse, but I don't want to be up for a ten stretch either, you understand?'

McKenzie swallowed back his burgeoning irritation. This was *his* show; he was the puppet master, the director. He didn't care to be questioned. The arm had been an accident pure and simple, the best laid plans and all of that; but it was just a minor problem, nothing McKenzie couldn't handle in a heartbeat. Their lack of faith, however, displeased him immensely. McKenzie needed, no, he *demanded* full compliance and unwavering praise and loyalty from everyone he was in contact with, lest his fragile ego be challenged or broken.

'Relax gentlemen,' he said measuredly, 'we have a surgeon waiting. He'll be good as new once he's finished with him. It's an open fracture, not heart surgery.'

He almost felt the palpable relief from down the line. 'I have to say though I'm somewhat disappointed; I was of the mindset that you would welcome such an unexpected twist. I mean, now is not really the time to have an attack of moral conscience.

Besides, isn't this what you signed up for? A once-in-a-lifetime opportunity to study the human condition when faced with adversity and moral dilemma. …?'

'I don't like surprises,' the American said flatly. 'We've got to remain in control.'

'Well, in that case please accept my sincerest apologies.' *Like hell.* The Yank was a deviant. He wanted tits and ass; McKenzie could tell. But he wasn't the only one of the Super Eight that needed pleasing in this pantomime.

The line sizzled like a snare above the silence that followed.

'So, what is next?' A French accent finally broke it, or perhaps German; he couldn't quite tell.

'What would you like to be next?'

'Let's get this party started properly, shall we? No more playing, how you say, *silly buggers*?'

'Yes … but before all that you need get that goddamn boy seen to, pronto.' The American was insistent.

McKenzie smiled thinly, though his telephone guests could not be aware of this.

'Like I said, relax. The rescue plane is already on its way.'

CHAPTER TEN

Mia Manhattan had regained full consciousness but as yet did not feel strong enough to stand. Instead she had dragged herself through the sand and debris over to where her very young lover was lying. His face was pale as a ghost's. She had not noticed the injury at first.

'Joshua darling, wake up. Come on now …wak–' She spied his arm and horror attacked itself to her aorta, nausea rising up through her intestines and threatening to spill out over her expensive designer kaftan, what was left of it. 'Oh dear God, no … oh, no, no, *noooooo*.' She collapsed onto his body, her chest heaving with gut-wrenching sobs, a primal scream rising from deep within her.

'Help!' she screamed, alerting the others who had gathered by the plane wreckage, 'Somebody *helllllp*!'

'Mia's awake,' Rupert remarked deadpan as her urgent screams rang out across the sand like a ship's horn.

Nate made his way over towards her, practically dragging a tearful Billie-Jo with him.

'He's hurt.' Mia was sobbing as they approached. 'His arm. … dear God. This is all my fault … all my fault. Is he going to die?'

Nate knelt next to her on the sand and placed a hand around her shoulder as Billie-Jo stood back, too fearful to go any closer, her stomach lurching, eyes unable to deviate from the bloody stump that was protruding through his skin. Nate didn't like to see a woman cry, least of all an older woman. He felt Mia's vulnerability as he put his arm around her, and something else as he held her: the need to protect her.

'It's OK,' Nate reassured Mia, as she had clung onto him, 'Shhh, it's OK.' He couldn't, however, answer her question. He looked down at JJ's injury; the tourniquet that Rupert had fashioned from strips of his shirt earlier was soaked burgundy with blood. The ugly truth was that unless they found help soon he *would* be in big trouble. And they all knew it.

Rupert joined them, Angelika close behind.

'The wound needs dressing,' Nate said, 'it will become infected unless it's cleaned.'

Rupert rolled his eyes.

'And here I was thinking you footballer's were a bunch of brainless buffoons.'

Angelika looked at Nate in horrified apology.

'We need to move him out of the sun,' Nate said, ignoring the remark, 'get him in the shade.'

'Precisely what I was thinking,' Rupert agreed, a trifle irked that the footballer appeared to be asserting control. 'Then we need to find some water.'

'Inside the wreckage?' Mia suggested. Her mouth was as dry as sandpaper, her lips beginning to stiffen as she licked them in a bid to keep them moist.

Angelika shook her head.

'We've already searched … nothing …'

'But there *must* be –'

'Didn't you hear her, Mia, or are you deaf as well as stupid,' Rupert snapped, turning away from her. 'We looked and couldn't find anything, no sustenance whatsoever.'

'Fuck you, Deyton,' Mia croaked, 'there's a man in distress here.'

'Child, you mean. Shame on you, Manhattan.' He shot her a derisive glance. 'If he dies, I will hold you personally responsible.' It was an unfair comment and Rupert knew it but Mia Manhattan was an easy target for his growing frustration.

'Jesus Christ, Rupert,' Angelika screamed, 'Just fucking stop, OK?! *Stop!*'

'I hold *you* responsible, Deyton,' Mia shot back menacingly, eyes like slits disappearing into her skull, 'I wouldn't have been on that goddamn plane if you hadn't destroyed my fucking career in the first place by being such an incompetent prick.'

She turned to Angelika, her enraged face streaked with black tears, her aging-yet-beautiful features defiant in their anguish.

'I feel sorry for you being married to such a bastard. You seem like a decent woman, as well; I'd get out while you can, while you still have both your youth and looks to rely on. Don't suppose he ever told you what really went on all those years ago, during the trial, did he?'

'Shut up, Mia!' Rupert boomed, lunging forwards as if to strike her.

Mia smirked, though she was more rattled than she let on.

'Ahh, so you didn't tell her, did you? Did you? Unscrupulous fucker –'

'Tell me, how is Richard these days, Mia? Oh yes, that's right, gold ol' Dickie is putting his *dickie* to better use with another woman, isn't he? A *younger* one. Saw the light eventually then. Always knew he had more sense …'

'You...!' Mia launched herself at him with what little strength she possessed but Nate wrestled her back, surprised by her considerable strength given her stature.

'Don't rise to it,' he said.

Billie-Jo watched the drama unfold from a safe distance. Usually she would have thoroughly enjoyed such a scene but this was all way too real to be pleasurable. All she wanted was to go home. She didn't even care about the Vuitton cases and watch anymore.

'Guys, please.' Nate was hyperventilating, holding a struggling Mia by the crooks of her arms. 'This is not the time to start evening old scores. We have to stick together; we *need* to stick together if we're going to survive this.'

'He's right, Rupert,' Angelia conceded, pleading with her husband. 'We have to find water … we need to take a look around … we need shelter, food. Please, let's think about Joshua … put him first.'

'It's not looking good,' Rupert looked down at Joshua with a sense of pitiful resignation, as he composed himself, he'd stopped groaning and thrashing around now and was pale and silent.

'How long has it been?' Nate wondered aloud, 'Since we came round from the crash, I mean?'

The light was beginning to change, the first suggestion of dusk hovering like a threat.

'It's difficult to say,' Angelika replied.

'Seems odd,' Nate said, 'It was dark when we were flying, right? The middle of the night? And we all came round about the same time … within a few minutes of each other. And now it's getting light …'

'Meaning what?' Rupert asked, his anger diminishing along with his hope.

'Meaning …I don't know,' Nate said, 'meaning something's not right …'

'None of this is fucking right,' Mia interjected, 'Pleasure Island, my goddamn arse … more like hell on earth.'

'Much the same as one of your concerts I should imagine, Mia.' Rupert couldn't help himself.

'Don't start, Rupert,' Angelika begged him, 'Please, for God's sakes, don't …'

'Look, we're going to get out of this, I know we are,' Nate said, 'I don't know where the hell we are but I'm pretty sure it's not where we're supposed to be. McKenzie would have expected us by now. He'll send out a search party; he'll have alerted the necessary services already – I feel sure.'

'Well, let's bloody well hope so,' Mia snorted derisively, 'because so far I see nothing *pleasurable* about this place.'

Her attention was suddenly caught by something above her.

Billie-Jo, a safe distance from the others, looked up and put a hand over her mouth, instinctively sinking to her knees.

She could only point as she struggled with the words that were forming in her mouth, a river of relief flooding her body and momentarily paralysing her facial muscles.

'Hey,' she said, though her voice, weak, lacked any projection above the arguing.

'Hey!' she was louder this time, enough to catch Angelika's attention.

'Billie-Jo…? Are you OK? What is it?'

Salty tears were rolling down Billie-Jo's face, stinging her eyes and blinding her as she pointed to the sky. 'P … P … plane!' she managed to say, before passing out on the sand.

CHAPTER ELEVEN

The pilot, a small, dark-skinned man in a white T-shirt and matching trousers said nothing throughout the mercifully short plane journey until it came to an end.

'The boy, he come with us … we fly to the hospital,' he whispered in broken English as they disembarked.

'Are you a doctor?' Rupert asked, protective of their wounded comrade, 'Who are you? Did McKenzie send you?'

'I'll go with him,' Mia said even though she was exhausted, lethargy claiming every inch of her.

The pilot shook his head. 'The boy, he fly alone.'

Nate felt lightheaded with adrenalin, high almost. He's wanted to speak, to object, say something, anything, but it felt as if the right messages were being sent to the wrong place inside his head.

'Did McKenzie send you?' Rupert repeated once more, he was struggling to focus, the situation too surreal, his mind confused, his mouth dry as the sand he stood upon. He felt a little woozy but above all he felt relief. They were on their way to Pleasure Island. They were saved.

'You sleep,' the pilot said, pointing in the direction of the warm, inviting glow of the luxurious cabanas that had just come into view.

'Oh, thank God,' Angelika breathed, 'we've made it.' Nate had been right; McKenzie had called out a search party for them. She hoped that by tomorrow this would all seem like a bad dream.

Through sheer exhaustion they'd surrendered to sleep in the end with little choice and minimal fuss. Angelika had struggled to keep her eyes open; she'd felt groggy, a little confused but even in the dark it struck her that the island was quite beautiful. An expanse of untouched, white sand illuminated in the inky blackness, a row of vast cabanas stood on wooden stilts in the shallow water's edge as if suspended in mid-air, welcoming warm, orange candlelight emanating from the vast terraces, enticing them in. Behind the villas, set further back from the shoreline was a huge mansion, colonial and majestic, a little sinister even, or so it appeared in the darkness.

A small welcome committee had gathered on shore to greet them; unfamiliar faces with comforting sounds and soft blankets as they'd finally made it onto sand. Angelika could not tell if they were men or women. It didn't matter. They were alive; they had made it.

A female member of the greeters began to gesticulate wildly, banging and crashing her hands together like cymbals, running her fingers up towards the sky and down again.

'What happened here?' Angelika asked her, watching as she continued with her silent mime. 'A storm?'

The woman shook her head animatedly.

'There's been a storm on the island?'

So a storm had caused the plane to crash. It all made sense now.

'I need to make a phone call immediately,' Rupert's authoritative voice severed Angelika's thoughts like an axe.

The woman simply shook her head, her expression apologetic.

'The lines?' Angelika attempted to communicate with her once more, 'The telephone lines are down?'

Nate sighed; he had never felt so heavy, so exhausted, as if his limbs were made of lead. Billie-Jo had already begun to follow one of the guides up towards the low-lit cabanas, her need to rest ameliorating anything else. She was safe, and for now that's all that mattered.

'You will let me know if you find my Rolex,' she said, her voice a husky rasp, 'It was a wedding gift from my husband you know. I loved that watch …' Her voice trailed off '… so pretty …'

'Where's McKenzie?' Rupert wanted to shake the man's hand and thank him personally for sending a rescue plane. It suddenly hit him just how close to losing their lives they had come but the woman simply continued to stare at him blankly.

'Let's go, Rupert,' Nate nodded at him, his arm draped protectively around Mia's slim, delicate shoulder, 'We can ask questions in the morning.'

Angelika came to with the sound of his voice.

'He's right, Ru,' she said, 'Let's sleep. We'll get our answers in the morning.'

Though in truth something told her not to be so sure.

'Feeling better now, my American friend?' Super8#3 enquired as he watched the group alight onto the island, bedraggled, exhausted, their faces pale and drawn in the moonlight. 'They've landed safe and the boy has been flown off to get fixed up so I guess you can relax now.'

There was a few moment's pause as Super8#3 adjusted his laptop screen to prevent glare which was threatening to ruin his voyeuristic experience; it was 90 degrees sunshine in LA. He kicked his espadrilles off and placed his sticky feet on his desk.

Although he didn't have the first idea who he really was, he'd taken an instant dislike to Super8#6. The guy came across as an arrogant dick.

'As a matter of fact Super8#3, yes, I am feeling much better thank you...though with the greatest respect, I am *not* your friend,' he replied.

'Suit yourself, asshole.'

Super8#6 hastily made to respond but wasn't quick enough,

'If you're unhappy, then why not come up with something better instead of complaining.' He disliked moaners; they were all the same; always quick to criticise while never offering an alternative.

'Gentlemen, please.' Super8#4 was also online and quickly waded in on the argument. 'Let's not bicker among ourselves; after all, we share a common goal here, don't we? Besides, now that they're on the island we have full control. McKenzie wants our input so let's give it to him.'

Super8#6 raised an eyebrow.

'You seriously believe that? McKenzie is the only one in control here, make no mistake about that!' He suspected that Super8#4, with whom he was conversing, was the woman and in all honesty he found her just as intriguing as he did the island guests. There had been something in her eyes when they had met that one time, something cold, something sinister and admittedly thoroughly delectable. He wouldn't have minded studying her too.

'OK, we know that gore isn't your bag, though personally I could watch it all day long. So, tell us Super8#3, what exactly *is* your bag?'

The American paused. Of all the members of the elusive Super Eight Club, he was the most sceptical. For him, this was a straightforward psychological experiment through which he intended to study the human condition. He was not a sadist, or particularly deviant, though he was rather pleased to see that the female guests appeared easy on the eye, but he had no particular desire to witness great pain and suffering, like he suspected some of his team members did, the woman especially so it seemed. This was not due to him possessing much empathy and more because it was not what he was in this for; it was confusion and conflict, moral dilemma and division he was after; he wanted to study how the guests would both react and interact when put in extreme emotional situations, like rats in a laboratory.

He smirked to himself. Whoever Super8#6 was he had under-estimated his supreme intellect. As it was he *did* have something 'better' in mind for their guests, something that didn't involve broken limbs and blood – well, at least not pre-meditatively.

'They need an ice-breaker,' he said flatly, 'something that's ostensibly fun but that's going to stir things up a bit. From what I can see already, Mia and Rupert –'

'Careful,' the woman interjected, 'we were instructed not to use their names remember? Play by the rules Super8#3, you naughty boy.'

Super8#3 stood corrected. McKenzie had been very straight about this from the off.

'Fair enough, though something tells me you're not one for rules yourself. The singer and the lawyer – we already know they have bad blood.'

'And … you have something in mind?' Super8#3 was reluc-tantly intrigued himself now.

'How about a little game of truth or dare?'

Super8#3 snorted derisively, though of course his fellow club member could not have heard it. 'Bit 11th grade, isn't it?'

'Not my version,' the American shot back.

The woman was smiling at her screen.

'And what's so special about *your* version?'

Super8#6's smiled malevolently. He'd compiled and used this particular 'experiment' in his practice sessions primarily to coax unhappily married couples he counselled to open up and confess their inner most feelings to each other. The results, while often hit and miss, were never dull. In the past he had seen couples kiss and make up and others come to physical blows; while the former was arguably the objective, the latter was undeniably more fun to watch. With some bespoke tailoring he felt it had the potential to make a truly insightful, not to mention explosive, introduction to the island.

'Well,' he relied smugly, 'let's just say the last time I witnessed this game being played, it broke more than just ice.'

CHAPTER TWELVE

'Fucking 'ell! You ain't gonna believe this!'

Billie-Jo had been known to try and disguise her harsh cockney accent in the past, particularly in company she felt could be of potential benefit to her, but it was a little like attempting to push a rubber ball to the bottom of a swimming pool, invariably it bobbed right back up again. Now that she was safe and on dry land, and following a half decent night's sleep, she was all set to put the horror of the past twenty-four hours behind her and turn her attentions to inspecting the luxury state-of-the-art villa that was to be home for the duration of the fortnight.

Billie-Jo King, as she had been before marriage, may have appeared fragile on the surface thanks to her diminutive stature and delicate aesthetics, with which she, ostensibly, manipulated men, but underneath the candy coating lay an inner steeliness that often went quietly undetected.

She was nothing if not one of life's survivors; but then when you'd spent your formative years watching your own father kick the living shit out of your mother every day of your life and had been sexually abused by your own uncle from the age of seven to fourteen you tended to grow skin as thick as a rhinos.

Martin McKenzie, Billie-Jo was convinced, was her fast track to the fame and the credibility she so desperately needed to bolster her cripplingly low self-esteem, an affliction that she would do almost anything to disguise, and she wasn't about to let yesterday's events, however much they'd rattled her, stand in the way of her achieving her aim. She was here to enjoy herself and make a good impression – and she fully intended on doing both.

'Nate … *Nate*!' her voice grew more urgent, demanding.

Nate reluctantly rolled over on the enormous bed complete with muslin drapes and what felt like cashmere sheets. Even he had noted how soft and inviting they had felt on his bruised skin as he had fallen between them in the early hours, exhausted.

'Come back to bed, Bee,' he murmured, aware of the sourness of his morning breath, the stench of his own body.

Billie-Jo pulled a face; Nate's lack of urgency irritated the fuck out of her sometimes. His emotions were the sonic equivalent of monotone. She could tell him she'd fucked all of his teammates in a gangbang and she doubted he would even raise an eyebrow, let alone his voice. Still, she knew there was something of his she *could* raise easily enough. *That* had never been a problem; after all Billie-Jo had been peddling her sexuality since she'd been an unfortunately knowing teenager. It was the only currency she had. Occasionally even now the memory of her uncle's depravities seeped into her subconscious, invading her dreams as she slept; the sour, rancid smell of his body, his hot alcoholic breath against her young neck, those long, stiff, spiteful fingers like hot knives tearing at her most intimate skin...

She had told no one, not even her mother, of the atrocities she had suffered as a child and instead had internalised those feelings, built an impenetrable wall around her emotions, a bog-standard coping mechanism by all accounts, or so the do-gooder social-worker bitch she had seen a handful of times kept telling her, not that it had done her any favours. By that stage her mix of narcissism and co-dependency had formed. Shit happens, right?

Billie-Jo's childhood may have been a fucking abortion but she would make sure that she would never suffer hardship again.

If men wanted her, and they most certainly did, well, then, they had to pay to get a ganders at the goods – a simple transaction when you thought about it. Being desired in the eyes of men and envied by women afforded Billie-Jo a sense of power, filling a tiny fraction of the gaping emotional void inside her.

Flashing her clout on camera had proved quite a lucrative gig so far too: calendars, lad's mag shoots, promotional events – it was all mounting up into a right tidy little sum. But she was already growing complacent and bored with being small fry; Billie-Jo had enjoyed an elevation to minor celebrity status since her nuptials to Nate. Frequenting various third-rate gossip mags and celebrity websites on a regular basis gave her a buzz, but if she played this one right who knew where it could lead?

She didn't want to be a pair of tits forever, or even a WAG; she wanted a bit of credibility and respect … to be someone in her own right. As 'famous as Persil', she'd once said in an interview. She'd lifted that quote from Victoria Beckham in her early Posh Spice incarnation. And look where *she* was.

'Oh, sod ya, then,' she muttered under her breath, wondering if there was anywhere on the island she might be able to score some coke. Her nose felt a little bruised where she had bashed it in the crash and she absentmindedly rubbed at one of the scratches on her leg, surprisingly small reminders of the past twenty four-hours, all things considering. She was starting to feel that familiar restlessness creep in. Still, she thought, as she began to inspect the cabana once more with wide, appreciative eyes, her attention caught by the sumptuous huge white floor cushions and sheepskin fleeces that were lavishly strewn throughout, checking out this place would keep her occupied, for a while at least. It was fucking huge!

The private accommodation was set over two floors, one being a mezzanine level which housed the huge, round, super king-sized bed surrounded by draped canopies that her husband still occupied and a vast wet room that had been hand-decorated by artisans in precious stone mosaic, not that Billie-Jo would've known that, or been in the least bit interested even if she had. She was more concerned with the abundant stock of Chanel bath products displayed on the floating glass shelves: soaps, body washes, perfumes, oils, shampoos and treatments. She'd squealed like a pig when she'd seen the in-built spray sun-lotion booth and the self-cleaning set of his-and-hers toilets, the huge fluffy white towels and matching bath robes with their initials, B-J S and NS, hand-sewn onto the front in fancy font.

Will you get a look at that lot, thought Billie-Jo as she momentarily sat down on one of the toilets to admire them; details; it's what separated the hoi polloi from the superstars and no mistake, you could've had a decent sized party in the bathroom alone. Exiting the impressive en-suite, she made her way past the bed to inspect the contents of the huge in-built wardrobes. She hoped there was something for her to wear; it had devastated her losing the best of everything she owned in the crash.

'Holy shit!' She screamed as she swung the doors open to see row upon row of couture dresses: Chloé, Chanel, Westwood, Cavalli, Versace, Prada, Hervé Léger … a vast colourful array of her favourite designers, and, on closer inspection, all in *her* size. She began rifling through them manically, pulling dresses from their rose-scented padded hangers, laughing and snorting with delight … and fuckin' hell! The shoes! There was a shop full of 'em: Jimmy Choos, Louboutins, Gucci, Pierre Hardy. And handbags too: huge, squashy Mulberry totes, sparkling crystal Alexander McQueen jewelled clutches, and the *piece de resistance*, a Chanel quilted number. *No. Fucking. Way.* There had to be millions of pounds' worth of designer clobber here, she thought, as she mentally totted it all up. Was it hers for keeps?

The very idea that it might be gave her a bigger buzz than any line of the cocaine she was craving ever could.

Energised by the discovery, she skipped down the hand-carved winding wooden stair case, her gasps accelerating loudly as she caught first sight of the lower floor properly for the first time, all vast white-leather couches offset by dark, shiny wood, scattered with animal-skin rugs, mink-fur throws and sumptuous cushions. The furniture was of Balinese influence, lots of dark driftwood, glass coffee tables, huge white hand-carved wooden floor mirrors, and an enormous ornate chandelier.

She clocked the Bang & Olufsen stereo system, the large, rustic-looking solid wood dining table with high back Perspex chairs, and fresh, exotic, floral display as an impressive centrepiece. The kitchen area was all black marble, granite and chrome appliances, bottles of Cristal neatly stacked one on top of the other inside a huge chiller next to a fully stocked bar containing every spirit save for the holy ghost himself.

Overwhelmed, she made a beeline for the chiller. She would crack open a bottle immediately; after all, it wasn't like she didn't deserve it after what she'd been through – and besides they were on holiday now. Snatching a fresh bottle she tore off the yellow cellophane and opened it with a satisfactory bang.

As she sucked the neck of the bottle to stem the overflow her eye was drawn to a small silver bowl of white substance on the granite work surface that on first glance looked like sugar only, hang on … fuck *off* … no, it couldn't be, could it? She licked her pinkie and gently dabbed a little of it on her tongue. It instantly turned numb and she squealed. Holy Mother of God, it *was* coke. And good shit at that. She'd shoved enough up her hooter in the past to know the difference.

Throwing a tentative glance up towards the mezzanine level where her husband was still sleeping, she took the small, silver spoon from the dish and loaded it with powder before snorting deeply. Within seconds she was greeted with the familiar rush, filling her with warmth like a long-awaited old lover's return, her exposed nipples stiffening as the Grade-A powder met her blood stream. Shit the bed, there had to be a kilo of the stuff in that bowl!

She swigged back some champagne from the bottle and began to giggle. McKenzie, it seemed, really had thought of everything! Lurking in the back of her murky unconscious mind, however, Billie-Jo did wonder why he would facilitate her in such a way, and how exactly did he know she had a penchant for the old yay-yo? But they were distant thoughts, like a half-remembered song. Her mum always told her she'd asked too many questions anyway; perhaps she was right. Billie-Jo eyes scanned the exquisite accommodation with delight once more.

For now she had all the answers she needed.

CHAPTER THIRTEEN

'Well, it's not exactly a mystery as to why he decided to call it Pleasure Island, is it? It's absolutely stunning.'

Angelika was leaning over the enormous balcony of the cabana that looked out across the eternal expanse of sea, her arms folded, fingers clutching her freshly washed, damp skin. She had scoured herself clean that morning, scrubbing every inch of her body with the abundant designer bath products until she was free from the filth and grime that somehow felt ingrained in her skin.

'I mean look at this place, Rupert; it's unreal.' She gazed, entranced by the crystalline water that was directly below her, the shoreline swirling in an out of the dips in the sand, the sun low on the horizon, casting a delicate, lace, crystal pattern across the sea as it made a gradual and majestic appearance – the promise of a new day.

Unspoilt beauty that was somehow luxurious in its simplicity, the bay-shaped island was sheltered by cliffs and bending palms swaying and nodding in the delicate, pine-scented breeze. A wood and rope jetty led down from the chalk-white sand through the transparent sea. A couple of small fishing boats rocking gently in unison with the tide moored to it, white string hammocks fluttered like feathers tied to more surrounding shady palms.

Angelika inhaled the perfumed air deeply, its raw natural beauty drawing her in and causing her to momentarily forget the horrors of the last twenty-four hours. To the left of the cabanas there was a cliff that housed a large, raised, wooden decked area complete with vast canopied day beds that were scattered with sumptuous, white, padded cushions shining like moonbeams in the glare of the harsh morning sun. Next to it a deep, azure-blue swimming pool complete with an in-built raffia-topped bar in the centre that seamlessly blended into the water's edge. Set back further up the mountain she saw the faint outline of a trail, a road perhaps, though it was difficult to tell without her glasses.

'It's not what I was expecting.' She turned to Rupert, watching as he removed the white fluffy towel from his waist and stepped into his underwear, wishing she felt some kind of emotional or physical reaction to his nakedness, *anything*. After all, he was still pretty fit for forty-odd.

'And what *were* you expecting, Angelika?' Her husband's tone was terse as usual. She only had to open her mouth these days and he seemed irritated, the provenance of which she could not pinpoint. They no longer held conversations like they once had, a long time ago, or so it seemed. Their conversations had left her feeling invigorated, and they'd had conversations where they actually discussed things and listened to each other, laughed and debated good-humouredly. These days everything was a prelude to a cross word, bitter snipes interspersed with caustic asides and snide remarks spoken in hushed, exasperated tones.

It was with deep regret that while Angelika loved Rupert she no longer liked him much, nor understood him. The years had seen her deep affection for him dissipate into bubbling resentment and repressed bitterness, stealthily creeping up on her like an undetected terminal disease. Her once dynamic, attentive husband had gradually become petulant and distant over the years, *unlikeable even*, a far cry from the brilliant man she had met and married. It was as if he had gradually become a different person with the passing of time, so gradual that she'd hardly noticed it happening until it was too late to do anything about it.

Rupert Deyton had been a face at Oxford university where they'd met as students and where he'd procured a reputation as being something of a cad: charming and charismatic. It was difficult to believe now, although he still knew how to turn it on when the mood, less frequently these days, grabbed him, but back then his reputation had preceded him. He'd admired her once, she was sure, and had pursued her relentlessly.

Angelika recalled the first night Rupert had asked her out with such clarity that it was as if she had witnessed it happening to someone else – that balmy September day that had slipped seamlessly into evening, the air chilly and deceptive. He'd offered to share a cab with her and she'd been so breathless with adrenalin that she'd simply nodded and got in. Rupert was smart and so terribly handsome then – still was, she supposed – his self-confidence that stopped only just short of arrogance had been devastatingly attractive.

As she'd stepped inside the cab she had been overcome by the sense that something wonderful was about to happen. Their courtship had been romantic and intense; lazy afternoons spent on boating lakes, his legs draped over the side as he recited sonnets to her – 'Shall I compare thee to a summer's day?' ('What, drunk and hot, you mean?') – and her responding with raspy renditions of Rimbaud and Keats. They had debated everything from politics and war to what merited a decent pop record over drunken, champagne picnics that invariably led to exciting, alfresco sex and listen to Lou Reed on his pre-historic (even then) record-player on the dirty carpet of his digs. High and giggly on marijuana, they would imagine they were Patti Smith and Robert Mapplethorpe, even though Rupert didn't really have an artistic bone in his body.

She had hung on his every word, captivated by his sharp intellect interspersed with offbeat, bohemian charm. He had been laid-back then – funny even – and less cynical … certainly more tolerant of the human condition. And while she supposed she could never have called their relationship passionate, they had been good friends.

It had been during a six-month sabbatical from their relationship (he'd needed to 'find himself', which she had roughly translated as 'shag other people') that Rupert had fathered a child with a French business student called Esme. Angelika had been heartbroken despite his insistence he was not complicit, or even consulted, on Esme's decision to go ahead with the pregnancy and that it had been a complete accident. He'd been just twenty years old when Serge had been born. For the first ten years of the boys' life Rupert had been what could be described as an absent father, or 'a complete shit' as Esme preferred. It was only when Serge became old enough to challenge his father on a verbally intellectual level that Rupert began to show a little more interest in the boy he would gradually go on to adore.

Aged twenty-three and twenty-five respectively, Angelika had married her handsome mastermind in a pretty church in Surrey near his childhood home. They'd been too young. She realised that now, but *je ne regrette rien*; isn't that what they said? And besides, the photos had been rather beautiful. Over the years they'd clung onto their marriage, largely through habit and lack of time to search for suitable alternatives, although Angelika suspected that she had predominantly been the glue in their union.

She supposed she still desired her husband; after all, he was still able to steal glances from strangers and took great care of his appearance but she wasn't entirely convinced that the feeling was mutual. Rupert rarely made love to her anymore and when he did she was usually the instigator. Sometimes she wondered if her husband was satisfying himself elsewhere, though with whom and when she couldn't imagine. Rupert was a workaholic and when he wasn't working he seemed to prefer the company of his polo and rugby pals. She trusted him though, and, whatever else, she knew he had her back. Perhaps that what's love really was at the end of the day, yet still it was a thought that depressed her. *Is that all there is?*

'You know, we really could sue the arse off McKenzie for this: post-traumatic stress and all of that. Maybe you should act like it's sent you off your rocker a bit – which shouldn't be too much of a stretch for you, let's face it darling – and we'll be looking at a six-figure sum easily. I might causally drop it into the conversation when we meet him, see his reaction. After all it's not like he can't afford it, and actually, I do feel like we should be compensated somehow for the terrible stress. We could've lost our lives, you know. In fact, we were bloody lucky no one was more hurt.'

'Assuming he's even here on the island,' Angelika mused, 'and, of course, I'm off my rocker, Rupert; I'm still married to you, aren't I? Anyway, someone was "more hurt" in case you had forgotten; a man died and God only knows what happened to that poor flight attendant.'

'Hmm,' Rupert agreed, 'well, we certainly need some questions answering, that's for sure. Anyway, what makes you think he isn't on the island?'

'Don't know exactly…intuition, I suppose. Something tells me he never had any intention of coming here.' Angelika felt a niggling suspicion, the lightest flutter of unease ever since she'd set foot on the island though she could not say exactly why.

'Women's intuition, eh?' Rupert raised a brow. 'Good job real decisions aren't made on that alone.'

'What are you talking about Rupert, your whole fucking career is based on hunches, intuition and gut feeling.'

'That and the small matter of evidence, Angelika.'

She grimaced at him behind his back.

'You said yourself you had a hunch about the rapist being guilty.'

'His name is Peter Cheshunt, as you very well know, and I never said any such thing!' Peter Cheshunt was the high-profile TV executive Rupert had recently represented during his much-publicised trial for the rape of a young PA who had worked for him.

'And as you also very well know he was acquitted.'

'You did! When you'd been at the Château Margaux one evening, you said to me you thought he probably was guilty but there wasn't enough forensic evidence to prove it. Terrible miscarriage of justice if you ask me; thanks in part to you a young woman's life and reputation is in tatters, and a guilty man walked free. He'll no doubt do it again, the arrogant bastard.'

'And that's the whole point,' Rupert fired back. 'There wasn't enough bloody evidence to convict, which is why he was acquitted, and rightly so. It's called the British Justice system.'

'Yes, but the circumstantial evidence was overwhelming, and you know it. You're just too bloody good at what you do, that's the problem. That's the only reason he's a free man. We both know he forced that girl to have sex with him, regardless of whether she'd had a drink, regardless of whether she went to his room with him, regardless of her revealing dress or whatever other misogynous bullshit you were peddling to create doubt. She still said no … no, no, no, no, no! What part of the word "no" do you think he didn't understand, Rupert?'

'It's a known fact that many women say no when they mean yes, or at least, oh, all right then. It's a trick they use to make it look like they're not the easy little sluts, when they know they really are deep down.'

She shook her head in disgust. He'd said it tongue in cheek to get a rise but she couldn't be one hundred per cent sure he hadn't really meant it.

'I will treat that comment with the contempt it deserves.'

'Yes, and will no doubt write a damning piece of journalism – and I use that term loosely – in that ridiculous rag you write for, saying just as much.'

When did you become so belligerent, Rupert, so small-minded, so *nasty*?'

'Our wedding day,' he quipped

'Touché.' Angelika shook her head as she stomped through the sumptuous cabana in her Calvin Klein pretty-but-functional nude underwear, the sudden knock at the door making her jump.

Rupert cast a derisory look as he peered around it.

'Yes,' he snapped at the small olive-skinned woman who greeted him with a subservient bow.

Saying nothing she simply handed him an envelope and retreated.

'Er, just hang on a minute!' he yelled out after her but she had scurried off and wearing nothing but cotton boxer shorts, he was reluctant to run after her.

'So British,' Angelika smirked.

'Didn't see you sprinting to catch her up in your bloody smalls.'

'I'm surprised you even noticed.'

'Get dressed,' he snapped as he began to read the contents of the small gold envelope, 'you were wrong; looks like we're going to get to meet the man himself after all.'

CHAPTER FOURTEEN

Angelika had, in fact, been right; there was no sign of McKenzie as they all gathered expectantly on the decked veranda of the wooden mansion, which was buzzing with staff carrying trays of champagne cocktails and canapés that looked like edible works of art.

'I don't know about a bloody drink, but I wouldn't mind some bloody answers,' Rupert snapped at one of them, swiping a glass from the tray anyway and immediately taking a large slug.

'Were you summonsed here as well?' He looked at Nate, who was now washed and dressed in a white T-shirt and denim three-quarter-length cut-offs, his dark, thick hair falling to one side, looking like something out of *Pour Homme*, a complete transformation since yesterday when he'd been a shabby, filthy, blood-stained mess. Rupert sized him up. Poncy-arsed footballers; how they managed to pull so many women when they all looked like one themselves he'd never understand, though he knew the real reason: money and status. The man could've had a face like a bag of spanners and they'd still flock to him. It was so … predictable. Still, he had to concede that Nate wasn't exactly hard on the eye.

'Yeah, the lady – she knocked on the door this morning – handed me the letter requesting we all convene here for welcome drinks.'

Rupert snorted. 'Welcome drinks … more like some welcome bloody answers, and they had better be good ones too. I said to the wife I'll be suing McKenzie's arse for post-traumatic stress for this fuck up. He's looking at shelling out millions in compensation, not least a decent chunk to that boy, Joshua. Any news on him by the way?'

Nate shrugged. 'Where's there's blame there's a claim, huh, Rupert?' He smiled. 'I was thinking more of thanking him for saving my life than suing him after all. He could've hardly foreseen such a tragedy, and no, none that I've been told, at least not yet.'

He smiled at Angelika, acknowledging her presence and she returned it with one of her own. He was struck by how pretty she was now that he could see her properly in daylight, her hair freshly washed and loose, sun-dried into natural waves, her skin clear and free of that gunk Billie-Jo covered herself in.

Today, Billie-Jo had dressed for the occasion in an Agent Provocateur cut-out swimsuit that was completely impractical for sunbathing but showcased her assets to their ultimate best nonetheless. She'd teamed the strappy, sexy creation with a pair of the vertiginous Louboutin gladiator sandals that were among the many she had discovered in the closet, piling on the gold and diamond jewellery that had been neatly displayed at her disposal. More was always more, as far as Billie-Jo was concerned. Her ears pricked. Rupert's use of the word 'compensation' had ignited her interest in the conversation.

'So you think there's a chance we might be in for a bit of compo then?' She wasn't able to conceal the avarice in her eyes, not even with a pair of oversized Chloé sunglasses on.

Rupert harrumphed. 'I'll say. PTS is big business and bucks these days.'

Billie-Jo made a mental note to herself to keep on his good side. He could be useful when the time came.

'So, was your wardrobe full of designer clobber an' all?' she asked Angelika, giving her the once over. She felt a slither of envy as she realised Angelika appeared both slimmer and more attractive now that she could see her in broad daylight. She possessed that quiet sort of natural beauty that usually photographed well, and she had good hair, skin and teeth, even if she was in her thirties. 'I swear down I nearly had a fuckin' heart attack when I opened mine!'

A waitress approached them with a spectacular-looking selection of breakfast sweets and savouries: mini Danish pastries that had been baked in the shape of hearts; canapé-sized muffins with crispy bacon, drizzled with maple syrup; eggs Benedict; and smoked salmon and cream-cheese bagels, which were warm and smelled delicious.

'How many calories are in those?' Billie-Jo pointed to the offerings. 'I'm a model, yeah, so I have to watch my figure. You know what I'm saying?'

The waitress smiled and nodded as they helped themselves. They were all ravenous, even Billie-Jo who'd already ingested a line of coke for breakfast.

Angelika had indeed been surprised to discover her wardrobe had been neatly stocked with beautiful designer clothes: Dolce & Gabbana capri pants in pretty colours with matching shell tops; neat graphic-print shift dresses by Victoria Beckham; denim cuts-off; and rows of soft, white, cotton shirts, cashmere cardigans and Breton tees – her favourites; wide-brim, straw fedoras with pretty ribbons; an array of floral tea dresses and boho-inspired scarves. It was as if it had all been hand selected by a personal stylist. It was the same for Rupert, too; even down to the pink shirts and paisley cravats he often favoured. McKenzie, so it seemed, had thought of everything and seemed to know more about their sartorial preferences than she could have anticipated. *But how?*

'Yes,' Angelika said, 'and I suppose it was a good job really seeing as though we lost everything in the plane crash. Bit odd, though, don't you think? How they could've known our individual styles and tastes.'

Billie-Jo blinked at her in quick succession. Odd or not, she certainly wasn't complaining.

'S'pose,' she murmured, wondering if Mia Manhattan had been given the same treatment. She suddenly saw Mia approaching the veranda. Seeing her all done up like a dog's Christmas dinner concluding that she probably had.

'So, where the fucking hell is that dreadful cunt McKenzie, then?' Mia certainly knew how to make a show-stopping entrance. Her colourful choice of language was enough to raise the most liberal-minded brow, not that she cared. Decades spent in the privileged position of being able to say and do as she pleased without question had afforded her carte blanche to be a rude as she deemed appropriate, even in the court room, as Rupert remembered only too well.

'What was she like?' Angelika had asked him at the time of the highly publicised trial; she had been keen for an insight into the superstar's behaviour on a personal as well as professional level. This was Mia Manhattan, after all.

'Exactly how you would expect someone who hasn't heard the word "no" for two decades to be,' he'd responded tartly.

The media had gone berserk for the Manhattan case and not least for the singer's choice of court attire, which had been religiously documented, discussed, dissected and debated at great length throughout the duration of the trial. Never one to disappoint her fans, Mia had faced such scrutiny with aplomb. Her shameless avant-garde sartorial choices – while deemed wildly inappropriate for legal proceedings – had gone down the proverbial treat with fashion editors the world over and made her something of an unlikely style icon in the process, particularly among the more camp members of society.

Today she had chosen to wear a white-and-gold floor-length Lanvin Grecian number reminiscent of Cleopatra, chosen from the impressive selection that had been at her disposal. If she was going to tear a strip off McKenzie, then she'd be sure she looked good while doing it. Besides, she hadn't seen the man for years, and, angry though she was, she still wanted to remind him of what he'd missed out on, all those years ago.

Mia had felt guilty experiencing a slither of joy as she'd dressed herself in the mirror that morning. She was glad to be alive, to have survived such an ordeal and come through it unscathed. However, as yet there had been no news on Joshua's condition, a fact that gnawed at her conscience. Hell, she didn't even know where he was. Moreover she had been incensed to find there was no phone inside the villa on which she could make the necessary telephone calls. As she'd inspected her svelte silhouette from every conceivable angle, she'd vowed to contact Richard as soon as she could locate a telephone. Dickie would bail her out, her *and* Joshua; she would get him to send a plane for them immediately, fly them away from this place. Even in spite of the bitter acrimony between them, following their highly publicised divorce, she knew deep down he would never see her in any real distress or danger. Then she would promptly phone that great dollop-of-shit agent of hers and fire his fat, useless, greedy arse once and for all. Screw Bailey, she didn't need him anymore, or McKenzie either for that matter. Bollocks to the pair of them; she'd sort out her own comeback; do *I'm a Celebrity…Get me*

Out of Here! if she had to. Hell if she could survive the past twenty-four hours then she could survive *anything*.

'That's what we're all here waiting to find out, Mia,' Rupert snapped at her, 'after all, we're hardly here for the free bubbly and canapés … or are we?'

'Pity you weren't flying that bloody plane, Deyton,' she muttered. 'You.' Mia pointed a manicured finger at one of the waiters buzzing past. 'I need a telephone.'

He stared at her, bemused.

'A *tele-phone* …' she repeated, waggling her hand in a universally understood thumb and finger sign. The waiter simply nodded before hurrying away back up towards the entrance of the house.

'You'd think he'd have managed to employ some English-speaking staff,' she scoffed, washing down a quail eggs Benedict canapé with a glass of champagne. 'Bloody miser, probably paying them slave wages.' She looked at Billie-Jo. 'Do you have a telephone in your suite?'

'No,' Billie-Jo replied, a little startled by Mia's abrupt question, 'I was hoping to phone me mum as well, let her know I'm OK; she'll be worried.' Though in all truth Billie-Jo knew that as long as her old dear hadn't run out of Johnny Walker and Rothmans she'd probably be right as Larry.

Not that she begrudged her, mind – Tracy Glynn had endured hardship and suffering like no one else she knew and it was little short of God's will her old mum hadn't drunk herself to death with what she'd had to put up with over the years. With four different kids from four different blokes – she wasn't even sure who had fathered Billie-Jo and had told her it was 'probably just as well' – it had been a lifetime of borderline poverty and hardship for Tracy, a stream of misogynists, alcoholics and junkies who were happy to put a fist in her face if the oven chips were served cold, or she'd bought the wrong beer, or there was a 'y' in the month.

Tracy had been a stunner herself once, just like Billie-Jo was now, but somehow it hadn't been enough to pull her from the clutches of the reprobates she seemed to attract and the gutter from which they came, her looks rapidly disappearing along with her human spirit.

That's what years of being ground down did to a woman; it robbed you of everything. Still, she'd done her best by her kids, by and large; they may have been shit poor but they had never been starved of affection and she had worked three cash-in-hand jobs to make sure they got the occasional treat.

Tracy Glynn loved her kids and she wanted a better life for them, actively encouraging her pretty daughter to cash in on her merchandise. 'If you got it, flaunt it, or better still, sell it!' Billie-Jo had never confided in her about the abuse she had suffered at the hands of one of her uncles but she was close to her mum and although resolute that she would rather sell her own eyes than end up like her, she secretly admired her.

In a funny kind of way, Billie-Jo knew that her tough upbringing had instilled in her some positive qualities, namely survival, ambition and unrelenting determination. Every cloud, she supposed.

Now she was seriously minted, however, it gave her no better buzz than to be able to bung her mum a decent chunk of change every now and again, take her out on lavish shopping sprees and spa days, pay for a car and holidays and treat her. Watching the grin on her old mum's boat-race as they rapidly melted one of Nate's many credit cards simply confirmed to Billie-Jo that it was a lorry load of bollocks when people said money didn't buy you happiness; that was something only rich people could afford to say. Yeah, but it could certainly buy you out of the fucking misery of poverty and Primark clobber, that was for sure.

Angelika sipped at her champagne glass tentatively, quietly observing her surroundings as the jets above them pumped out a spray of fine mist, presumably to keep them cool in a heat that what was already intense, even at such an early hour.

'Have you noticed?' she asked, addressing Nate mostly, largely because he was looking at her.

'Noticed what?' he responded. Her nose wrinkled when she was in thought. He liked it; it made her look cute.

'None of the staff has uttered a word, not even to each other …'

Before Nate could answer however, the door to the mansion opened.

CHAPTER FIFTEEN

'Please accept my sincerest apologies.' The woman was unsmiling but seemed ingenuous enough, 'I can only imagine what you've all been through these past twenty-four hours.' Her voice was low and masculine, her accent reassuringly British. 'I'm Elaine, Elaine McKenzie.'

'Where is your husband?' Rupert marched towards her. 'I'd be very keen to talk with him.'

'I'm afraid it's with great regret that my husband cannot be here to greet you all as planned,' she said in monotone. 'Please accept my deepest apologies on his behalf. It was his every intention to greet you in person, I assure you, but unfortunately the inclement weather conditions has prevented him from flying out –'

'Inclement weather … the storm, you mean?' Angelika met Elaine's steely gaze.

'That's right,' Elaine gave a succinct nod as if Angelika had passed some kind of test. 'We received a Met Office warning a couple of days prior of its imminent arrival, but were not quite prepared for the devastation it would cause.'

'So that's why the plane crashed?' Angelika mused. 'The storm …'

Nate looked sideways at Angelika. There was something considered about the lawyer's wife that he instinctively liked. She had been calm and dependable throughout the crisis they'd just faced, shown strength of character and capability, the total antithesis of his wife. He liked the sound of her voice, too, clipped Home Counties with the lightest northern burr. He found it strangely soothing. 'I suspect it was, yes.'

'You suspect? *You suspect*?' Rupert was repeating himself, which meant only one thing: he was irritated. 'You do realise the pilot's dead, *dead* … and the girl – the Jap – God only knows what happened to her…drowned I suspect, poor bloody bitch. We could've all died. Nothing short of a miracle we didn't, really.'

Elaine's face remained solemn as she absorbed his words.

'She's Thai, actually,' she corrected him. 'It was an unforeseeable tragedy about which I deeply sympathise. It must've been a dreadful experience for all of you. It's understandable that you're shaken and upset, which is why, on behalf of my absent husband, it is my responsibility to ensure your stay here, from now on, will be the most enjoyable, memorable experience for all the right reasons.'

Rupert was stunned. He hadn't quite known what he'd expected to hear but somehow this wasn't it.

'Where the hell has Joshua been taken?' Mia's voice cut through Rupert's incredulity like a pickaxe. 'Two men carted him off in that rescue plane last night. So I'll need a telephone, *Mrs* McKenzie.' Her eye caught Rupert's for the briefest second in a fleeting moment of solidarity. 'I need to contact my husband and agent and get them to send a plane for me and Joshua.'

'And we lost all our stuff, you know,' Billie-Jo joined in, 'my Rolex, iPad, all my Vuitton luggage. I mean, who's gonna pay for all that?'

Nate felt himself redden; that Billie-Jo was even entertaining matters of a fiscal nature in such a moment showed her up to be shallow and greedy. Sometimes he wished she'd at least have the grace to try and disguise it.

'A telephone.' Rupert reiterated Mia's request. 'I'm assuming you do have one?'

'Indeed,' Elaine McKenzie replied calmly, 'only I'm afraid all lines of communication have been down since the storm hit. We've no Internet access, no satellite signal, nothing I'm afraid.'

Billie-Jo's lip curled in protest. No fucking phones? No Internet? How would she brag to all her Facebook followers now? She'd been planning daily Tweets and had fully intended to post as many Instagram pictures as possible throughout her stay in a calculated bid to up her profile while pissing off a few haters to boot. She was gutted.

Angelika's eyes were drawn to the pipes that were pumping out fine mist above them once more. 'But there's light and hot water.' She could feel the beginnings of a headache, her thoughts starting to merge like watercolours in her mind.

'The emergency generator is working, we have utilities, running water, heat … we're lucky we didn't lose that as well.' She turned to Mia. 'As for the injured man, he was flown to a hospital on a local island, I believe. I know no more than that as there is no means of communication. Like I said, the network is down.'

'They took him in the plane, the same one that was used to rescue us,' Angelika said calmly, though her voice still conveyed some authority. 'If the plane was OK to fly, could it not fly us over to a neighbouring island as well?'

She thought she detected the slightest wry smile on Elaine McKenzie's otherwise-expressionless face.

'I'm afraid the whole north side of the country has been affected by the storm; you're safer here for now – besides, why on earth would you want to leave? We have everything we need here and more: food, drink, shelter, all in abundance. Besides, I know my husband would want business to continue as usual.

Our aim was always to make your stay as comfortable and enjoyable as possible, as was the original plan.'

'But if it was safe for the pilot to take off, to rescue us and then fly Joshua out –'

'I'm afraid there's been no contact with the light aircraft that took your friend,' Elaine McKenzie cut her off. 'The pilot took great personal risk in choosing to fly him off the island. We can only hope they made it to their destination safely.'

'And where might that destination have been?' Rupert had switched into professional mode, pacing like he did inside a courtroom when cross-examining a witness.

'Unfortunately I cannot answer that,' she replied, 'I'm assuming they either flew to the mainland or perhaps one of the neighbouring islands.'

She turned swiftly to Billie-Jo.

'I'm terribly sorry for any personal loss you've incurred; I do hope you will find everything you need within your accommodation, which I trust has met with your requirements?'

Billie-Jo nodded; she couldn't argue with that.

'So the gear's all ours then? The clobber and the jewellery and the bags and –'

Nate nudged her sharply. 'Shut up, Bee.'

'What?' she hissed at him, 'I got a right to ask, I lost practically every fucking thing I own in those cases.'

'Everything you find within your accommodation is complimentary. That's to say it's all yours,' Elaine drolly explained, the grim line of her lips broadening slightly, though you could hardly call it a smile.

She addressed the group as a whole once more. 'And so, I should really commence by giving you each a welcome pack which details everything you need to know about the island, its history, how my husband discovered it, the purpose of your trip here …'

'Well, yes, that would be good to know, because we've all been wondering exactly what that might be,' Rupert said, 'this whole charade has been shrouded in secrecy from the very beginning.'

'All will be revealed in good time I can assure you. Now,' Elaine said, 'this island lives up to its name, as I'm sure you will discover to your own delight in due course. It is completely without restriction; you are free to explore, roam and go where you please, whenever you please, as you please, though do take care to ensure you are wearing the appropriate footwear should you wish to go walking, climbing or indeed hiking. Champagne cocktails will commence here on the veranda every evening at half-past seven, followed by a six-course gourmet meal using the finest produce and prepared by some of the most-accomplished chefs in the business, giving everyone a chance to convene and socialise, discuss the day's events. Plus it's a wonderful vantage point to watch the sunset, though there are many places on the island that will afford you as beautiful a setting. Dinner is the only compulsory event of the day, the rest of which is your own to do as you so wish and take full advantage of the facilities my husband and I offer you. Regretfully the full entertainment schedule we had planned has been scuppered by the storm, so –' she paused momentarily '– I'm afraid you will have to make your own entertainment. Though this shouldn't be too difficult, I assure you. There is a plethora of activities available to you, including bicycles, mountaineering equipment, a state-of-the-art games room, steam, sauna, swimming pools, your own private Jacuzzis, a floatation tank, plus full and extensive complimentary spa and beauty treatments, for which bookings can be made here via reception. There is also a personal stylist, machinist and jewellers available should you ladies, or indeed gentlemen, require any bespoke alterations or designs made.' She clicked her fingers and on cue three practically identical brothers appeared, forming a military line behind her. Young and tanned, their torsos accentuated by tight white T-shirts, they were each carrying a shiny, black box, their Hollywood grins dazzling in the bright sunshine. 'And now I would like to introduce you to Remi, Rani and Raj, your personal butlers for the duration of your stay. Should you wish for anything, and I mean *anything*, day or night, then they will endeavour to meet your every need or requirement.'

'Does that include a telephone?' Rupert said, though this time under his breath.

'I should explain,' Elaine continued efficiently, 'that along with the rest of the staff here on the island, Remi, Rani and Raj are selective mutes.'

'Selective what?' Billie-Jo pulled a face. 'What's one of them when it's at home?'

Nate cringed at his wife's ignorance.

'They don't talk is what it means,' he whispered to her.

'They understand perfect English, of course,' Elaine continued to explain, 'but please don't attempt to engage them in conversation as this can cause them some considerable anxiety.'

'Is this some kind of joke?' Mia enquired.

'Not at all.' Elaine shook her head. 'My husband deliberately sourced them for their specific – how shall I say – lifestyle choices.'

'Bet the interview process was scintillating,' Rupert deadpanned. 'Just another of McKenzie's little quirks, eh? Whatever next, Oompa Loompas? Fire-breathing midgets?'

'What's inside the boxes?' Angelika couldn't hide her intrigue. She placed her champagne glass down onto the table. She felt lightheaded, a little giggly, even.

'There is a box here addressed to each couple. It's a surprise my husband organised. I'm afraid I can't say any more than that as frankly I don't know what's in them myself. What I do know, however, is that he left strict instructions for them not to be opened, at least not just yet.'

Elaine deliberately paused, satisfied that her guests had been duly subdued into submission by her announcement.

'Right then,' she said, smoothing her small, stubby fingers down her black slacks, 'are there any questions?' She scanned their faces, her narrow, grey, watery eyes evaluating them carefully.

'Yes.' Angelika raised her hand as though in a school room; she felt odd, her head a tad woozy, limbs light and airy, even though she'd only had a few sips of champagne. 'Where exactly are we?'

Elaine McKenzie smiled, finally, exposing a set of small neat teeth that didn't quite fit with the rest of her face. 'You're in paradise, my dear. Welcome to Pleasure Island.'

CHAPTER SIXTEEN

Martin McKenzie poured a generous measure of Glenfiddich 1937 into a heavy-bottomed crystal tumbler, a special treat from an exceptionally rare bottle of single malt Scotch, which he'd recently, procured at auction. At 64 years, the same age as himself incidentally, it was the oldest bottle of Scotch in the world and with a price tag at a little over £50k possibly one of the most expensive. Whiskey was his thing and he'd built up quite an impressive collection over the years becoming something of a connoisseur in the process. If it was a toss up between a rare bottle of Scotch and a shiny new Bentley, McKenzie knew where his heart lay.

Tonight, as he booted up his state of the art iMac and put his feet up onto the solid oak antique hand-carved Italian desk, he'd decided a nip of the best stuff was very much in order. It had been a bitch of a day: endless meetings with Japanese TV executives followed by the usual publicity and press junkets, a long and tedious lunch at Scott's in Mayfair with one of his PA's wittering on, endless telephone calls followed by a late dinner at Nobu, again with the Japs, and onto a very exclusive gentleman's club where he'd shelled out a little over £60,000 on distinctively average tits and arse and vintage Krug. Such vast wealth made anything and everything available to McKenzie but there was a downside to such infinite freedom and choice. Like a drug addict his epicurean practises needed to be bested each time to give him a buzz to match, or ideally exceed, the former and when nothing was forbidden to you, you were forced to get creative.

The computer screen flickered slightly as he went through all the necessary security checks to gain access to the Super Eight site and smiled as the action came into focus. He could see that Super8#6, Two and Five were also online.

'So, how is everyone faring today?'

He squinted at the images, all sixteen split screens playing simultaneously, and his eye was immediately drawn to screen three. Billie-Jo was taking a shower, soaping her nubile, naked body with alacrity, no crevice overlooked. Her nakedness wasn't especially arousing; he'd seen a million Billie-Jo's in his lifetime, it was her obliviousness to him that turned him on. She had absolutely no idea that she was being watched, playing a starring role in a highly exclusive soap opera for a selected few – there to be studied, observed and, above all, controlled.

'So, what's the schedule?' Super8#6 was keen to know if McKenzie would give his suggestion the go ahead.

Martin McKenzie smiled.

'All is in place number six. The game is being made and will be delivered shortly, in time for a little surprise party anyway.'

'Good show.'

He was chuffed. His idea had made the cut.

'Let's hope it is Super8#6.' McKenzie switched screens. Angelika Deyton and that dreadful husband of hers came into view. They were in the bathroom together, having a heated discussion from what he could make out. McKenzie turned the volume up. She was asking questions. Bloody Frenchman had been right; they would have to watch out for Angelika Deyton. Perhaps that bitch really was smarter than he'd given her initial credit for. Not that he was unduly concerned just yet, especially with the bombshell he planned to drop on her in good time.

She'd be asking a hell of a lot more questions soon enough. He took a slug of the expensive Scotch and pulling his lips over his teeth watched the couple intently.

'… it's like I feel a little … "tipsy" is the only way I can describe it …' Angelika said, 'even when I haven't been drinking …'

McKenzie gave a wry smile. She was the first of the 'players' to make such an observation, and he wondered how long it would take her to work out that the champagne was being spiked. Xanax, otherwise known as Benzodiazepine, was quite a multi-functioning little drug primarily prescribed for anxiety, panic attacks, social disorders, stress and insomnia. Low doses such as the ones he, or rather Elaine, was administering weren't quite enough to give an individual any noticeable high, but it was enough to take the edge off any anxiety and instil a little apathy. It was also known to lower inhibitions, something he was actively seeking to achieve. He made a mental note to ask Elaine to up the journalist's dose next time. She was a troublemaker – he could sense it – but then he already knew that thanks to the vitriolic biography the bitch had written on him. It had been this breech of his good nature that had secured her place on this little social experiment. No one got the better of Martin McKenzie, least of all some jumped-up, wannabe-controversial journalist with delusions of grandeur. Tonight, however, he needed them clear-headed and didn't want to arouse any more suspicion.

Enjoying himself, he flicked back to Billie-Jo who was busy attending to her bikini line with a razor, humming along to the surround-sound stereo, seemingly without a care in the world. Elaine, it seemed, had done a stellar job; her speech had been pitch-perfect, and just as he'd anticipated, aside from their initial griping, which was to be expected, once they had realised little could be done they had accepted her word with minimal fuss. McKenzie took another sip of his Scotch and contemplated a cigar to go with it. Human beings were so incredibly predictable; it was utterly fascinating just how quickly they had adapted to the situation and he hoped the other members of the Super Eight Club watching were just as pleased as he was by such insight. Safe and surrounded by luxury and comfort, it was as if the players had more or less erased the memory of the potential near-death experience he had created for them. Sunshine, safety and sustenance – that was pretty much all they'd needed to remain compliant, at least for now. The game hadn't even started properly yet.

Deciding upon a cigar after all – he'd been trying to cut back – McKenzie reached for his Cartier lighter. A strange sensation washed over him as Mia's unmistakable form came into view. Above all of the cast, her humiliation was the one he would personally savour and enjoy the most.

She was making her way down towards the beach, her glossy, black hair reflecting in the sunlight, the expensive kaftan he'd handpicked for her billowing behind her, exposing her slim legs as she strutted. She'd always been quite a beauty, he reluctantly conceded.

'Well, hello, Mia,' he said, sucking on the Cohiba and blowing rings of blue smoke into the air above him. 'Having fun yet?'

Mia Manhattan's name had been the first he'd thought of upon coming up with the whole concept of Pleasure Island. In a strange way she had, once again, become something of a muse to him. The bitter hatred he had harboured for her all these years had not waned with time. In fact, it was still so corrosive that it brought on an attack of acid reflux whenever she entered his thoughts, forcing him to reach for his omnipresent bottle of Gaviscon. Mia had done what no other women, nee, person, had ever dared attempt, not least achieve; she had turned her back on him. From the second he had discovered her, Mia had become McKenzie's prize possession, not to mention his golden goose, and her cutting all ties had cost him millions in potential revenue. For a man so fiscally driven, this was punishment enough but the real cost had been to his ego; deep down he had loved Mia. From the second he'd heard her sing, the moment he'd seen her face she had achieved something no other woman had to date, not even his wife – in fact especially not his wife. She had enchanted him completely. And although he had never confessed his feelings to her nor another living soul, what he viewed as her betrayal cut him far deeper than he was ever prepared to admit. *She hadn't needed him.* He'd lost control of her, something his narcissistic personality found truly unforgivable, even decades later. Even her well-publicised fall from grace in the courtroom – he had been heartily complicit in spreading derogatory rumours about her throughout the trial – and recent divorce had done little to ameliorate any feelings of retribution that he'd harboured all these years since. From the moment Mia had terminated their contract he had waged a private war against her, and like all wars there had to be some collateral damage: in this case Nate and Billie-Jo. They would be the fall guys for Mia's mistreatment of him. It couldn't be helped.

McKenzie drained the dregs of his glass. The plane, containing Mia's rock-star toy boy, was due to land on the other side of the island imminently and the thought made him smile.

He began to type an instant message.

Super8#1: 'Is everybody happy?' he asked.

Super8#4: 'So-so,' came the response.

'Good,' he wrote back, 'because it's just about to get interesting.'

CHAPTER SEVENTEEN

'Selective mutism? What the fuck is that when it's at home then?' Billie-Jo looked at her husband, nonplussed.

'I told you, it's when people choose not to speak, Bee,' he answered, silently wishing she could be struck down by such an affliction.

She pulled a face at Angelika as if to suggest that her husband was completely off his rocker. 'So you mean they *can* speak, they just don't *want* to?'

'That's right,' Angelika smiled at her, the three of them exchanging eye contact. 'It's a social disease that usually starts in childhood; most people grow out of it.'

'Seems odd that the entire staff force is affected though, don't you think?' Nate looked directly at Angelika and she raised an eyebrow. Now she thought of it, however, this hadn't been strictly true. Aki had spoken throughout the duration of their ill-fated flight, as had the pilot of the rescue plane, albeit in bad broken English. Rubbing her temples, Angelika still wasn't feeling right. Her head felt muddled, she'd only had a few sips of champagne and yet it felt like she'd imbibed the entire bottle, consciously struggling to find the right words when she spoke. It had to be the stress taking effect, she told herself; adrenalin and alcohol were a potent mix.

'There's plenty odd about this whole situation,' she suggested, 'though I'm starting to think that's McKenzie's whole MO.'

'MO?' Billie-Jo wished people would just talk normal, for fuck's sakes.

Nate felt embarrassed by his wife's ignorance. For some reason he was more conscious of it in front of Angelika. Her obvious intelligence merely highlighted his wife's lack of it.

'*Modus operandi*; it's Latin. It means method of operation.'

Billie-Jo shrugged still none the wiser.

'Well, whatever it means, it's well creepy.'

Angelika looked over at Rupert who was standing a few feet away. He appeared to be in deep, animated conversation with Mia Manhattan, though he was just out of earshot for her to ascertain what it was they were discussing. It was then through the fog in her mind that she remembered something Mia had said to her the night of the crash, while she and Rupert had been exchanging words. '*Did he tell you what really happened during the trial, hmm, did he?*' She made a mental note to herself to ask him when they were alone.

'Mutism, eh?' Rupert said as he approached the three of them, Mia close behind him, her expression sombre. 'You could take a leaf out of their book, darling.' He laughed.

Angelika grimaced. Rupert always took such joy in mocking her in front of an audience and she loathed him for it.

'I suppose there's really very little we can do until the telephone lines are up and working again,' Mia acquiesced. 'Until then we're stuck here so I don't know about you lot but I might just sample a little of what this place has to offer in the meantime.'

'You've changed your bloody tune,' Rupert snorted.

'Well, what other options do you suggest, Deyton?' she snapped back. 'We've no chance of getting off this island so I say we make the bloody best of it, and drink McKenzie dry and eat his expensive food...'

She placed the black box she was carrying down onto the table in front of them. She snapped her fingers in the direction of her assigned butler who nodded his compliance. 'Take this back to my apartment, will you, er – Remi, is it?'

'Mutes,' Rupert snorted. 'So typical of a man like McKenzie, pretentious arsehole.'

'Well, I'm not complaining,' Mia adjusted her Grecian gown, 'I like the strong, silent type.'

'Don't forget young,' Rupert smirked.

Mia smiled wryly. 'And tell me Rupert, what is *your* type?'

Angelika watched the cold exchange of eye contact between them carefully. She was well informed about the bad blood between them but instinct told her there was something else. Something she didn't know about.

'My wife's my type, Mia,' he shot back, placing an arm around Angelika as if to illustrate the point, surprising no one more than Angelika herself. Her husband rarely, if ever, indulged in any public display of affection anymore.

'Mia's right,' she said, feeling a little uncomfortable, 'there's nothing we can do other than stay here and wait. Hopefully there will be some news on Joshua soon … good news with a bit of luck.'

Back inside their cabana, Angelika was attempting to choose a bikini to wear: a daunting task given the vast selection. She had a good figure; better than she was aware of. She worked out three times a week and had not put her body through the strains of childhood. Her figure was petite, neat, and she'd always been naturally slim, and, thanks to a strict gym regime, gently toned. Though not blessed with an ample cleavage – something her husband occasionally unkindly reminded her of; she had come to believe over the years that this was a trade-off for being on the smaller side.

She had considered surgery, not that she was prepared to admit as much to anyone. It seemed far too vain and unbefitting for a woman of her age and status to even consider, yet she had, and at some length. The biggest stumbling block was her conscience and the fact that as she would probably have to write about it, thus throwing herself at the mercy of the general public's judgement, not to mention her husband's.

A woman like her – a well-respected high-profile journalist, a woman with substance and intellect – having a boob job; she couldn't even imagine the slew of criticism, the backlash from the feminist brigade, the drop in estimation. And yet she was still a woman; she still wanted to look and feel confident and happy.

Happiness, what was that anyway? Her mother once said to her that it was a habit: 'Just pretend to be good at it, and like any habit eventually you'll get good at it.' She realised now it wasn't such bad advice. She squashed her breasts together in the mirror forming a small, round cleavage. God, it had been so long she'd almost forgotten what it was like to feel sexy.

Angelika sighed. She suddenly remembered what she'd been meaning to ask Rupert. 'What did Mia Manhattan mean that time when she asked me if I knew what had really happened during the trial?'

'What are you talking about?' Rupert called out from the bathroom where he had gone to shave and prepare himself for a recce around the island.

'The night of the crash … you and Mia were arguing and she said something like, "did he even tell you what really happened during the trial?"'

Rupert winced in the mirror as he covered his face in shaving foam. Jesus, he looked as tired as he bloody felt. The fact that he should've been at home playing polo right now had not escaped him and he felt a wave of resentment towards his wife for ever having coerced him here in the first place. Frankly he could've kicked himself. He hadn't thought any of this through properly, he'd been distracted by the case he'd been on and Angelika had been so persistent. Now he was stuck on a bloody desert island with her for the foreseeable future with no means of any real escape, and if that wasn't enough to piss on his fireworks, then why not throw Mia Manhattan into the God damn mix as well.

Rupert looked into his own eyes and saw the worry in them. The trouble with Angelika was that she had a fucking photographic memory; he supposed it was partly what made her so successful in her chosen career. A talent it may be but sometimes, as in this instance, it was a real ball ache. Mia had made a stupid glib remark in anger and now Angelika was on his case.

Manhattan was a loose cannon; she had trouble written through her like a stick of rock. Her life had been one big, long drama and if it wasn't her drama then she'd be in the thick of someone else's, thriving on it like oxygen. Mia was the type of woman for whom the phrase 'all publicity is good publicity' was coined. She had no qualms about throwing anyone under the bus if it meant keeping her presence in the media buoyant. And the bloody big, old bitch had something on him, something potentially catastrophic.

Rupert was genuinely concerned she might open Pandora's Box, as well as the one she'd been given by Remi. He shuddered just thinking about it. Was Mia capable of being that vindictive? After all, she had kept his secret, somewhat surprisingly he had to admit, all of these years and had been granted plenty of opportunity to stitch him up in the past, yet she had never told a soul what she knew, or not that he was aware of. Was she saving it for an occasion such as this, one where it would create maximum drama and devastation, a situation where he would be backed into a corner, like shooting fish in a barrel? Well, two could play at that game; he had dirt on her too, weapons in his arsenal he could use if needs be, though admittedly would rather not. Perhaps that's why Mia had kept that great mouth of hers shut all this time, an unspoken vow of mutual silence between them. I won't tell if you won't, kind of thing.

He sucked his stomach in, his abdominals making a fleeting appearance before disappearing as he exhaled. The past twenty-four hours seemed to have aged him ten years. Rupert wearily dragged the razor down his face. He observed himself objectively in the mirror. Was he still attractive? He supposed he was. He still had his own hair at least and while he was no muscle man he could still remove his shirt in public without fear of scaring the birds. Still, he'd turned heads walking down the street once upon a time and couldn't help wondering had it anatomically shifted to stomachs instead?

'So?' Angelika appeared behind him in the bathroom wearing a bikini that was surprisingly skimpy for her usual taste, although admittedly he wasn't entirely sure what that was anymore, 'are you going to tell me what she meant?'

'Who knows what that woman means; she probably doesn't even know herself. No doubt referring to some imagined slight I am supposed to have made against her. You remember what she was like after the trial. She savaged me in the press.'

Angelika watched her husband's eyes in the mirror; she could tell he was lying. Fifteen years married had afforded her such a skill.

'How could I forget,' she replied, watching him closely while adjusting her shiny wet-look Gucci bikini.

'Bit racy for you, that, isn't it?' he commented, immediately wishing he hadn't.

She flashed him a look.

'You don't approve?' She didn't know whether it was the bikini, the light-headedness she had continually experienced since arriving on the island, or the fact they had survived a near-death experience but she suddenly found herself feeling amorous towards her husband for what felt like the first time in years. Angelika cast him a mischievous look in the mirror as she pressed her body into his from behind, sliding her arms around his expanding waist. It had been so long since she'd touched his naked skin in a sexual context that she felt a jolt of electricity between her legs.

'Racy, huh?' she said, gently biting his shoulder, 'now that's a word you haven't used since the 80s.'

She pressed her pelvis into the small of his back and made to slide her hand into the top of his Bermuda swim shorts but he squirmed away from her forcing her to take a step back.

'I'm shaving Angelika,' he said quickly, 'do you want me to cut my throat?'

Angelika's heartbeat quickened, her face burning; he'd murdered the moment brutally. 'I won't answer that,' she sneered, red with indignation. Why didn't her husband find her attractive anymore? She wanted to ask him but was too fearful of the answer. 'You don't like it then, the bikini?'

Rupert felt a little stab of guilt in his solar plexus.

'The bikini is lovely, Angelika,' he said. It sounded disingenuous, though it wasn't meant to. As it was she did look rather fabulous in it; she was after all still a very attractive woman.

'I knew McKenzie would be a no-show,' she said, changing the subject, not wanting to dwell on the emotions her husband's outright rejection had mustered. Was it her who turned him off or was it women in general? Had she imagined the way her husband had looked at Nate, his appreciate eyes scanning his toned body. Was it jealousy or something else? Angelika shoved the thought from her mind. She was being ridiculous.

'Well, yes, you know everything, don't you darling?' Rupert could hear the facetiousness in his own voice but was powerless to prevent it. It had become such a dreadful habit that he just couldn't seem to break.

'Yes, except for what Mia meant … I don't know that!'

Rupert felt a little hot behind the ears. His wife was the proverbial dog with a bone. She would never leave it alone now because that was Angelika.

'Don't you think it's all a little odd?'

'What is?'

'I've been thinking …'

'Ah, now you know that is dangerous, especially with your imagination.'

She ignored him.

'Isn't it a little odd how none of us, bar poor Joshua, were hurt in the crash save for a few superficial scratches and bruises?' she rubbed her hip again, the bruise, a little raised, was starting to make colour.

'Bloody good job too … we were lucky.'

'Do you think it was luck?'

Rupert looked at her.

'What else could it have been?'

'I don't know,' she answered honestly. 'I can barely remember anything before the crash … it's like my memory has been wiped.'

Rupert pulled a face. In all honestly though he hardly remembered much about the crash, or the lead up to it himself either. 'And ever since we've been on the island I've felt a little strange.'

'That's because you *are* strange, my dear.'

'I'm being serious, Ru.'

'So am I!' He managed a smile.

'It's probably post-traumatic stress; perhaps you won't have to act up after all when it comes to suing McKenzie's sorry arse.'

'I have felt permanently a little, well, tipsy, is the only way I can describe it I suppose.'

Oddly he knew exactly what she meant as he too had struggled with a slight malaise ever since they'd touched down onto the island. He'd put it down to lack of sleep and trauma.

'Maybe you ought to lay off the champagne then,' he remarked, welcoming the conversation's change in direction.

'Hmm … yes, perhaps the champagne's the answer.'

'Champagne's always the answer.'

Angelika began brushing her hair. 'What do you think is in the box he gave us?'

Rupert removed the last of the foam with the razor and shook it into the sink.

'God knows; nothing probably. It's just McKenzie's fuckery. You above all people know what a control freak he is. He's only done it so that we will have this exact conversation. It's a big PR stunt, the whole bloody thing.'

'Yes, but if that was the case then surely he would've only invited press people. Why invite Mia for instance, or Nate and Billie-Jo for that matter? He's a footballer and she's an –'

'Idiot? No to mention a little gold-digger and a slut.'

Angelika scowled.

'So judgemental, Rupert.'

'Come on, don't tell me you disagree.'

'I disagree with you being so judgmental. She seems nice enough.'

'Well, once thing's for sure, we'll no doubt get to find out! Until those bloody phone lines are fixed we're stuck here with the lot of them.'

CHAPTER EIGHTEEN

Never argue with stupid people, they will drag you down to their level and beat you with experience. This was the thought running through Mia's mind as she stretched out on the enormous egg-shaped sun pod in a cat-like manner and took a large slug of champagne.

She was sure McKenzie had done this deliberately – throwing her and Deyton together like this. After all, her dislike of her former brief wasn't exactly a big secret. Perhaps they were all in it together: McKenzie, Deyton and that bastard Bailey – she wouldn't put it past any of them, trio of unscrupulous fuckers. If only McKenzie had been brave enough to show his face she would've ripped it clean off. Instead, however, the big shithouse had sent his weird little wife to do his dirty work for him. Coward as ever. She shifted uneasily on the sunbed, unable to find comfort. Admittedly the setting was spectacular – he'd got that part right at least – the 360-degree view of tranquil crystalline ocean swathed in palms and sheltered by craggy cliffs and powdery, white sand was picture-postcard perfect in its simplicity, nature at its most breathtaking. For now she was content to bask in the unforgiving heat, the sun high and proud above the cliffs casting a white sheen over all it touched. In any normal circumstance Mia would've thoroughly appreciated the chance to rest and recuperate in such a spectacular location, and with all that was on hand too, but she couldn't relax.

What was McKenzie's *real* reason for inviting her here? He'd ignored her for years. Why now? Whatever it was she had a bad feeling about it. It was Bailey's fault for talking her into it. He had manipulated her, convinced her it would re-boot her flagging career, pave the way for a comeback and stupidly she had allowed herself to be seduced. She should've known better; Martin McKenzie was born with a hidden agenda. But what was that hidden agenda in this instance, and what did it have to do with her? She had history with him granted, but McKenzie didn't even know the half of it.

Their story went back over thirty-five years – practically a lifetime ago now, or so it felt – when she had been a terribly young, terribly beautiful and terribly talented wannabe star. McKenzie, a decade her senior at the very least, had already accrued a name for himself as something of an impresario in the entertainment industry, ostensibly in television broadcasting and talent spotting. He'd found her singing in a backstreet pub in Pimlico and promptly signed her on the spot.

'I'm going to make you the biggest star on the planet.' She would never forget his opening gambit. This was what she'd been waiting for from the moment she'd been consciously aware of her own existence. Recognition – and from someone with McKenzie's burgeoning clout – was like being given a golden ticket and it was only fair to say that he had made good on his word; for the next two years she had been his number-one priority in every sense, and had introduced her to anyone of any importance or sway in the business. He'd hooked her up with big name producers, people who'd worked with the likes of Diana Ross and Elton John and set about transforming her into a household name, a superstar with global appeal. 'You got the voice, baby, and that's all you need to worry about. You just let Uncle Mart do the rest, huh?'

Mia had never considered objecting, not to anything he said, ever, not even when he'd insisted on changing her birth name from June Longfield to Mia Manhattan. 'No one famous ever had the name June Longfield, honey.' McKenzie was the master, and she his slave. She had trusted him both professionally and personally, and with a naivety that was a preserve of her youth.

The affair between them had, with hindsight, been as inevitable as it was brief. He had taken her virginity with breathtaking self-entitlement and she had given it willingly, grateful to him for everything. She knew he was married and accepted it could never be anything more than what it was. He had even encouraged her to date other boys her own age, which she had done simply to please him and in a futile attempt to make him jealous. She supposed she had been in love with him. However, what had happened next had given Mia cause to despise the man, to loathe him with such raw hatred that she had willed him a slow, agonising death ever since. This secret, one she had carried and kept for over thirty years, had shaped Mia's entire existence and changed her life forever, the kind that never left you alone; it was always there, burning a hole through her heart, tormenting her thoughts, creeping into her consciousness whenever she found herself feeling happy and contented. Guilt was such a terrible affliction; it never let you forget. It was like a cancer, slowly corroding and gnawing away at her.

She had tried to forgive herself for it but guilt had a different agenda, its own life force, and no matter how much she had tried over the years to push it away it was always there, threatening, stealth-like beneath the surface, to remind of her of what a dreadful, cruel and heartless woman she really must be. Dickie was one of just three people who knew of her true past. McKenzie only knew half the truth but Rupert Deyton knew the lot. During her trial, when she'd been in a highly emotional state, she had confessed her terrible secret to him only to instantly regret such a moment of candour. Rupert bloody Deyton, of all people! What had she been thinking? She clearly hadn't been. And now he knew. And now he was here. However, while concerned, she wasn't overly so because she had dirt on him too. Shit, what she knew could be used as leverage should he ever threaten to spill the beans. He wouldn't though, would he?

The champagne had acted like a sedative, and sweeping her moribund thoughts out of her mind like ashes, Mia finally found herself drifting off in a fitful slumber – until suddenly she was aware of a shadow across her, an a drop in temperature as someone blocked the sun.

'Hey, babe,' the voice said, 'I didn't wake you, did I?'

Mia sat bolt upright.

Oh my God,' she gasped loudly, 'Joshua!'

CHAPTER NINETEEN

A scorching hot day had given way to a sticky, sultry evening where the guests had gathered, as per instructions, underneath the white, canopied terrace. Dinner, preluded by champagne aperitifs, had been a truly spectacular affair, a no-expense-spared feast of five-star cuisine displayed on sizzling silver platters: a plethora of fresh crustacean and melt-in-the-mouth meats; foie gras appetisers; and fresh fruits carved into elaborate works of art that looked almost too good to eat.

After clearing away the devoured dishes, one of the mutes brought a selection of digestifs along with a box and placed them onto the table before bowing subserviently.

'Mine's a brandy and lovage,' Rupert said, giving him the nod to pour.

'Another box?' Billie-Jo peered over at it. It had the words 'Play if you dare' written on the front. She repeated them with a raised eyebrow. 'Sounds like a challenge to me!'

'Looks like a board game or something,' Nate said opening it. 'Ah.' He pulled out a set of cards and some instructions. 'It *is* a board game.'

'Ooh, I'm in.' Billie-Jo clasped her painted hands. She loved playing games, of every variety, and anything that contained the word 'dare' in it had her vote. 'How about you guys?' She looked over at Mia and Joshua, who she noted had been surprisingly quiet since his return to the island just a few hours ago.

'Can't remember nothing,' he'd said honestly of being flown off the island to have his arm fixed up. 'I swear it's all a hazy blur, dude ... all I can remember is waking up to some nurse peering over me and the next thing I'm on a plane being taken back here.' He'd taken a swig of a cold cerveza and shrugged.

'You don't remember where they took you? Or if you had access to a telephone?' Mia supposed the poor boy had been sedated up to the eyeballs.

'Are you in pain?' Angelika had expressed her concern.

'Like I said, I don't remember nothing ... they pumped me full of morphine, man. I could've been in Tennessee or Timbucktoo, and no, no pain at all thanks to the liquid H.' He'd waved his cast arm as if to demonstrate. 'I kinda feel like a new man.'

Billie-Jo smirked. She knew the feeling.

Mia was glad he wasn't in any pain at least, but still she couldn't help feeling a little irritated by the fact that Joshua had not have the savvy to make a phone call from the hospital. If he'd alerted someone about the crash landing and who was here on the island, namely Rupert bastard Deyton, then it would eventually get back to Dickie and he would've sent a plane for her, she felt sure. But she was mindful of grilling him; the boy had been through the ringer and looked pale and tired. A relaxed supper and an early night was just what the doctor ordered, so to speak. Billie-Jo, however, seemed to have other plans.

'It's one of them truth-or-dare type games,' she announced, snatching the instructions from Nate and scanning them. 'An icebreaker it says here ...'

Nate glanced over at Angelika and gave a little eye roll. There was no stopping Bee when she got one in her bonnet.

'Icebreaker? How very … *American*.' Rupert couldn't think of anything worse.

'Actually, I'm feeling pretty exhausted,' Angelika said, 'and I'm sure Joshua here would like to rest, wouldn't you? After what he's been through.'

'What we've *all* been through,' Rupert chipped in.

Super8#6 watched the players from behind his computer screen. He felt apprehensive; it didn't look as if they were going to bite the bait and he felt a little panic rise within him. He had hoped to impress the club members with his psychological prowess; he knew that if they would only play it, then it would make for sensational viewing.

'Looks like you got all your timing wrong, my friend.' Super8#3 typed, unhelpfully.

Super8#6 felt his irritation spike. All the Super Eight club members had tuned in for tonight's anticipated action and he knew they would be disappointed to sign off unsatisfied, no one more than himself.

'Let's just see shall we, *my friend*.' It was official; Super8#3 was a complete jerk.

Billie-Jo gulped at a glass of Courvoisier.

'Aw, come on, you killjoys.' She continued to read the instructions. 'It's our first proper night all together on the island and look, it says here the winning couple are in store for a prize!' This was more than enough of an incentive for Billie-Jo. She liked the idea of a prize, especially one from the likes of Martin multi-billionaire McKenzie. 'Let's face it, we could all do with having some fun.'

No one could exactly argue with her.

'Suppose a quick game won't hurt before bed,' Angelika acquiesced, although something told her it wasn't a good idea.

Mia glanced at Rupert, up-lit by the candelabra. He was on his second brandy and lovage, and had an austere look on his face. This wasn't particularly unusual from what she could remember but still it put her ill at ease.

'So –' Billie-Jo picked up a small, white card from the pack. She had taken it upon herself to become task master '– I will ask the first question and I will ask …' She scanned the table quickly '… you!' She pointed at Angelika. Angelika decided to top-up her own Courvoisier glass; subliminally something told her she may need it.

'Truth or dare, Angelika?'

Billie-Jo shot her a sly smile though Angelika wasn't sure why. She had been nothing but pleasant to her from the moment they'd met.

Angelika hesitated.

'Come on, Angelika,' Rupert interjected, 'you've played spin the bottle before, haven't you?'

Actually, she wasn't sure she ever had.

'Truth,' she reluctantly replied. The truth couldn't hurt you after all, could it?

Billie-Jo grinned as she read the card.

'What's the worst lie you've ever told your partner? Two points for truth or forfeit one with a dare.'

Angelika's eyes widened.

'Does it really say that, on the card I mean?'

Billie-Jo held it up for her to see.

Super8#6 broke into a smile.

'What were you saying about timing #3, my friend?' he wrote, smugly. And so it had begun …

Angelika felt the heat of the other's eyes upon her, expectant.

'Well?' Rupert said. He looked almost amused by her discomfort.

Angelika knew the answer to the question right off but she was damned if she was going to confess her sins like this!

'And don't lie or I'll know!' he added, though he was careful to make it sound light-hearted.

She wracked her brains to come up with something plausible but her exhausted mind failed her.

'OK,' she said sheepishly, '… dare then.'

Rupert's eyes widened and Mia began to laugh.

'So you have a secret you're not telling me: a lie I don't know about … or that you don't want to say? What is it, Angelika?' he felt indignant, embarrassed; his wife had opted out of a confession and chosen a dare instead. What was so bad that she couldn't tell him?

'We all have secrets, Rupert,' Mia smirked, 'don't we?'

'Some more than others,' he fired back.

Nate sensed Angelika's discomfort and felt sorry for her.

'Dare it is then!' Billie-Jo was relishing this game already. She picked up a card from the deck. 'Point to a person here who you would most like to have sex with other than your partner … Oh my God!' She gasped excitedly. Now this *really* was her idea of fun.

'This is ridiculous!' Angelika objected, 'seriously?'

'Says here if you refuse the dare then you must "suffer the consequences".'

'Which are?' Nate said.

'Dunno, just what is says …' Billie-Jo shrugged. 'I'll have to hurry you, Angelika.' Billie-Jo was enjoying herself as she began to sing the iconic timed-out tune from the TV show *Countdown*.

'OK … OK …' She quickly pointed at Nate and felt herself redden.

The gesture burst Billie-Jo's bubble with a pop that was almost audible.

Mia and Joshua were looking at the three of them simultaneously. Billie-Jo's mouth was slightly agape, Rupert's expression was stony, and Nate, though Mia could tell he was making a stellar effort to disguise it, looked pretty-damn chuffed.

'Hey, so what's wrong with me then, Angelika? Not your bag huh?' JJ grinned at her. He wasn't exactly offended but his ego was certainly a little bruised. After all, he was younger, and a rock star. And was used to all the attention from pussy of all ages. So what was *this* chick's problem?

'No offence,' Angelika apologised quickly, 'it's just … well … there's not too much in the way of choice, is there? And … and … Nate's more my age,' she added, not daring to look in his direction. 'No offence,' she said again, this time looking at Mia. *How excruciating!*

Billie-Jo studied her husband's reaction carefully. Was that a half smile she could see on his face? She'd have to keep an eye out for Angelika Deyton. It was always the basic bitches you needed to watch out for when it came to protecting your assets. Surely he didn't fancy *her*?

Rupert fixed his wife's eyes and she widened her own as if to say, 'What was I supposed to do?'

'So …' Billie-Jo attempted to keep the animosity from her tone, 'your turn, *Angelika*.'

'Go on then!' Rupert said, as if to challenge her.

Angelika reluctantly picked up a card from the top of the pile with an unsteady hand. She wasn't enjoying this.

'Explain … ahem.' She cleared her throat. 'Explain your three least-favourite characteristics about your partner and why, and allow the others to guess which is your top least favourite.'

Mia's eyebrows rose. Some game this was turning out to be.

'I don't think I want to play this anymore.' Angelika placed the card back down onto the table and simultaneously sipped her drink.

'Don't be shy, darling,' Rupert mocked her. 'Things are just about to get interesting.'

Super8#4 smiled to herself.

'Aren't they just?' she typed. 'The lawyer is seriously pissed off that his wife wants to fuck the footballer … now you all know I predicted this.'

'Quite the clairvoyant,' Super8#2 wrote back.

'Well, where do I begin?' Rupert laughed. 'Angelika, Angelika, Angelika … hmmm … the three things I like about you *least* …'

'Oh, come on Rupert, it shouldn't be too difficult,' she humoured him in a bid to conceal her mortification.

'Ok, number one: my wife always has to be right about pretty much everything. If you've seen it, done it, or read it, then Angelika's seen more, done more, and read more.' He hardly paused. 'Two: she despises me having any interests, polo being the main one, and resents the enjoyment it brings me; number three: she doesn't listen. Having a conversation with Angelika is like talking to a cardboard box sometimes. She only ever hears what she wants to hear and can't see an alternative point of view, just her own. She's also always dragging me into situations or events which she knows I have no interest in attending and demands that I –'

'That four things,' Nate interjected feeling the need to prevent him from continuing. He could see the look on Angelika's face.

'No, please, carry on.' Angelika felt her heckles rising. How dare her husband say these things about in front of everyone, so blasé. And also so unfair.

'The second one,' Billie-Jo said. 'The polo ... I can see you're well pissed off about that! Am I right?'

Angelika shook her head. Rupert was clearly smarting about her dare and had wasted no time exacting his revenge.

'One point to Billie-Jo!' Rupert raised his glass to her.

'Nice one!' she squealed. 'We're winning, babe.' She turned to Nate and he looked at her unblinking. Billie-Jo always had her eye on the prize.

'What?' she said. 'It's only a game!'

'Your turn then, BJ,' Joshua said, reaching for a card with his good arm.

'What would be the one reason you would cheat on your partner? Would it be: a) money; b) fame; c) love. Your partner must guess your answer correctly for two points ...'

Mia smirked. Ha! That had shut the girl up.

Billie-Jo's mind revved like an F1 engine. She would have to be careful with her answer. She knew Nate would never believe that she'd cheat on him for love alone. He understood her too well and she didn't want to forfeit because then that would look like she didn't want to admit it would be one of the two former, as close a call as it was between them.

She glanced at her husband.

'OK, I have my answer.'

Nate shifted uncomfortably in his seat. What kind of a game *was* this?

'I really don't think this is a good idea,' Angelika said. 'I think we should stop playing it.'

'No,' Billie-Jo answered, 'I want to know what my husband really thinks. Nate ...?'

He sighed.

'Well, I'd have to say C then,' He was lying and they all knew it.

'Wrong!' Billie-Jo shot back looking quite pleased with herself. 'Because I would never cheat in the first place!'

JJ stifled a snigger. Yeah, right, and he didn't have a hole in his arse.

'But that's cheating,' Mia interjected. 'That wasn't an option! You'll have to take a forfeit now.' Mia was nothing if not competitive. She always played to win, even if she didn't like the game.

'For once I agree with you, Mia. Saying you wouldn't cheat was not an option on the card,' Rupert agreed.

'Like Billie-Jo said, it's only a game,' Angelika said, still reeling from her husband's invective.

'All right, all right, I'll do a forfeit then,' she pouted.

Nate read the card, his expression was cloudy.

'Tell each of your fellow guests your first impressions of them.'

'Easy,' she said, turning straight to Angelika. Nate squirmed in his seat. Careful Bee, he thought to himself. He knew his wife regularly didn't think before she spoke. She wasn't necessarily deliberately vindictive but she often hurt people through complete lack of consideration.

'I thought you was a bit stuck-up; you know, up yer own arse cos you're a journalist an' that. Reckon you think yourself a touch above … you was nice and everything but I felt like you was looking down on me. And it's obvious you two –' she pointed at Angelika and Rupert simultaneously '– have got more issues than *Vogue* in your marriage.' She switched to Mia. 'I didn't know who you were, though it seemed like you expect everyone to know exactly who you are. Thought you was glamorous though,' she added, thinking it a great compliment '– and that JJ here was your son.'

Nate inwardly groaned. Billie-Jo had been steadily attacking the alcohol all evening and as a result her inhibitions had gone out of the window along with all sense.

'Bit of a diva as well, but then I suppose you're knocking on a bit and have been famous for like, ever, so why the fuck not, eh? I probably would be an' all … and Rupert, well, you came across as a right stick in the mud, bit of grouch, old before your time … bit re– … what's the word …?'

'Repressed?' Mia offered helpfully.

'Yeah, and pretty horrible about your wife too, but then again maybe she deserves it.'

'Jesus fucking Christ, Bee!' Nate felt the need to stop her but she was having far too much fun now. She had been given legitimate carte blanche to say it like it was and wasn't about to waste a golden opportunity.

'I haven't finished yet. And JJ –' she looked at him and smiled '– well, I thought you were an arrogant knobhead who thinks way too much of himself but then again you are a rock star so and you're cute so you get away with it. I also wondered what the fuck you're doing with her,' she pointed at Mia like she wasn't really there.

'*Her!*' Mia pulled her chin into her chest.

'Well, thanks for such an eloquent insight into us all Billie-Jo,' Rupert was amused rather than offended. He couldn't give a rat's arse what this dumb little tart thought of him and had been called a lot worse both in and out of the courtroom. He was also on his fourth brandy and drunk as a Lord.

'Let's stop now, yes?' Angelika pleaded. However, she was rather hurt by Billie-Jo's observations, especially as some of them were true.

'My go!' Mia snatched up a card.

'Actually it's my go,' JJ said. He was kinda enjoying this in a perverse way.

'What would you be prepared to give up for a glittering career: money; motherhood; or your looks?'

Mia flinched.

'All three by the looks of it,' Billie-Jo muttered underneath her breath.

'What did you say?' Mia was almost out of her chair. The question had hit a raw nerve. 'Were you born a spiteful little bitch or has it taken years of practise! She looked at Nate. 'How did a lovely boy like you end up with a viper like this?'

Nate wasn't quite sure how to answer her himself. Bee really was her own worst enemy, especially when she'd had a drink. She was so full of venom sometimes that it worried him. He knew she'd been a messed up kid and that this hard-faced act was little more than a façade, but making friends with people wasn't high on her agenda, unless of course they could be of benefit to her. She really did herself no favours.

Mia picked up a half-finished glass of champagne and threw it at Billie-Jo. It was a knee-jerk reaction and the aim wasn't exactly spot on target, covering as much as Joshua as it did Billie-Jo.

'You stupid old bag,' she hissed. 'This is fucking McQueen, don't you know!' She dabbed at her dress with a spare napkin.

'Yes, dear, and you make it look like cheap tat. What is they say … ? You can't make a silk purse out of a sow's ear!'

'Ladies, please.' Joshua was laughing; he couldn't help it. Billie-Jo was something else and Mia was a pretty good match for her. It was almost turning him on.

'Look, I think Angelika's right. I really think we should stop this,' Nate interjected.

'I agree,' Angelika reiterated.

'You would,' Rupert remarked. 'But then again by the sounds of it you *more* than would.'

'Oh, do shut up, Rupert,' she retaliated, 'hardly in a position to start calling the moral high ground; any more rapists you want to set free?'

'Rapists?' Mia sneered.

'Peter Cheshunt,' she informed her, 'he knew he was a guilty as sin yet still he managed to get the bastard off.'

'Amazing,' Mia gave a wry smile, 'and you couldn't even get me out of a contract.'

'You didn't answer your question, Mia,' Rupert's eyes were ablaze. 'So, which would it be, money, looks or motherhood?'

'Fuck you,' she screamed, 'and fuck this!' Mia scraped her chair back and flounced from the terrace, the click-clack of her Jimmy Choos amplified by the canopied acoustics.

McKenzie watched with a grin on his face. He had added that particular question especially for Mia's benefit and her reaction hadn't disappointed.

Similarly, Super8#6 was basking in self-satisfied glory.

'Not bad viewing, eh, Super8#3?' he typed on screen.

'So, so,' he responded, though he had to concede it had all been rather fun to watch and terribly *awkward.*

'Well, I think we can say that certainly broke the ice,' Rupert snorted after a moment's silence.

Angelika stood. 'I'm going to bed,' she said, excusing herself.

'Me too,' Nate followed.

'Not together I hope,' Billie-Jo grimaced.

Rupert threw back the remainder of his fifth digestif and waited until Angelika had disappeared from view before standing.

'Well, it's been fun,' he said, adding, 'not.'

He made to place his glass heavily onto the table as a parting shot but missed and it smashed onto the expensive, wooden decking.

'Oops,' he said abandoning the mess with an unconcerned wave of the hand.

JJ turned to a rapidly sobering Billie-Jo. She was smoking a cigarette with a triumphant smirk and draining the last of her glass.

'I'm seriously pissed, man. No one got to ask *me* a question,' he said, indignant.

'Aww, didums,' she mocked him playfully. 'Well, I got one for ya –' Billie-Jo smiled flirtatiously as she reached for the bottle of champagne '–fancy another drink?'

CHAPTER TWENTY

Billie-Jo didn't do hangovers. You had to stop for one of them, and she was well on the way to being off her tits once more thanks to an entire morning spent quaffing champagne and snorting coke while indulging herself in a plethora of pampering treatments. Nate had barely said a word to her that morning and had scowled at her when she'd attempted conversation. She realised she may have overstepped the mark a touch at last night's little icebreaker but so what? Who were these people to them anyway? She couldn't remember what she'd even said, and as far as she was concerned if you didn't remember something, it didn't happen, right? Still, she thought it prudent to keep out of the way for a bit. She'd woken with a headache and thought a day of pampering her pretty ass would be just the antidote she needed. That a bit of the two C's. She was on holiday, for fuck's sake.

The spa had been so impressive that Billie-Jo felt like pinching herself, all marble and mosaic tiles, mirrored ceilings and inviting chaise longue daybeds with huge, lush cushions … if only she'd had her beloved Samsung she would've flooded Instagram with a million smug selfies.

'Bit of all right this place, ain't it?' she said to herself scanning the sumptuous treatment room and the comfy-looking white massage bed, the floating waterlillies in decorative glass bowls, soft, scented candlelight and hundreds of beauty products stacked neatly on shelves. A full-body aromatherapy massage was just the thing to round off what was fast becoming the perfect morning for Billie-Jo; she'd already done thirty minutes in the state-of-the-art gym followed by a dip in the heated, marble pool. Then she'd headed off to the floatation tank to chill out before treating herself to a deluxe paraffin mani-pedi, a wax and exfoliation, and an intensive anti-aging facial that had left her feeling like a million fucking bucks. Hey, she was worth it, right? This must be how the likes of Kim Kardashian lived, she thought, straight-up luxury on tap twenty-four seven, minions refreshing your glass every five minutes and catering to your every whim. They'd probably have wiped her arse for her is she'd asked them to.

'Where do you want me?' she enquired, sizing up the insanely fit-looking masseur. His dark smouldering looks bore a striking resemblance to that underwear model who was going out with that blonde one from that girl band she liked, David someone or the other. Hotter than a radiator on the blink, he was. Such a pity he was a fucking mute; she would've liked to have indulged in a little flirtatious banter with him. Billie-Jo glanced at him, doe-eyed, appreciating his impressive guns and the six-pack visible through his thin, white T-shirt, his large, masculine hands as big as shovels as he carefully prepared the oils he was about to rub all over her naked flesh. Happy days.

He nodded towards the bed.

Billie-Jo knocked back the remaining champagne from the ever-full glass she'd enjoyed throughout the morning. She was feeling more than a little light-headed and was glad of a lie-down. She couldn't be sure exactly how much champagne she'd thrown down her neck but was beginning to suspect it was far more than she'd thought. She opened her white, fluffy robe, displaying her naked body save for a tiny Victoria's Secret neon G-string, and let it drop to the floor.

'Front or back first?' she enquired breathlessly as she climbed up onto the table, aware of his eyes as they settled upon her impressive, enhanced breasts, and not in the least bit perturbed by it. She was exceptionally proud of her 32EEs, of her entire body, in fact, and with good reason. Getting naked was second nature to her, thanks to plenty of practise, and she enjoyed the reaction it provoked. After all, what was the point in looking as shit-hot as she did if no one could appreciate it? It didn't occur to Billie-Jo that her body might remain exclusively viewed by her husband in private. She was out to glean as much affirmation about her good looks as possible and judging by this fella's grid she would not be left wanting.

She glanced at his crotch. He was semi-hard already and extremely impressive with it, but while his obvious arousal gave her a sense of satisfaction, she had no real intention of acting upon it. Billie-Jo was the original cock-tease. As much as her outward portrayal suggested otherwise, she hadn't been as promiscuous as one might've naturally assumed. She'd not really been big on one-nighters, unless it was with someone with some serious clout, in which case she made an exception. After all, sex was just sex at the end of the day, a bargaining tool she had learned to use to her advantage.

But she was mindful of the adage, 'why buy the cow when you can get the milk for free?' Giving up the goods too early made you disposable before you'd had the chance to milk anything out of them yourself. Sex was just a commodity as far as she was concerned, enjoying it merely a lucky bonus. She'd once read in a magazine somewhere that there was supposed to be a big difference between the act of sex and making love but not as far as she bleedin' well knew. There'd been no 'deep spiritual connection' or whatever it was the deluded writer had reckoned, at least not for her. Sure it was nice enough fucking her husband and all of that, but that's just what it was at the end of the day – a means to an end, or a new handbag at least. She didn't understand why people made such a fuss about sex and love being mutually exclusive. It was a lie that society enforced to stop people enjoying themselves as far as she could see. That saying, Billie-Jo had never cheated on Nate, not yet anyhow, though this was largely due to the fact that she knew if he found out she'd been messing around behind his back he would divorce her, and she didn't fancy that idea much, at least not until she had something better lined up. Besides, Nate had showed her something none of the others ever had – kindness – and it was a feeling she rather liked, if only it didn't scare the living shit out of her so much.

Locking the door and dimming the lights, the masseur flicked the switch on the stereo, and soft elevator music piped into the room.

'Oooh,' she said as his warm hands got to work on her, firm but gentle, just the right amount of pressure, 'that feels *goooood*.' Billie-Jo relaxed as he began to silently manipulate her skin with expert fingers.

'You've done this before.' She sighed, her nipples stiffening in response to his touch. With one eye open she saw him smile and stifled one of her own as she closed her eyes and allowed the sleepiness she was feeling to begin to claim her. He set about her legs in long, soft, strong strokes, rubbing and pressing her calf muscles, easing away any tension in them, causing her to groan a little as he softly brushed her inner thigh with his magic fingertips, making the lightest contact with her intimate region as he stroked, so light in fact that she could not be sure it had happened at all. Billie-Jo began to drift off, her mind closing down as her body entered a state of such relaxation that she felt like she'd taken drugs, which she had of course, but this was different to the manic coke buzz she so favoured … this felt more like opiates or a sleeping pill or something. She felt strangely euphoric, small rushes of ecstasy flooded her system, causing her heartbeat and temperature to soar, her skin suddenly almost too sensitive to the touch. As she found herself falling into a strange, euphoric slumber, the masseur switched his attention to her torso, gradually working his way up towards her breasts, pressing his hands into the soft malleable skin, his palms brushing against her nipples as he worked on her, pressing, pushing, kneading her like a piece of dough. Billie-Jo felt a tightening between her legs as the blood began to flow. Fuck, what was happening? She had never felt so turned on in her life! She giggled softly, enveloped into a dream-like state, unsure of what was taking place; was this a massage or foreplay? She wasn't quite sure. Suddenly she wasn't quite sure of anything, only the sound of the music and his fingers, the touch of him. She felt herself float off somewhere in her mind as he took his time with her body, rubbing, pressing, his fingers dancing all over her skin, every imprint setting her on fire. She didn't, couldn't resist when after a while he turned her onto her belly and began rubbing oil into her firm, peachy buttocks, manipulating them, squeezing them, causing her to exhale deeply as the rushes became stronger and harder, her chest heaving, beads of sweat prickling the surface of her skin. She almost didn't notice his fingers at first as they gently slid inside her, it felt so completely natural, a logical progression, and she groaned in pleasure, entranced, paralysed by the intensity of it.

'Mmmm,' she responded as her gently played with her, teasing her, his fingers massaging inside and out in long, slow, sensual strokes. The man was a pro, and yet while she knew somewhere in the recess of her mind that it was wrong and should not be happening she felt completely powerless to stop it, her body and all the sensations it was giving her ameliorating any sense of moral outrage or objection.

Billie-Jo felt the warmth of his skin as it made contact with her own, the front of his hard thighs against her buttocks, the tip of him as he tilted her pelvis up so that he could enter her slowly, gently from behind, his hardness causing her to gasp as he parted her buttocks and held them, opening her up to softly glide himself inside her. Holy fuck! She could only gasp as he buried himself deep inside her, inch by inch by inch, slowly and with consideration, savouring each stroke, taking his time. Every nerve ending in her body was singing with such delight that she felt like crying out with happiness. He continued to rub her buttocks and back, as gently he pulled her up onto all fours, her limbs soft and pliable like a doll's as he took complete control, his hands so soft and tender as he manipulated her body, placing them around her tiny waist pulling her down onto him in slow rhythmic movements over and over, gradually, carefully, building momentum. She wanted to cry out but it was as if he instinctively knew this and put a gentle finger inside her wet mouth silencing her, maintaining a rhythm so methodical that it made her want to dance to it inside her head. She could feel the build up of her orgasm surfacing slowly, the climax gently pushing through her pelvis as he guided her towards it silently. Turning her over once more, he sat down onto the bed and gently lifted her down onto him with such ease, his strength at once both surprising and delighting her. She could see his face up close now and he kissed her: a deep, sensual exploration of her mouth with his tongue, savouring her, his lips pulling at hers gently with a quiet urgency that made her want to explode on him in a mad frenzy, except he was setting the pace, and every time she made to move things up a notch, he gently brought her back down to a slow, sensual rhythm instead, a place where he could be precise, explore her at leisure. Remaining silent, he dipped his head to kiss her dark nipples, circling them with his tongue, taking one gently between his teeth causing her to arch her back in ecstasy as he nibbled and kissed, licked and sucked.

Billie-Jo, by now, was now completely consumed in the moment, there was no thought of anything besides what she was experiencing right here right now. She was kissing him back as she gently rode him, devouring his face with her inflatable lips, moaning and gasping as his giant hands cupped her buttocks, lifting her up and down onto his impressive hard cock, her nipples brushing his solid well defined chest, her skin oily and hot with sweat, the music pumping like drum and bass in her ears as he bounced her up and down slowly in time to it. She felt it coming now, the pressure of it flooding every fibre of her body like a balloon about to burst, hot to the point of painful as it tore its way towards the surface. She was almost there.

'Oh. My. G*aaaaad*,' she said as the first crescendo of her orgasm hit, 'Ahhhhh, ahhhhhh, ahhhhhh.' It hit her belly first, causing her to bend double. 'Oh go-oh-god-oh *gaaaaaad!*' She could barely speak, rendered paralysed as it finally exploded inside of her in sharp, prolonged peaks of ecstasy, feel-good endorphins flooding her body, pleasure erupting like scatter crystals inside of her.

And in that moment Billie-Jo had an epiphany. She'd been wrong. Sex wasn't just sex; there was good sex, bad sex – and there was *this* kind of sex.

The little red dot blinked, undetected, concealed in the corner of the treatment room behind the infrared lighting. Not that the likes of Billie-Jo would've noticed it anyway, which was why she had been the perfect choice for this particular scene. Well, that and a couple of other reasons.

'Happy now?' McKenzie typed the words on his computer and sat back with a smile.

It had been some performance, not least by Billie-Jo herself, a consummate natural it seemed but then he supposed the MDMA she'd unknowingly ingested via all that champagne had certainly helped. He was impressed; the masseur, a professional porn actor, had cost him a decent sum to hire and he hadn't disappointed.

'Well?' he prompted them, keen for feedback.

'That's more like it, McKenzie,' came the response from Super8#4. 'So, what's next?'

CHAPTER TWENTY-ONE

Cody Parker's eyes darted across the computer screen, his nose practically touching it such was the intensity of his concentration. The network encryption of the private forum he'd been attempting to hack into for the past few days was new – like, never-seen-before new – and their OS was a few updates ahead of the big ones, which by rights should've made it easier when it came to password cracking in a strange kind of twisted logic that only he understood. He'd spent the past 48 hours solidly working on it but frustratingly had got nowhere. Now, however, it seemed as if he might have caught a break.

'Cody, honey, you want some milk and cookies?' his mom sang up the stairs, 'I got those white Oreos that you love from the store today … got them special … they all sold out in Walmart, or maybe they just don't stock them, so anyways I had to go down to the store on 5th, next to Walgreens, you know the one?'

Cody didn't answer her; he was far too absorbed in the moment. A fanfare of cheerleaders could've marched naked through his bedroom and he wouldn't even have looked up.

'Co-deeee,' she called up the stairs again with a weary sigh. She knew it wasn't healthy for her son to spend practically twenty-three hours out of every twenty-four holed away in his bedroom on that goddamn computer but she'd long been forced to accept it over the years because that's who Cody Parker was: someone was between 'genius and introvert', or so the people at the autistic society had said. To his mother, Lana Parker, however, he was simply her son.

Call it a mother's instinct, sixth sense or whatever you liked, but Lana had known there was something special about her only boy from the moment she'd first held him in her arms, bloodied and covered in vernix. There were small signs, pointers that flagged up questions that caused themselves to linger inside her head for longer than they should've: the distinct lack of eye contact even when he was on her breast; a noticeable sensitivity to light and sound; and as he grew, a lack of social interaction with other children, all of which had begun to support her fears that something wasn't quite right.

It being her first child, and therefore possessing no real milestone gauges, Lana put these fears down to being a cautious first-time mom. Didn't every new mom fret that her baby was A-OK? Rather than unduly worry herself sick she remained thoughtful of her son's 'quirky individuality'. It was only when the meltdowns at kindergarten started, the aggressive outbursts and self-harming began to happen, that such thoughtfulness escalated into genuine concern. She supposed it had come as no real surprise when finally Cody, aged seven, was officially diagnosed as being on the autistic spectrum; deep down she had always suspected it and yet having it confirmed was no less difficult to accept. A mother's denial was a powerful thing and sometimes she would watch her son through aching blurry eyes, a small person trapped inside a world in which she could never fully comprehend, a world in which he would forever remain alone, one where empathy and human comfort didn't exist. She had wanted to reach inside him and pull him out of himself, locate the real boy inside. Only he was the real boy. *Her* real boy.

Cut off from the 'normal' world, Cody Parker had gradually retreated into one of his own, one which consisted solely of computer games and technology, a world in which it seemed he displayed alarming expertise and one where he could lose himself; a world he understood and a place where he felt safe – Cody's world.

By the time he'd reached the tender age of ten he was solving mathematical equations that would stump a fifty-year-old university lecturer. 'High functioning', the Autism Society called it, though Lana preferred to think of it as both 'gift and tragedy'. By the time Cody had reached his teens Lana had given up attempting to steer her son's condition in any direction and had reached a sort of sad resignation, a reluctant acceptance of who he was and who he would ever be - her 'little *Rainman*'. Lana knew she would never see her son marry; there would be no white wedding, no one calling her Grandma, a sadness which never truly left her.

There would, however, be a first-class honours degree in Premier Engineering and Technology, and recognition as one of the country's youngest leading experts in his field. His condition had not affected him achieving, even if it had affected him in other ways. It was sad really because to look at him you would never know there was something not quite right. It was only on closer inspection, after spending some time in his company did you begin to see the strange quirks that made him 'different'. She was proud of her son, and fiercely protective of him; whenever he'd been challenged, picked on or berated, the lioness within her would protect her special cub. 'He's a freak, weirdo, psycho, creep, he's not *normal*' – she'd heard it all over the years and while the pain of ignorance and prejudice hurt, it had gradually slipped closer towards indifference. '"Is he autistic? Yeah, and his rising sign is Asperger's..."' But whatever he was, Cody Parker was, and always would be, her son.

Lana schlepped up the stairs in her carpet slippers, muttering to herself.

'I'll leave them here for you then, honey,' she said with a soft sigh, placing the cookies and milk next to him on the desk. 'What you up to anyway?' She glanced at the computer screen, at the rows of encryption in highlighted green text and shook her head. How he understood what it all meant she hadn't the first clue – it may as well been in hieroglyphics. Sometimes she wondered if his brain actually hurt with all the knowledge and numbers it contained, she worried that eventually he would combust and blow, like an overloaded plug.

'Intrusions,' Cody said, taking a cookie from the plate and biting into it.

'I'm sorry, Cody, I wasn't trying to intrude, but you know, baby – you gotta eat.'

'Computer intrusions,' he said, 'I'm past the scanner programme and the blog's network encryption is next ---'

'Uh-huh.' Lana ruffled his hair like he was five-years-old again instead of twenty-five. 'Don't stay up too late yeah?'

Cody nodded without taking his eyes from the screen. He'd discovered something, some kind of private network, a live stream that just a handful of people had access to by the looks of it and he wanted to know what it was. He'd hacked into and accessed some serious top security shit in his time, government files, FBI stuff, snuff and paedophile rings … real nasty shit. While Cody was aware of these things being wrong, his purpose was not to judge or even bring those responsible to task, it was simply a puzzle to solve, prove himself technologically superior by infiltrating their complex security measures; *that* was the buzz for Cody Parker. He wasn't out to expose or ruin anyone's fun, though if that was the outcome, which was more often than not the case, then it was of no consequence to him.

Dropping biscuit crumbs onto his keyboard, he blinked furiously at the screen, tapping in codes and encryptions like a man possessed, which he was really.

'Eureka!' he sat back as the PC prompted him; 'Please type in your unique pin code for access.' Pin codes presented no problem to a mind like Cody's; he was on a home run. After just fifteen or so attempts he was in.

The screen was split into six parts monitoring different areas like a security camera, and when he clicked on the first one a woman came into view. She was embracing a young man enthusiastically, covering his face in scattergun kisses... He switched screens quickly, kissing made him feel funny inside his belly. A woman and a man were taking a swim inside a beautiful azure blue pool; he watched for a few seconds and switched again. In the next screen there was a blonde girl with big tits. She was sunning herself in the smallest bikini he'd ever seen. Cody Parker was puzzled ... What the fuck was this? He wasn't sure what he'd expected but whatever it was he felt disappointed by it. No hardcore porn, no FBI files, no snuff ... the images on screen told him that whoever these people were there they were on some kind of holiday, somewhere hot by the looks of things. He watched them for the best part of an hour, switching manically between screens, listening into snippets of conversation, inane chat mainly, nothing too rad. He wasn't quite sure what he'd stumbled upon. The security measures had been pretty high for a bunch of people on vacation, so why the secrecy? It was probably just some kind of Big Brother-type shit, security cameras, although he was able to quickly surmise that whoever these people were – he didn't recognise any of them – they seemed unaware that they were being watched.

Cody began to tap away at his keyboard again. He needed to see who was transmitting this stuff, and more importantly who was it being transmitted to? As someone who had spent a great deal of his childhood being 'observed' and had suffered great paranoia as a result, he didn't much like the idea of voyeurism, even though he was more than guilty of it himself. Anti-establishment to the core, he justified his own needs to snoop and spy in the name of cyber vigilantism; spying on the spies. If Big Brother was always watching, then he'd be the biggest brother of all.

'Ah ha!' The sound of his fingers frantically tapping away on the keyboard was almost musical. He quickly established that this was a high security private forum broadcasting to a select few – wow, like just eight people by all accounts, a surprisingly small number.

In Cody's experience of private transmissions, all the sickos and freaks out there, of which there were many, who participated in high security driven snuff and porn and sex sites usually convened in treble figures at least, just eight was unheard of. The exclusivity of this intrigued and riled him in equal measures. Like, why had someone gone to all the trouble of broadcasting a few people on vacation? He'd need to track down the host for the answer to that one, and he would too, with a little more detective work.

'Mom!'

Lana Parker heard her son's voice from the kitchen below and went to the bottom of the stairs.

'Everything OK, honey?' she called up to him.

'I need more milk and cookies,' he said, his eyes still firmly fixed on his computer screen. It was going to be a long night.

CHAPTER TWENTY-TWO

'Eek!'

Angelika yelped as she dived off the edge of the rock plunging into the inviting blue lagoon beneath her. It was deeper than she'd anticipated, a little disconcerting, but the water was as warm as a bath as it met with her hot, oily skin. That morning she and Rupert had reluctantly decided to explore the island together, get a feel for the place, work out 'what was what' as he'd put it, and so far it had not disappointed. The lagoon she had discovered complete with rock pool and waterfall was like something out of *Endless Love*. Pleasure Island was certainly living up to its name.

Flowing in harmony with nature, the 300,000 square meter island was pervaded by idyllic country pathways and had been transformed, clearly no expense spared, into a kind of super-hacienda dream resort, the ultimate luxury hideaway, an A-lister's paradise. To the west coast of the island, not far from the exquisite stilted cabanas where they were staying, lay the exquisite beach, a horseshoe-shaped expanse of white, powder-soft sand, the shallow, blue Aegean sea gently colouring it golden as it licked the edge.

To the east coast it was mainly nature trails, shrubs and trees that sheltered pretty alcoves, one of which hid this stunning lagoon. As for the rest, well, she hadn't got that far yet. The north of the island was almost impossible to see unless you followed the trail behind McKenzie's imposing mansion house and were prepared for the long trek down to the harbour.

Boats! Angelika had what she could only describe as a flashback. She had seen boats, little fishing type vessels that she was sure had been moored at the harbour when they had arrived on the recuse plane. Only they were nowhere to be seen now and she wondered if she had just imagined it. Angelika squinted up at the rocks surrounding her, the sunlight cutting through her silted eyelids, salty water tickling her tongue. She could smell the pines and inhaled deeply as though the air were elixir, which it was, comparatively to London at least. She could hear birds chirruping in the brush above her, dense and thick like a fortress it surrounded the whole island, a fence protecting it. She was glad Rupert had abandoned the tour halfway through now, siting blisters as his reason to retreat back to camp leaving her to discover this place alone, though she suspected it was more likely because of a fat head from the previous evening. In keeping with most things in their marriage, Rupert had said nothing about last night's little showdown, brushing it firmly under the carpet. She wasn't sure if she felt annoyed or grateful for it. Perhaps a little of both.

The lagoon was so peaceful and untouched that she almost felt as though she were contaminating the water just by being in it. Angelika wondered just how many other places there were like this in the world; unspoilt, undiscovered islands just waiting for the likes of McKenzie to conquer it with their fat chequebooks.

Floating onto her back, the sun gently warming her exposed torso, she savoured the rare moment of solitude and attempted to clear her mind. So many things had been bugging her since she'd arrived on the island, not least of all her husband's shady behaviour around Mia. She felt sure something had transpired around the time of the trial that he didn't want her to know about. She tried not to think about it; perhaps whatever it was it was best left unsaid. But she didn't like secrets, not between husband and wife, it wasn't healthy, but then again neither she supposed was their marriage. Deep down somewhere on a murky subconscious level, Angelika felt as if she knew the real truth as to why this was; facing it, however, was another matter altogether. 'Time tells you all you need to know; don't rush it, just let it go.' These were words her mother used to say to her when she was young and impatient and she gave a melancholy smile as she thought of them. She could only hope her mother was right. She usually was; after all, weren't all mothers? In a moment of reckless abandon she undid her bikini bra, softly giggling as she discarded it with a flick of the hand. It felt so good that she untied her bikini bottoms and watched as they floated away too. It suddenly struck her that in all her thirty-eight years she had never, *never* swum naked before. A topless moment in a Jacuzzi in Ibiza during the early 90s was as close as she'd ever got.

Kicking her legs out behind her she began to swim, enjoying the sensation of the soft, salty water against her nakedness. Soon she was doing forward rolls, throwing her legs up in her air, her bare bottom exposed as she flipped and turned, splashing with joy. Lost in a private moment Angelika felt free for the first time in what seemed like an age and yet even so the questions still came at her, relentless; was she really happy? Had she achieved all she'd wanted to so far, what was missing from her life? She was well aware of her professional achievements; she was, after all, a successful journalist and writer with her own column in the UK's biggest-selling national newspaper. Her opinion counted, her voice carried weight; she was financially independent, owned a beautiful house and drove a luxury car;

she wanted for nothing, had a good family and a decent set of interesting friends. And yet ... and yet she couldn't quite connect to any of it. Something was missing, a void inside of her that no amount of money, success or prestige could fill. She pushed these thoughts from her mind but they bobbed right back up again, forcing her to contemplate.

On the surface she had it all, the perfect middle-class existence that her newspaper voraciously peddled; solvency, success, 'The White Company' lifestyle, bar the marriage and kids part anyway. Angelika thought of the abortion she'd had all those years ago. The child would've been eleven now, coming on for twelve, practically a teenager. She wondered whether it might've been a girl or a boy, she'd never thought about it much before and yet suddenly had a burning desire to know. Her life would've been different now of that much she was sure at least. But would it have been better; more fulfilling spiritually? Her friends with children had all told her how becoming a parent grounded you, gave you a sense of purpose, the feeling that there was something bigger, something greater than yourself – and secretly she'd scoffed at it. 'She's like my heart outside of my chest,' was how her friend Alice had described her newborn daughter, although as a writer she had quite liked that. Meaning: wasn't that what everyone was searching for? Her very existence suddenly seemed so pointless and futile, just a façade for others to look at and aspire to, a cardboard cut-out life with no real depth or substance, trapped by the trappings of social expectation. Had she made choices based on achieving the perfect outward perception? Good God, had she? Angelika swallowed some of the salty water and began to choke a little. She'd read somewhere once that everything you do is a choice and that everything everyone else does is a choice you hope is right for you. And suddenly this statement had resonance. She was pushing forty now: successful, yet childless; married, yet unhappy; and guilt-ridden that she felt as much. She *should* be happy, shouldn't she?

Angelika dived underwater and began to swim, holding her breath for as long as she could. The water was clear and, delighted, she saw a small shoal of fish just beneath her, their silver skin glistening rainbows as the sunlight bounced off their tiny scales. Gasping for breath as she broke the surface, she smoothed her hair from her face and spat out the salty water.

As beautiful as this place undoubtedly was, something about it gave her an instinctive sense of unease, a feeling she'd experienced from the moment she'd stepped onto the island. Alongside a general malaise, she had felt herself slip into a strange melancholy, her mood spiking in peaks and troughs. It was the plane crash for sure, or perhaps it was just that 'overactive imagination' of hers that her husband liked to remind her of, but she couldn't shake the feeling that she was being observed somehow – that she was being *watched*. She looked up at the cloudless sky, at the sun blazing from its centre, magnificent and majestic, almost arrogant as it cast a white blanket over everything. Suddenly sensing that someone was behind her, Angelika turned round. She *was* being watched!

'Hello?' Her voice echoed across the lagoon like a steel drum. She did a 360-degree spin in the water, eyes scanning the rocks for signs of life. 'Who's there?'

There was a slight pause.

'Hey.' He appeared as if from nowhere, as though he had been there all the time.

'Jesus, Nate!' she said, her breathing a little laboured, quickly followed by relief, 'you scared the shit out of me!'

'I'm sorry,' he apologised, smiling, 'I didn't mean to freak you out. I … I just …'

'How long have you been standing there?' Had he been watching her the whole … *Jesus Christ*! Angelika felt herself flush. She was *naked.*

'No … no … I – honestly, I just got here.' He pointed behind him, at something that wasn't there. 'I just found the place now a-a-and –' he was stammering '– and … I … j-just … now, right this second …'

She squinted up at him from the lagoon, one hand sheltering her eyes from the sun, the other attempting to cover her breasts, legs treading water furiously beneath her until her muscles began to burn.

'Honest,' he added again.

But they both knew he was lying.

CHAPTER TWENTY-THREE

'You were watching me?' Angelika continued to tread water, although she wasn't sure how much longer she could keep it up: her thighs felt like two barking dogs. Frantically she searched for her discarded bikini but it was nowhere in sight.

'No, I wasn't,' Nate said, climbing down the edge of the rock face surrounding the lagoon towards her.

Angelika wasn't sure if she was flattered or offended. Either way she *was* embarrassed. Had he seen her do the roly polys? She cringed at the thought.

'How did you find this place?' she asked.

'Same way you did,' he said.

'I'm naked, Nate,' she said, finally, suspecting he'd already worked that one out for himself.

'I know.' He tore his T-shirt off and threw it down to her. 'I'll turn my back while you put it on.'

'Thanks,' she said, watching as he turned away from her, his toned, lean, back muscles highlighted by the sunlight as it hit his skin. *The Golden Bolt.* His body was covered in tattoos, though he was too far away for her to tell what they were exactly. 'Must've hurt,' she remarked, looking for something to say while she scrabbled to put the T-shirt over her wet head, 'all those tattoos … not fond of needles myself.'

'Yeah, they did. The bigger ones in particular,' he said, his back still towards her. 'But I guess they were worth it. Where there's pleasure there's pain, right?'

'Ain't that the truth,' she said.

With the T-shirt sticking to her naked, wet skin, Angelika scrambled up onto the sheltered rocks, pulling it down as far over her thighs as it would stretch.

'Can I turn round now?' he asked.

'All decent,' she winced. *All decent.* It sounded like something her grandmother would say. She watched him as he carefully made his way towards her, navigating the rocks barefoot, naked himself save for a pair of battered denim shorts that sat dangerously low on his waist. His hair was ruffled, his expression pensive and at once she thought how he was both too young and too good-looking, though for what or who she couldn't say.

'I didn't mean to disturb your swim,' he apologised as he took up next to her on the rocks, though it sounded disingenuous.

The harsh sun was already causing the beads of water on Angelika's skin to evaporate, the outline of her nipples through the wet T-shirt gradually fading.

'It's stunning isn't it?' he said, squinting out across the lagoon, the sound of the waterfall churning in the background providing a musical backdrop.

'Spectacular,' she said, through a hundred-mile stare, mesmerised by it for a moment. She turned to him, snapping out of it. 'Have you seen much of the rest of the island yet?'

'I've been down on the beach this morning,' he said, 'for an early stroll. Watched the sun rise.'

'Bet that was something else,' she said wistfully, tugging at the T-shirt as she stretched her legs out in front of her self-consciously. It had been years since she'd been alone, semi-naked with a man, accidental or otherwise.

'Yeah, it was pretty special, quite romantic really. The whole place is, I guess.'

Angelika shifted uncomfortably.

'How's Billie-Jo faring? She put a fair bit away last night.'
Shit. Why had she mentioned last night? She'd been mortally
embarrassed and would rather forget it had happened.

Nate's eyebrows twitched.

'Billie-Jo is … Billie-Jo,' he said by way of an answer. 'Put it
this way, she's getting to grips with things.' Although he had no
idea just how or who his wife had been getting to grips with.
'Her bark is worse than her bite you know … she just doesn't
think before she speaks. She gets carried away, she doesn't really
mean to upset and offend people, not deliberately, at least not
all of the time. Anyway, she's gone to the spa in a bid to have her
hangover pampered out of her.' *And the rest.*

'Good, I'm glad she's OK,' she said, touched by the fact he
had defended his wife, only wishing her own husband possessed
such loyalty.

'And Rupert?' he returned the question. 'He seems like a very
capable bloke. Good in a crisis.'

'And terrible on the brandy.' She felt ashamed by her husband's little diatribe last night. He'd humiliated her by airing his
grievances like that. Why didn't he just talk to her, for God's
sakes? Why did they find it so difficult to communicate anymore?

She stifled a deep sigh. 'Rupert's … Rupert.'

They both laughed a little nervously as if an unspoken understanding had passed between them. There was a moment's
pause, a silence filled by the buzzing of crickets and the waterfall, the lapping of water against rock, gentle as a lover's sigh.

'Anyway, last night, I don't think anyone really said anything
they truly meant. It's the bloody booze I'm telling you!' she said,
making light of it.

'That's a shame.' He cocked his head and flashed her a small
smile. She tried not to return it, and pretend she hadn't a clue
what he'd meant, but she couldn't help it; it was instinctive.

'You know, I'm truly sorry for the way my paper … the way you found out about your adop–' She stopped herself short of saying it. She shouldn't have brought it up but it had seemed like the perfect opportunity to change the subject.

He stretched his legs out in front of him too, now, their feet almost touching.

'There's no need for you to apologise.' He dipped his chin. 'Wasn't you who wrote the piece, was it? You weren't the one digging up dirt on me … were you?'

'Good God no! … But still, I feel guilty by association. It must've been such a terrible shock. I can't imagine.'

Nate swallowed uncomfortably. It was still raw, still difficult to talk about. He'd hardly been able to process it all himself yet.

'That's an understatement. I mean, it's not every day you find out via national newspaper that your family isn't really your family at all, that the person you called Dad your entire life wasn't actually your dad, at least not by blood.'

She saw the anguish etched onto his brow, slightly furrowed, and felt compelled to place her hand lightly on his. It was a gesture that spoke louder than anything she could respond with.

'I've got a private detective working on it,' he said quietly, his voice low and soft, almost a whisper. 'Some ex-DCI dude. You see, I need to find out. I need to know who they were: my real parents. I need to know who they were so that I can know who I am, if that makes any sense.'

It did, perfectly.

'I owe the guy who brought me up – my dad – I owe him everything, I know that. He was the greatest bloke that lived, and I certainly don't think I would've had the career I did without him, but now that he's gone – and now that the career's gone – well, I'm just grateful that he isn't alive to have seen what the papers wrote. I think it would've destroyed him. But it's left me with so many questions.' He looked at her directly then, their eyes meeting, her hand still lightly touching his fingers. 'Like, why didn't he ever just tell me I was adopted?'

Angelika finally exhaled deeply. He had opened up to her and she was again touched by him.

'Perhaps he felt you were better off not knowing; maybe he knew deep down you would want to discover who your blood parents were and couldn't handle it himself, or maybe he was protecting you.' She wasn't sure if she was saying the right thing but felt compelled to offer some kind of explanation.

'How would you feel?' he said, 'if you discovered the woman you'd thought was your mother hadn't given birth to you?'

She tugged at the T-shirt once more. It felt like it was shrinking in the heat.

'God, Nate, I don't know how to answer that.' She thought for a moment. 'Betrayed, perhaps. Confused, angry, sad …' She looked out at the tranquil lagoon. 'All at sea.'

He nodded.

'All of those things,' he said, 'and more.'

Angelika's career had brought her into contact with a handful of adopted people over the years and mostly they had said they'd never wanted to discover who their blood parents were and that they considered their adoptive parents to be their 'real' parents; after all, they were the people who'd loved and cared for them unconditionally, taught them right from wrong, comforted their tears and supported them throughout their lives. Isn't that what made you a parent at the end of the day; that the child wasn't from your genes was merely circumstantial, wasn't it?

'Is it nature or nurture, I don't know,' she said, struggling with the complexity of it.

'Nothing natural about giving your child up for adoption,' he said.

'No,' she said, thinking of the abortion again, 'but there are always reasons, Nate, for everything.'

'Which is why I've got a PI on it,' he said, his mood lightening a little, 'questions I need answers to.'

'Speaking of which,' she said, 'what's your take on all of this?'

'This?'

'Everything … all of it. From day one I've been asking myself questions …'

'Like?' He ruffled his hair and rested back onto his hands, looking at her quizzically with one eye, watching her lips move intently, appreciating the shape of them, naturally full with a pronounced cupid's bow, and the way they parted to display her neat teeth except for the slight snaggle one at the front.

'Like … oh, God I don't know … the plane crash. I can hardly remember anything about it. And Aki, the stewardess – don't you think McKenzie's wife seemed completely unperturbed by her disappearance. And by the pilot's death, come to mention it? And then there was the rescue plane, the one that took Joshua off somewhere, God knows where. Why didn't it just fly us all off the island? And last night, that game … call me paranoid but it was almost as if it was designed deliberately to cause conflict between us.'

He was staring at her intently now and she felt a slight slither of something pass between them, though what it was she wasn't sure.

'Then there's the lack of outside communication, the fact the staff are all mutes and, oh, yes, I almost forgot the wardrobe full of clothes … all our individual preferences. Don't you think that's a little odd?'

'When you put it that way it's all odd,' he said, 'the whole damn lot of it.'

'I just can't seem to shake this weird feeling.' She shook her head. 'Maybe I'm just being silly … like we're being watched or something.' She looked around at the tranquil setting, nature in all its splendour and realised how absurd it sounded.

'Watched by who?'

'That's just it – I've no idea!' Even while she had been swimming naked she couldn't quite shirk the feeling that she wasn't entirely alone.

'Look,' he said, 'we've been through a pretty traumatic time. It's natural to feel a bit shaken.'

'S'pose,' she murmured, 'but why do you think we're here, Nate?' She fixed him with a direct stare. 'And I don't just mean for a promotional exercise ... I mean *really* here?'

'I don't know.' He shook his head with a degree of resignation. 'I guess we're going to find out though.'

Their eyes reconnected and she smiled coyly at him, her fingers gripping the T-shirt.

'I guess I should find my bikini,' she said, looking down at the lagoon, 'before it floats out to sea. I don't suppose it would look too good if we return back to base, me without my bikini and wearing your T-shirt.'

'No,' he smiled, 'I guess not.' Though in all truth in that very moment he didn't care; he was just happy to be in her company. There was something about simply sitting next to her that gave him a sense of peace. She had an easy tranquillity to her that made him feel as though everything was going to be OK. He began to renegotiate the rocks that led down to the lagoon, being careful not to slip barefoot.

'What are you doing?' she said.

'Protecting your modesty,' he called back at her, diving halfway from the bottom into the inky blue in a bid to show off.

She laughed as he thrashed below her.

'Hey, I've got the top!' he said, holding it above the water triumphantly like a trophy, diving back under in search of the bottoms. Angelika stood, one hand pulling the T-shirt over her intimate region, which it barely covered.

He was under the water long enough for a trickle of concern to slide down her oesophagus.

'Nate!' she called down to him, beginning to consider making a one-handed descent down the rocks herself. 'Are you OK?'

Eventually he reappeared, bobbing back up to the surface with a triumphant grin on his face.

'Ta-dah!' he said, swinging the bikini pants over his head like a lasso. He'd more or less forgotten the reason he'd come looking for her in the first place, which was to let her know that that they were planning a celebration that evening, a proper party for JJ's return. Somehow now, though, it didn't seem nearly so urgent.

She laughed out loud.

'Well done!' She reached the bottom of the rocks and stood, watching him, her bare legs slightly buckled and awkward. 'Throw them up then!'

'You want them?' He looked up at her mischievously from the water, his skin glistening, forgetting himself, forgetting everything as her blue eyes, shining, met his own, 'Then come and get them!'

Angelika blinked at him. A thousand thoughts rushed her mind: is he flirting with you; yes, he *is* flirting with you; he's younger; he's married; *you're* married; what would it lead to; what did she *want* it to lead to … She thought of Billie-Jo, of Nate's pretty-but-brash young wife who seemed so ill-suited to his gentle sensitivity and thoughtfulness. And then she thought of Rupert …

'Fuck it,' she said as she took a deep breath and jumped in.

CHAPTER TWENTY-FOUR

'Where the fucking hell have you been, Angelika?' Rupert snapped as she padded back through the cabana and out onto the private veranda where her husband was pacing up and down, a full glass of Scotch in hand.

'Well, seeing as though you abandoned me halfway through our little exploration, I decided to continue alone,' she snapped back. 'I didn't realise I was unable to make an autonomous decision without you, Rupert.'

'Don't be bloody facetious, Angelika. I'm not in the mood.'

'You never are,' she deadpanned. She made to fix herself a drink, too; she needed one after what had just happened, *a large one*.

'Bit early for you, isn't it?' he commented with mild disapproval as she decanted some champagne into a chilled flute.

'Ha! Hypocrite.'

Rupert rolled his eyes. There was no talking to her while she was like this.

'Cheers!' She practically threw the glass in the air before throwing half of it down her neck.

Rupert watched her carefully; she looked damp, like she'd been swimming and her bikini bottoms were inside out, the Gucci label poking out of the back of them, mocking him like a tongue.

'So, are you going to tell me where you've been, and what you've been doing and with whom or not?'

'No,' she said, before draining the glass and instantly refreshing it.

'Suit yourself.'

'I will.'

'Why break the habit of a lifetime, Angelika?'

'If you must know, I've been swimming down at the beach. The water is exquisite.'

'Alone?'

'Yes, alone – unless you include the fish, in which case –'

'Well,' he cut her off, 'I've been waiting for bloody hours for you to get back.'

'Really, darling,' she mused, sauntering past him towards the en suite in search of a robe, 'and why was that? Missed me, did you? Suddenly taken by the urge to –'

'Joshua is having a party,' he cut her off once more. He didn't want to have *that* kind of conversation with her again; it left him feeling way too uncomfortable.

'Really? When?' Angelika feigned surprise and hoped she sounded convincing. Nate had finally imparted the news about that evening's plans on their walk back from the lagoon.

'I meant to tell you sooner,' he'd apologised, 'but I was … I was side-tracked.'

'Don't be cute,' she'd said. Cute. She never used that word. 'Anyway, how is he today? His arm … is he OK?'

Nate had shrugged, 'No idea. He's holed up with Mia at the moment. I'm not sure whether to feel relieved or sorry for him.'

Angelika had laughed.

'I don't know what the beef is between her and your husband, but I can't help liking her.' It was true; he'd developed a bit of a soft spot for her and felt as though the feeling might be mutual.

'Their bad blood goes way back. Personally I think it's time they put the past behind them, but Rupert, well, he does like to bear a grudge. And yeah, she's something else is Mia, I'll give her that.'

'So are you, Ange,' he'd said, 'I can call you Ange, can I? Not too overfamiliar, is it?'

She'd smiled at him awkwardly. 'Ange is fine … makes a change from Ang-el-lika!' she said, mimicking her husband's voice and instantly feeling guilty. Could what had just happened between them constitute betrayal? She wasn't quite sure if it did. They'd swum together, both partially naked, she'd laughed as he'd ducked her under the water and she'd lunged at him playfully in response. Their bodies had connected; a brush of skin here and there, his fingers imprinted on her arms as he'd pushed her under the water. Thankfully, however, he'd been enough of a gentleman to turn his back as she'd dressed on the rocks.

'Is it safe yet?' he'd asked as he turned to face her once more.

'What?' He had been staring at her, and she'd tossed him his wet T-shirt.

'Nothing,' he'd said, though once again they both knew he was lying. 'I was just thinking how flattered I was when you pointed to me last night.'

She'd cringed; she had been hoping he wouldn't bring it up.

'Don't be.' She'd shot him a sideways glance. 'It was either you or Joshua and seeing as though he's an invalid right now, not to mention young enough to be my little brother.'

They'd both laughed.

'Sorry, I'm only teasing,' he'd said, wishing he hadn't said anything. He'd embarrassed her.

They'd walked along the sandy path in comfortable silence but for the sound of the ocean and distant birdsong.

'I wonder how Joshua made his way back to the island,' she'd said, finally breaking it. 'Must've been by plane, surely.'

'You'd think,' he'd agreed. 'Guess he'll tell us all about it tonight over dinner. We've all been invited to help celebrate his return, properly this time; they've organised a big party for him tonight'

'Hmm,' she'd said, as more questions presented themselves to her unstill mind. 'Planes need communication, right? Radios, transmitter waves …'

'Yes, they do.'

'Maybe he had access to a telephone while he was on another island,' she'd wondered aloud, 'in which case he may well have already alerted the authorities about the crash.'

'Who knows,' Nate had said, 'it's possible, although he says he can't remember anything of being in the hospital;'

'Yes, he did, didn't he? Another oddity.' She was starting to think that McKenzie wanted to deny them access to the outside world, keep them here as prisoners in paradise, but *why*?

They had parted company as the cabanas came into view.

'See you tonight, Ange,' he'd said turning to look at her, smiling over his shoulder.

'Yes, see you later,' she'd said casually, feeling anything but. 'Oh, and Nate.'

He'd stopped for a moment

'Thank you for coming to find me … to tell me about tonight. I appreciate it.'

'You're welcome,' he'd said before disappearing up the path.

'A party? What time?' Angelika feigned surprise as Rupert informed her of it.

'Aperitifs at sunset, it said, 8.30pm, and hopefully no damned games this time.'

Angelika looked at the clock, it was 6.10 pm already. She would need to start thinking about getting ready: showering, styling her hair and make-up, choosing an outfit. Suddenly it really mattered to her that she looked and felt good, and with a sense of impending guilt she knew exactly why.

CHAPTER TWENTY-FIVE

Cody Parker had been up for twenty-four hours solid and his eyes felt dry and gritty. He rubbed them furiously, red rims itching for a little respite from the relentless glare of his computer screen. The site he had discovered, which appeared to be a series of private webcams, had just eight IP addresses assigned to their network interface, addresses that had been configured manually by an administrator. He had run a few programmes, used some of his tried-and-tested trickery to track the host's identity but as yet had not succeeded.

Reluctantly he'd been forced to contact a fellow hacker in Ohio, someone he knew only as #cookthebook for his, or indeed her, assistance. As ever though, Cody knew it was simply a matter of time before that eureka moment happened, and meanwhile he must sit back and allow the programmes to do their thing. Patience had never been a personal strength, however, and he was pissed he'd needed to call on Cookbook's expertise in a bid to aid him. This was Cody Parker's discovery and he wanted full credit for it.

Cody had been watching the six people on camera intently on and off for a few days. He'd viewed the drama as it had unfolded through largely indifferent eyes, listened into their conversations, read their body language in his own unique way and had drawn the conclusion that these people definitely had no idea they were being watched. Whoever was behind this weird kinda soap opera was a voyeur, plain and simple. He had seen the pretty one with the big tits getting fucked real good during a massage; a cute brunette woman taking her clothes off by a lagoon later to be joined by a fit-looking dude who he had worked out was married to the big-titted blonde. The older woman was someone called Mia Manhattan, a seriously famous singer according to Google, although he'd never heard of her, but then music wasn't really his thing. Well, not unless it was death metal. Was this a swinger's site? He wasn't sure, but he *was* sure he would find out.

'Parker, you my friend r a fukin g-neus!' #Cookthebook's message flashed up on Cody's screen and he sprang forward.

'Tell me sumthing I dnt know.'

'I'm gonna … and it'll make you shit your pants man.'

Cody felt a slither of irritation travel down his spine. Cookbook had got a result before him.

'You found sumthing?'

'I sure as shit did my friend. And it's gonna blow that crazy mind of yours.'

'I'm waiting.'

Cookbook went offline for a few moments just to fuck with him. They liked to fuck with each other; it was a game they enjoyed playing, a battle to see who was the cleverest, the more technologically superior, although both of them knew that sometimes they needed to rely on the other's individual strengths to get the results they needed. Although they had never met or even conversed and knew each other only as their online handles, Cody considered cookbook to be his best friend. They communicated through cyber space on a regular basis on everything from social alienation and the theory of relativity to soccer scores and Dunkin' Donuts versus Krispy Kremes, while simultaneously hacking into high security systems.

Cookbook was as anti-establishment as Cody, perhaps even more so, and harboured a deep pathological hatred for those he considered 'successful through being fake', or 'pretentious phonies', as he sometimes preferred. Whoever Cookbook was (Cody had never considered discussing age or gender), they had often quoted Holden Caulfield together, the disenfranchised central character in J D Salinger's novel, *The Catcher in the Rye*. Two like-minded souls on a joint crusade to expose the phonies.

Cookbook was back online, his moment of fuckery complete.

'You been watching this shit?'

'Uh-huh. All week.'

'I'm hooked already … the blonde chick is seriously hawt, man.'

Cody felt irritated again. He knew cookbook was stalling just to string him out.

'They don't know they're being filmed.'

'No shit Sherlock...you know who any of them are?'

Cody smiled. He had made it his business to know.

'… yeah … I Googled them … minor celebrities from the UK: a soccer player, journo, lawyer, some dude in a band, a famous old singer and a titty model. Fuckin no marks, man … you gonna tell me what you know or you gonna be a prick all your life and hold out on me?'

'Be a prick all my life. Lol.'

Cody was ready to explode.

'Don't fuck wid me cookbook, what you got?'

There was a few seconds pause and Cody began tapping his fingers nervously on his desk.

Cookbook paused again for effect.

'D'ya know the show *Sing When You're Winning*?'

'Doesn't everyone?'

SWYW was a massive reality TV show hit in the US, prime-time Saturday night viewing that attracted millions. It was host-

ed by some real Jerk called Lester Reynolds, one of the biggest
TV stars in the United States today with a spray-on smile and
slicked-back black hair that reminded Cody of Adolph Hitler.
The show was created and produced by the most powerful media mogul on the planet, Martin McKenzie, the biggest asshole
that ever lived in his opinion. He resented men like McKenzie
for his arrogance and power. Men with God complexes who
thought they were doing the working classes a huge favour by
exploiting their talents to their own end, and then discarding
them like human garbage once they'd served their purpose (i.e.
making the exploiters rich).

'That crock of shit does my head in … all those sad wan-
nabes, man … and the dork that hosts it … what a douchebag
…'

'Lol …'

'What's that shitty show got to do with anything?'

Cody's heart rate was accelerating.

'Martin McKenzie, that's what!'

'Holy shit!' It was beating so fast now that he thought he
might have one of his fits.

His fingers hovered over the keyboard as his thought process
shifted up a gear.

'*McKenzie* is the host? He's the one broadcasting this shit?
You're sure?'

'Sure as eggs, buddy. I traced the IP eventually, though it
took some doing. Dude's security was tighter than a virgin's
snatch. Came up registered to a Mr Martin McKenzie, no less,
Hamptons address. I checked it out and it's legit. Besides, everyone knows that fucker has one of the biggest pads out there.'

'Holy crap,' Cody said aloud. This was insane. And exciting beyond belief. He thought for a moment, his mind revving
like a Ducati. McKenzie clearly had some fucked up secret soap

opera going on, a Big Brother private game show; one it seemed the contestants had no idea they were even playing.

'This is top security shit ...the real fucking deal. Tread careful bud, McKenzie is one helluva powerful man ...'

'One hulluva sicko u mean.'

'So what you gonna do now?'

Cody Parker sat back in his chair and took a swig of flat, diet Dr Pepper. His mom always bought the diet shit; it really made him pissed.

'Haven't decided yet,' he replied. But he had a good idea.

CHAPTER TWENTY-SIX

The pool party was a few glasses of champagne away from being in full swing. The air-conditioned, blue up-lit canopied marquee was decorated with hundreds of scented tea lights alongside lush exotic floral displays. A ten-tier champagne fountain took centre stage of the long table, its bubbles fizzing and cascading in a constant amber flow. Electric-pink bougainvillea swathed from hanging beams was offset by dishes of rainbow-coloured warm macaroons positioned next to silver platters of fresh Lobster, marinated in Cognac, and pink smoked salmon with edible gold champagne-soaked caviar and venison medallions. A six-tier Belgian chocolate ganache-filled cake sat proudly on the table, the base surrounded by white lilies and sprinkled with edible diamonds and emerald stones. No expense, it seemed, had been spared for Joshua's return.

'Wow!' he said, copping an eyeful of the feast of delights on offer, 'check this shit out … man I was only gone for a couple a days!'

Mia squeezed his hand.

'It's all for you, darling.' She smiled at him warmly. 'For your safe return.' She had been so genuinely happy to see him return alive and well, and had tried not to bombard the poor boy with questions, but to let him explain in his own time about what had happened. However, it hadn't been easy.

'I don't remember that much of anything, really,' he'd said truthfully. 'They doped me up to the eyeballs on morphine, man …. I was out of it.'

'Do you remember the crash?' Mia had asked as she had fixed them both a glass of champagne to enjoy on the balcony of their cabana, fluffing up the pillows on his sunlounger in a bid to make it more comfortable for him. It was the least she could do.

Joshua had shrugged, tapping her flute with his own and taking a generous slug.

'Nah, not a thing.' He ran his good hand through his long hair as he carefully lowered himself onto the sunlounger. His injured arm was in a cast and he was wearing a white sling but otherwise seemed perfectly healthy and lucid. 'First thing I remember is waking up inside a plane, some nurse looming over me. I was so out of it I couldn't really tell you what was going on … where I was … nothing.' He paused.

'You have no idea where they took you?'

He shrugged again.

'Well, it's all kinda hazy, really.'

'How did you get back to the island?'

'The plane,' he said, 'they took me back in some light aircraft.'

'It landed on the island? So where is it now?' Mia felt her heartbeat accelerate. If there was a plane, then there was a way off the island, although strangely the urgency she had initially felt to leave was somewhat on the wane now. It was a stunning place, after all, and she supposed she was even beginning to enjoy the luxury it offered. Besides, after last night's 'icebreaker' she was determined to show that little bitch Billie-Jo who was boss around here, not to mention that supercilious prig Deyton. Now that the horror of the crash had subsided, and with Joshua finally back, she was intrigued to find out what was next. What they were *really* here for.

'Apparently the engine practically gave out – failed a few seconds before we touched down on the island. The pilot said we were very lucky. I mean, fuck that; since I've been here I've survived a near-death experiences! Lucky for me I was medicated up on pills and booze. Not sure I ever wanna get on another plane in my whole goddamn life, though –' he looked at her sagely '– which kinda might be a problem when I'm touring, you know. I hope McKenzie's gonna shell out for some therapy … reckon I'll need it.'

Mia snorted. 'Ha, and the rest of us. We'll rinse that bastard once we're back on home turf. And your arm?' The vision of bone protruding through flesh flashed up in her mind and she felt her skin prickle.

He shrugged.

'It was a freakin' bad break, but it'll be good as new, they reckon.'

'You might want a second opinion on that. We should be thinking about getting off this bloody island and getting you seen to by a proper professional, someone in the States.' She gently probed him again; he hadn't been fully *compos mentis* last night and she hadn't wanted to push him too much. 'So you didn't get to make a phone call? There definitely wasn't one in the hospital?'

'No, I didn't. I didn't ask for one … like I said, I was flying on liquid H. Making a phone call didn't even register on my radar.'

'You didn't think of asking the pilot? Or the nurse? Or any-one else you came into contact with if they had a phone you could borrow?'

JJ heard the smallest amount of irritation in Mia's tone and felt his own rise to match it. 'You know, Mia, I was alone, in-jured, not knowing what fuck had happened to me … hell, I didn't even know my own name.'

'I'm sorry, darling,' she said. 'I was just so worried about you.'

'Anyways, the last thing I wanna do is get on another fucking plane, dude. Right now, all I wanna do is relax, recuperate and check this place out. It looks awesome.'

She couldn't argue with that.

'Did you miss me?' he asked her, with a cheeky smile. Now that the morphine had worn off, JJ's faculties – libido included – had returned with a burning vengeance.

Comparatively Mia's had done the polar opposite, at least as far as JJ was concerned. The horror of what had happened to him during the crash, watching as he'd lay there injured and bleeding – dying, for all she knew – had caused her to view him in an altogether different light. She wanted to take care of him, make sure he was OK, but she no longer wanted him between her legs. In fact, the very idea made her suddenly cringe with embarrassment.

'Cos I missed you,' he said, the bulge in his shorts becoming increasingly visible.

Mia sighed. Last night he had fallen into bed and slept like a baby. She supposed it would be terribly mean to deny him now that he was feeling better, and she duly opened the belt of her La Perla kimono, allowing it to slide to the floor.

'Be quick though, darling,' she said, as, now naked, she bent over the arm of the sofa, watching as he stepped out of his shorts, his undeniably impressive erection springing forward with alacrity, 'there's a party happening on the terrace by the pool and you're the guest of honour so we'd better get a move on.'

'So, how is he? *Really*, I mean?' Nate looked at Mia with genuine concern, and she was suddenly struck by what terribly kind eyes he had.

'Can't remember a bloody thing, poor love.' She sighed. 'Dosed up on morphine for the most part, by all accounts.'

Nate took a sip of Kir Royal. 'Ahh, the pain eliminator that is morphine.'

'Sounds like you're speaking from experience,' she said.

'They pumped me full of the stuff when I broke my leg on the pitch. I remember thinking no wonder people become addicted to this shit. It was like dying and going to heaven.'

Mia snorted softly. 'And that's just one of the reasons I've never tried it, darling. I've seen many people succumb to opiates over the course of my career, people who were looking for something to take the pain away.' At the mention of pain, her thoughts turned to Richard. When he had left her, Mia had used all sorts in a bid to kill the intense emotional agony she'd faced: drugs; alcohol; hypnotherapy; casual sex – all temporary fixes, the high simply masking the pain that would inevitably return with a renewed clarity and vengeance.

'If only there was a magic pill, eh?' she said, washing down her bitterness and regret with a mouthful of Cristal.

'If only,' Nate agreed.

'Now you really do sound as if you're talking from experience.'

She looked at him properly for the first time, studying his face; his large, grey-blue eyes and thick lashes, his full lips and neat bone structure. he was terribly handsome and young – late 20s she surmised – and he had a wonderfully calming presence about him … an easiness she found rather comforting.

'Must've been difficult for you,' she said, 'losing the career you'd worked so hard for because of an injury. It would be like me losing my voice.'

Nate cocked his head.

'Not as hard as learning you're adopted via national newspaper...' He was still hurting about it, it was always there.

'Ahh,' she said, suddenly understanding. She remembered reading something about it in the papers, albeit briefly. 'Well, I can only imagine how dreadful *that* must've been.' She pulled at her long, split-to-the-thigh, chiffon, Versace dress almost in protest. 'Bloody press have no morals, unscrupulous bastards all of them. Sell their firstborn to you for a fleeting headline, most of them.' The irony of her own words was not lost on her.

'The worst thing is not having anyone to turn to,' he found himself saying. 'Both my parents – adoptive parents anyway – are dead, and, well …'

Instinctively she touched his arm.

'I'm sorry, darling,' she said. 'At least you have Billie-Jo.'

Nate raised an eyebrow, causing her to smile.

Mia felt a sudden overwhelming sadness for him. It was the first time she had spoken candidly with him and she saw he was sensitive – gentle even – quietly intelligent and eloquent. Clearly there was more than met the eye and she berated herself for having judged him so quickly as a stereotypical footballer type; she should know better by now, really.

'You've been married long?'

Nate shook his head.

'A couple of years.' It felt like a lifetime already, he thought to himself.

'Well, marriages have their ups and downs,' she said, sensing trouble ahead for him; Billie-Jo had it stamped on her like a hallmark. 'As long as there's trust and respect then the rest of it is simply riding the storm.' She realised how incredulous that sounded. Who was she to give advice – newly divorced after twenty five-years of marriage – but it was nonetheless true. She and Dickie had ridden many a storm throughout the duration of their union, storms Mia reluctantly was beginning to concede were predominantly of her own making.

'I can't stand the drama anymore, Mimi,' Dickie had said, 'the crashing highs and lows, the euphoria and crippling despair. I'm creeping up on sixty years old and I'm tired, tired of being treated like my emotions don't count, wondering if they ever really did. It's all about Mimi, *me-me*, and it always has been. I've tried to fill the hole inside of you, Mia – Lord knows I've given half my life trying to – but I realise now it would never be enough, and the more I try and fill the hole, the deeper I realise it goes. My whole life has been about you and your career, and now, well, now I want something for myself. Is that so wrong?'

Something? *Someone* more like, she'd thought. Those words had wounded Mia so deeply that she would have traded an eye not to have been forced to accept them. Deep down she knew all of what he had said was true, but then he had gone and spoilt it all by shacking up with a bloody schoolgirl! That's when her rage had truly emerged – when all the blame and acrimony had begun. Anger was such a destructive emotion; it tore through her psyche like a nail bomb with revenge being all she could focus on. And yet really she had wanted to tell him that he was right, that she understood her part in it all, that she had been selfish and dominant, that there was a black hole inside of her that couldn't be filled. And the hole was in the shape of a tiny person she had met and held in her arms for less than a few minutes.

'Billie-Jo, she's very … *ambitious*,' Mia said, but then she understood that more than most. Despite having thrown a drink over the girl in outrage, Mia bore her no real malice. She'd dealt with the likes of Billie-Jo a thousand times over in her life and wasn't about to bear a grudge. They'd all been drinking the night of that stupid game and Billie-Jo was young and feisty, much like she herself had been at her age.

'Yep, that's Bee, all right. Fame's the name of the game,' he said, 'I'm only here because of her. I've never been interested in that side of things. I just wanted to play football.'

'Unfortunately talent and fame generally go hand in hand, though the two are not mutually exclusive, especially these days.

A girl's only got to wear a risqué dress to a party and she's the next big thing.'

She glanced over at Billie-Jo who was, by all accounts, already half-cut, swaying to a Bruno Mars track that was playing in the background, clutching a champagne flute as she attempted to coerce JJ into dancing with her, wrapping her arms around him provocatively, shrieking loudly and laughing as her Hervé Léger body-con bandage-dress rode northwards of her slim thighs. Mia clocked the look of resignation on Nate's face. She could see their relationship for what it was – the narcissist and the co-dependant – and knew the outcome already. Sometimes she wished she wasn't so old and didn't know or understand the things she had come to learn throughout her life. Youth and ignorance really were bliss, if only she had made the most of both.

'So, what's next for you, Nate?'

Mia took a swig of champagne, hoping it would wash away the lump of emotion lodged in the back of her throat. She was feeling a little tipsy herself now, even after all that delicious food, and was decidedly melancholy.

'Who knows?' He sighed, draining his own glass, his eye sill drawn towards his wife's inappropriate antics. 'Get drunk?' He laughed, acknowledging the speed of which it had been refreshed by a member of staff with a mock-shocked grin. Mia laughed with him. She wasn't bothered by JJ and Billie-Jo's brazen flirtatious display; that ship had already sailed.

'The journo's more your type, isn't she?' she asked, though she wasn't sure where it had come from.

'What makes you say that?' he said, a little taken aback. Was it that obvious?

Mia didn't know how to answer.

'Intuition,' she said, finally. It was the best she could come up with.

CHAPTER TWENTY-SEVEN

Angelika was giddy. Barefoot with her ditzy, floral, Chloé dress hoisted up to her thighs, she was dancing on the table with abandon, careering perilously close to the impressive five-tier cake.

'God, I love this song!' she shrieked, breathless as she sloshed champagne down the front of her dress, soaking her cleavage. 'Oops!' She laughed, putting her hand over her mouth. 'Come on, Billie-Jo! Let's dance!'

Rupert was watching his wife with unconcealed derision. What in God's name did she think she was playing at? He didn't recognise her. This wasn't Angelika; sociable she may be, but an exhibitionist? He eyed her curiously as she tossed her long, caramel hair behind her and ground her hips up against the gazebo pole, kicking her legs in the air.

'She's a better dancer than I thought she would be, I'll give her that.' Billie-Jo sniggered, watching Angelika's display through a mix of humour and mild jealousy. 'And check out her fella's face!' She laughed. 'He looks right pissed-off. Couldn't have fun in a prozzie parlour with a packet of Durex, that one.'

'Jeez, he should let the girl have some fun.' JJ was standing next to her, a little too close to be wholly appropriate. 'That dude has a real stick up his ass, man. He needs to lighten up.' He copped an eyeful of Angelika's thighs as she twerked on the table to the sound of Chris Brown.

Angelika was enjoying herself, lost in the moment, her head spinning as fast as her body around the pole. She felt light as a feather, as if she might float off into the night like a balloon if she didn't hold on tight.

'It's good to be back on the island with you guys,' JJ said, and he meant it. The past few days had been all but a blur, a kind of weird psychedelic trip almost. If it wasn't for the very real cast on his arm (he'd discarded the sling, too cumbersome and uncool), he might've written it all off as a bad dream. He wasn't even in any real pain anymore.

'Good to have you back,' Billie-Jo said, returning the compliment. JJ offered a more appropriate, appreciative audience for her narcissistic validation. She would enjoy him watching her perfect, young, fit-and-toned body as it paraded itself around the island in a perpetual state of near nakedness, his lustful wide-eyed stares and lascivious smiles as she did her best Halle Berry impersonations while exiting the swimming pool.

But she was worried; what had transpired between her and the masseur had seriously freaked her out and she was struggling to enjoy herself as a result. Following her unplanned intimate encounter, Billie-Jo had returned from the spa in a hazy state of shock and – something she wasn't used to experiencing – guilt. For all the layers of protection she had built around her fragile soul, manifesting itself in the form of selfishness, lack of empathy and general self-entitlement, she was not entirely without human conscience. She had not set out to cheat on her husband and certainly not in such a spontaneous and reckless manner, and now she was panicking. What would happen if Nate found out? She'd made a grave schoolgirl-error by shitting on her own doorstep, big style.

She thought about the question she'd been given in the game of truth or dare – '*none of the above … because I wouldn't cheat in the first place*' – and swallowed dryly. In her defence Billie-Jo had not been herself in that room. So she'd had a few lines of coke; that was no biggie, a regular occurrence, nothing she couldn't or hadn't handled before. She was a high-functioning user, and had never before found herself in such a precarious predicament. There had been plenty of opportunities for her to cheat in the past, men she'd been attracted to, men she might've considered fucking if it hadn't been for the fact that she'd already secured the golden goose itself. How had she allowed herself to have such a spectacular lapse of judgement and self-control? She swigged back some more champagne as she half-listened to JJ droning on in the background. To make matters worse, the sex had been the most incredible of her entire life, her orgasm more intense than any she'd ever experienced, so much so that it had fleetingly crossed her mind to go back for more. However, common sense had prevailed. What if the masseur told one of the other members of staff, confessed all after a few beers like blokes did? What if word got out she had screwed the hired help? Visions flashed through her mind of what it must have looked like when his impressive cock was sliding in and out of her from behind as she moaned with pleasure pushing himself slowly, deeply, gently inside her. *Fucking Jesus shit Christ.*

'I heard from Mia that all the staff here are like mutes or something freaky like that, man,' JJ said, continuing with the one-way conversation, oblivious to the chaos taking place inside Billie-Jo's mind.

A light switched on inside her head. *Fuck, yeah, of course; they were all fucking mutes!* Maybe that would just be enough to save her pretty, little ass.

'Do you think they talk to each other?' she asked. 'In secret, I mean?'

JJ shrugged. 'Fuck knows, dude. I mean, it's some kinda social disorder or some shit like that, isn't it, so I kinda doubt it.'

Billie-Jo gave him a smile of light relief which he translated as a sign she would probably, at some point over the course of proceedings, agree to sucking him off, just so long as Mia and her husband didn't find out, of course. He may have been doped up to the eyeballs the night he'd come back to the island and they had played that game, but he knew a sure thing when it saw it. He smiled at her as he threw back more champagne. He would look forward to it.

CHAPTER TWENTY-EIGHT

'What's the matter, Rupert?'

Mia sashayed towards him, her black, shiny bob swinging in time to her hips, her Heidi Klein kaftan flapping dramatically, affording him a waft of her cloying signature scent. It was the same perfume he remembered her wearing throughout the duration of the trial: Shalimar. He'd hate it then, too.

'Is she having too much fun for your liking?' she asked, nodding at Angelika, who was still throwing shapes on the table with gusto.

Rupert inwardly groaned, though in all honesty he was beginning to loosen up a little himself, his feet subconsciously tapping along to the deep, urban bassline that was pumping out of the state-of-the-art surround-sound speaker system. He, nor, in fact, any of them, had the first inkling that their drinks may have been laced with a little 'livener', as McKenzie had called it, and that, together with the music, a 'special substance' was also being pumped out via the air-mist sprinkler system above them that was supposedly in place to keep them cool from the sultry evening heat. For tonight's special occasion, McKenzie had given staff strict instructions to be most attentive towards Angelika, ensuring her glass was always full. Bloody inquisitive bitch had been asking far too many questions and needed to be kept in check.

'Do you remember that time you shut that mouth of yours and kept quiet, Mia?' Rupert addressed her with a saccharine smile, quickly adding, 'no, me neither.'

'Bothers you, doesn't it, watching your wife having a good time, indulging her sexuality?' She sipped at her glass, eyeing him from above the rim, enjoying his obvious discomfort. 'Such a hypocrite, Rupert,' she mused. 'Tell me, when was the last time *you* indulged *yours* …'

Rupert knew what Mia was getting at and resisted the urge to throw his champagne in her pious face. It would have been wasted on her.

'Haven't you got some babysitting to do?' he spat. 'Now that your manchild is back, shouldn't you be looking out for him? He's over there with the predatory WAG. I think he needs a chaperone.'

'Careful, Deyton, you almost sound jealous.' She raised a mocking eyebrow. 'Ahh, but of which one?'

Rupert sighed. He cut to the chase: 'What exactly do you want from me, Manhattan? Do you enjoy watching me squirm?'

Mia remained smiling, unfazed. 'Yes, Deyton, as a matter of fact, I do. I consider it karma.'

'Why can't you let it go?' he asked. 'It was all a long time ago now. And you do realise that blackmail carries a heftier sentence than murder and rape? Besides –' he leaned in closer to her '– don't forget I also know about *your* past Mia, and *your* dirty little secret.'

Mia felt her heart palpate beneath the delicate fabric of her Cavalli kaftan but held her nerve. She knew it was dangerous to goad him but he'd kept quiet for this long and Mia could never help pushing people's buttons. It was instinctive to her contrary nature.

'My secret – should it ever make the light of day – would no doubt illicit empathy, as indeed would your own "dirty little secret", only the empathy wouldn't be for you, would it, Rupert?' She glanced over in Angelika's direction once again. 'Poor girl.'

She gave an over-exaggerated sigh. 'She hasn't the first clue, has she?'

'Why didn't you die in that crash, you evil old witch?' he said, contempt billowing from his lips. 'You really are a spectacularly vindictive cunt, do you know that?'

Mia cackled.

'Oooh,' she said, mockingly, satisfied she'd got a rise from him, 'and less of the vindictive, if you don't mind.'

She realised, however, that she had probably overstepped the mark. Rupert's secret, should it be revealed, would undoubtedly destroy his marriage, and despite the loathing she felt for the man himself, she rather liked Angelika.

'Have you explored the island yet?' she changed the subject, attempting small talk, she wasn't in the mood to fight with him again. 'It really is rather spectacular, reminds me of one of the Greek islands. Santorini was a particular favourite of mine and Dick's … Anyway, now that Joshua's back safe and well, I may do a little sightseeing.' She paused. 'You could accompany us if you like,' she added in a spontaneous and uncharacteristic flash of olive branch.

'I'd rather contract Malaria,' Rupert remarked, though it lacked real contempt. He was tired of the banter between them already. Perhaps Angelika had been right; maybe it was time to bury the hatchet. 'And no, I haven't, not yet, though I intend to before we leave … if we ever bloody get to leave that is. Apparently the phone lines are still down.' Rupert pulled a face. 'Can't work it out myself. I mean, we're on an island. It's not the third world, though I'm beginning to wonder if it isn't the Third Reich.'

Mia laughed. Deyton had always been a wit. She reluctantly admired him for it.

'What do you think McKenzie really wants with us?' he said, genuinely interested in Mia's take on it. He might despise the woman but she was nobody's fool. 'If this was simply a PR exercise for McKenzie, then surely he would've invited the press exclusively. I mean, what can us mere mortals bring to the table?'

'Speak for yourself,' she quipped as Remi approached to refresh their glasses with more fizz, though she had to concede that Rupert did have a point. 'Who knows what goes through that bastard's mind … personally I'm not sure I even want to.'

'Hmm … indeed.'

Rupert strained to recall the small print of the contract he had scan-read before his stupid bloody wife had gone behind his back and signed their lives away, almost quite literally. He was sure it had said something about being required to partake in all publicity requested of them prior, during and following the duration of their stay on the island.

'Well, he'll certainly make headlines if that's what he wants. We could've all died in that crash. No doubt I will be forced to go on some ghastly talk show to relive it all once we're back in Blightly.'

Rupert shuddered at the idea and Mia once again laughed, although she herself was beginning to ruminate on what a great press opportunity the air crash may potentially afford. *Global singing sensation cheats death at 30,000 feet!* There would inevitably be myriad TV and media interviews desperate to hear about her brush with mortality, giving her the chance to make headway with her comeback while exposing her to a whole new audience in the process. Every cloud, Mia thought, suddenly quite enamoured by the whole idea.

Rupert smiled at Raj as he refreshed his flute and thought he caught a familiar look in the man's dark, chocolate eyes as they briefly met, though he could not be entirely sure. It was a look he'd only been privy to on a couple of occasions.

He glanced over towards Angelika again, suddenly seeing her celebratory antics through slightly different eyes. Perhaps he *was* missing out on something fun and exciting. Billie-Jo had already stripped down to her barely there crochet string bikini and was submerged in the sunken Jacuzzi next to the pool swigging Cristal from the bottle, JJ was struggling to undress himself with one good arm in a bid to join her and Nate was behind the DJ decks seemingly unperturbed by his wife's close proximity to the guest of honour and instead smiling and laughing as Angelika entertained him with her risqué impersonation of a stripper. Rupert necked his glass of champagne in one.

'You'll probably only ever hear me say this once,' he said to Mia, adrenalin suddenly buzzing through him like electricity, the need to move his feet to the music reaching the point of unbearable, 'but would you care to dance?'

CHAPTER TWENTY-NINE

Martin McKenzie sat back into the plush, cream, leather seat inside one of his fleet of private jets and prepared for take-off – destination Beijing. Flipping his iMac open, he loosened his Tom Ford silk tie and settled down to enjoy a little in-flight entertainment. The party was kicking off just as he'd planned, his guest's inhibitions disappearing as quickly as the ground beneath him. He sipped his drink, a smooth, vintage cognac, pulling his lips over his teeth as the strong liquid scorched his palate, and watching intently as the blonde discarded her pink bikini top with a shriek and that dumb American fuck began to fondle her impressive tits with his good hand. Soon enough that bitch journalist woman practically fell into the Jacuzzi next to them, closely followed by the footballer, already in a half-state of undress, his shirt discarded along with all sense of morality. The blonde, the footballer, the journo, the uptight lawyer, the rock star and the has-been; to refer to them by name would be to humanise them. These people were simply actors, players in his latest production. And right now they were headed for a collective Oscar.

He hoped the Super Eight were relishing the show with as much anticipation as he was. An orgy in a Jacuzzi would round the day's proceedings off nicely. But where was that bitch, Mia? And the journo's husband for that matter? He clicked on another screen to search for their whereabouts - and it wasn't long before he found it.

'Well, well, well,' he said aloud, viewing the scene with morbid interest. This was far better than even he could've hoped for. Ahh, the wonder drugs that were MDMA and Rohypnol, they really did get to the truth of a person. The champagne had been spiked with a measured amount, just enough to loosen everyone up, but not enough to be traceable in the blood after forty-eight hours, according to Elaine's research anyway, and as an added bonus he'd arranged for amyl nitrate to be pumped out through the water sprinkler system that was hidden underneath the shady bougainvillea-covered pergola. McKenzie finished his drink, clicked his fingers to request another and settled in for some decent viewing content in the knowledge that the Super Eight Club were all glued to their screens at this very moment. Still, if they thought they were getting their money's worth now, they were soon to be in for an even bigger surprise.

Cody Parker was feeling pleased with himself. In less than twenty-four hours the link he had posted to a select few had already caused a major stir within the higher echelons of the hacker community, fast-tracking him to the top of his game and affording him the praise and admiration he so voraciously sought from his special 'family'.

He grinned, clicking a ring pull on a diet Dr Pepper and guzzling back half of it in celebration. He had sent the link out to a selected few of his contemporaries, hackers he knew would be impressed not just by the content itself but by his ability to have found a way in. He'd added the message: 'Dear friends, my latest discovery: a game show with a difference; one where the contestants have NO idea they're being filmed...viewing figures (present company excluded) eight. The source: TOP SECRET!' Cody knew he couldn't take all the credit for uncovering the site's host, but he wanted to give the impression that he had, and steal the lion's share of the glory. It was risky, however; he knew that by sharing his find with fellow hackers there was a chance of it being leaked. As insular as the world he operated in was, and as much as there was a code of conduct between fellow hackers, a discovery such as this was too good not to share, in which case it wouldn't be long before it infiltrated the mainstream. If this shit hit social media anytime soon, the exclusive Super Eight would be looking at adding a healthy few noughts onto its membership within hours. Hell, now that was PR for you right there. However, Cody was keen to keep it within the hacker's secret society, for the time being anyhow. In spite of his glory-seeking fantasies, he was still aware that he might get into trouble and would need to remove all trace of himself before this thing went public, which it would, eventually. And when it did, Cody wanted to be able to sit back and watch McKenzie's public fall from grace with a sense of *schadenfreude* and bask in the glory that it was he who had brought such a powerful man down. 'I'm making a polite request for you keep this one on the low-down, guys, so just sit back and enjoy in private,' he'd added, 'for now at least.'

As it was though, he was already too late.

CHAPTER THIRTY

Angelika woke with a start.

'Jesus Christ, I'm going to throw up.'

She sprinted from the bed to the en suite, dropping to her knees and grasping the rim of the toilet before emptying the contents of her guts into it.

'Ange?' The sounds of her retching had caused Nate to stir awake. 'Ange, are you OK?' Unsteady on his feet, he pulled himself up and shuffled into the bathroom after her. 'Fuck,' he whispered, kneeling down next to her, pulling her long hair from her face and rubbing her back as she violently convulsed. '*Fuck.*'

Nate thought he heard the door to the cabana open. It was Rupert; he was pale and dishevelled, his hair sticking up on end almost comically, the buttons on his white, muslin shirt askew, pool sliders in his hand.

Rupert was not prepared for the sight that greeted him. Billie-Jo was spreadeagled on the white, leather couch, naked, her hair a tangled straggly blonde mess, limbs protruding awkwardly at various angles, her mouth open. She looked like a mannequin, a blow-up doll, and for a horrifying second he thought she might even be dead – that was until he saw her large breasts heaving. *Thank God.*

JJ was slumped on the armchair opposite her, his body leaning to one side. He was, at least, wearing boxer shorts. Empty bottles of Veuve Clicquot and Jack Daniels were scattered around the room like bowling pins. There was shattered glass on the floor, a marble ashtray upended on the table next to remnants of white powder, rolled notes and other paraphernalia discarded besides squashed cigarette butts. *Aftermath*.

Rupert swallowed dryly, his anger beaten down by his own sense of shame. It seemed like he wasn't the only one with some explaining to do. Instinctively he walked over to the glass coffee table and with a shaking hand up-turned the ashtray and an empty bottle next to it. He stepped over Billie-Jo's discarded bikini bottoms and made his way towards the bedroom. Where the hell was his wife? Where was Angelika? He was torn between calling out her name and turning and leaving the carnage behind him, his own guilt following like a shadow. He needed time to think about what he was going to say to her. He was scared that his face would project the truth – that it would silently confess his own terrible sins from the night before.

God almighty, what had happened to them all last night? He wasn't sure what but *something* had … something bad. He could recall Angelika dancing, that he himself had begun to dance at one point, a pastime he hadn't indulged in since his student days. Last night, however, he had been compelled to move himself around to the music, lost in it like it had somehow become part of him.

Images flashed up in his mind, grainy and sketchy; he'd been dancing with Mia, *Mia* … the sound of human noise, of chatter punctuated by the chorus of crickets in the air, the music – God, the music. It was like he'd been born deaf and was hearing it for the first time; the clarity of the drums, the pulsating bass and hiss of hi-hats … he'd been in tune to every cymbal, every note. And it had enchanted him, hypnotised him like a snake charmer, forcing his body to respond, to move and react in time to it.

He'd watched Billie-Jo enter the Jacuzzi, her narrow, tiny body almost like that of a child's, were it not for the shop-bought air bags making a splash on entry. JJ had followed her, dancing, his good hand in the air, lost, too, in the music.

It had occurred to Rupert that his wife might be sexually attracted to Nate Simmons; he had been briefly aware of fleeting clandestine exchanges between them, how she seemed slightly looser of limb in his presence. Naturally he'd been jealous. After all, Nate was a good deal younger, fitter, and aesthetically blessed than him – these days at least.

Rupert struggled to admit it to himself but his feelings of envy were based less on the fact that his wife might lust after another, and more that someone as ridiculously attractive as Nate was would actually consider her an option. It was a competition; everything between them always was: who was the more successful, witty, popular and attractive. Well, two can play that game, he'd thought at the time, watching as they had begun to fool around in the Jacuzzi, Angelika practically impervious to his existence. Rupert had never seen her like it in all their years together; she was behaving like a common slut, dancing like a hooker displaying her wares in a brothel window; stripping down to her underwear and jumping into the pool like a teenager on drugs.

Good God! The thought suddenly hit him like a comet. Had their drinks been spiked with something? It seemed too absurd an idea to entertain but it would explain things. Dismissing the thought more or less instantly, Rupert made his way up towards the bedroom where he was met with the sound of his wife's vomiting.

He looked around the bedroom. Had Angelika and Nate spent the night together? Had they fucked each other's brains out? The carnage and discarded items of clothing would certainly suggest that *something* had taken place. Not that he was in any position to start creating even if they had.

Rupert stopped short of the en suite, hovering outside it. He caught sight of himself in the ornate wall mirror, a look of anguish etched across his tired face. This was all Mia Manhattan's fault, he decided. Whenever he was around that woman bad shit happened. She was a fucking omen, make no mistake. He'd been dancing with her; *him*, dancing, with *Mia*, twirling her around to the sound of Nicki Minaj's latest, dross he would otherwise have switched off the second it came on the radio.

'He's looking at you,' she'd said with that half-raised-eyebrow mocking expression of hers.

'Who is?'

'Raj.' She nodded at the handsome dark-skinned mute with the washboard stomach, his ice-white teeth illuminating his face in the low, night sky as he looked on obediently.

'Can't say I noticed,' he replied tartly. 'Besides, why would he be looking at me?'

Mia had fixed him with a knowing smile, her blood-red lips parting, almost Machiavellian.

'One indiscretion,' he'd eventually said quietly.

'Didn't look much like an indiscretion to me at the time.'

'Leave it, Mia. It was a long time ago.'

During Mia's ill-fated trial, Mia had been driven to and from court by a young man called Michael Curtis whom inevitably Rupert had come to know. Michael was vivacious, attractive and out, though not overly camp, and the two had struck up an unlikely friendship, a friendship that had turned into a quiet obsession, for Rupert at least, and he had begun to grapple with emotions he had never experienced before. He'd been attracted to Michael – sexually attracted – and it had left him feeling both elated and unhappy. Was he gay? Had he always had homosexual leanings that he'd buried, refusing to recognise in himself? He'd loved women all his life: Angelika being the ultimate. He was engaged to be married to her when the inevitable happened and he'd given in to his desires and slept with Michael. The sex had been incredible, had made him feel whole and alive, more than any sex he'd had with any woman, his wife-to-be included. But gay? Rupert didn't think so. If only that spectacular cunt Mia hadn't walked in on them, then it would've been an experience to have savoured, a memory to treasure and remember fondly before burying. Only Mia wasn't about to let that happen. When the case collapsed and her vitriol was at its worst, she had threatened to out him, to tell Angelika, go to the press. And he'd been in no doubt she would've had he not known about her own secret. Rupert didn't feel particularly gallant about using it against her but she'd backed him into a corner. She'd confessed all to him one very drunken evening when she'd been in one of her highly emotional and vulnerable states during the case, possibly even using such tragedy to try and make him work even harder on her behalf. Who knew that damned woman's motives? What he did know, however, was that she didn't want her confession leaked to the press, and so there they were, adversaries, each with something on the other, bound by respective secrets, each holding the others over them like a weapon.

And now he'd gone and given Mia the upper hand. How he'd felt last night, Raj … He'd been powerless to deny those emotions once more. Only now it was a thousand times worse. Rupert felt like physically crying. It had been the three of them – him, Raj *and* Mia – at one point. Flashbacks seized his mind, strong arming him to remember, Raj's hands on his own, the touch of his skin, the look on his face as he had entered him from behind, Mia standing over them, her black, shiny bob, her red-lipstick stains on his own body … was it all jut a diabolical nightmare? Rupert couldn't recall if he and Mia had done the ugly deed. If they had then he had promptly blanked it out and hoped it would remain that way. But she had definitely been there, involved, watching, observing, encouraging. The very idea made him physically sick to his stomach.

'Angelika!' Rupert almost screamed her name as he took a breath and marched into the en suite.

'What in God's holy fucking name,' he said as Nate looked up at him, startled, his hand still on Angelika's back as she threw up for England inside the toilet bowl. She was naked save for her nude underwear.

'It's not what it looks like,' Nate said calmly as his eyes met with Rupert's.

Rupert swallowed. Frankly, a part of him hoped to God the man was lying.

CHAPTER THIRTY-ONE

The evening air was rich and warm, almost palpable, alive with a chorus of crickets and birdsong. She was sitting on the edge of the pool looking out across the sea, the low light forming a halo around her silhouette, her bare legs stretched out in front of her, hair hanging past her shoulders in loose, beachy waves. The pool was tranquil and smooth, blending seamlessly into the ocean, the sunset projected upon it, ombre reds and purples melting like watercolour on its mirrored surface.

He wished more than anything that he had a camera to capture her in that very moment: beautiful but with a certain vulnerability. He stood for a second and watched her until she became aware of his presence behind her.

She turned, her eyes briefly meeting his. 'Nate,' she whispered, before looking away.

'Is it OK …?' He stared at the empty space next to her.

She smiled faintly and nodded.

'Spectacular, isn't it?' he said of the view, as he took his place beside her and she nodded again.

'I needed to get away,' she said after a moment's pause. 'I needed … to think.'

He wanted desperately to hold her but knew that he shouldn't, that it would be unwise to instigate any physical contact. He thought he might be falling in love with her. Whatever it was he couldn't explain it; just being around her made him feel content, the opposite to how he felt around his own wife.

'Last night ...'

'I wanted to talk about ...'

They spoke simultaneously, both laughing through the nervousness lingering between them.

'You first,' he said.

'No,' she said, 'you first.'

Nate stared outwards at the perfect view and paused for a long moment.

'When I was young, you know, just a little boy, I wanted to be a photographer. I was always obsessed with cameras, taking pictures of family and friends, used to drive them all nuts.' He smiled wistfully. 'I got a Polaroid camera for my eight birthday and thought it was the business: this thing that took pictures and processed them there and then ... none of the hassle of putting the film in the chemist. Just, snap, boom, there they were – instant gratification.' He paused again and she turned to him slightly, a sign he took as encouraging. 'I never really wanted to be a professional player, you know ... but I was just ... just so good at it, I suppose, and my dad – well, the man I believed was my dad – he was just so made up with the fact that his son had been picked to play for a professional team. He was so proud of me and I was so happy to please, you know. That's all kids really want to do at the end of the day, please their parents.' His voice trailed off. 'The footballing world wasn't really for me, though. Don't get me wrong, being part of a team – being accepted, praised, adored – it's pretty addictive.' He brushed his thick fringe from his face; it was beginning to stick to him in the sultry heat that was still gently persisting. 'And the money ... well.' He sighed. 'But the lifestyle, what it all came with: the girls and the cars, all that stuff ... it made, well, it *makes* me uncomfortable.'

She didn't know what he was trying to say.

'I don't know who I am, Ange,' he said quietly, his large eyes glassy as they met her own, and she saw the sunset in them. 'It destroyed a part of me when I found out about the adoption. The questions, Ange, my whole existence … like, I'd always thought I had my dad's eyes, similar mannerisms, only I didn't, not really, I couldn't have. I wonder where, or who I got my eyes from, my determination, sense of humour even – all that stuff that makes you who you are.'

'I'm so sorry,' Angelika said softly, 'perhaps the private investigator will have something for you when we get back home. But you know, Nate, sometimes you should be careful what you wish for. Sometimes there are things best left unknown … unsaid …'

They were silent for a moment, the sound of the crickets' musical language providing an aural backdrop.

'What happened last night …' Angelika's heartbeat escalated, her bare foot began to twitch.

'What happened last night …' She repeated the words but could not bring herself to add to them.

The truth was she couldn't remember much; it was blank in her mind, wiped out like chalk on a blackboard. She was biting her lip nervously and instinctively he touched her hand, grateful when she didn't recoil.

'I haven't been that drunk in my entire life,' she confessed. Had they made love? The situation she had found herself in upon waking up would certainly suggest so. She'd been wearing underwear, a small relief, but Nate had been next to her in her bed in only his Calvin Klein boxer shorts. After vomiting violently, she had locked herself away in the bathroom, the low sounds of Nate and her husband's hushed conversation from behind the door almost drowned out by the sound of her retching. Did she feel any different? She had touched herself intimately in a bid to try and gauge. Would she have felt him on her still, would there be signs? Shame had swept through her like fire. Had she cheated on her husband without recollection? Had they indulged in some kind of four-way sex orgy with Billie-Jo and JJ? The very idea made her blood run to ice. To add to the surrealness of the situation, Rupert had remained perfectly calm upon his return to the cabana. He told her he had woken Billie-Jo and given her a robe to cover her nakedness before Nate had seen her, then he'd set about rousing JJ. Once the three of them had left he had knocked on the bathroom door.

'Are you OK, Angelika?' he'd asked and the familiarity of him had undone her completely.

Guilt and shame, embarrassment, regret, confusion; she'd been flooded with all of it.

'I don't know, Ru,' she'd said, panic evident in her voice, 'last night … I don't know what's going on.'

'I think I do.' Rupert paused. 'It's possible our drinks were spiked with something.'

To her shock and surprise he had taken her in his arms, a gesture so rare that it simply compounded her guilt and she had struggled not to cry.

'Where did you go?' she'd asked him and she'd felt his body sag in response to the question. Her last memory was that of watching as Rupert had danced with Mia, twirling her around to the music with abandon, and then he had gone. In fact, now she recalled it, so too had Mia.

Rupert had swallowed so hard that she'd heard his throat click.

'I … I don't remember much myself,' he'd said. They'd stood together in the beautiful en suite bathroom with its gold taps and shiny marble floor, the ornate mirrors duplicating them from every angle, his long arms stiff around her small frame. And in that moment she'd felt for the first time in ages that her husband needed her and that whatever else was missing between them, trust and friendship still remained. *Why wasn't that enough?*

'I think we may have been drugged, that our drinks were spiked.' She looked at him, still chewing her lip nervously. 'It would explain … my behaviour, so out of character. Even Rupert said as much and he's not prone to wild imagination, let me tell you. If he smells a rat it usually means there is one.'

'It's OK, Ange,' he said, 'if you're worried that we … well, we didn't.'

'We didn't?' She blinked at him with a confusing mix of disappointment and wide-eyed relief.

Nate felt a little deflated.

'Would it have been so terrible if we had?' It was a stupid question and he wished he'd not asked it. They had kissed though, that much he *could* remember, and he had held her as he'd slept next to her, felt her skin against his own, soft as cashmere. He'd been so scared to touch her in case she'd disappeared like a dream.

'I'm sorry.' She looked down at her legs awkwardly. 'Not terrible at all, just not ideal given the situation: the fact we're both married.'

'Not that my wife would know it, at least it certainly didn't seem that way last night from what I can remember.' He had a look of resignation on his face, like he'd half expected it.

'But that's just it, Nate,' she said, 'none of us *can* remember. Don't you think that's odd? I really do think Rupert may be right and that we may have been drugged.'

'But why? And by who? Elaine McKenzie? Why on earth would she want to spike our drinks?'

'I don't know,' she said, wondering if it wasn't such a ridiculous thought now that she'd said it aloud, 'but I'm telling you, there's something not right about this place, Nate. It gives me the heebeejeebees.' She thought of how calm Rupert had been despite having walked in on his semi-naked wife in bed with another man. Instead of the scene she had expected, one in which her husband rightfully lost his shit, he'd been a picture of composure and had even comforted her. Was he not even the least bit upset or jealous to have found her in such a compromising situation? He had not grilled her over what had happened, not properly as one would expect anyhow. Did he not care? Was the bond between them now so platonic that sexual jealousy was no longer part of the equation? Or, she wondered, was it because he himself had something to hide? His whole demeanour had been one of malfeasance that morning, his reticence disconcerting. Rupert liked to have the upper hand, always, and the scenario had presented it to him on a plate. Only it seemed that morning he just wasn't hungry.

'Can I ask you something, Ange?' Nate looked at her intently, forcibly refraining himself from brushing the hair from her face with his fingers. 'Do you love your husband?'

Angelika pulled her chin into her chest, suggesting the question impertinent.

'Of course,' she said without hesitation. 'What a question to ask!'

'Only last night, after we kissed, you told me that you weren't in love with Rupert anymore. That sometimes you loathed him and wished you had left him a long time ago.'

She blinked at him in shock, her heart beat rapidly escalating.

'We kissed? But I thought you said we didn't —'

'— make love? No, we didn't, but I wanted to Ange,' he said, suddenly feeling braver than he'd ever felt with a woman before. Unlike his wife, being with Angelika fed his soul rather than his ego. He was, however, too much of a gentleman to admit to her that it had been she who had instigated the kiss. They'd both been intoxicated, though she seemingly more so, and he'd been cautious not to take advantage of this fact, but she was just so human and real, so unlike Billie-Jo, her hair damp and loose and natural, her skin luminous and that snuggle tooth … he'd only had eyes for her the entire evening, impervious to his wife, to JJ, to Rupert or Mia. As far as he'd been concerned they were invisible. She was all he could see and when she spoke he absorbed every word, savouring her tone of voice. It had intoxicated him so entirely that he didn't care who knew it; he'd just wanted to the feeling never to end.

'We shouldn't have done that,' she swallowed dryly, wishing she meant it. Angelika knew that if she'd been stripped bear, metaphorically speaking at least, if the myriad barriers had not presented themselves then she would be in his arms right now, but there were just too many of them.

'But we did,' he said, flicking his hair from his boyish face. If only it wasn't so boyish. *Forget it Angelika, this is absurd, you're married, he's married …*

'What about Billie-Jo? She's your wife.'

Nate shook his head.

'You've seen Billie-Jo. Look at her, most men's dream … just not mine.' He shook his head. 'It's not her fault, it's my fault. I married her because she is who she is, what she is, what she represents. I thought … I thought that's what I was supposed to do. The world I lived in, the trophy wife, I'm ashamed to say it, Ange.'

'Then don't,' she said, pleading with him. 'If things were different, Nate …' It sounded like a cliché but she meant it.

'Don't get me wrong, I care about Bee; she's what she is, the product of a screwed-up life, making money from the only assets she has. I don't blame her, don't hate her, but I know what she is.' His voice faltered as he caught the expression on Angelika's face.

She'd stopped listening to him and was leaning forward, her attention caught by something, something deep within the brush nestled on the side of the cliff. The pool was at sea level, built into the side of the bay which, like the entire island, was shrouded in shrubbery, brush and wild flowers, tiny buds that somehow flourished in the biting heat.

'What is it?' he asked, turning to look, 'what have you seen?'

'There!' She said, her light summer dress falling mid-thigh as she abruptly stood.

Her sudden movement startled him. 'What?'

'There in the bushes.' She grabbed his arm, the sensation of her touch sending an electric current through his body. 'There's something flashing.' She was up on her feet now, moving towards it, dangerously close to the edge. 'Nate, look. See it?'

She pulled him towards her, the warmth of her skin touching his own as she pointed at the shrubs.

'What am I looking for?'

'In the bushes, down there.'

He crouched down, squinting.

'I don't see any … Oh, hang on …'

The tiny red light, practically a dot, was buried deep beneath the brush, but it was there, flashing silently, a claret spec almost invisible to the human eye.

'How the fuck did you see that?'

'Hold my ankles,' she said, dropping to her knees.

'No,' he said, 'let me do it. Just make sure I don't fall.'

They looked down at the rocks below them. The drop was 200ft at least, and it was getting darker now, the light low and atmospheric casting shadows around them.

'Be careful,' she warned as he lay down onto his belly and snaked towards the edge. She grasped his ankles firmly, the feel of his cartilage stiff against her palms, his pulse detectable on her fingers.

'Jesus, it's buried deep whatever it is.' He was stretched out like a plank now, his arms straining as he scrabbled around in the bushes. 'I can't … it's attached to something. Jesus.' He made a low grunt, using all the strength he had, tugging at it until it came loose and snapped off. 'Got it!' he said triumphantly as he recoiled backwards. Angelika pulled him from the edge.

'What is it?' she asked, her curiosity peaking as he brushed himself down. They stared at the piece of plastic in his hand.

It had stopped flashing now.

'I'm not sure,' he said, inspecting it closely, 'but at a wild guess I'd say it was some kind of camera.'

CHAPTER THIRTY-TWO

Billie-Jo was inspecting her fingernails as she lay stretched out on the white egg-pod sunlounger. She'd bitten them to the quick.

'Hey!' she called out in a bid to catch the attention of her personal butler, Remi or Ranjit or whatever his name was. 'Can you book me in for a manicure and gel polish as soon as? But before you do, send over a large Bloody Mary, will you?' She needed hair of the dog, or something anyway. He nodded obligingly and Billie-Jo sighed as she settled back into a horizontal position, her colourful crochet Missoni bikini displaying a generous amount of side boob. She knew she was in the shit big time and needed to think, only she had the mother of all comedowns and couldn't concentrate on a single thought for longer than a few seconds. What the fuck did she think she was playing at? What was happening to her? First that business with the masseur, and then last night she'd woken up naked, *stark bollock naked*, remnants of coke on the table, discarded bottles of champagne and JD scattered around her. JJ had passed out opposite her as good as starkers himself. Thankfully Rupert had seen fit to throw her a robe so she could cover herself up, but still she wondered if Nate had seen them. *Holy hell*, you've really surpassed yourself this time, Billie-Jo, she thought, vowing to lay off the drink and drugs for the rest of her duration on the island. How could she have been so indiscreet? So she'd fancied JJ. Who wouldn't; he was right up her boulevard: young, tanned, smoking-hot body, covered in ink and, the *piece de resistance*, a bona fide rock star.

Maybe she'd fucked him, in which case she was furious at herself because she couldn't quite remember. Had she really drank and snorted that much gear that she'd had a total blackout? A party pro, Billie-Jo knew her limits and she had a high constitution when it came to recreational drugs. She felt sure she'd indulged way more in the past and still retained full clarity so what had been so different last night? More pressing, however, was how the hell was she going to talk herself out of this one? Her addled mind raced in time with her heartbeat. Would Nate flip out when they finally got round to speaking? She supposed she couldn't blame him if he did. They had walked back to their cabana together that morning, him two steps ahead, in complete silence. Was he going to divorce her? If so, on what grounds? She wasn't even sure she'd committed adultery, at least not with JJ anyway. Billie-Jo groaned. It was all going wrong for her and she didn't know why. Nate would never have to know about the massage, days had passed and nothing had come to light which had led her to believe that she'd gotten away with it, and anyway, it was just one little oversight, the first real slip up she'd made since saying her vows. Everyone was allowed one mistake, weren't they?

'If in doubt, say nought.' She thought of the seasoned advice her poor downtrodden mum had often given her. Good advice, she now conceded. Deny, deny, deny, yeah that's what she'd do. Forgive herself and move on. They'd all been off their tits last night anyway, Nate included. In fact, her husband had been all over that Angelika bird like the clap if her sketchy memory was correct – something she'd not been best pleased about. She'd worked hard to ensnare Nate Simmons and get him up the aisle and she wasn't about to give up her investment without a fight.

Deep down, however, Billie-Jo knew that he didn't truly love her, or that they were particularly well-suited, at least not beyond the façade. Nate was happy to let his star fade into obscurity, while hers, she felt, was on the ascent. But she still needed him; he still possessed clout on the celeb circuit, was still receiving offers of advertising deals and invitations to A-list events. In a few years' time she hoped it would be a different story. By then she planned to be a household name in her own right, in which case if he wanted emancipation from her, to slip back into being a nobody with the hoi polloi, then on he could go. Billie-Jo ended up hurting everyone she'd ever been close to in her life; it was all she'd understood and felt comfortable with. It was damn or be damned, as far as she was concerned. Yet she did care about Nate, more than any of the other geezers she'd known. Maybe it was as close to love as she'd ever been. But if he had to be collateral damage in her bid for fame then *que sera, sera*, although she wished it didn't have to be that way.

Inside her fragile heart, Billie-Jo knew that Nate Simmons was a good man, too good for her really. He was gentle, empathetic and sensitive; everything she wished she could be. But there was no good in being sentimental, that shit saw you chewed up and spat out for the dogs. You had to play hardball in this life to get what you wanted, and undoubtedly this meant a few casualties along the way. Nate was slipping away from her and she knew it but she had to make things right with him for now, while she thought of plan B.

Looking up, Billie-Jo saw JJ approaching. He was holding a beer in his good hand and waving at her, his long bed-hair flapping in momentum as he slunk towards her with that insouciant rock-star swagger.

'Ah,' she said quietly to herself, 'speaking of plan B.'

'Drugged?' Elaine McKenzie looked up at Rupert, her cold, steely eyes unblinking.

He felt she had a slight smirk on her face and it made him feel like smacking her across it.

'What on earth would make you think such a thing?'

Rupert sized her up calmly. As a formidable barrister he had, over the years, represented and prosecuted everyone from child murderers and rapists to tax-dodging celebrities, and just about everyone else in between; nothing truly shocked him anymore. He'd seen a life-time of heinous crime and degradation perpetrated by pure evil and come face-to-face with it on many occasions. He was versed in cross examination, used to dealing with narcissists, liars who'd tell you the moon was square and almost convince you of it, too, but he was not about to be fobbed off by this ugly, wizened dwarf.

'Being drugged would make me think such a thing, Elaine,' he replied.

'Really, that's quite absurd.' She looked at him with horrified incredulity. 'How, for one thing, and why, for another, come to that?'

'All questions I put to you, Mrs McKenzie,' he replied.

Elaine shook her head and walked towards the wooden antique desk that formed the centrepiece of the vast colonial study.

'Frankly, I'm a little shocked, not to mention offended. That's a very bold accusation to make – as a man of your profession would well know – and completely unfounded.'

'Last night,' Rupert said, 'none of us have any recollection of it whatsoever.' Or so he hoped, praying he was speaking for Mia as well. 'It's a total blank. And my wife, she was sick, violently sick. And my wife is never sick, Elaine. That woman hasn't thrown up on alcohol since the 1980s. Something's amiss.'

Elaine gave a thin smile, careful to maintain eye contact as she did.

'I realise a lot of alcohol was consumed,' she conceded, 'but Pleasure Island is a special place, Mr Deyton. It can have a very intoxicating effect on a person. I'm sure you all needed to let your hair down a little and ...'

Elaine was an accomplished liar but then again so was this man, and no more to anyone than himself, it seemed, having watched the footage of him from last night's little soirée. She hadn't had Rupert Deyton down as a closet fag, and it had given cause for a wry smile. Just went to show you could never judge a book by its cover. However, she was a touch unnerved by the conclusions he'd drawn, not least because they were true.

Elaine had researched the correct dosage of drugs meticulously and made sure they had been administered methodically. In hindsight, however, she realised that perhaps she had not policed the amount the journo had been given overall, but then she had been under strict instructions from her husband to pay special attention to Angelika Deyton. Now Rupert Deyton was suspicious and Marty would be angry with her.

Even if she wasn't even aware of the fact, Elaine McKenzie was under her husband's complete physical and emotional control. Over the duration of their twenty-five year marriage, the woman she had started out as had gradually been whittled away and replaced with a virtual 'stepford wife'. It had been a prolonged process of manipulation and subtle cruelty over the years, withholding affection and money in turn for complete subordination, alienating her from family and friends, cutting her off from society until she was solely and completely dependent upon him, not even so much as having an autonomous thought of her own. Elaine couldn't so much as take a dump without Marty's say so, yet in his own way her husband respected her; he had transformed her into a formidable and fiercely loyal ally upon which he could put upon without question, rewarding her with praise and entrusting her with his dirty work. This in turn afforded Elaine a sense of importance and self-worth, her sole purpose being simply to please and appease her husband in any and all ways possible. As a result her own moral compass no longer existed; over the years she had gradually taken on Martin McKenzie's persona as her own and now they were practically one and the same.

'Where exactly is your husband?' Rupert asked through narrowed eyes, 'It's been over a week now. This is the twenty-first century, Elaine. You can't tell me all lines of communication are still down: no phone, no internet … no means of getting off the island to get help.'

'Help from what?' she answered him coolly, lighting a thin, brown cigarette from a packet on the table.

Unsure exactly how to answer, he moved closer towards the desk, placing his hands upon it like he would when cross-examining a witness. He could smell her perfume, musky and unpleasant, almost cheap. Her practical no-nonsense white shirt, buttoned to the neck, was clearly tailored, designer probably, yet teamed with loose grey slacks gave her the overall sartorial look of a prison warden, which he was beginning to think she was, of sorts.

'Aren't you a little pissed off that he's left you in the lurch, here, alone, to deal with your guests, tend to our myriad whims? I know I would be. And if he's expecting positive publicity on the back of all of this …' He snorted. 'He can bloody well think again. We were almost killed in that crash. Two people died, Elaine … *died!* And, frankly, it's rather worrying, your lack of concern.'

Elaine struggled to maintain composure, though Rupert was not aware of it.

'One person,' she corrected him, adding, 'that we know of.'

'Drop the act, Elaine,' he said stoically, 'you can't kid a kidder. Tell me why we are here?' Rupert addressed her slowly, his eyes fixed upon her in a fierce glare. 'What's the *real* purpose of this exercise? And don't fob me off with all that promotional bullshit because I don't buy it. I want – no – I *demand* you tell me straight, Elaine? I've smelt a rat from day one, and I'm not talking about that rancid perfume of yours either.'

Elaine didn't much care for such a personal remark and was offended. Marty had bought her this perfume back from the Middle East on one of his business trips and she thought it was rather exotic. She would need to speak to her husband about this; she had expected questions, complaints even, but she didn't want a mutiny on her hands. What was wrong with these people? They were enjoying luxury of the like only those with the most-colourful imaginations and deep pockets could possibly envisage and yet *still* they were bitching and moaning like a bunch of spoiled children. Elaine McKenzie had genuinely believed that, in spite of the crash, or perhaps even because of it, they would actually be *grateful* to her and realise just how lucky and privileged they were to be alive.

'You don't like the island?' she mused.

'What's not to like,' he replied sharply, 'it's paradise. Only that's not the issue and you know it.'

'You really ought to explore a little more, go fishing perhaps, snorkling... Maybe you should spend the day at the spa, pamper yourself, or watch a film if sunbathing isn't your thing. And I trust the cuisine has met with your high expectations, although I understand you have already sampled *some* of the delights on offer.' She smiled again, the corners of her thin lips twitching.

Rupert's jaw clenched. What was she insinuating?

Elaine smiled, more affably now.

'Please don't look so concerned. Whatever happens on Pleasure Island stays on Pleasure Island, I can assure you of that.'

Rupert felt his blood run to ice. Did she know something? He struggled to hold his nerve but years of practise kept his core from collapsing.

'The only thing I'm concerned about, McKenzie, is getting out of this Goddamn place. And when I do –' his voice was low now, menacing even '– I'm going to file the biggest lawsuit in history against you and that twisted control freak you're married to, bankrupt the pair of you. You've endangered six people's lives, killed a pilot and *possibly* a flight attendant, poisoned us with God knows what, and have refused to allow us to make a phone call. Strip you of all that wealth of yours and you're nothing but a pair of common criminals.'

Elaine picked up the receiver from the old-fashioned antique telephone on the desk and held it out to him.

'Check for yourself. The lines are still down. Perhaps you haven't quite understood,' she explained slowly, her tone falling somewhere between disingenuous and patronising, 'this is a remote place Rupert, one that my husband has gone to great lengths to make inhabitable but nonetheless still quite rudimentary in parts; the storm destroyed all the cable lines we had put in. I'm afraid they were very basic and could not withstand the battering they took. I'm hoping they will be fixed imminently and that we'll soon have satellite signal again but you must understand, this is a slow place...the pace of life, everything is *mañana*.'

'I think you're forgetting just who're you're talking to.' Rupert raised his chin defiantly. 'You may think you can try and pull the wool over my eyes but really this would be a foolish mistake, *Elaine*.' He accentuated her name with a smirk. 'And frankly I'm sick of talking to the organ grinder; I want to see the monkey face to face.'

She dismissed his invective with an affable smile.

'Well, that makes two of us,' she said, 'but as I've already said, it's not safe for my husband to fly here while the weather is still inclement and we're on alert.'

Rupert shook his head. 'The breeze wouldn't even knock your hat off; it's been the epitome of calm ever since we got here.'

'That may be, and long may it continue, but until we have the official go ahead –'

'So what happens when the food runs out, hmm? When there's no more champagne and lobster? What then? And what about the staff? Don't they have families who'll be concerned about their safety, worried when they can't make contact home? You insult my intellect, McKenzie.'

'Your concern for the staff is touching, I must say. It'll just take a little longer to be fixed, and then … all will be well. These people have come to expect such inconveniences in life, Rupert, unlike you and I. A little more patience is perhaps a good lesson, no?'

Rupert chortled.

'Well, they do say you have to meet the wrong people to teach you the right lessons in life, so perhaps you've got a point.'

She laughed too now, a manic sound that made him feel edgy.

'I appreciate your cereal-box sentiment, Rupert, but I fear your profession has made you somewhat cynical and suspicious.'

'What's in the boxes?' He met her steely gaze with his own. 'Those big, black, metal boxes you gave us all at the start of the week … not to be opened until you get the "nod from God".'

'I really have no idea, I'm afraid,' she said, honestly this time. The boxes had been Martin's plan, a plan she hadn't been privy to. All she knew was that she was not to distribute the keys until he said so. Frankly she was as intrigued as her guest.

'I'm sure once the phone lines are up and running …'

'And what if that doesn't happen?'

Questions, so many damned questions. He was beginning to irritate her. But then she supposed she might be as uptight, too, if she had to carry around the secrets he did.

'Will we be stranded here forever, for the rest of our natural days. Will we *die* here, Elaine?'

This was not really an idea Rupert had truly contemplated but it had dramatic effect in driving his point home nonetheless.

Elaine McKenzie undid the top button on the collar of her shirt, white bespoke Givenchy poplin, and lit another brown, foul-smelling cigarette. She looked up at him. Stupid, pompous, arse of a man, she thought, forcibly blowing smoke in his direction.

'I never had you down as a drama *queen*, Rupert.' She sighed, her eyes fixed intently upon his own. 'Besides, I could think of a lot worse ways to go, couldn't you?'

CHAPTER THIRTY-THREE

The moribund silence during aperitifs was deafening as all but Mia convened, as they did every evening, underneath the shaded, canopied patio on the grounds of the McKenzie mansion. Set back into the mountains at some considerable height, the position afforded perhaps one of the most-stunning views over the entire island, though this was subject to debate; the sea stretched out eternally into the distance like a shimmering, rippled blanket, the last of the days rays dancing on the surface like silver fish, surrounding shady trees casting intricate black crochet shadows around them like a web. The sun was beginning to descend now, slowly slipping behind the water, dripping its final throes of maroon light into the giant expanse of sea.

'Not even a boat,' Angelika said, her thousand-mile stare unbroken by her words. 'Just the perfect colours of nature, untouched … the sun and the sea …' Her words trailed off along with her gaze.

'If only a blasted boat.' Rupert's brittle tone shattered the moment. 'I mean, have you even seen a boat?' He addressed no one in particular and no one answered. 'Exactly. It's been over a week and none of us has seen anything pass this godforsaken place, sea or air.'

The mention of a boat once again sparked something in Angelika's memory. She felt sure she'd seen one, possibly two at some point but couldn't quite remember where or when. Perhaps she really had just imagined it after all and it was just wishful thinking. Or perhaps they had been on the far north side of the island that was obscured from view by McKenzie's mansion and gardens. Access to this part of the island wasn't straightforward; you had to pass through McKenzie's grounds and on a descending rough trail that led down to the other side of the beach. She vowed to take a look soon.

'Ah, who gives a shit, man,' JJ said, swishing his long hair from his face in a *laissez-faire* manner, 'who cares where the fuck we are. It's awesome here. And we're supposed to be having fun, right?'

Jesus, JJ wondered, did this dude ever stopped complaining? From the moment JJ had returned to the island, Rupert had not stopped bitching about something or the other. Whiney-assed Brit. Like, what did he have to complain about anyways? After all *he* was the one who'd almost lost his freakin' arm in a plane crash. *He* was the one with his digits in fucking plaster unable to wipe his own ass properly. If anyone had cause for griping it was *him*, but why bother? It was done, right? He'd survived, they all had, and his arm would mend. Besides, this place was six-star luxury of the like he'd never see again in ten lifetimes. What's not to like? While admittedly the accident had been a real bummer, the welcome-home party in his honour had more than made up for it in JJ's eyes.

Still, in a way he'd wished he'd not put so much of that shit up his nose because it had clearly fucked with his head, he couldn't remember a damned thing and was pissed about it; he would've liked to have had some recollection of boning Billie-Jo. Whatever was up the British dude's asshole he didn't know but he was certainly enjoying himself.

'How's the arm, JJ?' Nate asked. He thought it best to make small talk with JJ, act ignorant to his obvious designs on Billie-Jo. There was every real chance JJ had already screwed her: a fact he was oddly resigned to and not nearly as upset about as he should've been.

JJ waved his good arm in the air.

'Never better, dude,' he laughed, amused by his own wit.

Billie-Jo giggled. Having already broken her promise to Nate – one she'd no genuine intention of keeping forever, if she was honest with herself – she felt the warm rush of the line of coke she'd secretly snorted before drinks circulate her bloodstream and resurrect the remnants of last night's intoxication on its journey. Nate had made her promise that she would never touch the stuff again after he'd seen the remnants of it on the table but the truth was she needed it to get her through the night, and most of the day, or so it had become anyway.

'Sound, I'm glad,' Nate smiled, 'we were pretty damned worried when they whisked you off on that light aircraft. I think I can speak for us all on that.'

JJ shrugged.

'Don't remember a thing, bro, from the moment we stepped on that plane and pretty much ever since, but hey, that's rock 'n' roll!'

'Or being drugged up to the eyeballs,' Rupert muttered.

Nate glanced at Angelika who appeared still deep in thought. Tonight she was dressed in a long, slightly translucent, white, maxi dress, the outline of her small breasts just visible through the flimsy, cotton fabric, delicate arms adorned with stacks of gold-and-silver bangles and her long wavy hair hung loose to her shoulders partially covered by a battered straw Stetson. She reminded him of a 70s love child, like she would rather have flowers in her hair than diamonds on her fingers and he resisted the urge to playfully steal her hat. It was childish perhaps but he wanted her attention, to see that smile of hers, get a glimpse of that snaggle tooth that did strange things to him. In direct contrast to Angelika, tonight Billie-Jo had opted to wear a Ca-valli playsuit in acid brights, the plunging-neckline and tiny-hot pants combo as ever leaving very little to the imagination.

In that moment Nate understood the adage that less is more. Undeniably Bee turned heads, but her 'look at me' sartorial ap-proach inevitably drew all the wrong kind of attention, but then again he suspected perhaps that was the whole point. Angelika, however, was more of a wrapped present that gave you just a subtle hint of the gifts inside. He thought about the time he had seen her naked, swimming down by the cove, lost in a moment of abandon, the curve of her belly and soft round hips, her small breasts and the arch of her back, her naked bottom as she had rolled over and over in the water …

'Admiring the view, babes?' Billie-Jo's voice dripped with sar-casm. She'd been watching her husband stealing glances at An-gelika ever since they'd sat down. Regardless of her own antics, the sight of Nate showing an interest in anyone else was enough to consume her with jealousy. Why the fuck was he interested in *her*? She looked at Angelika. Stuck up bitch looked like a fuck-ing gypsy who wouldn't know what to do with a cock if it came flat-packed with instructions.

'Perhaps we should tell them, Ange,' Nate said.

'Oh, *Ange*, is it now?' Billie-Jo sneered, unable to contain her green-eyed monster any longer.

Rupert's lips curled. Angelika and Nate were clearly on very friendly terms and admittedly it bothered him. Whatever else Angelika was still *his* wife. These bloody footballers all thought they were God's gift and could have any woman they wanted thanks to their extortionate earnings and the fame that went with it, yet he knew deep down Angelika was not the sort to have her head turned by either of those things. Rupert was about to say something when a scene from the previous evening flashed up in his mind of the tanned, toned, bronze Adonis that was Raj, naked and erect standing over him with that salt-white smile. Even if the man could've spoken, in that moment he'd not needed to say a word. He savoured the image for a moment until it was shattered by the recollection of Mia's shrill voice ringing like a round of bullets through his mind: '*Well now, aren't you two a pair of very, very naughty boys …*'

He took a slug of his Scotch miserably and kept quiet.

'Yes, *Ange*, do tell us,' Billie-Jo continued, her heckles raised. 'Bit over …' she struggled to find the word she as looking for and felt her anger accelerate. 'Bit over … friendly … bit … *familiar*, ain't it?' That was it! *Familiar*.

Angelika shifted awkwardly in her seat.

'Where's Mia?' Rupert asked suddenly. In spite of the knot of dread he felt in the pit of his stomach, he was surprisingly hungry and wanted to eat, only the rule was they all had to be seated before dinner could commence. 'That bloody woman would hold up her own funeral,' he muttered.

'She couldn't decide what to wear,' JJ said, slipping his hand underneath the large, wooden banqueting table and sliding it onto Billie-Jo's bare thigh. He was still feeling horny even after the quick knee trembler he'd had with Mia over the sofa the previous day, who, he'd noted hadn't seemed quite as into him as she'd previously been. This had pissed JJ off no end. Just a few days ago the old lady couldn't get enough of him. He was getting the brush off from Grandma and it wasn't a cool vibe, man. He put Mia's fluctuating libido down to her age; she was probably having hot flashes or something. Being aware that their relationship had been purely based on her wanting a bit of young cock and him wanting to cash-in on her celebrity status, he wasn't sure what his role was supposed to be anymore. Did this leave him open to being fair game, like if she didn't want the goods any more would she be down with him going elsewhere?

Billie-Jo flinched a little as his hand connected with her inner thing but didn't remove it. She had even more reason to keep JJ sweet now; he was her plan B, after all, and the way things were headed it looked like plan B may well soon need to be upgraded. Besides, she had the hots for him big time and was upset that she couldn't remember if they'd already had sex or not.

The night had been one long blank, pretty much, which was exactly the excuse she'd given Nate that afternoon when he'd finally questioned her about it.

'You were naked underneath that robe, Bee, not a stitch of clothing on … sprawled out on the couch opposite JJ and you'd been snorting coke! Coke, Bee! Where the fuck did you get it from? Did you bring it with you?' Nate detested drugs, always had. He'd seen what they did to people, likeable people who started out decent enough and then turned into monsters with enough toot inside them. He's seen that shit wreck careers, relationships and reputations over the years and as such had made a vow never to touch the stuff himself. Drugs really were for mugs. He'd suspected that his wife occasionally dabbled with the party powder but he thought she'd have more sense than to get a serious habit, or more vanity at least. Now, however, it was slowly dawning on Nate that he really didn't know the woman he'd married at all.

'I swear it was here when we arrived,' she'd explained, honestly this time, 'a fucking sugar bowl full of it. I never said nothing to you because I know how much you hate drugs, babe. Would you believe me if I told you it was just one line?' She'd looked at him with saucer-like blue eyes, her lips subtly pouting. She had been wearing one of his shirts, unbuttoned, the curve of her high-profile implants visible on her chest. She'd played with her hair childishly as she'd posed on the bed, twisting and curling a lock around her finger, only the innocent baby-face routine hadn't washed with him. When he'd looked at her that afternoon he'd felt nothing but indifference – pity, if anything at all. In contrast he only had to think of Angelika's face to experience the exact opposite emotion. It had floored him how he felt more for a woman he'd known practically a matter of days than he did his own wife, yet he could not deny it. His thoughts had left him both elevated and depressed and in that moment he'd wished he'd never met Billie-Jo.

'No, Bee, I wouldn't,' he'd replied sharply.

'Well, I'm not bloody lying!' she'd screeched. 'It was here, in the cabana when we arrived … and last night … I don't know.' She'd shrugged. 'It's just a blank, babe, all of it. I don't know what happened.'

This much Nate had believed. He'd felt like his own memory had exploded and random, scattered fragments had been all that remained. He had, however, recalled his wife getting rather familiar with the injured guest of honour.

'Anyway, you can't talk,' Billie-Jo had snapped, wrapping his shirt tightly around her naked body defensively, 'you were all over that fucking Angelika bird like a rash.' Attack had always been Billie-Jo's first form of defence, as in most cases involving a guilty conscience. 'Last thing I remember was you and her in the Jacuzzi making eyes at each other.'

Nate had shaken his head.

'Don't be ridiculous, Bee,' he'd replied feebly. 'We were all drunk. Besides, I'm surprised you even noticed … you were so busy getting all up on Joshua.'

Billie-Jo had laughed. Some jealousy. *Finally.*

'More your type, is she, *Ange*? Got one of them Octopus complexes, have ya?'

'Edipus,' he'd quietly correctly her.

'Yeah … that thing where you wanna fuck your mum or whatever it is.'

'She's not old enough to be my mother,' he'd said.

'Ooh, 'ark at you, defending her.' Billie-Jo was enraged. How could Nate possibly fancy that plain Jane in favour of her? While Angelika had been nothing but pleasant to her throughout the duration of their stay so far, and admittedly she had been the one to comfort her during the aftermath of the crash, she was hardly Nate's type. If anything she was a bit bland really, certainly not brimming with charisma, sexiness and charm like Billie-Jo was. 'Well, you know how the saying goes, why go out for McDonald's when you've got *filet mignon* at home?'

Nate began fumbling with the small plastic device in his pocket that Angelika's beady eye had spotted in the bushes up by the affinity pool.

'If I catch you doing coke again, Bee, I'll divorce you,' he'd said flatly. 'I think you should go into rehab when we're back in London. Get cleaned up, get that shit out of your life once and for all because I'm telling you, there's not room for both me and the coke. Do you understand? I want to help you, Bee; that shit will destroy you from the inside out.'

The D-word alone had sent fear down her spine like a hot rod. Rehab? Fuck that shit. There was no way she was checking into some glorified nut house to have it all washed out of her arsehole and brainwashed to boot. She knew friends who'd done the whole Priory thing, and they'd all claimed it was a living hell. Besides, her habit wasn't that bad, was it? He was overreacting as usual. She'd immediately switched to charm offensive mode. Allowing his shirt to fall open and expose her full-frontal nakedness, she'd smiled sweetly as she had walked towards him on her knees across the bed. Looking up at him, eyes wide, she had slowly begun to pull his shorts down and had taken him in her mouth.

'You won't, babes. I promise,' she'd said, winding her tongue around him, watching as his head rolled back onto his shoulders and he began to stiffen. *Catch me, I mean.* This was nothing a half-decent blowie couldn't put right, she'd decided as she set her lips and tongue to work around him. After a few seconds, however, he had sharply pulled away from her.

'Get dressed, Billie-Jo,' he'd said, his erection floundering. 'We'll be late for dinner.'

At dinner Nate ignored his wife's comments and kept his eyes fixed on Angelika's. Frankly he was done with Billie-Jo; if JJ wanted to take her off his hands, he was more than welcome to. In fact, he secretly hoped he would. They were better suited and far more compatible; they even looked right together, the inked-up rock muso and his Barbie-doll arm candy: perfect tabloid fodder. Much the same as Nate knew that Bee had only been interested in him for his status, the same could be said of JJ and Mia. It was obvious to everyone, no doubt even Mia herself, that Joshua Jones was only stepping out with her to garner publicity for himself. Mia Manhattan may be knocking on a bit and hadn't had a record out in years but she was still something of an institution, and the press had always had a fixation on her. They were both social climbers; users; cut from the same tree. It would be a match made in heaven for them, and hell for everyone else.

'Tell us what exactly?' Rupert's eyes shifted between the pair of them, butterflies gently settling upon his empty stomach.

'I think we should wait until Mia arrives,' Angelika said. 'I think this is something we should all see.'

CHAPTER THIRTY-FOUR

Mia Manhattan had always insisted on making an entrance wherever and whoever she was with, and tonight she'd decided would be no exception. In fact, in light of what had happened the previous evening, from what little she could recall, it was imperative she put on an unrepentant display of self-confidence, however mortified she felt. She was a professional after all. Mia closed her eyes. Images of limbs intertwining, naked flesh and erect penises – though whose exactly, she could not be sure – had been coming back to her in sharp, unpleasant, little flashbacks, growing in clarity throughout the day as the fog had gradually lifted from her mind. How on earth had she participated in something so … so sleazy? And with Rupert Deyton of all people! Had she gone temporarily insane?

Admittedly Mia had made some mistakes over the years, not least at the height of her fame when she'd indulged in a few extra marital flings predominantly fuelled by a mix of ego, booze and blues, but this particular epic moment of indiscretion spectacularly stole the cake. At the pinnacle of her career Mia's status had given her access to some of the world's most-eligible bachelors (and some not-so eligible), a position of which she had occasionally taken full advantage, though in hindsight sometimes it had also been the other way round. Dickie had always turned a blind eye to her 'misdemeanours', the ones he knew of anyhow, the golden rule between them being never to be seen in public with anyone else, never in the marital bed, and never, ever, give the heart along with the body. They'd even indulged in a few *ménages à trois* together back in the day. Well, it was the 70s, after all – who hadn't – and they had been so terribly young, beautiful and rich. But the truth was she'd only ever truly loved Dickie and had always stuck to the rules. How ironic then that in the end, all those years later, he would be the one to finally break them. Mia felt the resentment of her ex-husband's deceit resurface once more. Dickie had committed the ultimate betrayal by abandoning her at an age where it was particularly difficult for a woman to start again. She was past her 'best-before date' – even she had to admit it – and while she was still considered 'famous' of sorts, her kind of celebrity was no longer relevant to today's movers and shakers. She'd slipped into comparative obscurity, defunct, a dinosaur, trading on the last of her faded-and-jaded looks, staring down the barrel of fifty with the menopause knocking at the door.

Mia looked at herself in the mirror and swallowed back self-loathing; surgery could only do so much. She inspected her face critically, now predominantly constructed from fillers and Botox, the mini facelift she'd undergone as a post-divorce gift to herself giving her a smooth finish, but it couldn't turn back the clock. She looked like an older woman 'in good nick', as her father would've said, and had been forced to concede that there really was no magic procedure or potion to give you back what time had robbed you of. No matter how much shit they stuffed into your cheeks and lips, puffed you out, sucked you in or tightened you up, that fresh-faced 25-year-old plump, youthful, glow could never truly be recaptured, gone forever in an underappreciated and painfully short-lived moment in time.

Mia sighed heavily. Who would be a woman? she asked her reflection, engulfed in a moment of self-pity largely brought about by a post-chemical comedown that she wasn't even aware of. It was all right for men; they were allowed to age, many even improving with the onset of time. There was no ticking, biological clock for those bastards; no career breaks to have children, which subsequently left you out of the game and saw you spending the next ten years playing catch up while you watched your tits go south. There were no periods or menopause for them, watching as a slew of younger, more-fertile females climbed up the ranks behind you, nipping at your heels and your husbands, waiting to replace you while you hurtled towards tan tights and TENA Lady, gradually becoming invisible.

Mia thought of Billie-Jo then, the girl's pretty-but-not-especially-remarkable face flushed with the springy firmness of youth, although she had seen the hardness behind the girl's eyes that had made her think she would not age well. Though they were aesthetically very different and she hadn't much taken to the girl, Billie-Jo reminded Mia of herself in some ways. There was a steely determination to her that she related to, even admired. Billie-Jo had only one destination in mind: planet fame. She was hungry for it, focussed, obsessed with getting on, just as she herself had been and Mia sensed the girl was prepared to do anything to get it. No doubt she'd do well as a result of such tenacity, but the industry, even more cut-throat and unforgiving than it was in her heyday, would chew her up and spit her out by the time she hit thirty, if she wasn't careful.

Mia sighed as she thought of JJ and Billie-Jo's brazen flirting in the Jacuzzi the night before; they'd been all over each other like herpes. She supposed she had been somewhat jealous, though not especially surprised. They were, after all, far more suited age-wise and she had to admit that they made a rather-attractive pairing. Why hadn't she just invited the girl back to their cabana – there was enough of JJ to go round, after all – instead of getting embroiled in a Caligulan nightmare with

Rupert and Raj? Stupid, *stupid* old woman, she berated herself. Still, she imagined she couldn't feel any worse than Rupert did right now; if she was filled with dread and regret, she could only imagine the velocity of his self-loathing. Good job his wife had been preoccupied with Nate and vice versa, by the look of things. It had not escaped Mia's watchful eye that Nate Simmons had something of a crush on Angelika Deyton and the very idea left her tickled pink.

'Oh, the wicked webs we weave when we choose to deceive,' she muttered underneath her breath. Last night had been little more than one, big, seedy, swinger's convention. Perhaps it had been too much for them all, the sun and alcohol and the euphoria of Joshua's return, a touch of post traumatic-stress maybe, or perhaps it had been something else, something in the air, something she couldn't quite put her finger on. Whatever the reason for their collective tawdry antics, she suspected tonight's dinner would at very best be awkward as hell.

Well, she supposed, attempting to find a bright side, at least she now had something else on Deyton, another stick to beat him with; every cloud, eh? Upper hand or no, she'd still rather none of it had happened. But what's done is done and can't be undone, Mia told herself and not for the first time in her life either. No regrets; well, perhaps just the one. She thought of her child in her arms then, the moment she had held her son for the first time, an image that hadn't faded along with her youth and looks and fought back tears.

Pulling herself together, she smoothed her hands over her neat, shiny, black bob, a trademark style she'd had since time immemorial. 'Well, if it ain't broke, don't fix it,' as her stylist would say. Bobs never went out of fashion, even if her music had; look at Anna Wintour and Jennifer Anniston. She adjusted the tie on her Diane Von Furstenberg animal-print, silk-jersey-

and-chiffon wrap dress, opening the neckline a little to reveal a more cleavage and then pulling it back again. Why was she bothering to try and compete? She'd come here with a boy young enough to be her son, grandson even, and it was clear that he had turned his attentions on Billie-Jo. Who was she kidding anyway; she had been nothing more than a stepping-stone to Joshua Jones. Now that his band was signed to a high-profile label she had been expecting his gradual departure, and frankly he had served his purpose anyway – only it was a bit bloody brazen of him to openly make advances on another woman, another much *younger* woman, and married at that, right under her nose.

Feeling sidelined, Mia slipped on a 54-carat diamond Boodles bracelet and spritzed her entire body with Shalimar perfume. She slipped on her 9-inch Louboutin snakeskin sandals and sighed heavily once more.

'The show –' she said, smacking her red lips together one last time in the mirror '–must go on.'

CHAPTER THIRTY-FIVE

'Finally,' Rupert deadpanned as Mia sashayed to the table in a bluster of strong scent and bravado, 'No, really, Mia, there's absolutely no need to apologise, none of us are hungry or anything.'

'Good evening, Rupert,' she shot him a sideways glance, 'and may I say how well you look this evening. Clearly a little fun last night did you the power of good.'

Rupert swallowed hard. He had expected this – an evening of subtle, snide innuendo from her – and she had not wasted a moment.

'You too, Mia.' He flashed her a mock gracious smile. 'And you're only an hour late as a result of it. Miracles do happen then?'

'Fuck you very much, Rupert.' She grimaced as she took her place next to Joshua on the vast wooden table which had been lavishly decorated with a stunning selection of floral displays that wouldn't have looked out of place at a royal wedding. 'Beautiful flowers,' she remarked, admiring the lush, exotic, fragrant, fresh mix of bird-of-paradise, bottlebrush, heliconia, frangipani, flame of the forest and blue passion flower. 'A different display every evening.'

Angelika's mind clicked. Mia was right. As someone who had an account with a local florist, delivering freshly cut blooms on a weekly basis to display in her vast hallway, she had over time become versed in recognising certain plants and flowers. She had all but explored the island in its entirety now, with the exception of the far north side and had spotted everything from fragrant orange trees to lurid red poppies, a few wild irises and even an apple blossom or two, but she had not come across anything quite as exotic as the assortment adorning the dinner table. These were tropical flowers that couldn't withstand harsh heat. So where had they come from?

As anticipated the atmosphere was tense and despite her misgivings about any more damned alcohol consumption, Mia decided to accept the champagne cocktail immediately offered to her to take the edge off her nerves. Just the one wouldn't hurt, although she'd pretty much said the same thing last night and look where that had got her. She inwardly cringed. Still, at least she hadn't been the only one whose moral compass had gone askew; there was some small solace in that, at least.

'I'd be careful drinking that, Mia,' Nate warned her gently.

Mia met his eyes, such a handsome boy, well, man really, and his countenance was always polite and gracious, so unindicative of his profession. The football players she had come across (quite literally, on a couple of occasions) had always been rather brash and uncouth. This one, however, had been well brought-up, she could tell.

'I do appreciate your concern regarding my alcohol consumption, darling,' she said, 'especially in light of –' she stopped herself short '– but I don't think Betty Ford will be spinning in her grave anytime soon … hair of the dog and all of that, cheers!' She raised her glass to him.

'Who's Betty Ford?' Billie-Jo asked.

'Seriously, Mia, please don't.' Nate looked at her ingenuously and she felt a pang in her chest.

'We've reason to believe that the alcohol may be spiked, Mia,' Angelika cut in.

Regardless of their concerns, Mia contrarily took a sip anyway before carefully replacing her glass on the table and lighting a cigarette. Rupert pulled a face, as if the woman didn't smell bad enough. He was convinced he could still detect that perfume of hers on his skin even after scouring himself in a hot shower for some considerable length of time.

'Spiked, you say?' Mia humoured her but the truth was such a thought had actually crossed her own mind already, albeit fleetingly. 'With what, by who?'

'Are you serious,' Joshua piped up. 'Like, why would anyone wanna spike our drinks, man?' He supped on his ice-cold beer as if to make a point he didn't buy a word of it. These people were so damn paranoid they seriously needed to lighten-the-fuck-up.

'The same reason were all being watched.' Angelika gave Nate the nod and he duly threw the little black plastic device in the middle of the table.

Mia looked at it blankly.

'Am I supposed to know what this is?'

'Nate and I found it in some bushes down by one of the pools. It was buried deep in the brush. I saw it flashing.'

Billie-Jo pushed JJ's hand from her thigh where it had rested from the moment she'd sat down.

'*Nate* and *I.*' she mimicked Angelika's voice, her jealousy resurfacing. 'Oh, yeah? And what the fuck were you two doing in the bushes together anyway?'

Rupert was inclined to encourage her line of questioning, only he remained reticent in case it somehow sparked Mia's vicious, loose tongue. That Angelika may or may not have been getting up to something with Nate Simmons was humiliating enough but it was nowhere near the league of the shame he would experience if Mia's mouth ran off with her, which, given her track record, was more likely to be a case of when than if.

'It's really not like that, Billie-Jo,' Angelika said, her face flushing, attempted to explain, 'it's not what you think, we were just –'

'Which is exactly what people say when it *is* what you think, or else why would they be thinking it?' Billie-Jo said, not sure even she understood what she meant herself. She turned to her husband sharply. 'Are you fucking her or what, Nate?'

At least the girl didn't sugar-coat it, Rupert thought to himself, watching Mia's reaction closely. He was on tenterhooks; it was like waiting for a firework to go off.

Raj suddenly appeared at the table and silently attempted to refresh their glasses.

'No, thank you. Not for me.' Angelika shook her head as she covered her glass with her palm.

'Me, neither,' Nate followed suit, more out of respect for her than anything. She really seemed to believe there was something suspect going on, and while he agreed there were questions to ask he wasn't entirely as convinced as she was. At least not yet.

'Jesus, you *are* paranoid.' JJ laughed. 'Like, seriously? Spiking our drinks …? You guys have been watching too many detective shows. I know you journo types are paid to be inquisitive, man, but you're freaking me out with this shit.'

Rupert felt his body stiffen as Raj brushed past him, not daring to look up until he had passed. Mia was staring at him, an eyebrow gently raised. *Don't you dare, you evil bitch.*

'Well?' Billie-Jo eyes were aflame.

'Of course not!' Angelika was bright red, hot behind the ears, her heartbeat accelerating along with her awkwardness. 'We just happened to be there at the same time and …'

Rupert allowed a small snort to escape his lips.

'I didn't fucking ask you, did I?' Billie-Jo snarled at her in full-blown confrontation. 'I was talking to MY husband.' She glared at Nate.

JJ watched as the drama unfolded. Jeez man, he was surprised she'd had the front to say anything at all after what they'd got up to themselves, or at least what he *thought* they'd got up to because he still couldn't damn-well remember exactly. The girl had some kahunas, but then again he liked a bit of fire in a chick. Maybe he'd get the chance to fuck her again, and remember it this time.

'No, Bee,' Nate replied, calmly, 'it's like Ange said. She was already at the pool when I got there and, well, then she spotted this, didn't you?'

Angelika nodded, thinking it best not to speak lest it set Billie-Jo off again.

'Ooh, *Ange*.' Billie-Jo's crimson face was clashing with her neon onesie now. 'You're talking like you've known the woman your whole fucking life instead of five minutes.'

'Don't, Bee. OK? Just don't,' Nate warned her.

'Don't what?' She was standing now, her body forming a Z-shape, attitude oozing from every pore. 'Don't make a scene …? Don't upset anyone … ? Don't object to you being all over Miss Prissy Pants over there like you were last night, though fuck knows why. It's not like she's got anything I ain't.'

'Aside from a little class,' Mia muttered under her breath.

'What was that, Grandma?' Billie-Jo had turned hood. 'Got summit to say, have ya? Spit it out then but be careful your false teeth don't come with it.'

Mia laughed, which disguised her outrage.

She looked at Nate pitifully. 'You need a muzzle and licence for this one in public.'

Angelika was mortally offended, though did her utmost not to let it show. Miss Prissy Pants …? Jesus, was that really what other women thought of her?

Nate shot up out of his chair.

'Sit down, Bee. NOW!' he said, raising his voice.

JJ gently pulled Billie-Jo back into her seat.

'Chill out, babes,' he whispered to her, not wanting the argument to get round to the point where he might be expected to explain himself. He had hoped they could all be kind of British about it, and sweep it under the carpet. Like, if you didn't remember it, it didn't happen, right?

Mia glanced at Rupert expecting to see a self-satisfied smirk on his face, but he wasn't smiling.

'Going back to the camera,' Nate said, his voice returning to normal pitch and the matter at hand, 'I'm no expert but it looks to me like it's some kind of recording device – some kind of camera.' He would deal with Billie-Jo later. For now her histrionics would have to wait; this was more important.

Rupert picked up the device and inspected it closely. Admittedly he suspected Nate was right. It did rather resemble some kind of camera, closed-circuit CCTV or the like, not that he was any expert but as an educated guess …

'And you found it down by the swimming pool, and removed it?'

'Yes, though I suspect I wasn't supposed to find it at all.' Angelika looked at her husband expectantly.

'It's just a security camera, Angelika,' he said dismissively. 'No doubt the place is full of them.'

'If it's just a security camera, why go to the bother of hiding it?'

'Jeez man,' JJ said, 'it's just a CCTV camera. For protection, what else?'

'Hidden in a bush?' Nate asked, without looking at him.

'You said yourself that you thought our drinks had been spiked.' Angelika leaned forward across the table towards her husband. 'None of us can remember last night. I know I certainly can't. Can you?'

Billie-Jo was listening now, her temper gradually dissipating. The conversation was starting to creep her out at little.

Rupert sighed, wearily.

'So what are you trying to say, Angelika?'

'Yeah, Miss Marple,' Billie-Jo joined in, 'what are you saying?'

Ignoring Billie-Jo's remark she looked at her husband with visible disappointment. She had hoped he would have her back on this.

'I don't know exactly.' She felt herself flush once more. 'Just that ... well, something's not right, Ru. I've ... just got a bad feeling, that's all.'

'Maybe it's your conscience,' he remarked, instantly wishing he hadn't. He just couldn't help himself, especially where Mia was concerned. While he was wholly accustomed to airing other people's dirty linen in public, his own was a different matter altogether. The last thing he wanted was to open Pandora's Box, or any damned box come to think of it. He just wanted to go home, play polo and forget this nightmare ever happened. Pleasure Island had thus far proved to be nothing more than a bittersweet misnomer.

'Anyway,' Rupert said, dismissively, 'I've had it out with Elaine McKenzie already and she's assured me the phone lines will be up and running shortly, in which case the moment they are whoever wants to can arrange to have themselves flown off this place and back to civilisation. I'll charter a bloody private jet myself if I have to. So in the meantime try and keep a hold on that wild imagination of yours, won't you, *darling*?'

Rupert had shot her down in flames and Angelika felt humiliated. In hindsight she should've known better than to rely on his support. Any opportunity to belittle her he seized with alacrity these days. The rare moment of intimacy between when he had held her in the bathroom had been very short lived and only served as a painful reminder of how it had once been between them. But her intuition told her that her sense of unease was not without foundation. They were being watched; she was convinced of it.

'Ah, at last,' Rupert said as he watched the staff appear with an array of steaming silver platters, 'dinner is served.'

CHAPTER THIRTY-SIX

'Champagne!' Elaine McKenzie clasped her hands together in appreciation as her husband instructed the private on-board butler to open the bottle of Krug Clos d'Ambonnay 1998, a snip at $2000 a pop, quite literally. She watched as he meticulously decanted it into two cut-crystal Tiffany flutes, a light, oily sheen forming on his brow thanks to the intense midday sun and the fact that he was dressed in full formal livery as per strict instructions from his boss.

'Congratulations, darling,' he said, 'you're doing a stellar job so far in taking care of things. I'm proud of you.'

Elaine preened; a compliment from her husband was akin to a shot of amphetamine. She took a slurp of her vintage champagne. She never usually drank alcohol – she liked to keep her wits about her at all times – but today she would make an exception. Mart had returned from his business trip in the Far East and had chartered one of his yachts allowing them to spend a little quality time together. The boat, aptly named '*Small Change*', at 40 meters long was one of McKenzie's most understated motor yachts in a progressively impressive fleet that he'd collected over the years like Tonka toys. Today he'd chosen this particular vessel specifically for her distinct lack of wow-factor and unremarkable aesthetic, much like his wife he supposed. He was hoping to keep a low profile as they cruised around the island of Santorini for the afternoon; it wouldn't do to alert the paparazzi of his whereabouts. With breath-taking hypocrisy, McKenzie loathed having his privacy invaded. He was also mindful of drifting too far south of the island where there was the potential to be spotted on the horizon. He had handsomely paid off the locals to avoid them taking any route by boat that could bring them into clear view of Pleasure Island, lest his prestigious guests attempt to flag them down and so far they had willingly complied. Ahh, the power of the pound, or Euro in this case.

'So, how was the Far East?' Elaine enquired, 'I trust you've been well looked after these past few days?'

Indeed he had. In fact once the business side of things had been wrapped up he had done a little detour via Thailand on his return journey and had been thoroughly entertained by a selection of prostitutes for some 36-hours straight. Martin McKenzie gave a small, satisfied smile. He did so appreciate the Thai whores, they were so much more submissive than their Afro-Caribbean or Eastern European counterparts, therefore allowing him to fully indulge his most debased desires without too much objection. He enjoyed degrading the diminutive women, instructing them to engage in all manner of deviant sexual behaviour and had paid them well to whip each other's naked bodies until they'd screamed out in agony.

'Business as usual,' he lamented, 'although the hospitality, as ever, was unfaultable.'

Elaine adjusted her functional swimsuit; it was cutting into her meaty thighs beneath her sarong.

'I take it you've been keeping abreast of events on the island?' she enquired carefully. Her husband would expect a full debrief and this made her a little nervous. She was concerned he would consider his earlier praise as having been somewhat premature.

'Of course,' he said, clicking his neat, manicured fingers high in the air. 'Hors d'oeuvres,' he barked to the liveried butler, who by now was perspiring profusely in the 95-degree heat. McKenzie placed a small, white bag tied with ribbon onto the table.

'A token of appreciation, my dear,' he explained, 'for your most loyal service.'

Elaine giggled, an act that appeared somehow incongruous with her dour, pinched features.

'Really, Marty, you shouldn't have.'

'Call it gratitude for keeping things ticking along nicely …'

Elaine was stunned; this was high praise indeed.

'Well, it's certainly been interesting. I mean, who'd have thought that the lawyer was gay! I have to say I didn't see that one coming – and neither will his wife by the looks of things.' She gave a wry smile. 'You think you know someone …'

'Ah, but does anyone really know anyone?' he replied.

'Husbands shouldn't have secrets like that from their wives; it's morally reprehensible,' she said, oblivious to her own situation.

McKenzie inwardly smirked.

'Not like us, dear, all our cards on the table.'

The McKenzies had been actively swinging throughout their marriage, although he had kept her in the dark as to the full extent of his sexual desires which had become increasingly more depraved with each passing year. Besides, Elaine really didn't do anything for him anymore. That particular ship had sailed long ago. These days she was little more than a lackey to him, a PA he had doing his dirty work and who he occasionally bent over the bedpost to scratch an itch. His only real regret was that Elaine hadn't given him a child; he'd always liked the idea of having a son in particular, someone to own completely, even down to their DNA, but it had never happened. The woman was baron, in every sense.

She began to open the gift, her stubby unpainted nails clumsily fiddling with the ribbon.

'Perhaps you have that intuitive thing,' she said, 'whatever they call it these days … gaydar!'

'Yes, perhaps!'

As it was McKenzie had known all along about Rupert Deyton's sexual persuasions. He had made it his business to, or his team of people had. They had been instructed to dig up as much dirt on him as possible, on all of them, and at the first flash of a fat wedge of green Mia's old chauffeur had coughed the lot. Money really was a universal language that needed no interpretation. Throw enough of the stuff at people and they'd tell you *anything*, however sordid or unflattering. It had taken months of meticulous research undertaken by a privately hired investigative team to unearth his chosen guest's most unpalatable secrets. And soon, in the ultimate final act, he planned to spectacularly reveal exactly why.

'Oh, Marty.' Elaine gasped as she opened the box and saw the Cartier watch inside. The huge encrusted diamonds forming the circumference of the rose clock-face glinted back at her in the sunshine. 'It's … exceptional.'

Her heart sunk faster than the boat's anchor. She would never wear it; it was it was far too ostentatious – vulgar even – although hell would freeze over before she ever told him as much. In all the years her husband had been gifting her jewellery he had never once got it right. As a result she often forced herself to adorn the presents he had given her on special occasions, mindful of hurting his feelings. Only she needn't have worried; he didn't have any. McKenzie had, as usual, given one of his PAs (young, always attractive, usually willing) a wad of cash and instructions to pick something out for his wife; unbeknownst to her he had never once personally chosen a present for her in over two decades.

'Put it on then,' he commanded and she duly obliged. It looked ridiculous, its overstated opulence merely highlighting the rest of her plain, unremarkable ensemble.

'Thank you, Marty,' she said, admiring it with a smile, which didn't quite reach her cold, dead eyes.

Having already lost interest in the watch, he changed the subject. 'And what about the girl, eh? She gave an exemplary performance with the masseur, I must say. The Super Eight were most impressed.'

'She's been putting on quite a show with Joshua, too.' Elaine swallowed her champagne with a raised eyebrow, wondering if now was a good time to discuss the conversation she'd had with Rupert. It had been troubling her.

Elaine McKenzie was a formidable woman; she did not suffer fools gladly and was capable of being an extremely fierce adversary, tricks she had learned over the years from being married to a monster like McKenzie. She gave very little of herself away in social company, unless of course that company happened to be her Lord and Master – and husband. Very little either fazed or scared her; Marty managed to do both.

'The Deytons concern me,' she finally said, 'they're asking questions, Mart. Too many questions. And –' she paused nervously '– and it seems they've somehow cottoned on to the fact that their drinks were spiked the night of the party; they're suspicious.'

Sweating like a man on trial for murder, the butler appeared carrying a solid silver cloche containing a mouth-watering selection of hors d'oeuvres including freshly prepared sea urchins wrapped in Parma ham, gazpacho, crabmeat-and-sour-cream Asian spoons and foie gras-sprinkled Beluga-caviar filo parcels.

McKenzie inspected them with a fiercely critical eye before giving him a disdainful nod to serve.

'Did you hear what I said, Mart? Angelika and Rupert Deyton – they've been asking questions about the night of the party, about the drinks, the telephone lines … they're growing impatient. They want answers about the crash, about the staff, everything, and they want *you* to answer them. I mean these people, aren't idiots – the Deytons especially it seems.' She swallowed more champagne and debated whether or not to inform him that she'd seen Angelika locate one of the hidden cameras down by the infinity pool. There were at least 200 hundred of them spread across the entire island, all strategically placed and expertly hidden inside and out, but that bloody inquisitive bitch had somehow managed to locate one of them, which she now had in her possession and had shown to the rest of the guests, potentially throwing the whole operation into jeopardy.

McKenzie smiled at his wife amiably. Elaine was worried, he could tell and he knew exactly why, because he'd been keeping a close eye on her, too. She had fucked up, royally. And now she would have to pay.

'Screw them.' He waved a hand dismissively, the diamond signet ring he always wore on his left pinkie catching the light with the momentum. 'What about Manhattan? What's that bitch had to say?'

Elaine bristled. She knew very little of her husband's relationship to Mia Manhattan other than what was already in the public domain. Intuitively she suspected there was more to it than that but had never dared to ask. If her husband wanted her to know something he would tell her. Experience had taught her this lesson the painful way.

'All that woman is concerned with is a mirror and the minor she brought along with her, although it does seem like she has gone off the boil with him somewhat, now that his attentions are on the Simmons girl.'

Her husband was deep in thought; she could tell by the way his right leg was swinging slightly over his left. 'And obviously she and Rupert Deyton don't see eye to eye, not that you'd have known that after they'd ingested all that MDMA though.' She smiled wickedly. 'They were really somewhat *friendly* after that.'

'Exactly how much of the stuff did you give them, Elaine, on the night of the party?'

'Only what you'd instructed me to,' she replied quickly, feeling the unease of his eyes upon her. 'A little more to the Deyton woman, like you said. But I'm not a doctor, Mart; everyone's metabolism is different. It's not an exact science. How was I to know how much would be too much, that it would make her sick … start to ask questions …'

McKenzie looked his wife in the eyes and wondered for a moment if it wouldn't be just to beat her to death with the cloche there and then, throw her overboard and claim that she had drowned. He could buy the butler off, no problem. The idea quickly gathered momentum in his mind. She was practically superfluous to needs now anyway, now that he'd thought he'd found a potentially willing and suitable candidate to replace her in the young British woman who was part of the Super Eight. With a little grooming he felt she really would make a rather satisfactory replacement. He thought about the moment she had taken him in her mouth that time they had met, savoured it in his mind for a few seconds. Elaine had had her day and in truth he'd been looking for a reason to emancipate himself from her for some while; she was getting old and sloppy and had let him down. What had started out as a little bit of 'fun', a pastime in which he and few like-minded souls could indulge their voyeuristic perversions – not that McKenzie viewed them as such – plus exact a little revenge in the process, now had the potential to blow up in his face, thanks to his wife's incompetence.

'They'll be a mutiny if we're not careful,' she said, relaxing a little now that it seemed he wasn't as furious with her as she'd anticipated. Only she had lulled herself into a false sense of security and unwisely continued to seal her own fate. 'Unfortunately I think Angelika may have found one of the cameras, too.' She chewed her thin lips tentatively, watching as he devoured another of the delicious hors d'oeuvres, waiting for his reaction.

McKenzie looked past his wife and out onto the blue behind her. Such a perfect day, he thought, cloudless sky, high sun, the temperature perfect, for him at least.

'She found one the cameras?' He feigned surprise as he looked over at the butler hovering in the background. The man was the colour of lobster and he found his obvious discomfort somewhat gratifying.

'Yes, though as yet she hasn't come to me about it … she just shared the information with the others. Anyway, it's speculation,' she said, downplaying her concerns. 'It could easily be a security camera, which is pretty much what the general consensus was among them all, anyway. They put it down to paranoia.'

'I see.' McKenzie kept his simmering rage contained. He'd personally guaranteed the Super Eight total anonymity throughout this whole experience, protection from any culpability and he could not afford a scandal of which there would undoubtedly be one if that journalist bitch went to the press with her accusations and suspicions. Potentially he could be investigated, even go to prison if she had enough proof, an idea that he refused to entertain for longer than a few diabolical seconds. Damn Elaine. He had made the fatal mistake of trusting her to keep things tightly under control, keep the guests in a euphoric, submissive, relaxed and happy state in which they could be easily manipulated, and she had fucked up royally. He looked at her, concealing his utter contempt carefully behind his bespoke-made gold-mirrored Ray-Bans.

'Perhaps we should open the boxes,' he said casually. 'I think it's time.'

Elaine's eyes flickered with relief. He wasn't angry with her.

'Ok,' she agreed, 'I'll do it tomorrow night.'

'Grand,' he said.

'Fancy a swim before lunch, dear?' he asked.

'Why not,' she said, a little surprised by the sudden suggestion. Marty wasn't much of a swimmer.

McKenzie stood and Elaine duly followed suit.

'Ladies, first,' he gestured with a florid bow.

'It's the perfect spot for it, at least,' she remarked, looking out
onto the small, sheltered cove where they had moored for lunch.
There wasn't a soul insight. 'The water looks divine.'

'Doesn't it,' he agreed.

The butler watched from his assumed position as the pair
abandoned the dinner table he had so carefully and lovingly prepared earlier. His vision was becoming a trifle blurred from the
sweat that was dripping into his eyes, causing them to sting, and
he felt a touch lightheaded. He needed some water, to take off
this damned, heavy, woollen, coat-tail and loosen his bow tie.
He was beginning to feel rather unwell and somewhat unsteady
on his feet.

'I'm terribly curious to know what's in the boxes, Mart,'
Elaine said with her back to her husband as she untied her sarong and made her way to the edge of the boat, peering over the
steps that led down into the inviting crystal-clear water below.
Her husband followed close behind. 'Rupert Deyton has been
asking me about them and I genuinely couldn't give him an answer. Told him I had no idea myself which is true.'

'Well, you know what they say about curiosity, dear,' he said,
raising the silver cloche and smashing it down onto the back of
her head with considerable force, watching as her skull exploded, a deep burgundy pool of liquid quickly forming on deck.
There was a look of genuine surprise and despair etched onto

Elaine McKenzie's face as she half-turned to look at her husband before falling sideways into the water.

'It killed the cat,' he said calmly.

McKenzie made his way back to the table, popping the last hors d'oeuvres into his mouth before replacing the cloche back on top of the silver platter and wiping his wife's blood and brains from the rim with a starched white napkin. Sighing, he turned to the butler, only he wasn't there. His eyes darted across the boat.

'Ah!' he said, spotting him. Poor bastard had passed clean out in the heat dressed in all that heavy livery and was lying in a hot sweaty heap on the deck. Still, this made things much easier all round.

'Sorry about this old chap, nothing personal,' he said to him as he took the man by the wrists and began dragging him towards the edge of the boat and straining to roll his dead weight over the side, 'but you look like you could do with cooling off.'

CHAPTER THIRTY-SEVEN

'What *are* you doing, Angelika?' Rupert watched her as she manically searched the cabana, pulling back the shutters and rifling through the closets.

'I don't know exactly,' she replied, shortly. 'Looking for cameras, I think.'

Rupert shook his head. This place had sent them all round the twist.

'Well, I highly doubt they'd be under the bed,' he mused as she scrabbled about on all fours, searching the mattress.

'So, where do you suggest I look, Columbo?'

Rupert snorted softly.

'Look, I realise things have been a little … odd since we've been here, but aren't you taking this all a little too far? I mean, spy cameras? Whatever McKenzie's reasons for this madness, filming us without our permission … well, it's a very serious criminal offense. Even a man like McKenzie wouldn't do something so insane. He'd never get away with it. Besides,' he said, pouring himself a finger of Scotch, 'why on earth would he want to film a bunch of no marks like us?'

'Speak for yourself,' she shot back. 'Anyway, you said it yourself: the man's a control freak, a maniac …'

Angelika noted the whiskey glass in her husband's hand. It was 10.30 am. Rupert was worried about something; in all their married life she had never seen him imbibe alcohol before lunch. He clocked her staring at his glass.

'It's enough to turn a man to drink all this –' he gestured around him to nothing in particular '– and all this secret camera talk is making me nervous, Angelika, so please stop it. Anyway, I'm on holiday.' He drained his glass and poured himself another.

'If you've nothing to hide, then there's nothing to be worried about,' she said. 'And I have no idea why McKenzie would want to secretly film us but I'm convinced that's what he's been doing.' She padded defiantly across the wooden floor in her bed shorts and white vest, her nipples visible through the cotton fabric. Her long hair was messily piled high onto her head and her face make-up free and lightly tanned. It was no surprise Nate found her attractive really, Rupert thought objectively; she was the antithesis to his high-maintenance fake wife. A woman like Angelika would be a refreshing change, he imagined. Funny how people always seemed to want the opposite of what they already had. He swallowed his Scotch and closed his eyes as the fiery liquid hit his empty stomach and spread its warmth throughout his churning guts. He hoped to God Angelika wasn't really onto something with this whole camera debacle. If, and he held onto the word hopefully, her suspicions had grounds then someone somewhere would have seen *everything*. The very idea made him want to gulp back the entire bottle of single malt in one hit.

'I may go fishing today,' he suddenly announced. 'There's really not much else we can do until the phones are back up and running, which Elaine has said will be any day now. May as well make use of what's on offer while we can.'

'And how will you go fishing without a boat?' *The boat* ... damn it, she just couldn't locate inside her mind; it was so frustrating. 'Don't you think it's odd that there are no boats here on the island, not even a fishing one, especially since McKenzie collects the damn things. You'd have thought he'd have one of this yachts moored here at least, something to take us all out on and impress us.'

'I don't know, Angelika,' he answered sharply, sick of all her questions, 'perhaps he meant to, perhaps the storm prevented it, or perhaps you ought to stop being so damned paranoid and asking so many questions. Anyway, I was thinking of navigating the rocks down by the beach, they go quite a way out, I'm bound to get a catch eventually.' The idea of some peace and solitude appealed to him. He would grab some fishing gear, request a packed lunch and finish this bottle of malt while he was at it. It was becoming an increasing struggle to look his wife in the face. Besides, he wasn't sure he could stomach another day of Mia Manhattan's supercilious remarks and knowing smirks. The fear of the woman opening that great gate of hers had him on tenterhooks the whole time and he couldn't relax. Jesus, he looked forward to going home, getting back to reality, back to hiding behind a mask of middle-class respectability. He was even looking forward to making a return to the courtroom, not to mention the bloody polo playing field where by rights he should've been in the first place.

'Suit yourself,' she said, 'I think I'm going to go on a little trek around the island again. I haven't been up beyond the house yet, on the north side. It's the only part I haven't seen.'

'Looks pretty baron to me,' he said, 'nothing but rock and brush.'

'I'd still like to check it out, see what's up there. I may have missed something.'

'Rather you than me, Poirot.' Rupert's eye was drawn to the black box on the kitchen table. It had been sitting there on the shiny marble kitchen counter almost mocking him since their arrival and he'd had a terrible feeling from the beginning that whatever was inside it was not going to make for a happy discovery. Perhaps he would take it down to the beach with him and throw it off the rocks, yet his own curiosity, he knew, would prevent him from doing so. He took another sip of Scotch, only he wasn't convinced that it was helping. If anything it was facilitating his maudlin thoughts and burgeoning ill ease. If they could just make it through these last few days without any more drama, then he would never complain about anything again. Not even his wife. What had happened here on the island would stay here with it when they left and with a bit of luck he would never be confronted with any of it ever again. He comforted himself in the knowledge that soon this experience would simply be a distant memory, with the exception perhaps of one remissible sin – that he would *not* forget, though it would be a whole lot easier if he could forgive himself for it. The sketchy encounter with Raj flashed up inside his mind once more, of the man's strong, soft hands and glistening lips as they'd wrapped themselves around his …

'Do you think it's a good idea to go trekking alone?' he said, shaking the memory from his head. 'It's not as if you can call anyone should you run into difficulty. And you'll need to take plenty of water.'

'Careful, darling, you almost sounded as if you cared then.'

'I do care, Angelika,' he said. And although he knew he might not show it as he should, he wasn't lying.

Angelika was preparing herself to shower now and had wrapped herself in a robe before stepping out of her bedclothes. Although Rupert had seen her naked body more times than she could count she suddenly found herself feeling more self-conscious than usual around him. Something had shifted between them, an uncomfortable distance she could not explain.

Rupert, a touch inebriated now, followed her into the en suite and stood behind her as she began to wash her teeth over the ornate mirrored basin with one of the state-of-the-art electric brushes. If he could just force himself to desire her again, make love to her and *feel* something …

'What are you doing, Rupert?' She looked at him in the mirror as he slipped the robe from her shoulders, exposing her nakedness. 'You're drunk!'

'So what?' he said as he ran his fingers down her arms.

Angelika was shocked; this was the first time her husband had displayed any intimate intensions towards her in over two years. As little as a few weeks ago she would've welcomed such attention with open arms, and legs, but now she wasn't so sure.

Willing his erection on, Rupert closed his eyes and thought of Raj as he parted his wife's thighs. She did not stop him but instead watched his face carefully in the mirror as he entered her from behind, moaning in pleasure until she too closed her eyes and followed suit. After a moment he turned her around, lifting her by the buttocks into the shallow basin and she wrapped her legs around him, arching her back, releasing her long hair from her top knot as he began to kiss and nibble her small breasts, caressing her neck with his hand as he pushed himself into her, harder, building momentum, his breathing deep and shallow in time with hers.

'Oh, go … yeah … yeah …' she found herself softly saying, her orgasm building as she watched the defined, thigh muscles working in his legs, 'fuck me …'

Only she wasn't really talking to him; she was imagining her husband was Nate Simmons, that it was *his* body pressed against her own causing her to groan with pleasure, *his* lips around her nipples, her legs around *his* strong, taut abs …

Pulling her down onto all fours upon the soft sheepskin rug in the en suite, Rupert held her by the waist as he slid into her from behind once more, only it wasn't Angelika he was entering with increasing frenzy, it was Raj. It was Raj's dark cocoa-butter skin he felt beneath his fingertips. It was the scent of Raj's masculine sweat that he could detect lingering in the air between them. He felt Angelika's body buckle beneath him as she came in a crescendo of short sharp bursts, her muscles contracting around him, squeezing. He was close himself now, the power of his orgasm almost paralysing him as it finally took hold.

'Ahh, yeah, that's it … you bad boy … you dirty, fucking bad boy …'

Angelika froze, wondering if she'd heard him correctly.

'What was that you just said?' She sat upright, her heartbeat refusing to slow down. Rupert was hyperventilating, beads of sweat dripping from his brow. Thinking of Raj had made him come like a train.

'What?'

'"You bad *boy*"? That's what you just said to me … "you dirty fucking bad *boy*"!'

Rupert panicked, his post-coital euphoric rush evaporating rapidly like liquid nitrogen.

'Did I? I'm sorry,' he apologised, 'I … I was talking to myself. I meant *I'm* a bad boy … *I'm* a dirty …' His voice trailed off. The moment had passed and reality hit him like a wrecking ball. Angelika blinked at him as she reached for her robe and quickly covered herself up. She wasn't entirely sure what had just happened, but she didn't feel particularly good about it.

'I'm taking a shower,' she said quickly, which he rightly translated as 'please leave immediately'.

Rupert stood, awash with self-loathing and made to leave but turned to her at the last minute.

'I'm sorry, Angelika,' he said.

'What was that?' she called out, pretending she hadn't heard him; she was already in the shower, washing the scent of him from her skin. She felt strongly that whatever had just taken place between them during those few minutes of spontaneous passion shouldn't have. It had felt so wrong, so disconnected. While physically present, spiritually she had been somewhere in her mind, *with* someone else. And what was clearly evident was that so too, it seemed, had her husband.

CHAPTER THIRTY-EIGHT

The woman stepped out of the shower and began to roughly towel dry herself in haste. As usual she was running late for a lunch appointment with her 'boyfriend', and as usual she didn't really give a flying fat fuck, only she sensed she'd been pushing her luck with him lately and this was enough to ensure she got a move on – not because she gave a shit about him, because she absolutely didn't. In fact, like all of her 'boyfriends', she felt very little other than contempt for him; he was a pathetic, snivelling, woefully inadequate ass-clown, but she couldn't afford to lose him, not yet anyway. As one of her most lucrative 'boyfriends', their long-standing 'understanding' had allowed her to give up her day job and purchase a bijoux apartment in Belgravia, not to mention fund her recent investment into Martin McKenzie's latest pay-per-view 'project'. Reason enough to be on time then, if there was any.

Their arrangement was pretty straightforward; he was older, married, loaded and liked to be dominated. She was comparatively younger, single, enjoyed administering pain and humiliation and relieving him of a large chunk of his salary for the privilege. As well as the most generous, this particular 'boyfriend' was also the most subservient, pathetically grateful to be punished for the smallest of imagined slights. And she did so enjoy his pain and suffering. There was, however, one downside to this agreement and it manifested itself in the form of an obsessional intolerance towards bad punctuality. The man went completely crazy if ever she was late to a 'date', and in a spectacular moment of complete role reversal would tear her a new arsehole if she was even as little as five minutes overdue. It pissed her off but she was wise enough to suck it up and make sure it didn't happen too often. She had a good number going with this particular piece of shit and didn't want to jeopardise it. After all, it beat working for a living.

She began to dress herself from the assortment of attire on the bed starting with his favourite Agent Provocateur stockings, followed by some French lace *ouvert* knickers, a waist-cinching corset and a skin-tight leather Alaïa dress that accentuated her dangerous curves. It was Thursday, Doggie day, where he liked to fashion a diamond studded collar while she dragged him around the bedroom on a leather leash before strapping him into a harness and whipping his naked behind senseless. She particularly enjoyed the part where she got to make him eat Pedigree Chum from a plastic pet bowl as he crawled around the floor like the pathetic turd he was. She stepped into her 8-inch studded Louboutins and reminded herself to walk through as much of the city's grime on her way to meet him; it gave her such sublime pleasure watching him licking the shit off her red soles with his tongue. Occasionally, weather-permitting, they would take a trip out to the countryside together afterwards to some infamous beauty spots, admire the great outdoors before indulging in a little dogging. They would alternate between being the voyeurs and putting on a show for other doggers, depending on what mood grabbed them. Personally she preferred the former. Voyeurism was her bag, although she could be anything you wanted if the price was right; dominant, submissive, as deviant as you were prepared to go; a good all-rounder, she like to think. Still, she enjoyed Thursdays; her 'boyfriend's' particular preferences allowing her to release any pent-up aggression she had accumulated during the week.

She opened the door to her closet of tricks, which contained all manner of devices and fetish gear, and reached for the 12-inch rubber dildo he liked her to use on him so forcefully. The man really was a sexual degenerate, as well as a respected private medical practitioner to the exceptionally rich and famous. The contrast always made her smile; if only his patients knew what their hero surgeon's sexual perversions were when he cut them open, they'd probably have a heart attack right there on the operating table. Still, it took all sorts.

Applying blood-red lipstick and spritzing herself with his favourite perfume – Rive Gauche, a somewhat old-fashioned smell that apparently reminded him of his grandmother – and mindful of the time, she grabbed her black, studded, Jimmy Choo shoulder bag and made to leave, only her eye caught the laptop that was open on the dressing table and she hesitated. *Just a little sneaky peek …*

She threw her handbag down onto the bed and went over to it. Clicking on the screen she inputted her unique pin code and smiled as the action came into view.

'Well, hello my little friends, and how are we all today?'

Admittedly she was finding the antics on Pleasure Island utterly addictive. Watching it had become something of a guilty pleasure, money well spent as far as she was concerned. This was her kind of show, a soap opera for voyeuristic sadists, one in which the actors had no idea they were performing for the cameras and where she also had a say in the storyline. After a hard day's spanking and administering humiliation, she had enjoyed nothing more than coming home, switching her computer on and catching up on the events unfolding on the island. She had been particularly pleased with Billie-Jo's storyline. The masseur seduction scene had been her idea and McKenzie had executed it with great aplomb, hiring in a professional to get the job done. The feeling of control it had given her to watch the action unfold had been enough to bring her to an earth-shuddering orgasm; the sex itself was largely immaterial, it was the feeling of the power she had over a bunch of complete strangers that really flicked her switch.

Now she was keen to see what could happen next between Angelika Deyton and Nate Simmons and had been busy thinking of various scenarios that would potentially push them together. She wondered what the rest of the Super Eight might be concocting, rightly sensing there was competition between them as to who could push things the furthest, whose ideas would make it to the final cut and get the almighty McKenzie's seal of approval.

Playing with other people's lives was such fun. It was only a pity she couldn't throw on some PJs, order in pizza and spend the afternoon tuned in. Listening in on a conversation that Mia and Angelika were having about Rupert while simultaneously watching Nate Simmons use the bathroom – he was certainly blessed in *every* department – she wondered which of the other club members were watching and checked the bottom left corner of the screen to see who was currently on-line. Inadvertently she dropped the lipstick she'd been holding. That couldn't be right, she thought, frowning. Her phone suddenly beeped, startling her. It was her 'boyfriend' demanding to know where she was.

'Chill the fuck out, arsehole,' she muttered, her eyes transfixed on the bottom left of the screen. It was clearly a mistake. McKenzie had given their private exclusive little club the moniker it had for obvious reasons – there was just eight of them. In which case, she wondered – a feeling of unease suddenly settling upon her tightly encased stomach – how come it now said: 'users: 112,478'?

CHAPTER THIRTY-NINE

'Aren't you worried about getting caught?' Billie-Jo stood opposite him in the sea, the water waist height, the sun and light breeze causing her big nipples to harden like diamonds beneath her gold-and-silver Agent Provocateur Mazzy bikini. 'What if we're seen?'

'Isn't that part of the buzz?' He grinned at her. 'Anyways, why the fuck should I be worried? I'm not the one who's married.'

'Yeah, but you came here with Mia, as her … I dunno, what would you call it, squeeze? Date? Grandson impersonator?'

'Cheeky little fucker you, aren't you?' He laughed. 'Mia's all right. She's been pretty good to me really, I s'pose. Helped introduce me to some influential people, you know, producers and stuff, guys who've worked with some big names, people like Pink Floyd and Led Zep and those dudes. I can't say that stepping out with her hasn't helped my profile either. She might not have had a tune out in years but man, the paps still gotta thing for her.'

'Led Zep? Never heard of them,' she said dismissively, 'and for that you have to fuck her in return, right?' She swished her long, blonde hair back from her face in dramatic fashion. 'Must be like eating out your nan's pussy. Eww.'

She pulled a face and Joshua laughed again. She was so crass, and so damn sexy with it. He kinda liked it. Billie-Jo was all front, literally, yet he sensed there was more going on underneath the bravado. Still, at least you always knew where you were with a girl like that. He hated all that second-guessing bullshit most chicks played. This one was nothing if not direct. It made a refreshing change.

'I'd rather eat out *your* pussy.' He raised his eyebrows at her, his dirty, blond hair hanging just below his shoulders, giving him the look of a young, fairer Jim Morrison. 'Anyway, a boy gotta do whatta boy gotta do, you know what I'm saying?'

She did. Exactly.

'Your cast is getting wet,' she said.

'The only thing I give a shit about getting wet is your pussy,' he retorted.

'Ha, dream on,' she said. 'Anyway, like you said, I'm the married one.'

'So what you doing here then, sugar tits?' he replied cockily, 'checking out the view?'

Billie-Jo snorted. She did so love an arrogant man, one who presented her with a challenge; she thrived on it.

'I'm asking myself the very same question,' she replied facetiously, placing a hand on her hip. Actually she knew very well why she had agreed to meet JJ down by the beach at such an early hour and why she had stomped round the cabana that morning creating as much of a din as possible; she wanted Nate to know that she was off somewhere; she wanted him to search for her and ideally find her, catch her alone with JJ. It was a test. If he came looking for her then she knew all was not lost and that he did really love her.

At the end of the day that's all Billie-Jo had ever really wanted; to be loved. She knew deep down that life had hardened her, making it almost impossible for her to obtain true intimacy with anyone. She trusted no one, not even her own mother. In her experience, both sexes were out to get her in one way or another; men to use her for sex and women because men wanted to use her for sex. She couldn't win but she sure as shit was gonna put up a damned good fight.

Billie-Jo was of the school of thought that you had to leave someone before they left you; first sign of trouble and she was out the door and into the arms of the next awaiting car crash. It had been a diabolical pattern all her life but the alternative – giving herself to someone fully, loving someone unconditionally – was far scarier. Einstein she may not have been, but she was far more emotionally intelligent than she cared to let on. She understood that in order to have a successful relationship with a man, with anyone, she would need the balls to tear down her barriers and learn to love herself. After all, if she didn't love herself, then no other fucker was going to. And that was the bit she struggled with most. When you'd been treated as if you were a worthless piece of meat since you were a kid, it was difficult not to believe it in the end.

Nate felt sorry for her but she sensed he did not love her. How could he? She hadn't exactly made it easy for him. They wanted different things; him to settle into obscurity, become a nobody and her polar opposite. He'd experienced fame and it had left him with a bitter aftertaste. For her it had been like nectar on her tongue; it had made her come alive, feel special for the first time in her life, the attention giving her flaccid self-esteem a permanent hard-on. Was it so wrong to want to be adored, to be admired by others, celebrated and imitated? People were always saying how fame and money doesn't make you happy. Like, who the fuck were they kidding? Did Kim Kardashian have a miserable face when papped on board her husband's yacht? Did she fuck.

Nate Simmons was the closest Billie-Jo had ever been to a man – hell, to anyone really – and yet she knew relatively little about what really made him tick. He had been kind to her, though. He'd never given her a slap like some of the others had; never unashamedly engaged in all that roasting and prostitute-shagging that many footballers were want to do, humiliating their wives and girlfriends in the process. On the contrary he'd been respectful, placid even, tolerant of her often-destructive behaviour, supportive while she'd been starting out in the glamour game, even encouraged her. Their marriage had been sedate and relatively drama-free – and yet, she felt ashamed to admit, largely boring as fuck because of it. Unless she was in an intense state of emotional agony or a crazy euphoric high then Billie-Jo wasn't feeling anything at all. She didn't do middle ground. Nate was just too good for her, and she was just too good at being bad.

Although she sensed her marriage was little more than a farce coming apart at the seams, Billie-Jo had felt irritated with her husband's indifference towards her since they'd arrived on the island, his attention somewhat pre-occupied by that fucking toffee-nosed writer-bitch, *Angelika*. She still couldn't get her head around that one, the possibility that he might actually prefer the likes of *her*. It had been the first time she'd been faced with genuine competition for any man's affection, let alone her own husband's, and it was not sitting well with her. One thing Billie-Jo had always relied upon was being the prettiest, most-desired girl in the room and it had been a huge bruise to her ego that Nate's attention seemed to have become focussed elsewhere. Still, Joshua Jones was shaping up to be a suitable replacement if needs be, and besides, she actually quite liked him.

JJ splashed her playfully, lunging forward and linking his good arm around her tiny waist.

'Cool it, mister,' she said, backing off, 'all breakages must be paid for.'

JJ laughed. 'Bit late to start playing it cool, isn't it? Like, that ship sailed a few nights ago, babe.'

Billie-Jo snorted in a bid to disguise her nervousness. Had it, really? If so, then she sure as shit had no recollection of it.

'So you say, Jose,' she remarked, 'but then again we were all off our tits. Cement would've had a job getting hard the amount of shit and liquor we shovelled up our noses and down our throats.'

She was right; he couldn't quite remember the details himself, but he was pretty sure *something* had taken place. They'd woken up naked next to each after all.

'What do you think of Angelika?' Billie-Jo asked, interested to get JJ's take on her. 'Do you think she's attractive?'

'Sure,' he shrugged, 'bit girl-next door for my personal preference, but pretty enough face and a smokin' hot lil' body. Could have a bigger rack, I suppose, but I wouldn't kick her out of bed, put it that way.'

'No, please, tell me how you really feel! And you wouldn't kick *anyone* out of bed,' she said, mildly aggravated. 'You're just a dog with two dicks like the rest of them.'

'And you're just the kinda bitch this dog likes. Anyways, don't be jealous, you're much more up my boulevard, babe. She can't hold a candle to you, which is a good job really I suppose since you might go up in flames with those plastic tits.' He laughed. He liked this chick, genuinely. There was something about her.

'And here was me thinking you yanks didn't do ironing.'

'Irony, dumb ass.'

'That's what I said!' she shot back.

'Ironing is what you'll be doing for me soon enough; keeping my shit nice to take on tour with me; I can just see you in your house coat now, hair in curlers, sucking my dick while you press the creases in my jeans.'

'Piss off!' she screamed at him. 'Anyway, who the fuck under fifty puts creases in their jeans anyway?'

The both started laughing now, hard, and for a split second Billie-Jo found herself lost in the moment, enjoying herself for real. She'd never laughed like this with Nate before; she wasn't sure she'd ever laughed like this with anyone.

'Anyway, screw that, you won't need to do the ironing; we'll pay some maid to do that shit for us, I'll be needing you for *other* things though.' He was face to face with her in the water now, their noses almost touching, his hands linked around the small of her back. She felt his hard on pressing against her wet thigh.

'Oh yeah, and what's that?'

'Every good frontman needs his woman on tour with him, keep the groupies in check,' he said, his lips almost upon hers. She felt his breath against her face, warm and salty, the faint smell of cigarettes and alcohol.

'I'd be on tour *with* you?'

'You bet your ass,' he whispered, their eyes locking. 'You think I'd leave a knockout like you at home? No freakin' way!'

Billie-Jo smiled happily. Now this was much more like it she thought as he finally pressed his lips against hers, his warm tongue gently sliding inside and meeting her own. 'But I'm married …' she was about to say but thought better of it. Oh fuck it, she said to herself, surrendering fully to the kiss, pressing her large, hard nipples against his lean, tattooed torso, it wasn't as if anyone was watching.

CHAPTER FORTY

Andrea Levinson was weighing up her lunch options. Should she risk the wrath of her bitch-face editor by doing a Pret run and treating herself to a no-bread sandwich (surely a misnomer, right?) and a skinny, soya latte, or snatch five minutes to grab a fat bacon-buttie and a cappuccino from the subsidised staff café for a fraction of the time and cost? Fuck it, she thought, scanning the immediate vicinity for any signs of her formidable superior. Cath Redmond had eyes like a shit-house rat and had been known to time her taking a piss in the past, let alone daring to go out and grab some sustenance. But what the hell, it was Friday and she was feeling reckless. Besides, it had been a relatively slow news day so far, at least on the entertainments desk. Aside from a boy band member 'allegedly' caught smoking a spliff, a Victoria's Secret model spotted on board Leo Di-Caprio's boat (yawn), a pathetic spat between two Z-list glamour models which resulted in the loss of some hair extensions, and another non-story on Kim Kardashian's ubiquitous arse, there was little doing. She clicked on her Facebook page, time to check up on this weekend's events she thought, spying the familiar red envelope that told her she had mail. One was from her friend and fellow entertainment hack, Sam Long, asking if she was going to be at the party tonight, the launch of some new reality TV show that listed an entire cast of other reality TV shows rejects, aptly titled 'The Biggest Loser.' She supposed she might go; after all it wasn't like she was inundated with better offers and at least that was her evening meal sorted. No wonder she was struggling get into her size 12 jeans, she'd been practically living solely off a diet of canapés and cheap fizz for the past two years.

She clicked through the remaining messages, scan-reading them for relevance and importance and then ... hang on, what was this?

The message was from 'Facebook user' suggesting that whoever had sent it was no longer active. Odd, she though, opening it. There was no private note, just three links. Spam, she decided, absentmindedly clicking on the first. Her thoughts returned to her lunch dilemma once more; maybe she'd swerve Pret after all and get some soup from Eat instead. That was healthier, wasn't it? She'd need something a bit hearty if she was going to go to this party and sink half her body weight in Zinfandel. She tugged at the roll of fat on her belly that she was convinced wasn't as substantial this time last year, but then she supposed this time last year she'd been on the heartbreak diet. She'd lost nearly three quarters of a stone thanks to her lousy cheating bastard ex and had summarily put it straight back again on the moment she'd been over it. *Totes annoying.*

The link opened and a title appeared on screen: 'Billie-Jo Gets a Massage'. Andrea stopped thinking about her lunch immediately. Billie-Jo? The only Billie-Jo she knew was the Z-lister wag that was married to the ex-footballer Nate Simmons. She'd given Billie-Jo quite a few column inches recently, documenting her outrageous outfits and nightclub antics; the girl was a train wreck, a rampant attention-seeker with a pretty face and big tits. Intrigued, she watched the silent sixty-second clip of Billie-Jo having no holds barred hard-core sex while getting a massage. It was definitely Billie-Jo, all right; she'd recognise those double D's anywhere. After all, they'd been on display enough times.

Shocked, yet utterly compelled, Andrea quickly clicked on the second link with alacrity.

'Nate Simmons scores again', the rudimentary font appeared on screen. The footage was grainer this time forcing her to squint. It appeared to be some sort of party, outdoors, a Jacuzzi just visible in the background, again there was no sound or colour. Nate's image came into view closely followed by a woman with long, dark, blonde who was most definitely not Billie-Jo. The pair of them were close, smooching she supposed you could call it, and then they kissed and then …

'Holy fuckamoly!' Andrea knocked her handbag from her lap and onto the floor in haste as she sprang forward in her seat, her heart knocking into her ribs. She recognised the woman! If she wasn't mistaken it looked very much like the newspaper's revered columnist, Angelika Deyton. She didn't know the woman personally but she'd seen her strut in and out of the office on numerous occasions full of her own piss and importance, smug in the knowledge that she was getting paid more than anyone else on the job.

'No fucking way!' What the fuck was Angelika Deyton doing kissing Nate Simmons? And where in God's name were they? Come to think of it she hadn't seen Angelika Deyton in the office this past couple of weeks. Was she on holiday? Her appetite dissipating rapidly. Andrea blinked at the screen. Pret could wait; this was all the fodder she needed!

She replayed the 20-second clip again. This time she noticed another woman in the background, an older woman with a bobbed haircut who struck her as familiar but who she couldn't quite place. Andrea gave a little squeal of delight. If this little gem didn't see her on a fast-track promotion then nothing would! The third link directed her to what appeared to be a live webcam. What in God's name was this? A woman was sunbathing on a lounger, drinking from a giant coconut, nothing too risqué. She watched the screen enthralled as a man who appeared to be Nate Simmons came into view and took up a lounger next to her. The screen suddenly switched to another man showering – he was naked, of course, lathering himself up, his image unclear due to steam from the hot water. Keen to get a ganders at the goods, Andrea held her breath and when he eventually stepped out of the shower she gasped. She was sure it was Joshua Jones, Sony's new signing and her most-current celebrity crush, she'd recognise those tattoos anywhere. Sizing his naked form she raised an eyebrow; so the rumours *were* true then.

'Got anything interesting for me, Levinson?' Cath Redmond suddenly appeared behind her, startling her, her expression the usual mix of smug displeasure.

Andrea smirked.

'As a matter of fact, Cath, I think I might have.'

CHAPTER FORTY-ONE

John Kirkbride, group editor of the *Daily Voice*, replayed the footage for the fifth time in succession. Stroking his chin, he contemplated his professional and moral dilemma carefully.

'Well, there's no denying it's her,' he said, 'unless she's got a doppelgänger somewhere.'

'Well, they do say we all have one of those though, don't they?' Andrea added enthusiastically. She was incredibly excited to be inside the group ed's office for what had effectively been the first time in her career on the *Voice*.

Cath shot her a disdainful look that told her to shut up.

'And this came directly to you on your private Facebook page, right?'

'Yes,' she answered brightly, mentally spending her pay rise in Ibiza already.

'And you've no idea of the recipient?'

'None. It just said from Facebook User. I'm guessing that means whoever sent it is no longer active. Probably created an account for the purpose of sending it and then deactivated it.'

'It may well have been sent to my account as well,' Cath interjected, 'although I haven't checked it yet.'

Andrea stiffened. Her bitch of a boss was trying to snatch the credit for herself. Well, this was Andrea's break and she wasn't about to let anyone steal her moment of glory, let alone Rancid Redmond.

'Well, check,' Kirkbride said quickly. 'We'll get IT onto it pronto. We need to authenticate the source.'

'Agreed,' Cath seconded his motion.

But then she would agree to selling her own eyes, thought Andrea, if it meant looking good in front of the big cheese. She really was an epic glory-seeking arse kisser.

'Where do you think they are?' Cath asked. 'Some kind of holiday destination? Did Ange say where she was going?'

John Kirkbride chewed his lip silently, deep in thought.

Ange? Cath was talking like they were bloody besties or something, the stupid cow. Andrea knew that Angelika Deyton had rarely uttered a word to her, and that Cath was always commenting on what a snooty bitch she was. Hypocrite.

'And you do know who the other woman is, don't you?' Kirkbride said. 'The one with the dark hair. That's Mia Manhattan. She's obviously there, wherever there is, with that toy boy, Joshua ... whatshisname she's been stepping out with ...'

'Jones,' Andrea added helpfully, 'Joshua Jones from *The Dopamines*.'

'Yes ... Jones, and no,' he said, 'she didn't say a word about where she was going. Has anyone tried calling her?'

'Straight to voicemail,' Cath replied. 'Phone must be switched off.'

'So who do you think is filming them?'

Kirkbride shook his head.

'No, idea. Is this stuff viral already?'

'I'd say so if it's being circulated on Facebook,' Andrea said, basking in her own self-importance.

'Right. And has any of the competition got wind?'

'Very likely, I'd say. And if not, then it's only a matter of time.'

'Are we going to publish?' Cath asked with nervous excitement.

John Kirkbride got up out of his seat and began to pace the scruffy office which was indicative of his appearance. A greying, old, school hack in his mid 50s, Kirkbride had been at the helm for the best part of ten years and despite appearances suggesting otherwise, he was a seasoned news hound and consummate professional, a grass-roots journalist who had been reluctantly dragged kicking and screaming into the age of social media.

'Publish what exactly? I mean, what's the actual story here? OK, so there's a sex tape. We can definitely run with that. But as for the rest – the footage – it's just a bunch of people on holiday.'

'Well, not exactly just a bunch of anybody,' Cath reminded him.

'But she's one of us, Cath.' Kirkbride ran his nicotine-stained stubby fingers through his grey thatch, his grubby shirt stretching across his expanding middle, gained courtesy of one too many boozy lunches at Langan's on expenses.

'Careful, John, you almost sound like you care.' She smirked at him.

'You need to see the archive footage,' Andrea said, 'there's loads of it. Some of it's pretty interesting. I'd say, albeit in my professional opinion, that these people have no idea they're even being filmed.'

Cath scoffed. *In my professional opinion.* She had pairs of knickers older than this girl, fucking little upstart.

'Moreover, the name Elaine McKenzie has been mentioned a few times.'

Kirkbride's eyes widened and his heart began racing inside his chest, no doubt playing havoc with his high blood pressure.

'Martin McKenzie's wife? Jesus, you think this could have something to do with the McKenzie's?'

Andrea shrugged. 'It's possible. Looks like a luxury holiday resort on an island somewhere … maybe he invited them there and somehow someone's got hold of the security footage.'

'From the bathroom of their private accommodation? Hardly.'

Kirkbride could smell a story from a thousand paces. And this one stank like overripe Camembert. Shit was going down and anything that featured Martin McKenzie – one of the most famous, powerful and revered men in the business – was potential dynamite. That's why he needed to think how to play his hand carefully.

'I want the whole team on this,' he said, 'I want the source of the link located and I want you to get in touch with friends and family to find out just where the hell this bunch are and what they're doing there. I want that sex tape authenticated – who, what, why, when and where – and try and identify the massage guy, and get an interview, yeah? Let's report it but not publish until it's been through a thorough legal OK. I'm serious, now. This story is potential gold dust and as we all know the bigger the story the bigger chance of making a major fuck up. If McKenzie's involved in this then we need to tread careful, and I mean tiptoe … 'kid-gloves' careful. If McKenzie sues then none of us will ever work again. Report the facts; don't speculate or get creative, and don't try and flesh out the bones, you got me?'

Cath and Andrea nodded, their combined adrenalin almost palpable.

'And what about the footage of Angelika and Nate Simmons?' Cath asked. 'What do we do with that?'

Kirkbride kissed his teeth and thought about lighting a cigarette but was mindful of setting off the blasted alarm. He still hadn't managed to remove the damn thing's batteries, despite numerous attempts.

'Jesus.' He exhaled deeply. 'I mean, Ange is our girl, Cath.'

Andrea bristled. Why wasn't he addressing her? *She* was the one who'd found the damn story after all.

'And she's married...' As dedicated as he was to the job, Kirkbride liked Angelika Deyton – liked her a lot, in fact. He'd often fantasised about what she might look like in her underwear, bent over his desk, though he was not deluded enough to think such a fantasy would ever supersede anything other than the realms of his imagination. She was a bloody good columnist too, responsible for a healthy chunk of reader revenue and had won the paper some prestigious awards. Could he afford to potentially fuck her in the arse, for want of a better expression? It would need to be managed carefully.

'Whatever happened to fair game?' Cath flashed him an almost-Machiavellian smirk.

Bloody ruthless bitch would sell her own son down the river for a headline, he though. He supposed that was why she was his second-in-command.

'At least this way we can be … sympathetic towards her?' Cath said.

'What's the splash today?' he asked without giving her a straight answer.

Cath rolled her eyes.

'The Killer Food Bug scare …'

'Drop it,' he said abrasively. 'Get to work on this before the bloody *Sun* get their nasty gnashers into it.'

Cath beamed. 'Yes, boss.'

He stared at the pair of them.

'Well, go on then, what are you waiting for? Fucking Christmas is months off yet.'

He waved the two women from his office and ran his fingers through his hair, a small cloud of dandruff visibly swirling in the sunlight that was streaming in through the cheap, plastic blinds. He shut them immediately.

'Oh, and Angela …'

'It's An*drea,*' she corrected.

'Well done.'

Andrea almost exploded with pride, savouring every moment of her immediate boss's seething displeasure.

'Thanks.' She grinned.

Closing the door behind them, Cath Redmond clapped her hands together loudly to alert the chattering news team.

'OK, everybody,' she boomed authoritatively, 'hold the front page.'

It was a line she had been waiting to say her whole career.

CHAPTER FORTY-TWO

The sound of the doorbell ringing sent a jolt of foreboding through Angelika's chest. She waited, her breathing shallow, adrenalin coursing. Her palms were sticky with sweat and she rubbed them onto her light, floral, Chloé playsuit before pushing the bell once more. Nothing. She pressed it again, harder this time and rapped on the door with her knuckles, the momentum of which caused it to open a crack.

'Helloooo, is anyone here? Elaine?' Angelika hesitated as she tentatively stepped inside into the vast hallway, the acoustics of the shiny wooden floor amplifying her slow, careful footsteps. The house was eerily quiet, the silence almost sinister. 'Elaine!' she called out again. 'It's Angelika Deyton … I need to talk to you. The door was open …' There was no answer.

'I need to talk to you about this camera, Elaine … and about the night of the party. It's important.' Her voice rang out like gunshots through the open space, bouncing off the walls and echoing back at her. 'Elaine, are you there? Anybody?'

Spurred on by her need for answers, Angelika pushed open a door to her left and peered inside. It was a study of some sort; there was a large wood and leather desk with books stacked neatly on surrounding shelves. A giant vase filled with fresh flowers scented the entire room, brightening up what was otherwise an austere setting. The swivel chair was a little way back from the desk and turncd to the side as though someone had abandoned it in haste. She spotted a telephone, one of those old-fashioned

50s types, like a film prop on the desk, and immediately went to it and picked it up. There was no dial tone and she sighed, replacing the receiver with a click. The desk was neat and in order. A notebook, pen and laptop computer, closed, sat perfectly symmetrical next to Post-it notes and other office paraphernalia. A vintage, leather, Chesterfield sofa was positioned in the corner of the room; not even the large, velvet, scatter cushions made it look inviting. An oscillating fan squeaked and churned above her, adding to the general feeling of unease.

Angelika ran her fingers over the laptop and, glancing at the door, she opened it and pressed the button to boot it up. Suddenly she heard voices. Springing back from the desk, she quickly took cover behind the door and listened; there were people outside in the hallway.

'So where is she then?' a deep, male voice enquired.

'No fucking idea, bro,' another male voice answered. 'She was around yesterday and then … hell, I don't know where the old bitch's gone.' Their accents sounded British, perhaps one was American.

'Yeah, well, she would want to turn up soon because it's pay-day tomorrow.'

'She's probably gone to the island for something. Is her car still here?'

Car? Angelika's breathing was so loud she felt sure they would hear it from behind the door.

'Yeah, it is. I checked this morning.'

'And she said nothing about taking a trip out anywhere?'

'Dude, I told you. I saw her this morning and haven't seen her since.'

'Did she look like she was going somewhere?'

'She was wearing a swimsuit, that's all I can remember. And she told me to keep an eye on things until she was back.'

'So she was going somewhere?'

'Well, I guess so. But she said she'd see me later and to keep a check on the Deyton woman. That's it.'

'I'd happily keep an eye on the Deyton woman.' One of the men chortled. 'Looks like she hasn't been fucked properly in a decade.'

Angelika was shaking.

'Yeah, and we know why! Anyway, Billie-Jo's more my cup of tea, bro, though right now I wouldn't say no to anyone. With all this tits and arse on display, I got a permanent hard-on.'

'Same be said for Raj as well, eh?'

The men laughed.

'Yeah, how come he got to break the rules and fraternise with the cast?'

'Must've been in the script, though I have to say, keeping up this silence in front of them 24/7 has been the biggest challenge of my fucking career. Every time that Rupert snaps his fingers and demands a Scotch I wanna tell him in no uncertain terms where to stick it, only by the looks of things he'd probably enjoy it!'

'Ha ha, you're not wrong. Still only a few more days and we're done. I'll be glad to get out of here. This place gives me the shits, man. Weirdest gig I ever done. Anyways, we getting the boat into town tonight or what? Grab a few drinks, check out the fresh pussy … there's bound to a new planeload by now. You on for it?'

'Yeah, man, why not? I'll see you round the back of the harbour around midnight, yeah?'

The voices grew distant.

Script? Fraternising with the cast? Boat! So she had been right about what she'd thought she'd seen. There *was* a boat on the island! She was sure it had to be somewhere on the north side of the island, obscured from view. Angelika's mind was revving like a car stuck in first gear. And the mutes weren't mute at all. It was just an act they'd been putting on. And Elaine had a car – transport off the island. She had been lying to them, keeping them here under false pretences, little more than prisoners, albeit in five-star luxury. But in God's name, why? She took the camera from her pocket and looked at it. *Cast* … one of the men had used the word 'cast'. Could it be that … ? But before she could continue her thoughts, the door to the study opened.

CHAPTER FORTY-THREE

From the confines of his private residence, Martin McKenzie watched Angelika Deyton hiding behind the door of his study downstairs with a smirk.

A message flashed up on his screen. It was from Super8#4.

'What the fuck's going on, McKenzie? There appears to be thousands of new users on line. Have we been hacked?'

What? McKenzie looked down at the bottom of his screen and sure enough saw the user count was now in the hundreds of thousands.

'It's a mistake.' He dismissed it instantly. 'There is absolutely no way this could happen. It's an impossibility; you have my absolute assurance on this. It's a technical error. No need for alarm.'

'It had better be,' Super8#7 chipped in.

McKenzie was not taken with the man's tone, and neither was he concerned. He'd had this private forum built by the world's most-competent software and technical specialists and security had been of paramount importance. He'd been personally assured that the firewall he'd had built especially was the most technologically advanced of its kind anywhere on the planet. 'Weapons of mass destruction couldn't penetrate this protection – you have my absolute guarantee on this.' That's what he'd been told, and certainly what he'd paid for, and McKenzie had absolute faith in the statement he'd been given because the man who'd given it knew that he'd signed his own death warrant otherwise.

Still, he thought it prudent to message his tech people and let them know there had been an error and to get it fixed without delay. He didn't want the club unnerved, and he certainly didn't want them up his arsehole about it. First things first, however, he would have to deal with the hack. Snapping his laptop shut, McKenzie made his way downstairs.

'Mrs Deyton, what an unexpected surprise.' Martin McKenzie greeted her with a smile so disingenuous that it sent an icy chill the length of her spine, and for the briefest moment she thought about making a run for it.

'McKenzie,' she said struggling to compose herself, 'I … I wasn't expecting to see you.'

'Evidently,' he mused, making his way over towards the desk. His whole demeanour conveyed an air of unimpeachable authority, just as she had remembered.

'How did you get here?' she said. 'Elaine told us the island was on a weather alert and that there were no planes landing or taking off.'

'And she was right,' he said. 'Only I'm an incredibly rich man, as you know, Angelika. I may call you Angelika? After all, we're already acquainted.'

She nodded, squeezing her fists tightly to prevent him for seeing her hands shaking,

McKenzie continued: 'And so I managed to eventually, how can I put this, *persuade* the right people to flout the restrictions and allow me to take a private jet here. Landed just now.' He moved over towards a small cabinet and pulled out a bottle of

Scotch, aged single malt, of course, and held it up. 'Drink? You look like you could use one. I know I could.'

'No … thank you,' she said, though he was right in his assumption. 'I don't drink Scotch.'

McKenzie scanned her with his dark eyes. She was prettier than he'd remembered, more feminine and petite, quite attractive, all said, standing there in her summer playsuit and wedge espadrilles, her long hair falling past her shoulders in silky waves. No tits, though. Still, you couldn't have everything.

'No, no of course you don't. It's a man's drink, I suppose. A brandy then, perhaps?'

'You've twisted my arm.' Her nerves were in shreds. His unexpected presence had completely blindsided her. Suddenly she couldn't think of a single thing to say, the plethora of questions she'd wanted to ask abandoning her like Scotch mist. He handed her a large cut-glass tumbler, half full.

'Cheers.' He raised his glass, his eyes still lingering upon her. 'I trust you've been enjoying your stay, that Elaine and the staff here have made you welcome, made sure your every need has been catered for? I take it that's why you're here, to see Elaine about something?'

'You don't know about the plane crash?' Deeming it safe to do so, she moved away from the door towards him and took a sip of the dark liquid. She had watched him pour it straight from the bottle and figured it was kosher.

'Plane crash?' The corners of his mouth turned outwards. 'What plane crash? I'm afraid Elaine and I have been incommunicado since your arrival. Damn phone lines were down and I've been unable to reach her on her mobile.'

'And that didn't concern you, that you couldn't get hold of her for the best part of a fortnight?'

'Well, yes, it did. Hence … here I am. I was aware of the weather conditions, of the flight restrictions, but as for any crash … that's news to me, I'm afraid. Nothing was reported. Besides, I have every faith in my wife's capabilities, Angelika. I left her in charge. I feel sure she would've found a way to contact me should she have felt the need to.'

'Felt the need to? We almost *died* getting here, McKenzie,' she said, 'and the pilot, he *did* die – a horrible, dreadful death, too.' The sight of the man's face embedded into the control panel flashed up inside her head like the trailer of some gruesome horror flick. 'And the attendant, Aki, her body … we never found it. We suspect she drowned.'

McKenzie shook his head but remained calm and composed – too calm and composed for her liking.

'And as for Joshua Jones … well, he could've lost an arm.'

'But he didn't?'

'No, but that's not really the point.' She stared at him, incredulous.

McKenzie shook his head again and tutted. 'Dreadful. That's really quite awful, especially for a musician. I do hope he's on the mend.'

Angelika was still as a statue. Was he mocking her? Was this all some elaborate joke at her expense? Suddenly she did not feel safe.

'Take a seat, my dear. You look a little jaded.'

She ignored the request. 'I want to know what's going on … why we're being kept here against our will.'

McKenzie took a seat in the leather swivel chair behind the desk and sipped his drink, savouring it by pulling his lips over his teeth and making an 'ahhh' sound.

'Against your will?' he eventually said. 'Whatever do you mean?' He drew his chin into his neck.

'I overheard the men talking, outside.' She pointed to the door awkwardly. 'Some strange things have happened …' She realised she wasn't making much sense. 'We had a party for JJ, for Joshua, the night he was flown back to the island, although he doesn't remember a thing. None of us do.'

'Good night, was it?'

'That's just it, McKenzie,' she said, 'none of us know. We think we may have been drugged, though why we have no idea.'

'Why on earth would anyone want to drug you?' he asked dismissively. 'That's really quite absurd, my dear. Were you injured in the crash? Perhaps you have a concussion. I can arrange to have you seen by a doctor if you wish.'

Angelika gulped back a mouthful of brandy. It was smooth as it slid down her throat but the afterburn almost took her breath away.

'I don't need a doctor. I need answers,' she said flatly, a trickle of confidence returning. 'Why are we being filmed, McKenzie?' She waggled the small plastic recording device at him. 'I found this buried deep in some bushes up by the infinity pool. And why did Elaine lie and say she had no access to transport when in reality her car was here all along. And –' she paused for breath '– how come the selective mutes are suddenly having full-blown conversations with each other? I just heard two members of staff talking quite clearly outside in the hallway. They mentioned the word "cast" like they were referring to us. What did they mean?' Angelika deliberately omitted mentioning the fact she had heard the men talking about a boat. It could be their ticket out of there and she didn't want him to know she knew about it.

'Too much champagne can turn even the best-behaved girls bad, you know. I've had many a champagne blackout in my time. Or perhaps you're choosing not to remember on a subliminal level. The mind, after all, is the most powerful organ in the body.' He was calm, affable even. 'I can only imagine how the crash affected you all. I really can't apologise enough. Please, won't you sit down?'

'I'd prefer to stand if it's all the same to you.' She watched him carefully in an attempt to read his body language, searching for silent clues that might give something away. He was dressed in a deep-blue three-button wool suit, a replica of the one he'd worn the day she'd interviewed him, sharply tailored, the detail subtle, his pristine white shirt offsetting the inky hue. The cuf-flinks were diamond, of course, to match the impressive time-piece on his wrist: Cartier – platinum by the looks of it – and covered in rocks. He was immaculate, carefully groomed, yet somehow giving the impression of the casual effortlessness of someone who wasn't trying too hard. She couldn't read him.

'As a narcissist – your words, if I recall, my dear, not mine – I would hardly be likely to film my guests. What would be the point in that, if, as you have previously suggested in your rather unflattering biographical interview of me, I'm my own biggest fan? Surely I would have a camera crew filming *me* if that was indeed the case.' He paused momentarily. 'That piece of plastic you have in your hand is in fact an electric water timer with an inbuilt temperature sensor that works on the principle that should the ground get too dry it triggers the sensor which trips the water sprinkler system. I care very much about this island, Angelika. It's taken me almost a decade to make it wor-thy of prestigious inhabitants much like your good self. I spent hundreds of thousands of pounds planting the trees, shrubs and plants across the entire island. As you have no doubt seen for yourself, the climate here is harsh and unforgiving; rain is a rare gift. When I first arrived here there was little more than brush and a few hardy perennials that could survive in such temperatures. But with a team of horticultural and agricultural experts on board we came up with a technologically advanced system that would ensure moisture could get to the dry soil, allowing the plants to flourish, part of which you're holding in your hand.'

Angelika hesitated, processing the information. It was a feasible explanation, she supposed, and for a moment she doubted herself. Was it all really just in her head? Was she, as Rupert kept reminding her, simply suffering from an overactive imagination … paranoia brought about by the trauma of the crash?

'And in response to your other concerns,' he continued apace, 'the staff here are indeed selective mutes. With hindsight, perhaps, this was not my finest idea, but really Angelika, as a man who travels the world and for whom everyone he meets has a question to ask, I came up with the idea through personal preference, taking 'the speak when spoken to' ethos one stage further if you will. I'm not one for small chat; I find it rather tedious, particularly if I'm relaxing on a luxury vacation. And admittedly I felt it might add a little, well, mystique I suppose. I am a showman, after all. I supposed it could be construed as a touch pretentious, like your husband suggested. And perhaps some of them were faking it just to get a gig out here; after all, who wouldn't want to spend a fortnight on Pleasure Island? But rest assured I will be looking into it. I don't like having the wool pulled over my eyes, Angelika. I was guaranteed their authenticity and went to great pains to have them sourced and flown here from all corners of the globe.'

'And what about Elaine's car?'

'It was already here on the island, the Range Rover, ghastly thing guzzles gas like an alcoholic in a distillery. I should imagine she had very little juice and wished to keep it in case of a serious emergency. As it is she appears not to have made it back to the island which concerns me somewhat that she may have run out of gas somewhere along her outward journey and without her mobile phone, well... I assume her reasons for keeping this information undisclosed was to avoid hysteria, especially since I am now aware of your most unfortunate introduction onto the island.'

Angelika felt the heat of his eyes upon her and took another sip of her brandy. He made her want to look away but she stood her ground and kept her eyes firmly upon his.

'I can think of no greater emergency than a plane crash, can you?'

McKenzie smiled thinly. 'One of which you all survived I'm happy to see.'

'All but the pilot ...and Aki, I presume. We never found her body.'

He sighed heavily. 'I've no doubt that lawyer husband of yours will have something to say in the way of compensation and frankly I can't say that I blame him after this. I will have a full investigation conducted as to what went wrong and why – you have my word on that – and if it appeases your conscience, I will ensure the pilot's family are fully compensated for their most-tragic loss.'

'*My* conscience? Ha!' Angelika snorted, the heat from the alcohol stinging her nostrils.

'If you do decide to sue, and frankly I couldn't blame any of you if you did, I won't take it personally. Besides, I'm a businessman, Angelika; it's standard practice to make sure you're insured to the hilt, to make allowances for every eventuality. Even unforeseen air accidents.'

'What happened to the plane that flew Joshua out of here and back again? Why couldn't it have flown us out of here, too?'

McKenzie shook his head. He was growing tired of her relentless questions.

'Unfortunately I have no idea.' He poured himself another drink in an excuse to turn away from her, lest she see his irritation. 'But as I've said, I will conduct a full and thorough investigation, which will result in the answers you need in full clarity.' Of course he had no intention of doing this whatsoever. After tonight, the plane crash and question marks it had brought about would be the least of this inquisitive bitch's concerns. After tonight it would be all about damage limitation for Angelika Tippie-toes Deyton, the hack with a knack for asking the wrong questions and sealing her own fate. All she would be worried about would be protecting her privacy, keeping her dignity and reputation intact; it would be the same for the rest of them, too. Once those boxes were open they would have nothing but happy memories to share about the island and they would praise him in the press, voluntarily enforcing the original Vegas motto that 'whatever happens on Pleasure Island stays on Pleasure Island'. And if, though he had calculated it being a very big if, any of them *still* had the minerals to take him on, then he would do what he'd always done and buy their silence. As far as McKenzie was concerned, it was a win-win situation.

CHAPTER FORTY-FOUR

Lennard Bailey gulped back some Pepto-Bismol straight from the bottle and washed the pink gloop down with a tot of cheap whiskey that he kept in the top drawer in case of emergencies, of which there seemed to be an alarming frequency. His heartburn was giving him serious gyp. He'd been putting off making an appointment at the doctors for months now, afraid of the dreaded 'I'm afraid it's not especially good news' line he sensed was due his way.

Absentmindedly scratching his backside and pulling at the waistband of his cheap slacks, he checked his diary for the day ahead. Client meetings followed by more client meetings. He didn't know why he'd even bothered looking. The telephone rang and belching painfully, he picked it up.

'Bailey.'

'Bailey, it's John Kirkbride from the *Daily Voice* in the UK.'

He raised his eyebrows in surprise and checked his watch. It would be 11pm in London now. Bit late, wasn't it?

'Kirkbwide, to what do I owe the pleasure?' He hadn't heard from this unscrupulous motherfucker in a while and was all the more grateful for it. They had history that went way back, a reluctant relationship born of mutual necessity; Bailey had needed Kirkbride to feature stories on his clients and Kirkbride had needed stories to sell in his newspaper: a simple enough exchange, one would think, but that hadn't always been the case. Kirkbride's irresponsible journalism had given Bailey cause for some real ballache over the years, namely defaming some of his biggest client's, often sullying their reputations, even outing their sexuality, and usually without the good grace of a little forewarning. Bailey remembered how Kirkbride had been a mere wet-behind the ears junior hack during Mia Manhattan's sensational trial and had made his name on the back of it, thanks to his especially unforgiving reportage. His scathing negativity of Mia had, Bailey felt sure, been partly responsible for her steep public decline. While it was all a long time ago now, he had never truly forgiven him for it. The man couldn't be trusted.

'Courtesy call, Bailey,' Kirkbride said, forgoing any niceties. 'Tomorrow's headlines. I take it you've heard about the footage doing the rounds?'

Bailey dropped his feet from the desk and sat up straight.

'What footage doing what rounds?'

Kirkbride snorted. 'You're getting sloppy, Bailey. Mia Manhattan and the webcam footage … it's all over the Internet.'

Bailey felt his sphincter muscles relax, panic tightening around his stomach like a gastric band.

'Fuck off, Kirkbwide, you're winding me up. Mia's on vacation, a *priyvate* destination …not even the paps know where she is.'

''Fraid you're wrong there, Bailey. How about I send it over to you? Seems as though Mia's been – how can I put this – *enjoying* herself on her little island retreat. I don't suppose you know where she is exactly, or if you've been in touch with her?'

How the hell did Kirkbride know where Mia was? Even he had no idea. A private, secluded island McKenzie had said, although he hadn't given an exact location. He had, however, given Bailey no room to manoeuvre when it came to convincing her to agree to it.

'It's imperative that bitch agrees to accept my hospitality, Bailey,' McKenzie had said, 'and it's up to you to make God-damn sure of it.'

Bailey hadn't wanted to challenge the almighty Martin McKenzie. Keeping a man such as him happy was par for the course. He was just too powerful to upset. McKenzie had the sway to make or break anyone in the industry. Hell, he *was* the industry. If he came to you and asked you to jump you asked, 'how high?' Besides, there was something about the man that gave him the bloody willies. He'd heard rumours over the years, unpleasant stuff about his sexual preferences and a ruthlessness that bordered on the plain psychotic. And one thing Bailey had learned in life; there was rarely smoke without fire. On the few occasions they'd crossed paths, Bailey had noted the unhinged look in his eyes, giving him cause to believe that Martin McKenzie was not a man you fucked with.

As it was he'd been given no choice in the matter. He thought back to the conversation they'd had some weeks back.

'I can tell you now it won't be easy to persuade her,' he'd nervously explained. Mia despised Martin McKenzie with an unfettered rampant passion that was borderline unnatural.

'I don't care how you do it, Bailey, but you will get that cunt to agree, do you understand?'

McKenzie had paused as the line crackled like the embers of a bonfire.

'Rumour has it you're under investigation by the IRS, if I'm not correct?'

Bailey had been affronted. How the hell did McKenzie know about that? It was his private business and he was most keen for it to remain so. The last thing he wanted was any attention on himself; he saved that shit for the catalogue of limelight-hoggers he represented. Despite his lack of sartorial finesse and speech impediment, Bailey was respected and revered as being a bloody-good agent. Something like that getting out would be very bad for business indeed.

'Are you blackmailing me?'

'Call it what you will, Bailey,' McKenzie had said, 'but actually I want to help you. I hear you're looking at a serious fraud charge, somewhere in the region of $450K?'

Bailey had sighed. It was little wonder he'd got a bloody ulcer; in all honesty, with the stress he'd been under since the audit he was surprised he hadn't dropped dead of a heart attack.

'What's it to you, anyway?' he'd muttered miserably. It couldn't really get much worse than it already was. If the IRS found him liable, which of course they would, then it was all over for him, anyway. Sometimes he wished he'd never relocated to the States; the tax office here was made up of even bigger bastards than in the UK, and that was really saying something.

'Make sure Mia Manhattan is on that plane next Thursday and I'll foot the bill. Once she signs that disclaimer whatever you owe will be written off by me.'

Bailey had struggled to comprehend what he was hearing. McKenzie was going to solve all his problems just as long as he convinced Mia to go and stay on his luxury island for a couple of weeks. It should have been a no-brainer. It was a no-brainer. Only Bailey knew that there had to be more to it than that.

'Why Mia?'

'Why not?'

'What's the catch, McKenzie? How can I weally twust you?'

'How can you afford not to?'

It was a fair point. Sill, getting Mia to agree would be a task in itself. That woman was unmovable when she didn't want to do something, no amount of transatlantic phone calls and begging in the past had proved it. He'd not wanted to sell her down the river, which he sensed was exactly what he would be doing. Despite their turbulent relationship over the years he was still fond of the old diva.

'I need your assurance that she'll come to no harm, McKenzie,' he'd said, his gastric juices bubbling.

McKenzie had laughed horribly.

'As soon as she signs up, the money's yours. Then you can kiss goodbye to your financial woes, my *fwiend*,' he'd said mockingly. And, surprisingly, he'd been as good as his word.

'So, what's the story exactly, Kirkbwide?' It was a question he'd rather not have to have an answer to but he needed to know what the damage was.

'Mia's part of a much bigger picture; she's on holiday with Joshua Jones, Nate and Billie-Jo Simmons and Rupert Deyton and his wife, one of my columnist's, Angelika Deyton. Tell me, Bailey: why would Mia Manhattan be on holiday with Rupert Deyton? We both know there's zero love lost between the pair.'

'Rupert Deyton.' Bailey's stomach lurched. 'Jesus Christ.' Mia would have his balls on a plate for this. So that's why McKenzie had refused to confirm who else would be on his special little trip … his *power* trip. Mia would never have agreed and McKenzie had known it.

'Don't tell me you know nothing about this, Bailey, because you've always been a spectacularly shit liar. I can see straight through you like a pane of glass.' Kirkbride hesitated a little. Thinking about it, Bailey had actually sounded genuinely shocked. 'Cut the shit, Bailey; you're telling me you seriously didn't know about this?'

Bailey cleared his throat.

'The fact that Mia was away with Joshua, yes. That she was on vacation with Rupert Deyton, no.'

Surprisingly Kirkbride believed him. 'Do you know where they are?'

'No, I'm afraid I don't,' he said. It was a half-truth.

'Has this got anything to do with Martin McKenzie?'

Bailey felt his panic reach fever pitch.

'McKenzie? What on earth makes you say that?'

This time Kirkbride didn't believe him.

'A little birdie, Bailey.'

'So what's on the footage? What's Mia done?' He was already pre-empting damage limitation.

'See for yourself,' Kirkbride said, 'I'm sending you the link now. It's live footage, Bailey … seems as though your client has signed up for some kind of reality TV show she knows nothing about.'

Bailey gulped back some more of his pink gloop followed by the last of the whiskey.

'You mean they don't know they're being filmed?'

'Watch the stream and make up your own mind.'

Bailey groaned. Suddenly an afternoon filled with demanding client meetings didn't seem such a bad thing at all. 'I'd advise you not to run with this story, John. Seriously, you're opening a can of worms.'

Now Kirkbride was really intrigued. Bailey had used his Christian name. This *was* serious.

'And why's that, Bailey?'

'You don't know who you're dealing with.'

'So it is McKenzie?'

'Selling out one of your own, too … are there no depths you people won't sink to?'

Kirkbride laughed.

'Dance with the devil, Bailey, and your feet get burned. You know how it works.'

As he'd suspected, McKenzie had stitched Mia up, placing her on a secluded island with her nemesis and filming the results. But why? What would McKenzie possibly gain from it aside from enjoying Mia's obvious discomfort? He frantically thought how he might be able to turn this around to her advantage and save his sorry arse in the process. She wanted a comeback, right? Well, perhaps Kirkbride getting hold of this footage, whatever it was, would be a blessing in disguise. He sure as shit hoped so because compared to what Mia would do to him when she discovered the truth, financial ruin suddenly seemed like the soft option.

CHAPTER FORTY-FIVE

Wearing only a matching Victoria's Secret bra and thong, Billie-Jo was energetically twerking in the bathroom, Beyoncé blaring out from the Bang & Olufsen surround-sound speakers as she racked up a line of coke on the tiled surface and quaffed back yet more chilled Cristal. Grinning at herself in the large full-length mirror she took a hit, snorting up a long, fat line in one deep inhalation. She'd promised Nate she would never touch the stuff again but then she'd also promised to forsake all others on her wedding day and look how that had turned out. Oh, well, she sighed resignedly, in for a penny … Anyway, screw Nate, she decided, he was just too fucking square for her. He was only in his early 30s, for fuck's sake, yet the way he carried on you'd think he was ready for his pipe and slippers. Nate's trouble was that he didn't know how to have fun, and moreover it seemed he didn't want to either. All Nate wanted to do was hide away from the world, wallowing in self-pity about being adopted while disappearing into obscurity. Billie-Jo just didn't get it. She didn't understand what the fucking deal was; Nate was still young, he was fit, in every sense, and he was loaded. He had everything he wanted at his feet, yet still he was miserable. Some people were never happy. It was so unfair really; Nate had access to real fame and fortune and yet wasn't arsed about either, whereas she was desperate for both and had neither – at least not quite, not autonomously, although all that looked set to change if she played her cards carefully over these next few months.

While it was not an option she'd initially wanted to consider, Billie-Jo had to concede that perhaps time was running out on her marriage to Nate Simmons. Whatever else this 'holiday' had revealed, the cracks in their relationship had certainly been one of them. Joshua Jones, however, was fast shaping up to be a half-decent proposition in terms of a suitable replacement. With a single due for release which had already been tipped to be a global smash and an album to promote, plus a major tour in the pipeline, Billie-Jo was starting to ruminate on the idea of trading in her WAG status for that of rock-star wife, or girlfriend to start with, at least. The more she thought of it, the more she warmed to the idea. WAGs were so yesterday, so passé. Now a rock star's wife: that had real cachet and kudos. Moreover, JJ knew how to have fun – proper fun, her kind of fun – sharing a love of hard partying, coke and champagne. And he was hung like a donkey, not that she had any complaints about Nate in that department but when she weighed it all up JJ came out on top; they certainly had more in common. And he made her laugh which, while not being a prerequisite in a potential husband, at least for her, was most definitely a bonus. All JJ needed to do now was make some serious wedge and she'd be cool with a trade in. Divorcing Nate would be a doddle. She doubted he'd make a fuss; Nate was just too nice to put her through any bitter acrimony and plus he wouldn't want the exposure. With a bit of consideration she would come out of it with a decent lump to see her right, a nice property and a smart motor, plus some fabulous jewellery and clobber to boot.

Billie-Jo wasn't sure whether it was the coke, the champagne, or the fact that her plan B was coming together nicely but she felt damned good. Perhaps it was all three, that and the fact that spending the morning with JJ had given her a real buzz. She had enjoyed his company more than she'd enjoyed anything in a long while, well, aside from the mind-blowing sex she'd had with the stranger in the spa. It was odd that she hadn't seen the horny masseur about the island since their encounter, leading her to believe that he was keeping a low profile. Still, she didn't give it too much thought; that ship had seemingly sailed without any repercussions and her focus was now firmly on Joshua Jones. Billie-Jo racked up another line of gear and turned the stereo up. She'd cajoled Nate into coming here, much like she cajoled him into doing anything worthwhile and despite everything that had happened she was now very glad that she had. If Nate wanted that boring bitch Angelika Deyton then he was welcome to her. They were welcome to each other. They could bore each other shitless slipping into a mundane middle-class existence while she toured the globe partying with a famous front man. Fuck yeah! Flo Rida came on the stereo and she wacked up the sound with the remote; this tune was sick! Whipping off her bra and thong, Billie-Jo stepped into the shower with a renewed vigour and began lathering herself up in Chanel Coco Mademoiselle body wash. She didn't hear Nate enter the bathroom.

'Billie-Jo?'

'Shit!' Nate was back. She could've sworn she'd locked the door. Holy fuck, the gear! She'd left it out on the side with a rolled up bank note next to it.

Nate pulled the glass door to the shower open causing a rush of cold air to hit her naked body.

'What the fuck is this, Billie-Jo?' He was holding the bank note up in his fist, waving it at her, eyes aflame. 'I thought I asked you not to touch that fucking shit ever again? Are you stupid? One line, you said … yeah, right, and the rest!' She'd never seen him so angry.

'Nate! What are you doing? Shut the door, you're spraying water all over the floor!' Her eyes began to sting as soap slid down her face. 'Jesus,' she said angrily, 'can't this wait until I'm out of the shower!'

'You lied to me; you said you wouldn't touch this fucking shite ever again. I told you I'd div–'

Angry herself now and charged up on champagne and coke, Billie-Jo grabbed a fluffy, white towel and wrapped it around her nakedness before stepping out of the shower, her buzz disappearing as fast as the steam from the hot water.

'Told me what, Nate, that you'd divorce me … yeah, I remember. Well, what you waiting for, on you go.'

'Just how out of hand has your coke habit got, eh?'

He looked down at the small pile of white powder next to the matching his-and-hers sink, and promptly blew it all into the basin before running the tap.

'You fucking idiot,' she hissed.

Nate shook his head.

'Now that is rich,' he snorted. 'You know what this stuff does to people. How many more times do I need to ram it home to you?'

'Oh, lighten up, killjoy – it's just a line of coke. It's not heroin or crack … just a bit of a livener, that's all. We're on holiday, Nate. You need to take that stick out of your arsehole and relax a little, have a little hit yourself. You never know, you might even enjoy it. Miracles can happen.'

He felt like slapping her face.

'How long have you been doing this stuff really, Billie-Jo? And be honest, if you're even capable of honesty, that is.' He looked at her contemptuously. He knew she had dabbled in the past, but he was beginning to realise he may have sorely underestimated the extent of her habit.

'Since before we were married,' she sneered, 'well, I needed something to relieve the boredom, didn't I? And in case you're wondering, yes, I was coked off me tits on our wedding day, too. How else did you think I was gonna get through it?' She didn't know why she was being so mean; the words were just tumbling from her lips. She'd been cold-busted and was panicking.

'So this is what you spend my money on, is it? Handbags and coke.' He was looking her up and down like he'd stepped in her. 'That's the thanks I get from pulling your arse out of the gutter, is it, Bee? A junkie for a wife? Thanks … thanks a lot.'

'Out of the gutter? Ha! Oh, the Golden fucking Bolt. I've got more balls than you'll ever have, Nate Simmons. If only you could've been such a hit off the pitch as well as on it. But you're a lame duck, now aintcha? In every fucking sense. Couldn't have fun on a fucking bouncy castle, you couldn't … too busy wallowing in your own misery, pining after Mummy and Daddy, whoever the fuck they might be. My money's on a pair of gutless drips. After all, you must've got it from somewhere.' Billie-Jo had gone too far and she knew it, but she couldn't help but be vicious when cornered.

'*Your* money? *My* money you mean, sweetheart,' he shot back, 'the pocket money you make getting those fake tits of yours out only just makes enough to keep you in bras, and no doubt more of this shit!' He threw the note at her but it fell short. 'You know what,' he said, leering at her, 'it was a mistake to marry you ,Billie-Jo. Yeah, that's what *I* was thinking while I was saying *my* vows. And as it turns out I should've listened to my gut. You're little more than a strung-out coked-up gold-digger with a vicious tongue.'

Billie-Jo's face contorted in anger and hurt. How dare he speak her like that! Dropping her towel she picked up a full shampoo bottle from the side and threw it directly at him. But Nate's reflexes were too quick and he dodged it. The sound as the bottle impacted with the mirror was ear-splitting and they both winced as the glass exploded, shattering into pieces onto the marble floor.

'Now look what you made me do!' She glared at him. 'I'm going to the beach.' She flounced from the bathroom, leaving him to clear up the mess.

Nate looked down at the shattered glass on the floor and then up at the huge mirror frame.

'Jesus Christ,' he said, moving towards it. There was something … something behind the mirror. He stared at it, its lens in full view, red light still flashing as it followed his movements. 'Well, I'll be damned,' he said, 'now that *is* a camera.'

This time there was no mistaking it.

CHAPTER FORTY-SIX

'He's here, on the island.' Angelika was so breathless by the time she'd reached the pool that she could hardly get the words out. Mia, who was rocking gently on one of the enormous hammocks next to JJ, lazily opened one eye.

'Who … who's here on the island?'

'McKenzie.' Angelika felt lightheaded with adrenalin, her nerves jangling like a wind chime in a gale. She needed a drink, a proper drink. 'Where's Rupert?'

Mia sat bolt upright, using one arm to prevent her untied bikini top from slipping clean off as she practically fell out of the hammock. 'You've *seen* him?'

'Just now at the mansion. I was looking for Elaine.'

'How long has he been here?' Mia was already snatching up her belongings and throwing them haphazardly into her Heidi Klein raffia beach tote.

'He says he flew in today, not long ago.'

'Flew?'

'Apparently he bribed a pilot to bring him.'

'Nice one,' JJ chipped in, 'guess this means we get to meet the man in person, after all.'

Mia and Angelika exchanged stony glances.

'So does this mean the telephone lines are up and running?'

Angelika shook her head.

'He claims he hasn't been able to get hold of Elaine since we arrived, who, by the way, has had a car here on the island all along.' Once again she deliberately decided not to mention the boat, at least not yet, not until she'd spoken to Nate, not until they'd found it first.

Mia blinked at her.

'A car? That fucking bitch had *a car* ...'

'McKenzie said she went out in it earlier today and hasn't been seen since. Gave me some cock-and-bull story about her wanting to save the gas for a real emergency. How she didn't want to create hysteria by telling us about it ...'

'It's a fucking set-up!' Mia screeched. 'That bastard ...' Her eyes met Angelika's. 'He's been fucking with us all along. Well, now he'll have me to deal with. And we've got old scores to settle.'

Angelika didn't argue with her, though she was intrigued to know just what those scores might be. Raj appeared with the ubiquitous tray of champagne, nodding at her, and she thought about having a glass but decided against it. She kept replaying the conversation she'd had with McKenzie in her mind, something he'd said about the mutes. '... *I suppose you could call it somewhat pretentious ... just like your husband said ...*' It suddenly struck her: how would McKenzie possibly know that Rupert had said such a thing?

'Where's Rupert?' she asked again.

'Fishing,' JJ said, wondering if Billie-Jo had a heads-up on the latest news. She'd gone back to the cabana to freshen up, for him he assumed, for the round two he hoped they'd have later on this evening. Though he'd have to be discreet judging by the tricky conversation he'd not long had with Mia.

'So, you have your eye on the little cockney sparrow then, darling?' She'd mused as she'd sipped a strawberry mojito and made herself comfortable on the white, string hammock next to him. She didn't waste any time in getting to the point, he gave her that much.

'Difficult not to, really,' he'd replied awkwardly, 'I mean, she's been up in my face since I got here.'

'Ha!' Mia had snorted into her glass, though she bore no real malice by it. 'Please don't insult my intelligence, sweetie. I've kept library books for longer than you've been alive.'

JJ had been duly silenced.

'Take my advice: she's a married woman, Joshua, and regardless of whether that marriage is a happy one, which is clearly debateable, it wouldn't do to start rubbing people's noses in it, mine included. Be a little discreet, there's a love, or better still, wait until we're back on home ground before you start swinging that delectable dick of yours around, hmmm?'

It was more command that polite request and he got the message. After all, it was only a couple of days ago he'd had Mia bent over the leather chaise longue. Now she was offering him relationship advice and it made for uncomfortable listening.

'Just a bit of harmless flirting, babe,' he'd said, playing it down. 'I've only got eyes for you, you know that.'

Mia had thrown her head back and laughed, sloshing more of her mojito down her cleavage in the process.

'Oh, please, Joshua,' she'd said, lowering her head, cocking it to one side, a gesture that made him feel stupid. 'Do what you will with the girl but at least have the decency to wait until I'm out of the picture, OK?' She was saying it for his own good and for Nate as much as herself. She felt a little protective towards Nate Simmons. He was sensitive, much more so than his hard-faced wife and she genuinely had begun to think a lot of him.

JJ had nodded a little pathetically. He supposed he owed her that much at least.

Mia turned her thoughts back to what Angelika was saying.

'He wants to invite us all up to the mansion at midnight where he says he'll answer all our questions as fully as possible.

Aperitifs on the roof terrace. Formal attire. He says he has a big surprise for us.'

'I didn't even realise there was a roof terrace on the mansion,' JJ mused. 'Wow, man, the view must be awesome!'

'Screw the view,' Mia hissed, 'if that man thinks he can just roll up after everything and start dictating, I don't think so! View … I'll give him one he'll not forget in a hurry.'

'We should let Nate know he's here, and Billie-Jo, of course,' Angelika quickly added.

'Sure, I'll go find her.' JJ pulled himself up out of the sun-lounger with his good arm, 'Tell her.'

Mia flashed him a look.

'I mean tell *them*,' he quickly added.

'No need, darling.' She shot him an asinine smile. 'Look, they're headed this way.'

Rupert had been fishing off of the peninsula for the best part of the afternoon and hadn't even so much as had a gentle pull on the line.

'Couldn't catch a bloody cold here,' he grumbled to himself. Still, as far as beauty spots went, this one was pretty spectacular, the Mediterranean Sea stretched out in front of him like a glistening, aqua blanket, rippling in the gentle breeze that seemed to whisper around the small, sheltered plane he'd found for himself upon the rocks. He'd watched it for some time, mesmerised by the eternal ebb and flow of the water's surface, ever constant in a world of such inconsistency. It had given him a tranquil – almost humble – sensation; a peaceful sense of solitude and calm, which was somewhat ironic as in that very moment he was unknowingly being watched by thousands of strangers across the world.

Rupert shifted his body towards the direction of the sun and basked in the sensation of the heat against his naked stomach. Looking down at himself he thought about how he might've lost a few pounds since he'd been on the island, which again was somewhat ironic given the delights he had imbibed. He'd allowed his facial hair to grow out a little too and had even begun to feel less conscious in his island attire of rolled-up chino shorts and open muslin shirts. It wasn't just a shift in his physical appearance that had taken place, though; he felt different too.

Slowly, painstakingly, he was beginning to reconcile with the truth within. Complete denial, he realised, was no longer an option; two weeks in paradise and the events that had occurred had forced him to evaluate. Being 'gay', or even 'bisexual', was something Rupert had never allowed himself to consider, not even for a split second. The word 'homosexual' had always sounded somewhat unpleasant to his ear, much like an incurable disease or affliction. He was aware that times had significantly changed since his youth, though, and that these days being gay almost carried a certain cachet. No one really batted an eyelid if you batted for the other side nowadays, only it wasn't as straightforward as 'coming out of the closet', at least not for him. He was, as far as appearances went, a straight, married man in his 40s, a high-flying, high-achieving barrister; what would his family think, his colleagues, his son, and, of course, Angelika? As much as she irritated him to despair sometimes, he did care about her so much and wasn't sure he could ever drop such a bombshell upon her.

The emotional detonation would just be too catastrophic: the humiliation, the hurt and shame, the sense that their entire marriage had been a sham, which incidentally he didn't feel was entirely true. Despite everything theirs had been a solid partnership on many levels, only to his great sadness and regret his heart had never truly been in it 100%, and it was only now he could finally bring himself to admit it.

Part of Rupert even wished that Mia had outed him all those years ago like she had threatened to do; it would've all been over and done with now and perhaps he and Angelika would've been respectively happy, though not with each other. Perhaps she would've gone on to have had a family, a relationship with a husband who appreciated her physical attractiveness instead of a repressed, bitter, shell of a man who she was forever at logger-heads with, unspoken resentment and mutual competitiveness forever simmering beneath the surface of a carefully constructed façade.

Angelika was 38 years old; it wasn't too late for her; she was young enough to start again without completely destroying his conscience in the process, wasn't she? At least that's what all those bloody magazines she wrote for were always saying: 'never too late to start again'; '40 is the new 30'; 'black is the new white'; 'gay the new straight'; or whatever bullshit it was they peddled to make women feel better about their shambolic, unfulfilled lives.

Would she forgive him? Could he ever forgive himself? Rupert sighed. Who was he kidding? They could barely say a civil sentence to each other as it was already. No, he'd lived with, and largely successfully buried, this part of himself for long enough; he would just have to carry on regardless. In a couple of days' time it would all be over and back to business as usual, his drunken sexual misdemeanour with Raj banished to the annuls of his memory bank next to Michael. Perhaps it was easier to live a lie when the truth was too unpalatable for all concerned.

Too late in the day to be gay, Rupert thought as he gave a little snort of mirth. And yet deep down he knew that he would never truly be at peace until he learned to accept himself. Part of the problem was the fact that Rupert was actually something of a sexual prude; he found the idea of people looking at him and wondering if he was 'giver' or 'receiver' completely abhorrent and found his own sexual desires distasteful, even shameful. He stared out onto the horizon once more, at the sun high and blazing, majestic in its glory, unrepentant, a force of nature that brought with it such joy and pain in equal measures, much like being on this island itself; much like *life* itself.

'Penny for them.' The voice startled him so much that he momentarily dropped the fishing rod he'd been holding.

'Raj.' Rupert stared up at him in shock, his heartbeat galloping inside his chest. 'What on earth are you doing here?'

He shrugged. 'Came to find you.'

'And how did you know where to look?' He stood up, placing the rod down by his side, sucking in his exposed stomach, suddenly feeling self-conscious about his state of undress.

'Call it a sixth sense,' Raj said, smiling, his salt-white teeth off-set by his smooth, mocha skin.

He has such kind eyes, Rupert thought. Eyes that seemed to answer questions before he'd even needed to ask them.

'And you *do* speak?'

'Only when spoken to,' he replied, with a wry smile.

His accent was British, clipped, and came as a surprise. Rupert tried to avert his eyes from his perfectly formed abdominal muscles. He suddenly felt emotional and wanted to bury himself into his chest, to let go at last.

'But I make exceptions...' Raj continued.

'For who?'

'Exceptional people,' Raj replied, his dark, chocolate eyes shining as they held Rupert's own in a fixed gaze. 'People like you.'

Rupert swallowed dryly.

'I think I preferred it when you didn't speak,' he said quietly.

'In that case,' Raj said, taking a step closer towards him, 'I won't say another word.'

CHAPTER FORTY-SEVEN

Martin McKenzie's phone was about to blow up. It had been buzzing all day and eventually he'd had to switch the damn thing off just for a little respite. The moment he'd turned it back on, however, it was at it again, vibrating like a hooker's faulty dildo. Pressing it angrily, he looked down at the screen, 67 missed calls in 24 hours. Someone wanted to get hold of him badly. Well, whoever it was they could wait, he thought contrarily, throwing it across the room. He had important things to attend to here now that Elaine had been 'relieved' of her duties. After all, someone had to clean up the mess that incompetent bitch had left behind.

McKenzie poured himself a crystal tumbler full of Scotch and took a generous mouthful. It was unlike him to feel nervous, and the feeling unsettled him. Still, he supposed it was natural for one's feathers to be a trifle ruffled having just done away with your wife. He sat back into the old, leather chesterfield and put his legs up onto the seat, kicking off his hand-stitched Italian brogues. They made quite a satisfying sound as they hit the polished, wooden floor. He booted up his screen, ostensibly to view the players but also to check to see if the tech guy had got back to him regarding this little user error that had been brought to his attention. Sure enough he had.

'I'm on it, sir, right away,' the email read. 'Please be assured that my original testimony stands. It's impossible for even the smartest brain to have penetrated the security on this. There's zero cause for alarm. I put my life on it. However, I will rectify this error immediately and report back as soon as it's investigated.'

McKenzie relaxed. It was just as he thought; this was just a technical glitch. As a precaution, however, he typed a message to the club members copying the tech's words in a show of reassurance.

'This is absolutely no cause for concern. I have been given 100% authority on this. It was a technical error that has now been rectified. We need not discuss further.' He wrote, calling an end to it.

McKenzie sighed with fatigue. It had been a trying sort of day and he couldn't help wondering if now, perhaps, he'd been a tad hasty in murdering Elaine. The image of his long-standing loyal wife's skull exploding as he had brought down the cloche onto it with such brute force flashed up in his mind – and her expression: one of total surprise and ultimate despair as she realised in that nano-second what he'd done to her. Poor old Elaine. He wondered what her last thought had been before she'd made impact with the water, if the blow had been enough to kill her outright or if she'd subsequently drowned. Ah, well, no matter; the outcome had been inevitable anyway. Still, it was unlike him to act in such a spontaneous manner and it was this lack of forethought that had given him the jitters.

McKenzie was still very much aware that murdering one's wife was illegal and that as such he could be held accountable should he not cover his tracks most thoroughly. He liked to be meticulous about things, plan them to the nth degree. Acting spontaneously ran the risk of being sloppy and overlooking things that couldn't afford to be overlooked, and it was for this reason he was a little cross with himself. He wished now that he had waited. Still, recriminations were futile. What was done was done and couldn't be undone. Elaine was in a watery grave and he had business to attend to.

Sinking more of his Scotch, McKenzie sat up, replaced his shoes and suit jacket, and slicked back his carefully dyed hair with the palm of his hand before opening his laptop. Clearing his throat and switching on his webcam he smiled as his face came into view.

'Good evening, lady and gentlemen. It is with my immense personal pleasure that I welcome you to the final act …'

CHAPTER FORTY-EIGHT

'There's nothing here,' Angelika whispered quietly as she looked at Nate, her blues eyes wide with disappointment. 'Round the back of the harbour, they said. I heard them clearly. We have to find it, Nate. We have to see if there's a way off this island.'

He heard the urgency in her voice, his heartbeat mirroring it.

'Perhaps they've already left in it,' he said. 'Maybe we're too late.'

Nate scanned the deserted harbour. It was dark, though not pitch-black quite yet, and the stillness was disconcerting.

'Do you think we're being watched, right now, I mean?' Angelika felt the heat of a thousand hidden eyes upon her and her skin prickled.

'Who knows,' he said. 'It's a possibility.'

Spurred on by a mix of adrenalin and determination, she began to navigate her way barefoot further down the rocks towards the edge, holding her Havaiana flip-flops in one hand and balancing herself with the other.

'Be careful, Ange,' he called out to her in a hushed voice. 'It's dark down there. Tread carefully.'

Nate's revelation of his grim, bathroom discovery had confirmed what she had suspected all along, that McKenzie *had* been spying on them, or at least someone had, invading their most intimate moments and violating their privacy in a way that seemed unimaginable. The thought that 'they', whoever 'they' were, had watched her take a shower and use the toilet, maybe even seen the rare, intimate and not-altogether-pleasant moment which had taken place between her and Rupert in the en suite made her flesh crawl. She had been right to listen to her intuition, to trust her instincts. If they could just find a way off Pleasure Island without alerting suspicion then they could go to the authorities, get them to send a plane for them all and have that bastard McKenzie bang to rights. The man was sick –

a criminal.

'He won't get away with it, Ange,' Nate said, as though reading her thoughts. 'Whatever he's done, we'll make sure he gets what's coming to him through the proper channels.'

Only she wasn't so convinced. Men like McKenzie had a habit of getting away with *everything*. And the six-billion-dollar question hanging over everything still remained paramount in her mind. *Why?* She suspected that at midnight tonight they were about to find out and, as much as she was horrified, unnerved and scared to death, she needed to know. First, however, they had to find this goddamn boat.

'Well, fuck-a-doodle-do, dude … ho-ly shit!' JJ gave a loud whistle as he and Mia made their entrance onto the roof terrace. 'It's like something out of Tony Montana's place in *Scarface!*'

The roof-top terrace of the mansion was indeed nothing if not ostentatious. While the mansion itself was testament to McKenzie's exorbitant wealth with its lofty, high ceilings, abundance of marble pillars, gold fixtures and intricately decorated ceilings, he had, Mia concluded, saved the best until last, or the top in this case. They had reached the terrace by glass elevator, stepping out onto a white-and-gold marbled expanse of floor that was shiny enough to reflect the low sunlight that was quickly disappearing upon it. In the middle of the huge terrace was a pool, within it a large, ornate sculpture depicting the Greek mythological scene of Narcissus starring at his own reflection, his mouth the fountain piece from which water poured, beautifully up-lit by tiny lights and shrouded by carefully pruned box tree. An array of seating was thoughtfully positioned throughout: huge, white, leather chesterfields scattered with sumptuous, gold cushions in an assortment of the finest fabrics; striped chaise lounges surrounded by gold statues of cherubs and angels; a pair of porcelain tigers, six-foot high stood either side of the seating area, their regal, feline faces flickering in the light provided by a number of gigantic free standing gold candelabras that towered above them.

Positioned at the furthest north point into the mountains, the view afforded an unparalleled backdrop out to sea. The sun was setting at eye level, its pastel colours painting the 360-degree view like a Monet and appeared so close it felt like you were part of the picture itself. Underneath a large, white canopy was a long, banqueting table dressed to an exquisitely high standard, solid, silver cutlery glinting in the throes of the fading light, fine china and crystal cut glass. Countless magnums of Vintage Krug, Dom Pérignon and Cristal sat inside large, silver, ice buckets on huge piles of crushed ice.

On closer inspection, Mia saw that there were also platinum, hand-engraved name places, and noted that she was seated next to Joshua, a small but welcome relief. To the right of the table, a large video screen had been erected as though they were about to enjoy a film premier and her interest spilled over into unease: they were going to watch something. Music was playing in the background, just low enough to be heard and she suddenly recognised it was one of her songs: 'Pretty Little Lies', a smooth, soulful ballad she had written at barely 22 years old. She hadn't heard the song in many years; it had never been one of her greats, yet it had always remained one of her favourites. It stopped her in her tracks, flooding her with a million memories, transporting her back to a time in her life when she had been so young, so beautiful and naïve, so … *hopeful*. Swallowing hard, Mia's maudlin thoughts were broken by a member of staff offering her a glass of champagne, which she duly took. It was chilled to perfection.

'Well, the sculpture is apt, if nothing else,' she remarked.

'Huh?' Joshua gave her a blank look.

'It's Narcissus, the scene from Greek mythology …?'

He shrugged and she sighed.

'This suit is uncomfortable man.' He pulled a face as he fiddled with the cummerbund. 'I feel like a douche.'

'Yet you look divine,' Mia said. 'Get used to it, darling. Black tie means just that … rock star or not.'

'Yeah, well screw that,' he grumbled, wondering why he couldn't have just done the whole 'white T-shirt and cool suit' combo. He bet Adam Levine didn't have this kinda problem. Mia, however, had gone all out in an embellished, couture, Marchesa gown that was split to the thigh to reveal matching, bejewelled underwear.

'So then –' she'd done a 180-degree twirl for JJ earlier, once he'd managed to pour her into it '– what's the verdict?'

The verdict was that the gown was probably two decades too young for her, but he knew the drill by now.

'You look da fucking bomb, babe.'

Mia had been horrified. *Da bomb*? God, how she missed her Dickie in that moment, a man who knew how to give a woman a proper compliment. Da bomb indeed! Age inappropriate or not, Mia had been happy with her choice of attire. She had always known how to give good gown.

Rupert greeted her with an asinine smile, ubiquitous glass of fizz in hand. 'Playing one of yours, I hear, Mia?' He was smoking a cigar and looked far more comfortable in such formal dress than JJ did, but then she supposed he'd had more practise.

'Surprised you even noticed,' she said.

'Incredible dress,' he said in a bid to avoid any frosty exchange.

She wondered if he actually meant it.

'You can borrow it, if you like,' she quipped, 'but then again, you've a wardrobe full of them, I should imagine. After all, you wear a gown every day to work, don't you?'

Just then Billie-Jo joined them – having taken in as much of the view as she could enjoy – resplendent in a lime-green and leopard-print Versace dress, the neckline plunging all the way to her bellybutton and showcasing the high, round firmness of her enhanced assets.

She knew she looked incredible, if somewhat overstated dripping in make-up and jewellery, but then she was determined to make an impression on the impresario she hoped to finally meet this evening. McKenzie would remember her; she would make sure of it.

'Looking fly, BJ,' Joshua remarked.

'Not looking bad yerself,' she returned the compliment, aware of Mia's watchful eye.

'So, do you think we're gonna get to open them boxes tonight, then?' she said. They'd been instructed to bring them along to this evening's proceedings and her need to know what was inside had reached fever pitch.

'I should imagine that's the idea, dear,' Mia said.

'What do you reckon's inside them? Jewellery, perhaps? Keys to a soft-top Merc?'

Rupert raised an eyebrow. The greedy girl was nothing if not hopeful.

'Your wife not joining us this evening, Rupert?' Mia asked, noting Angelika's absence.

Now that she'd mentioned it, Rupert had started to wonder just what, or who, was keeping Angelika. She had said that she would follow him up onto the roof terrace imminently.

'You go on ahead,' she'd suggested as she'd applied her make-up in the ornate mirror back at the cabana. 'I'm not quite ready yet and we don't want to be late, we might miss something important.' She'd smiled at him, adding, 'I won't be long.' Never one to wait around, not least for his wife, he had not needed telling twice and hadn't given it a second's thought until now.

'She should be here any minute,' he said.

Billie-Jo's facial expression clouded over. Now that she thought of it, Nate had also agreed to catch her up. He'd complained of feeling unwell and had gone for a walk in full black tie to supposedly 'clear his head' before dinner. Had he and Angelika sloped off somewhere together?

'No, Nate either,' Mia remarked dryly, 'although I'm sure it's just an innocent coincidence.' She kept her eyes firmly upon Rupert's.

'If he's gone off with that bitch, I'll fucking kill him,' Billie-Jo hissed underneath her breath.

'Chill, babe,' JJ whispered in her ear. 'Like, do you even give a shit?'

Billie-Jo bristled. After all, she supposed she wasn't exactly in a position to start bitching about her husband's suspected infidelity, not when she'd spent the afternoon bouncing all over JJ's hard dick. But still, at least she'd been discreet about it. Nate, it seemed, hadn't even gone to any length to cover his tracks; brazen bastard, she would nail him to the wall after this.

Rupert sucked on his cigar in a bid to soften the sense of foreboding that was gnawing at him.

The three of them all stood staring at each other, none of them wanting to ask the question they knew they were all thinking: where the fuck were Nate and Angelika?

CHAPTER FORTY-NINE

'I want to make love to you in the boat, on the way back ... Jesus, Ange, I want to make love to you here, in this club, right now!' Nate looked at her like a blind man seeing the sun for the first time. Angelika smiled at him, her eyes sparkling, up-lit by the neon lighting of the packed bar. She could not remember a time a man had so obviously desired her and she only wished that she could give him her full concentration, but her mind was elsewhere, a thousand unanswered questions wrestling for space inside her head, answers she sensed were imminent, answers she felt lay somewhere on this island, with the pressing mission being to find the boat.

They located it eventually, tucked away inside a tiny alcove, carefully hidden between rocks, and boarded it with a mix of elation and unease, their collective adrenalin fizzing like electricity between them. They hugged instinctively, triumphantly. As she made to break away, he stopped her, held her there in his arms.

She smiled at him through her eyes, deep and blue, and he felt as if he could dive into them, swim in them. She parted her lips a little, displaying her teeth, neat aside from that slight snaggle that he had come to adore; a tiny flaw in an otherwise-perfect smile, or perfect for him, at least. She was so beautiful to him in that moment that he could not prevent himself from wanting her. She made sense to him; her skin soft and a little aglow in the moonlight, eyes shining like the ocean, her hair sun-and-windswept into soft, messy waves. She didn't flinch as he pulled her closer, her body soft, feminine, pliable as it lightly pressed against his own.

She was shaking slightly, and he wondered if it was because of him or the evening chill from the water. He felt the heat of her breath as his lips slowly reached hers, eyes closing as they finally connected, the lightest touch to begin with, the scent of her skin in his nostrils as his mouth began to explore her. She tasted so good, so different to Billie-Jo, like he had known her lips all his life, or at least should've done. He pushed his tongue gently into her open mouth and she responded with her own.

'Oh, God, Ange,' he said breathlessly, his arms gripped tightly around her now, his hands touching her exposed skin as the kiss escalated into a passionate frenzy. He was hard for her now. Jesus, since he'd met her he'd been hard for her, and he could not stop himself from pressing up against her, his pelvis touching her own. Gently, their lips still upon each other's, he laid her down inside the boat and in that moment Nate could think of nothing other than her: making love to her; touching and tasting her; smelling her intimate scent. He had never felt sexual desire like it before in his life. He wanted his woman – *really* wanted her – in every sense. She would be his wife one day, he thought as his hands began to explore her small, pert breasts, her nipples stiffening to his touch, his mouth around them, gently nibbling and sucking as she began to gasp in pleasure underneath him.

'Nate … oh, Nate …' Angelika surrendered completely. It was inevitable; she could no longer deny the desire she felt for this man: a desire that she'd felt from the beginning; an unspoken connection that she could neither understand or explain. She had tried so hard to do the right thing, to hold back, repress her feelings because she was, after all, a married woman, but finally she gave in to the heat of her desires, the ache she felt between her legs, pulsing, throbbing, needing him there.

Her dress was open, her bare breasts exposed, lit up in the darkness as he gently, softly worked his mouth around them, circling her nipples with his tongue until she felt she might cry out. Nothing felt more right in that moment than their bodies touching, the smell of his hair as his tongue travelled from her breastbone to her hips, slightly damp, fresh from the shower, like mandarins. And she realised just how it felt to be wanted by a man, really wanted and desired, a feeling she had been missing her entire marriage, it felt, as his lips touched her intimately, causing her to moan in pleasure as he buried his mouth into her, her legs naturally opening wider to accept him, giving herself to him at last …

A sharp noise – a crack in the air – startled them and they both bolted upright, killing the intensity of the moment.

'What the hell was that?' she asked, breathless, her chest heaving. She pulled her dress together.

'Jesus, I don't know,' he said, his head darting in all directions in a bid to locate the source.

'Let's get out of here, Nate,' she said, suddenly remembering that they could be being watched right this very second. Panic seized her. 'Let's go … they could be watching.'

Reluctantly he agreed.

'And we have to be back by midnight,' she reminded him. Whatever they were about to discover she would not miss the chance to confront McKenzie face-to-face with what she now knew.

Nate could not contain his disappointment but he knew they had to leave. She was right; they may be watching and he did not want the moment violated. They would have to wait.

'You got it, Cinderella,' he smiled at her as he pulled up the sleeves of his suit and began to row.

'I can't believe we made it here, Nate,' she said, her body close to his in the confined space of the heaving club. She felt the heat of him against her; his strong body pressed tightly against her own, her heart thudding in time to the base line of Ne-Yo's 'Closer' – an irony that was not lost on her. What had happened on the boat, the intimate moment between them that had felt so right, was still lingering on her skin, her desire undampened.

'Do you realise what this means? It means that we can go back for the others, let them know that there's a way off the island. We were so close all along we could've practically swum it.'

They had only been rowing for ten minutes when thousands of tiny lights came into view, illuminating the sky, twinkling like diamonds and causing her to gasp aloud: 'Nate! Look!'

He'd glanced behind him and began to row faster. The island had been there all along, hidden from view behind the huge mountains and rocks.

Angelika looked down at her wrist, at the watch that wasn't on it.

'Don't panic, we've got plenty of time. Let's just enjoy ourselves now that we're here, get a drink, shall we?' he said, pulling her through the gridlocked crowd towards the bar that groups of young women were dancing upon with careless abandon, lost in a moment of hedonism, stolen by the music.

He ordered them two Jagermeisters and two gin and tonics, consumed by a sense of freedom and relief at finally being off the island, boyed up on endorphins, the taste of her still on his lips. It was only then he realised he didn't have the means to pay for them and signalled to the barman but as luck would have it he'd moved onto the next reveller and so he slipped away quietly with the drinks. Let's celebrate, Ange. Let's celebrate the fact that in spite of everything that's happened we found each other; that among the madness and mayhem we found each other. Because none of it matters to me anymore – what happened on the island – now that I've met you.'

He downed the shot and she followed suit, conscious of eyes upon them. People were staring. The noise was deafening and the music went through her like it was attached to her aorta, almost painful. She felt conspicuous in her evening dress, more befitting for the opera than a night's clubbing in a sweatbox, and it only added to her paranoia. It was too much too soon – the music, the lights, the crowd – complete sensory overload, the antithesis of the comparative solitude of the island.

How quickly one adapts to one's surroundings, she thought. How quickly one accepts a situation in which one has no control.

'Have you noticed, Nate?' she asked, enjoying the bitter taste of the alcohol as it slipped down her throat. It felt good to drink something other than champagne. If she never had another glass in her life it would be a day too soon.

'Noticed what? How beautiful you are? How much I think I'm falling in love with you?'

She shook her head, unable to help but smile at his exuberance, at his sudden candidness. Suddenly she was serious once more. 'We're being watched.'

Nate consciously looked at the faces around them – faces that appeared to be nodding in recognition as they observed them.

'We think you make a really lovely couple,' a young girl said as she danced close, bodies touching through lack of space, the crowd moving in unison, a human wave.

The girl beamed at them, her neat, white smile aglow in the neon lighting.

Angelika looked at him. 'You see,' she said, 'it's like they know who we are, Nate. *How* do they know?'

'Maybe it was just an observation.' He beamed at her, his handsome features lit up. 'Maybe we *do* really make a lovely couple.' He pulled her closer into him, swaying his hips in time to the beat, grinding his pelvis into hers once more, losing himself in the stolen moment; a moment he hoped would last forever. It was finally just the two of them, together and it felt right; *she* felt right.

Angelika scanned the club; it was hot and sweaty, nothing chic about it, just pure hedonism in a box. For a moment it felt like she had jumped from the frying pan into the furnace.

People know who we are, she said again, only this time more to herself.

'You want another drink?' He was smiling; lost in the moment, almost forgetting the reason they were there in the first place.

'No, Nate, I just want to sit down … to think.'

'I'll get us another,' he said. 'You find a table and I'll bring them over.' He squeezed her fingers between his reassuringly and she nodded, realising it futile to argue. She wanted to tell him her theory as to why McKenzie had invited them all to the island in the first place … only she could barely allow herself to think it, let alone say it. Besides, she couldn't prove it. She could prove nothing. *Not yet.*

Throwing back her gin and tonic, Angelika surveyed the erupting room. So many young, beautiful people having the time of their lives, their lack of cynicism almost palpable. Would she do any of it differently if she had this time over again? Ha! Only regret the things you didn't do rather than the things you did, right? Yeah, well, what if you regretted both? What if you regretted *everything*?

'We need a phone,' she thought, 'maybe someone here will lend us one?' She was conscious of time and it occurred to her that it was late and they had no idea where they were. Who would she call anyway: the police? And say what? She wasn't even sure a crime had been committed. With her despair growing, Angelika frantically tried to think what to do next. And then it came to her: Kirkbride – her boss! She'd call him, get him to book them a flight on the company, explain later. If she promised him an exclusive, then he'd probably fly the damn plane himself.

'Hey –' Angelika smiled at a couple of young guys who were dancing drunkenly, staggering along to the music as they spilled beer down their slogan T-shirts and whistled at every girl who came within spitting distance '– where are we?'

'What you say?' one of the young men lurched forward, his breath smelled of strong alcohol and weed. Thankfully he spoke English.

'I said where are we?'

'The Scandinavian Bar!' He announced this to her as if she had died and gone to heaven, his eyes wide, like he was on something. 'Best fucking disco on the planet, yeah!'

'No, I mean where are we? What's the name of this island?'

The guy stopped for a moment and looked at her as if she had just come down with the last shower. But, before his brain could register such confusion, the DJ shouted over the mic: 'Mykonos! Let's go fucking *craaaaazzzzzy*!'

'Did you hear that, Ange?' Nate was back and shouting over the music which seemed to be getting harder and louder by the minute. 'He said Mykonos ... we're in Mykonos.'

'Can I borrow your phone?' Angelika gave the boy the best seductive smile she could muster under the circumstances.

'My phone?' The guy gave her a look that clearly said he thought she was weird. 'For what?'

'Please, it's an emergency. I just need to make a quick call.'

The guy stared at her blankly wondering if he recognised her from somewhere; she had a familiar face. He handed it over reluctantly but without much argument.

'Hey! Oh, my fucking God!' Another young reveller had approached them, her mouth wide, eyes like saucers, her crop top barely containing her pert, bouncing tits, her toned midriff on proud display as she bobbed up and down in time to the beat excitedly. 'I can't believe it!' She turned behind her, checking to see if anyone else had spotted her find. 'It's *you!*' she squealed excitedly.

'*Me?*'

And then she saw him through the crowd; it *was* him, wasn't it? The boot-polish dark hair slicked to one side like something out of *Bugsy Malone*, the crooked smile that had instantly made her feel uneasy the moment she had boarded that godforsaken plane, and those shifty eyes. His head was thrown back in abandon, laughing; he was dancing, throwing shapes with alacrity. He looked happy to be *alive* …

'Excuse me –' Angelika pushed past the girl, making her way towards him through the crowd.

'Yeah, well, screw you, too!' the girl called out after her. 'Think you're someone special now that you're famous, right?'

'Hey! My phone!' the drunk guy said. 'That bitch just took my phone!'

But Angelika was gone, lost in the crowd. She was moving towards him with tunnel vision, pushing her way through clammy bodies, paying scant regard for manners she had always been so meticulous about, her heart knocking against her ribs half a beat faster than the music. It *was* him. She gasped as she grew closer, her hand automatically covering her mouth in shock. He was dancing – with *her*. It was him *and* her … together. And in that moment it all suddenly made terrible, diabolical sense. In that moment she understood everything so clearly.

'Well, well, well,' she said as she approached him head on, his euphoric expression dropping like a stone. 'Don't you guys dance pretty well for a couple of dead people?'

CHAPTER FIFTY

'Lady, what the fuck is your problem?' At first he hadn't recognised her but then suddenly he remembered exactly who she was; it was the woman from the plane, and the guy, too: McKenzie's guests, the ones who had been in the staged plane crash, actors he'd presumed, although he had never asked because when McKenzie requested you to do something you just did it. You didn't ask questions, not if you wanted to keep your job anyway. And he did, as did his wife Aki. McKenzie had paid them a small fortune for what he called their 'invaluable contribution', enough for them to buy their own place outright with change left over, and he'd been more than happy to sign a confidentially agreement once he'd seen the fiscal rewards for such loyalty. Hell, for that kind of money he would've crashed the plane for real and done a stint in the hospital if needs be.

'What the …' Nate stared at them as he reached Angelika, his mouth forming an O-shape in disbelief. 'The pilot … but … but you were dead,' he said. 'I saw you myself.'

Angelika saw the panic on Aki's face as she began to back away from them.

'How did you do it?' she asked. 'How did you stage the crash?'

'Hiro, let's go,' Aki spoke quickly, her eyes searching for the exit.

'Hiro …' Angelika snorted with mirth, though it belied her nervousness within, 'now there's a misnomer if ever I heard one.'

'Listen, lady, you've got the wrong guy,' he said but it sounded lame and they both knew it.

'Were we drugged? Was there something in the champagne? Is that why we can't remember properly?'

Hiro looked at her through his dark, narrow eyes. 'Lady, you don't know who you're dealing with … If I were you, I would go quietly. Don't make a fuss now … it'll do you no good.'

Aki suddenly made a run for the exit, pushing a young partygoer to the floor in her haste.

'Jesus!' the girl screamed after her. 'Don't fucking mind me, bitch!'

Hiro was quick to follow her and Angelika lunged in a bid to prevent him but he slipped from her grasp.

'Leave them,' Nate said. The crowd was just too dense. It was pointless trying to give chase.

Angelika looked at the phone. It was 11.38pm.

'Let's get out of here, Ange,' he said, grabbing her hand he began pulling her through the bustling throng. 'We've need to get back to the island, tell the others what we've seen, and decide what to do.'

'It never happened, Nate.' Angelika felt tears of frustration prick her eyes. 'He staged it all … the crash … faked the pilot's death and took all our possessions, kept us virtual prisoners … goldfish in a bowl.'

'I know, Ange,' he said gently, as he dragged her towards the exit of the bar, 'I know.'

The music was deafening now, hard core trance pulsating in her ears until they felt like they might bleed, yet still it could not drown out the question that was screaming inside her mind.

But why? *WHY*?

The water was slightly choppier on the return journey and Nate's muscles were burning as he struggled to control the small, wooden boat.

'C'mon … *come on* … Oh, God, Nate, there's hardly any signal.' Angelika held the phone above her in blind panic. 'One bar at most.'

'Just keep trying, Ange,' he said, breathless; it was pitch-black now and he prayed he was rowing in the right direction; if he took them further out to sea they would be screwed. The air was chilly now and he could see she was shivering. He took off his suit jacket.

'Put this on.'

'No really it's –'

'Please.'

She wrapped it around her shoulders, and then punched in the digits. There was a long, protracted silence while she waited.

'The number you have dialled has not been recognised. Please check and try again.'

'Shit, Nate, I can't remember the bloody number.'

'Yes, you can, just don't panic … stay calm … take your time.'

His voice momentarily soothed her and she took a deep breath and dialled again.

'For God's sake, John –' she held her breath '– please still be there … *please* …'

CHAPTER FIFTY-ONE

On a busy news day it was not unusual for John Kirkbride to do what he referred to as a 'writer's all-nighter'. 'News doesn't stop because you need some shut-eye': that's what he told his exhausted team between coffee breaks anyhow. Besides, in his years of experience, it was always while you slept that the best stuff seemed to take place, which was probably why he looked more like 65 than his 55 years, and why a bottle of Brandy never even touched the sides.

As expected, yesterday's headlines had sent every news desk on the planet into a virtual feeding frenzy. Anything to do with McKenzie always made headline news but this ... this was the scandal of the century. McKenzie had links to a lot of people in high positions, including politicians, judges, celebrities and royalty, and the establishment was quite rightly shitting itself lest it be exposed. Many had already begun the process of disassociation. Now it was simply a battle between the rags over who could get the latest scoop. The links had gone viral by now, and with the competition having equal access, it was a race to come up with the next sensational splash.

McKenzie's people weren't talking, however, and had closed ranks but the very fact that the high courts had already put an injunction out there to shut down the live feed spoke volumes. That dirty bastard had been filming his guests for his own perverted pleasure and now, with his reputation in steep decline, he had a *lot* of questions to answer, if only anyone knew where the fuck he was.

John Kirkbride looked at his phone. It had been ringing off the goddamn hook ever since they'd broken the story and during the past 24 hours he had spoken to everyone from the PM's right-hand man to Billie-Jo Simmons' mum, who was clearly willing, if not keen, to sell a story on her daughter. The high-court writ from McKenzie's people banning him from publishing anything they deemed 'defamatory' against their client had already hit his desk, and as such his hands were tied until he could garner more evidence, another side of the story, ideally from the guests themselves.

Kirkbride was pushing his luck and he knew it but he'd run with this because his gut told him it was the real deal, and there would little more pleasurable experiences in his career than to go down in history as one of the men who brought down the great Martin McKenzie, exposing him for the twisted, psychotic, ruthless fucker he'd always suspected him of being.

Cath Redmond poked her head round the door. She looked like he felt: shit.

'Starbucks run,' she croaked. 'Coffee and a muffin?'

Kirkbride shook his head.

'Liquid supper,' he said, opening his top drawer and producing a half bottle of cheap cognac.

She pulled a face. 'That stuff'll kill yer.'

'Could think of worse ways to go … Any news on the hacker yet?'

'Yep, some kid called Cody Parker in the US, but he ain't talking … yet. It's gonna be a difficult one, John, because the boy – well, he's a man really – is autistic. They're protecting him already. But we're on it; I've offered the mum some serious wedge and a huge charity donation, said we'll fly them over here and put them up in the fucking Ritz if we have to. It won't be long … '

'Make sure it isn't, Cath; if those bastards at the *Sun* usurp us on this I'll piss nails.'

'Drink too much of that shit and you'll be pissing blood.'

'Like you give a shit.'

His phone rang and she shot him a wry smile before closing the door.

He rubbed his gritty eyes.

'Kirkbride.'

'John! John, oh my God, you're there! He's there, Nate!'

Kirkbride sat bolt upright in his knackered, old office chair, knocking his bottle of brandy clean over.

'Jesus shitting Christ … Angelika, is that you? Angelika?'

The line crackled like the embers of a bonfire and he winced, placing a finger in his ear in a bid to hear her better.

'Yes, John, it's me! Listen, John, I really need your help.'

'Where are you? Angelika can you hear me?' The line was atrocious.

'I can hear you, John … just about … I'm in a boat … listen, John –'

'Who are you with? Is McKenzie with you? Ange … Ange, we know what's been going on.'

'What?' Angelika strained to hear him. 'You know? What did you say, John … John?'

'Yeah, I'm here, Ange. Are you OK? Is everyone else OK? Listen, you need to get the hell out of there. McKenzie has been filming you all. You need to leave. Immediately.'

'There was plane crash, only it wasn't real. He staged it and –' Angelika suddenly paused '– how did you know we were being filmed, John?' Icy fear shot through her body and Nate's jacket slipped from her shoulders.

'We had to run with the story, Ange. We did our best to protect you … the Simmons girl … a sex tape … Where are you?'

'You need to send a plane, John, as soon as you can.'

'Yes … yes, of course, of course.' He was almost hyperventilating. 'But where to?' He picked up his pen, poised.

The line fizzed and sizzled.

'Are you still there?' he asked. 'Where to, Ange? Where are you?'

There was a delay on the line, the signal dipping in and out making her sound like a dalek.

'We're on an island just north of Mykonos … I don't know exactly. The boat's not big enough for all of us. Please John, send a plane!'

'Yes, yes, it's OK. I hear you, Ange. It's going to be OK. Is McKenzie with you?'

'No, he's meeting us at the mansion, tonight. Listen, John, what did you mean when you said you *know*?'

John Kirkbride picked up the brandy bottle that was lying on its side and attempted to drink the dregs. *Jesus Christ alive*, he thought as he took a deep breath, the poor bitch doesn't have a clue.

CHAPTER FIFTY-TWO

'Are we too late?' Angelika burst onto the roof terrace, her gown hoisted in one hand, her Alexander McQueen sandals in the other. The Havaianas had gone overboard. She was almost hyperventilating, her chest tight with adrenalin. Nate followed close behind her, his expression equally dire. They appeared shocked and dishevelled, her face a sea-salty mess of smudged mascara, his hands dirty, shirt rolled to the elbows.

'Jesus Christ, Angelika –' Rupert cut her off '– where in fucking God's name have you been?' He stood abruptly, abandoning his dinner plate with a clatter, his appetite long since passed. His anger completely disappeared, however, when he caught the look of genuine anguish on his wife's pale face. 'What is it?' he asked. 'What's happened?'

Angelika wasn't sure how she was going to tell them what Kirkbride had told her. She wasn't sure that she could.

'Did you know you were being filmed, Ange?' Kirkbride had asked her, 'that McKenzie has been spying on you all, though for what purpose … well … God only knows.'

'Yes, I've had my suspicions all along.' Her voice was breaking up and he struggled to hear what she was saying, 'I found a camera, and confronted him. He denied it, of course. But John, how do you know? How do you know that he's been watching us, unless –' and it had hit her full force and she gasped, instinctively putting her hand to her mouth '– you've been watching us too …'

'I'm so sorry, Ange.' John Kirkbride had sighed heavily, . 'I'm afraid it's not just me who's been watching,' he'd said, wishing he didn't have to, 'it's the whole Goddamn world.'

That's when Angelika had become hysterical.

'Nate?' Mia stood up from the table now, her heartbeat knocking against the heavy necklace she was wearing. She sensed something was wrong … terribly wrong.

'You cheating pair of bastards.' Billie-Jo launched herself at her husband drunkenly before Angelika could answer them. Secretly seething she'd been steadily knocking back the champagne and slipping off to the restroom for her usual coke fix all evening and was ready to explode. 'No fucking shame, the pair of yous.'

JJ held her back. 'Take a chill pill, babe,' he said in a bid to calm her down.

Billie-Jo was having none of it. 'Headache, you said.' She pointed a long, accusing fingernail at Nate's chest. 'Yeah, well you'd better get used to having one of them because the first thing I'm doing when we get home is contacting a solicitor. In fact, Rupert here has already agreed to represent me when I take you to the fucking cleaners, ain't cha, Rupert?'

Rupert was still staring at Angelika; he'd never seen her look so frightened in all the years he'd known her and it sent a chill down his spine. He thought about reaching out to her and putting his arms around her but he couldn't bring himself to.

'Angelika?'

'We'll rinse him for everything he's got' Billie-Jo ranted, fired-up on booze and coke. As hypocritical outbursts went it was pretty spectacular but she felt genuinely wronged. She may well be doing the dirty with JJ on the sly, not forgetting the afternoon with the well-built masseur, but at least she'd had the integrity to try and cover her tracks and keep it on the low-down. These two brazen fuckers … they didn't seem to care who knew, sloping off like that and rubbing everyone's noses right in it without a red face between them.

Furious, she struggled from JJ's grip.

Holy shit, JJ thought, this chick is *insane*.

Rupert could see that Angelika was shaking.

'No … no, you don't understand,' she said, 'we have to get out of here … we have to leave *now*. Right now!' Her voice was low and husky, and Nate spontaneously put his arm around her. 'Something terrible has ha–'

'You fucking bitch!' Billie-Jo screamed, pushed over the edge by Nate's action. As the slap made contact with Angelika's face it resonated through the night air with a sickening crack. 'He's my fucking husband! Stay away from him, you slag!'

'Leave her alone!' Nate roared at Billie-Jo, pushing her away as Angelika brought her hand up to her face in shock. 'You don't understand, you stupid bitch!'

Mia looked on, horrified. 'Children, please!' she exclaimed. 'This really isn't the time or –'

But before she could finish, the video screen suddenly lit up and McKenzie's image came into view.

CHAPTER FIFTY-THREE

Martin McKenzie felt a strange sense of relief as the private jet made a smooth take-off from the farthest – and most sheltered – northerly point of Pleasure Island in a calculated bid to ensure his guests would not detect his departure. He glanced at his Cartier watch. It was 11.57pm. The pre-recorded footage he had made would appear on the video screen at any moment now and his prestigious players were about to unwittingly enact the final curtain call in his master plan. With a bottle of aged malt beside him and a celebratory Cohiba already lit, he flipped the lid of his laptop and booted it up in anticipation.

This was the moment he had been waiting for – the pinnacle of the entire exercise, the crescendo – though the build-up had been somewhat dampened by a terrible hallucination he'd had the previous evening that was still lingering fresh in his mind. Elaine; she had appeared at his bedside during the night, her skin dripping with water, seaweed matted in her hair, her prefrontal cortex missing, blood and tissue smattered on her conservative swimsuit. Her fingernails were black, like she'd had been clawing at debris, her facial expression fixed in the one of despair she'd had as he'd brought the cloche down onto her skull.

'Why, Marty?' She had shuffled towards him in small, juddery, unnatural steps, her familiar voice gravelly as though her lungs were filled with water. 'Why? Why did you do it?'

'Elaine …?' Perspiring profusely, he'd rubbed his eyes, the apparition almost rendering him blind with terror. 'No … no … get away from me … Noooo!'

He had pulled the expensive, cotton sheets over his head and screamed. He had been unable to close his eyes again for the rest of the night.

McKenzie swallowed a few fingers of Scotch and decided to check his phone messages. He needed to get a grip; people had been trying to reach him. Once he was back in the UK it would be business as usual, plus he would have to declare his wife missing, and then there would be press to deal with, policemen to talk to, and an international search to embark upon. He would be forced to draw on his acting skills to convey a convincing role of the concerned husband. Damn that woman; even in death she would cause him consternation and bother. McKenzie located his phone and switched it on. It beeped immediately in quick succession and he cursed. The 67 previous missed calls had now escalated to 215. There were 16 new voice messages. This was his private number, all business calls were usually filtered through one of his many overworked PAs. Whoever was trying to reach him must've been desperate.

Knocking back the remainder of his Scotch, he filtered through them. The majority were from his legal representatives, Larry Goldenburg & Co. What did *they* want? Larry was a good friend but the kind you only called upon in an emergency. McKenzie felt the lightest flutter of concern settle on top of his Scotch as it slid into his guts. The messages went back a few days. He'd ignored them of course because deep down McKenzie knew he wasn't going to like what he was about to hear.

'Martin, yes, hi, it's Larry Goldenburg.' The man's nasal, Jewish tones irritated his ear almost instantly. 'Um, we got a bit of a situation going on here and I need to speak with you urgently. Can you call as soon as you pick up this message? Thank you.'

McKenzie puzzlement slipped seamlessly into concern. Like himself, Larry rarely, if ever, contacted his clients direct, not as a first point of call, anyhow. This would have to have been a matter of extreme importance. The remaining messages simply compounded that something was indeed very wrong:

'McKenzie, yeah, um it's Larry again. Listen, I have to speak with you as soon as possible. Please, the moment you get this message, call me'; 'Martin, it's Goldenburg again. Look, some serious shit has hit the fan. I really don't want to have to do this in a message. Call me. *Now.* Please …'; 'McKenzie, Goddamn it, man, call me! You're in it up to your neck, and I need your instructions. My fucking phone is ringing off the hook … *where are you?*'

McKenzie had begun to shake now as he listened to the messages one after the other. There was a different caller.

'Yeah, um, Mr McKenzie –' the voice was as urgent as it was unfamiliar '– this is John Kirkbride from the *Voice*. I need to speak to you in connection with some footage we've reason to believe took place on an island that you own. It's regarding Mia Manhattan and Joshua Jones, Angelika and Rupert Deyton, and Nate and Billie-Jo Simmons. We'd like to get some facts straight before we go ahead and run with anything, and were hoping to ask you a few questions if possible. We've tried your reps but no one's getting back to us. I hope you don't mind my calling you directly. My private line is 0207 …'

Hyperventilating, McKenzie scrolled through the myriad messages from his press team.

'Please call the office. It's URGENT!' There were at least 30 more.

Even Bailey had given him the heads-up. 'Your number's up, McKenzie. You're *weally, weally* in the shit now. We all are.'

Panic gripped him like a hand around the throat. Why the fuck would a filthy muck-peddler like Kirkbride want to speak to him about Pleasure Island? No one knew where it was. The guests had had no contact with the outside world since their arrival. Even if the likes of Bailey had sung to the press, which was unlikely given the fact he'd settled the man's exorbitant tax bill, all he knew was that Mia had been invited to a private holiday destination. No one but he and Elaine and the Super Eight knew the identity of the other players. There was little if any chance of one of the club members having gone public; to do so would mean exposing their own identities and deviances, and unless the dead had somehow learned to speak from the grave …

So how did Kirkbride know? Unless, of course …

McKenzie, massaging his heart with his hand in a bid to stop it thudding, logged into his computer using his private access code and watched as the images of the island came into view as usual, clicking on his internal message system which allowed him to speak solely with the Super Eight club members.

'Super8#4 is no longer active … Super8#2 has left the conversation …'

He looked at the bottom of the screen in a bid to check who might be online, and could shed some light on just what the hell had happened here. He saw that the current online users had rapidly escalated since he had last checked … to an astonishing 1,678,356.

But that just couldn't be right; his technical people had given him their complete reassurance that it must just be a glitch, a mistake, a technical error. He clicked on his private email, ostensibly to contact that walking-dead man who had built the forum and who had claimed it to be 'unhackable'. There was a message from him already waiting.

'I need to speak to you with the utmost urgency, sir,' it read. 'I'm afraid something seems to have gone horribly wrong.'

There was another message underneath it. One from Super8#4, the female deviant who had pleasured him so willingly in his office. It simply read: 'You're fucked.'

McKenzie dropped the laptop, and the bottle of Scotch went down with it.

'Fucking shit!'

Alerted to the din, Aki came running through the red, velvet curtain.

'Is everything OK, Mr McKenzie?' she nervously enquired, scrabbling to clean up the mess.

'A newspaper,' he said, his lips were suddenly dry as sandpaper and he struggled with the words. 'Bring me a newspaper … and another bottle of Scotch.'

Aki nodded profusely. She had never seen Martin McKenzie in anything other than a state of complete control and restraint and she hurried off, frantically rushing back with a pile of newspapers and a fresh bottle of Macallan single malt.

Snatching the papers from her grasp so violently that she gasped in shock, McKenzie stared at the front page as horror seeped into every crevice of his body to the point where he thought he might have a seizure.

'Oh, fuck …' he whispered as he read the headline. '*Fuck …*'

Aki hovered next to him, a look of genuine fear on her small, flat face.

'Can I … can I get you anything else, sir?' she squeaked through her terror.

'Yes.' McKenzie said. 'Bring me my gun.'

CHAPTER FIFTY-FOUR

'Firstly, I must apologise for not being there in person.' McKenzie cut a sharp image on-screen with his slicked-back hair and trademark dark suit, reminiscent of a fading Hollywood actor. 'But I'm sure you can appreciate, or certainly will after this speech, why I felt perhaps it prudent not to be.'

'He's had a facelift,' Mia remarked dryly.

Angelika was still as a statue, the sound of her heartbeat ringing in her ears, her hand still holding her stinging face.

'Is this a live recording?' Rupert blinked at the screen. 'Because if it is —'

'Shhh!' Mia snapped. 'Let's just listen to what the bastard has to say, shall we?'

Nate slipped his fingers into Angelika's and she gripped them tightly. No one noticed; they were too preoccupied.

'We have to tell them now,' she said quietly, but the truth was she wanted to hear what McKenzie had to say as much as the rest of them did.

'I suppose you're all wondering why I invited you here to Pleasure Island in the first place.' McKenzie cleared his throat loudly, like a politician addressing his crowd. 'Well, I am about to explain, but before that I would like to thank you all personally for providing myself and my fellow club members or, as I prefer to call them, "the Super Eight" with such excellent footage over the duration of these past two weeks, it's been —' he paused, thoughtfully '— riveting to observe.'

'What's he talking about?' Billie-Jo's faced crumpled. 'Observe? Observe what?'

'Us, you stupid girl,' Rupert said, without taking his eyes from the screen.

'Some of you, that is to say the smarter amongst you, have rightly already suspected that you were being watched. Of course, the question you are no doubt asking yourselves right this very second is why exactly?'

Billie-Jo swallowed back nausea. This was a joke, right? A sick joke.

McKenzie paused again, though his cool composure remained intact.

'Some time ago I had an idea for a new reality game show, one in which the contestants had no idea they were being observed. The premise of the initial concept was to place a group of people onto an island and ... how can I put it?' He stroked his chin. 'Put them in various situations in a bid to see how they would react. Place temptation in their way, obstacles for them to overcome, secrets to divulge ... that sort of thing ... thus affording the viewer a psychological insight into their individual personalities. A social experiment, if you will.'

'Oh my fucking God.' Billie-Jo exchanged nervous looks with JJ.

'The plane crash,' McKenzie continued, 'was pre-designed to put you on the back foot. We wanted to test your metal, myself and my fellow viewers, see what you were made of, which of you would sink and which would swim, metaphorically speaking, of course.'

'*Fellow* viewers?' Rupert's hands were shaking violently. '*Super Eight?*' He rubbed his temples. This wasn't really happening. It was all a horrific nightmare, wasn't it? *Had McKenzie witnessed his tryst with Raj?*

'As it was, all of you somewhat surprised us with your individual capabilities and survival instincts. Though perhaps now would be a good time to express my apologies to young Joshua for the business with his arm. That particular incident wasn't supposed to happen, but the best-laid plans and all of that. Anyway –' he smiled jovially '– the champagne was laced with a strong sedative which allowed the operation to run smoothly, or as smoothly as possible anyhow. And, shall I say, no real *arm* was done.' He laughed then, a horrible sound that showcased him as the psychotic maniac he really was.

'Of course, my wife Elaine was fully briefed and privy to all plans and the staff, the pilot and the flight attendant on my payroll, and the men and women who have helped make this experience a truly luxurious one, are all trained actors who, while aware of the cameras, were not aware of *your* lack of awareness of them, so please, don't blame them should any of you feel the need to vent any frustration.'

'I need another drink,' Mia said to no one in particular.

'Frustration? Is he for real? Angelika could barely believe what she was hearing.

'And so,' McKenzie continued, 'to the bit you've all been waiting for. Why us?' He stood then, clearly revelling in being the centre of attention, albeit by proxy. 'This was no random selection process. There really was a method to the madness.'

He paused for a moment, took a sip of his Scotch before carefully placing it down on the desk and addressing the camera once more. 'Revenge –' he said the word as though he were recording a TV commercial and explaining to the viewer why they should buy his product '– is of course a dish best served cold. But I feel it one of the most underrated of the sins, if one can call it such a thing. Let me elaborate. Many years ago, decades in fact, I discovered a young singer –'

Mia froze.

'Ahhh, the beautiful Mia, or should I say June? I do hope you're listening, I want you to savour every word of this.'

'*June?*' Billie-Jo stifled a snigger.

'June truly was the find of my career: young, beautiful, supremely talented, I'm sure she won't mind me saying.'

Mia gulped back her drink, swallowing down nausea with it.

'I made her an overnight sensation, a household name. I gave her everything she was, and still is to some extent today. June had – has, in fact – me to thank for the life she's been privileged enough to experience: for the glittering career; the riches and the adoration and success; the cars and the homes and the places she has travelled. None of this would have been possible without me.'

'He's absolutely insane, a despot, completely certifiable … He's going to prison, you know that, don't you?'

'Shut up, Rupert!' Mia snapped. 'I need to hear this. We all do.'

'Only instead of her loyalty, instead of the gratitude due to me in abundance, dear June decided there was something better out there for her and so she dismissed me … betrayed me by taking up with a rival label – an unforgivable act of treachery that I am sure you can all comprehend. *I* made Mia Manhattan the person she is today. It was *I* who bankrolled her first-ever world tour. *I* who convinced some of the world's greatest artists to collaborate with her. *I* who changed her name, took her from a plain, frumpy nobody and turned her into a mega star *and* it was *I* who fixed it all for her when got herself pregnant with a son, whom incidentally she went on to give up for adoption. But I digress slightly, for now at least.'

Mia swallowed. She felt lightheaded with rage. *That bastard*, how could he? Given up for adoption? Forced into it by that evil heartless cunt more like! Mia had been just nineteen years old when she discovered she was carrying a child, news made all the more bittersweet by the fact that on the very same day she had also scored her first UK number one with 'Dreams Like These'. Terrified, she had concealed the truth for six weeks before finally plucking up the courage to break the news to her formidable mentor.

'Get rid of it,' he'd instructed her coldly. 'You have that child and you can kiss goodbye any hopes of a glittering career, Mia, because it won't happen, you hear me.' She had begun to cry then.

McKenzie's shocking brutality had blindsided her; her tears replaced by silent sobs. How could he be so cold, so cruel? She had thought that he loved her. How stupid she had been.

'I'll arrange it all, pay for a private doctor, make sure you're looked after. You'll be back at work within the week.'

Only it wasn't as simple as that. Mia had lied to him about how far gone she was and had left it too late; and had felt the child kicking inside her belly, the sensation of arms and legs connecting with her body, causing a deep bond within her. She was attached to the child already, the desire to see the pregnancy through as strong as her ambition.

'I'm having this baby; I'm already twenty-five-weeks gone, maybe more.' She didn't tell him that the child was his. How could she now? He didn't want her, didn't love her.

McKenzie had looked at her with such disgust that she'd felt ashamed.

'You fucking foolish girl.' He'd rubbed his temples in angst, struggling to think. ' I can keep you in the studio away from the limelight, build up a bit of mystique until the child's born, but once you expel that thing you put it up for adoption and it's back to business.'

On the twenty-first day of September 1981, two weeks ahead of her due date, Mia Manhattan had given birth to a tiny baby boy. The sound of his cry as he'd entered the world for the first time haunted her like a recording to this day. Those lungs! He was her son all right! She had made to put him to her breast instinctively, an overwhelming rush of endorphins contaminating her with such intense feelings of love that she never wanted to let him go. She wanted to protect him, comfort him, feel the warmth and newness of his skin against her own, her boy, her son. And in that moment Mia had understood everything clearly; her own parents, her own mortality and what real, unconditional love felt like.

'Kit,' she'd said the name softly to him, her fingers lightly stroking the softest downy fuzz on his warm bloodstained head. It had been her grandfather's middle name and she had always loved it, just as she'd loved him, a gentle, kind man who had always adored his 'little singing princess'.

'Welcome to the world, Kit.' She'd kissed his little head, breathed him in as he'd snuffled and snorted around for her breast. And that's when they had come for him; two stony-faced women in suits, their stiff fingers brutally prizing him from her loving arms.

The weeks that followed post-partum had seen Mia sink into the darkest abyss of deep depression, plagued by images and dreams, the scent of her newborn son omnipresent in her nostrils. Even sleep offered little solace; she would hear his birth cry inside her mind, the trilling of his virginal lungs as they had met with air for the first time. She would awake in the night and search for him thinking she could hear him, smell him, aching for his tiny body against her own. She had never experienced pain like it – emotional pain so intense it had manifested into the physical, rendering her bed-ridden and paralysed. And the tears, oh, the crying … she'd sobbed until her skin was tender and raw to the touch, her diaphragm on the point of collapse.

It had been thirty-three years since Mia had given up her son. Although time had seen her with little choice than to come to terms with it, it had not eased the pain she felt whenever she thought of that grey abysmal day in September, a day that by rights should've been one of the happiest a woman could experience. She'd often contemplated searching for him; the need to know he was alive and safe, happy and looked after had never waned. She'd endlessly daydreamed about him: how he might've looked as a toddler; did he have her eyes, her smile, her determination? Was he married with children himself? She had driven herself half-mad with thoughts of 'what if'. And now, suddenly, there was a strange, new thought running through her mind. What if her adoptive son was closer then she thought…?

CHAPTER FIFTY-FIVE

Rupert shook his head. He didn't understand what Mia's shameful secret had to do with anything. Surely, this wasn't just about settling old scores? Mia's deflection to another record label had taken place years ago, and McKenzie was a businessman, if nothing else. Surely he understood that all was fair in love and business. But he realised in that moment that McKenzie was worse than a narcissistic maniac; he was truly psychotic *and dangerous*.

'This leads me on nicely to the fragrant Angelika Deyton.'

Angelika almost crushed Nate's hand as she squeezed it tightly. It was her turn.

'I can't watch this, ' Billie-Jo said, although she couldn't take her eyes from the screen.

'Once upon a time, not so long ago, I very graciously accepted the lovely Ms Deyton's invitation to interview me for what she herself described as a 'first-person insight' into my good character. After much due consideration, I made the – with hindsight – unwise decision to accept her offer and welcomed her into the realms of my private inner sanctum. However –'

'I knew it.' Rupert turned to Angelika. 'I knew it was that bloody piece you wrote on him. I told you so, didn't I?'

Angelika ignored him, her eyes transfixed upon McKenzie's image; it was the proverbial car-crash that she couldn't look away from.

'– instead of the "insightful and thoughtfully written biography" that Ms Deyton had so carefully duped me into believing she was planning, she instead produced the most unflattering, defamatory portrait of my entire career, and subsequently caused me great embarrassment and considerable distress; a truly unforgiveable act of betrayal.' He paused again momentarily. 'I'm afraid your husband has simply been collateral damage in this little experiment of mine, Angelika. I only hope he can forgive you for dragging him into your mess. Although it does seem he has exacted his own revenge somewhat already –'

Rupert felt weak. *Oh God, here it comes …*

'– but this you will discover in good time,' he added quickly, smiling affably.

'So where the fuck do we fit into this fucking pantomime?' Billie-Jo shrieked at the screen. 'What about me and Nate?'

'And as for Nate and Billie-Jo,' McKenzie said as if he'd heard her question, 'well, the contents of the boxes will explain. Though I would like to say to Nate Simmons how truly sorry I am for what you are about to discover, genuinely so. This was never anything personal against you. In fact, I rather like you, Nate. Out of everyone you appear to be the most likeable. And as for the divine Billie-Jo, well, what a fine performance indeed. You, my dear, are a star in the making, something our specially hired masseur can certainly vouch for.'

Billie-Jo felt a disconcerting mix of fear and elation at the same time. McKenzie had called her 'a star in the making' but … the masseur … So he *had* seen what had taken place at the spa that time.

'Why is he apologising to me?' Nate said. Whatever the reason, he got the distinct impression he wasn't going to like it.

'The keys to the boxes are underneath the cushions of your dinner seats. I do hope you will accept my parting gifts with the good grace in which they were intended. At the very least I hope you will find them most *insightful*. Tomorrow, the telephone lines will be reconnected and the staff will duly arrange for a plane to take you back to reality – that is, your new reality – in the comfort and luxury of one of my private jets. Now I know what you're all thinking, and the distress you may be feeling at this very moment in time, so perhaps it would be prudent of me to remind you of the confidentiality clause, number 7a, and the agreements you, plus every member of the team, all signed before coming into the island, which clearly stipulates that there shall be no public disclosure following your return. Oh, and Rupert, as you well know, this clause is recognised quite clearly by the law. So should you have any inclination to go to the press or even the police, then I am fully within my rights to sue you for breach of contract. But let us hope that it will not come to this. After all, I think you'll all agree that it is in all of our best interests to adopt the motto that "what happens on Pleasure Island stays on Pleasure Island".' He beamed broadly into the camera as it panned in for a close-up. 'So, all that is left for me to say is thank you all –' he placed a hand onto his chest in mock sincerity '– for being the most entertaining and enlightening of guests on my new pilot TV show, which I think you'll agree is bound for future success. None of it could've happened without you. Adieu, my friends. Until we meet again.'

The screen went blank, the silence deafening as they all stood staring at it, paralysed.

Rupert was the first to speak.

'I think we all need to be philosophical about this,' he said, adopting a professional tone as if to offer a panacea. 'And as much as I am loathe agreeing with that sick piece of shit, I think perhaps he is right. We really should think about keeping this to ourselves. I mean, if we let this get out, then we'll all be under scrutiny, won't we? Our privacy invaded even more than it already has been.'

Angelika knew what her husband was saying and more over why he was saying it.

'Taking on a man like McKenzie is akin to taking on the establishment; if we keep calm, stick together, then we may all come out of this better off yet.'

'But he's been watching us!' Billie-Jo was incredulous. 'Dirty old perv, him and his little gang of nonces, the Super Eight or whatever the fuck he called them. And he's been putting drugs in our drinks ... he can't get away wiv it!'

'Well, it seems to me you don't have too much of an issue when it comes to narcotics, Billie-Jo.'

'I do when I've no idea I've been taking them,' she shot back. Rupert's stance had surprised her. She thought he'd have been the one screaming the loudest blue murder and threating McKenzie with all sorts. Now it seemed he wanted it all brushed under the carpet.

In that moment Billie-Jo realised that she'd probably been under the influence of something in the dalliance with the masseur and the thought knocked her sick. She'd shagged that bloke while she'd been unwittingly off her face. That was tantamount to rape, weren't it?

'Yeah, but ...'

'He's had his fun,' Rupert interjected, 'his twisted little revenge. Him and his little club of voyeurs. Perhaps we should all just try and put this nasty little experience beh –'

'Only it's not just him that's been watching us, Rupert,' Angelika interrupted him.

'So there were eight of them in this sick little club.' Rupert shrugged. 'Strangers, people we'll never meet. They're nothing to us, nor us them. They've had their sick fun, these eight freaks, whoever they are.'

'Eight.' Angelika squeezed her eyes tightly together for a moment. 'If only it was just those eight.'

'What you chatting about?' Billie-Jo said. 'Don't tell me there's more of them?'

'Yes,' Nate said, looking at Angelika's pained expression, seeing that she was struggling, 'much more than eight.'

'Much more …?' Mia was confused. 'How many more have been watching us, Nate. Tell me?'

He looked at her with weary resignation.

'The whole world.'

CHAPTER FIFTY-SIX

Gifts. This was the one word from McKenzie's speech that had stood out in Billie-Jo's mind and she rushed to her seat to locate the key to the box. She hoped that whatever was inside would be enough to compensate her for what she had just learned, that the world had watched her getting fucked by her husband, the massage dude *and* Joshua Jones, not to mention shovelling coke up her nose like there was no tomorrow. She was finished after this.

'Open it, Nate.' Her fingers were shaking so much that she couldn't quite manage it herself.

'I'm not sure I want to do this,' Angelika said, 'I don't think I want to know what's inside them.'

'Are we being broadcast now?' Rupert looked at his wife despairingly and she wished she could go to him and comfort him but it was too late for them now; too late for them all.

'Kirkbride says the high court shut down the links some days ago.' She didn't tell him that Kirkbride had also told her that he had seen the footage of her husband with a dark-skinned man down by the rocks; that conversation was for another time. 'I think we're safe.'

'Let's open them in unison,' Rupert said.

'I agree,' Mia said. She took the black box in her hands and began to unlock it.

'Let's finish this sick game once and for all.'

'She's right, Angelika,' Rupert said. 'We need to see this through.' He was clinging on desperately to the hope that his afternoon with Raj was not now something of an Internet sensation. He thought about McKenzie's speech and evaluated it in his mind; something in the man's demeanour told him that McKenzie knew nothing of the fact the footage had been leaked at the time he had made that recording. Had the injunction been made active in time? He, above all people, knew how quickly these things could be turned around and he grasped onto this thought like a comfort blanket. Had he been outed via the Internet, for the whole world to see? He'd be a laughing stock, a figure of public ridicule, or maybe even hate. Would he lose his job, the support of his family, his son's respect. Good God, his own son may have seen. He wanted to throw up and thought he actually might, bile rising up through his diaphragm, his mouth watering, consumed with self-loathing and humiliation. He knew he had no choice but to come clean.

Miserably it also occurred to him that perhaps Raj had actually been paid to find him attractive; that their encounter had simply been an act, albeit a convincing one, and the very idea was somehow more painful than the thought of the entire world watching him getting fucked in the arse.

Mia opened the lid and pulled out the document that was inside it.

'Oh my God.' She began to cry hysterically, her hands shaking violently as she read it. 'Oh dear God, no ...'

McKenzie had picked his PC up off the floor, rebooted it and was watching the drama unfold while swigging neat Scotch from the bottle. The years he had spent planning this whole operation, the expenses he'd incurred buying the island and making it habitable, the research and private investigations … it had all culminated this very moment and yet he could not bring himself to enjoy it as he had hoped he would: the sublime sense of *schadenfreude* as he watched that bitch Mia's face, to feel her pain and suffering first-hand; witnessing Angelika Deyton's life implode as she realised her entire marriage had been a farce – it had all been marred by the thought of the impending fate that awaited him. Still, he attempted to reassure himself; he was one of the richest men on the planet – he would find a way out of this thanks to his chequebook and some considerable blackmail. First, however, he had some TV to watch. He wasn't going to miss this final episode for anything.

CHAPTER FIFTY-SEVEN

Billie-Jo stared at the photograph of a cute-faced baby – a newborn, practically, by the looks of it, in the arms of a young woman with dark hair and a pretty face – and peered into the otherwise-empty box. There were no jewels, no car keys, no platinum membership cards to private clubs or luxury hotels, no hard cash … nothing. Just a Goddamn fucking dog-eared old photograph of some kid. Her palpable disappointment erupted into uncontrollable rage.

'What the fucking hell is this shit?' she shrieked, throwing it to floor, incensed. It fell on its face and she saw there were words written on the back of the picture: 'Kit. September 21st 1978.'

'Kit?' She was hysterical now, the ramifications of everything only just beginning to sink in. 'Who the fuck is Kit?'

Nate snatched the photograph from the floor with shaking fingers. 'September twenty-first, nineteen seventy-eight. That's my birthday.' He stared at the photograph, at the woman holding the baby. Was it him? Was this his birth mother? Was it … he looked up. Mia was standing in front of him, her face a mess of mucus and mascara.

'Yes,' she said, her voice low and calm as she handed him the birth certificate that had been inside her black box. 'Hello. Kit. I'm your mother.'

Nate visibly stumbled backwards.

'Holy fuckamoly,' JJ said. This had been some fucked-up vacation and no mistake. If he'd been a gambling man he would have put money on the idea that they'd just entered the fucking twilight zone.

Rupert reached inside his box and pulled out the contents. It looked like a press-cutting and a hospital-scan picture.

The cutting was taken from the obituary pages, for a Michael Curtis. He recognised the name instantly. Apparently some months ago Michael had hung himself.

Shaking, Rupert discarded it and looked at the hospital scan. It had been taken at the Marie Stopes clinic in 2007, and the small-print read: gestation, 16 weeks … the name on the top: Angelika Deyton.

Silently, they sat around the table. It was a while before anyone spoke.

'I never wanted to give you away.' Mia looked at Nate through blurry eyes. 'I was so young … on the brink of stardom. I was forced to choose and I … I made the wrong choice.'

Nate stared at her blankly. His whole body had gone into a state of paralysis as he struggled to comprehend. Mia Manhattan? His blood mother?

'Can you forgive me, Nate? Please say you will forgive me. A day has never passed when I haven't thought of you. I have carried you in my heart from the moment I held you in my arms. Those few short moments before they took you from me … they were the happiest of my life. Please, Nate,' she begged him, 'please believe me.'

She was on her knees now, her beautiful Marchesa gown gaping open to expose her bejewelled matching underwear, her face a blacked mess of MAC make-up and years of regret. She had dreamt of this moment, fantasised about it her entire life, and yet here it was, delivered in the most brutal fashion by the very man who had fathered him, a man so insidious and sick and evil that she wished she could go back in time and re-write history so as never to have met him. She would have traded it all in now, the fame and the riches, the adoration and success. The day she had met Martin McKenzie had shaped her entire life, and blighted it too.

Billie-Jo made to put her hand on Nate's but he moved it away.

Oddly, he felt relived somehow, like a particularly persistent boil had been finally lanced. They'd been sharing the same space for the past two weeks, neither of them aware of the revelation that was to come. *Mia Manhattan was his mother.* McKenzie had known all along, orchestrated this whole charade for the purpose of throwing them together, watching them, observing them, with the intension of dropping the final bombshell for his own voyeuristic pleasure in a bid to cause maximum pain and humiliation. It beggared belief, like something out of a twisted fairy tale. Still, if they had got through these past couple of weeks, then somehow he figured they could get through anything. McKenzie wouldn't win; he'd make sure of it.

After a long moment's silence he looked up at her.

'Who is my father?' His voice little more than a whisper.

Mia shook her head and gave a small howl, a low, primal scream.

'Mia, please …'

'Oh, God,' she moaned as though she were in physical pain. 'Oh, Nate. I'm so, so sorry.'

She was holding onto his knees now; the poor woman looked wretched and, despite himself, he touched her hand.

'Will you ever forgive me?' Your father is Martin McKenzie,' she said, before collapsing at his feet.

Martin McKenzie had been watching Mia's performance with elation but as soon as she said those words he stopped laughing. *He* was Nate Simmons' father? That lying cunt. Frantically he cast his mind back. Mia had been stepping out with that American chap at the time she'd got herself in the family way, if he remembered rightly. Brogan ... Chad Brogan ... yes, that was it, some flash-in-the-pan overrated young actor. He'd assumed he'd been the one to father the child, although now that he thought of it Mia had never actually confirmed this, and the timing of their own brief affair ... he supposed ... No, she was bluffing, wasn't she?

McKenzie unbuckled his seat and picked up the Colt M1911 pistol that Aki had duly brought to him on request. He kept one in every aircraft he owned – a man of his wealth and status could never be too careful – and made his way, unsteadily, through the red, velvet curtain.

'Turn the plane around,' he instructed Hiro. Aki's wide eyes were drawn to the gun in his unsteady hand and she said something to her husband in their native tongue.

'Is impossible right now, Mr McKenzie,' Hiro replied. 'The visibility is poor. It be too dangerous. We need more height, better vision –'

McKenzie wasn't interested in the details that accompanied the word no.

'I'm not asking you, you stupid nip, I'm telling you, turn this damn plane around right now! Take me back to the island immediately. That's a command!'

Hiro and Aki began conversing quickly, their expressions animated.

'Is no safe, sir,' she explained, 'my husband say if we do, we die.'

'And tell your husband that if he doesn't he's dead anyway.' McKenzie pointed the gun at Hiro's head. He had a son … *a son*. A decent, successful, talented, handsome son. *His* son. It was what McKenzie had always wanted: a child who would continue his legacy, someone to which he could pass down his knowledge and wisdom, who would follow in his footsteps, look up to him in awe adoringly … the unconditional love of a child which would offer the narcissist his purest source of supply.

'No, sir, no!' Aki made to seize the gun and began to grapple with him. It went off almost immediately and she screamed as the contents of her husband's head exploded over the small cockpit.

'Bloody hell! Now look what you made me do, stupid bitch!' he pistol-whipped her face and she collapsed on top of her husband's corpse. Ironic really, McKenzie fleetingly observed; it was almost an exact re-enactment of the death they had staged. Well, they did say life imitated art. And then it struck him: with the pilot decorating the cockpit who was going to fly this damned plane? He pulled Aki from her husband's body, and she fell lifelessly to the floor. He took up a seat, cursing to himself as he irritably wiped the blood and grey matter from his pristine, white shirt. He searched the control desk for autopilot mode. For a man with such an impressive collection of private jets, McKenzie surprisingly knew very little about how to operate one. He did, however, know that in an emergency, for which he felt this qualified, an aircraft could fly itself for some considerable time, giving him opportunity to contact the necessary people to talk him through landing the blasted thing.

Aki groaned on the floor beside him and he resisted the urge to put a bullet in her, kicking her in frustration instead. He'd deal with her later. She was silent once more. Women; they complicated the most simple of tasks. If this silly bitch hadn't made a rush for his weapon then it wouldn't have gone off, Hiro wouldn't be distributed all over the cockpit, and they wouldn't be in this mess. He stared at the control panels, attempting to make sense of the myriad lights and switches and buttons but reluctantly he was forced to concede he didn't have the first idea what he was doing. Randomly he began to press things and when nothing erratic happened he pressed more, flicking switches and lights with purpose. He hit the ALT mode and the aircraft began to descend rapidly, dropping vertically.

'Fucking hell!' McKenzie screamed, frantically pressing and flicking. What he didn't know was that when first turned on, the ALT mode immediately tries to maintain the current altitude of the aircraft and that this can cause serious control issues, particularly if the vessel is climbing or descending too rapidly. Shaking his head he thought he felt the plane steady itself for a moment and stopped pushing buttons. A light suddenly came on signalling that the aircraft was in 'Infinite flight Mode' and he felt the aircraft stabilise. He began to laugh manically.

'Eureka!' His warranted panic began to neutralise almost instantly, his heart rate beginning to slow down to a more natural rhythm. 'Thank fucking God for that!' he said aloud, just as Aki pulled the trigger at the back of his head.

CHAPTER FIFTY-EIGHT

'If I never fly again it will be a moment too soon,' Angelika said to no one in particular.

Kirkbride, as promised, had sent a plane for them. They were going home, although somehow the word meant something different to all of them now.

Rupert looked at Angelika. They had all been in complete shock but now it was starting to wear off…

'You had an abortion and never told me.'

'Yes,' she said quietly.

'Why?'

'Because … I don't really know, Rupert. Because something told me it was the right thing to do at the time…something inside told me it was.'

He looked down into his lap in resignation. This time there would be no smart comeback.

'Who is Michael Curtis?' There was no anger in her tone, just a deep sadness that had wrapped itself tightly around her throat like a vice. His denial and deception hurt beyond words, no one more so than himself, she could see, and so her anger had tempered more into pity for him really; for both of them.

Rupert stared at the cutting he still held between his fingers. There was no point in denial now; McKenzie had seen to all of it. He glanced over at Mia, slumped in her seat, still wearing in her finest evening attire, her crumpled face indicative of her once magnificent dress.

She briefly met his eyes and he saw the anguish in them as though it were his own. Sighing heavily he took a swig of champagne.

'He was Mia's driver during the trial,' he said. 'It was a dalliance …' He looked at her, met her in the eye. 'We were lovers, briefly.'

Angelika nodded. 'Lovers …' The word trailed from her lips and oddly she thought of a phrase she had remembered from the Bible. She'd read it as a child, many years ago now, and had largely forgotten it, but somehow these words came to her: 'the tongue is a small thing, but what enormous damage it can do.' It all made perfect sense to her now, the years of bitter resentment, his physical despondency, his growing indifference towards her.

'Yes,' he said, 'I'm gay, Angelika. I think I always have been.' He had said it aloud, thus making it real at last. Even if she could not understand, he hoped she would forgive in time, just as he hoped he could forgive himself, and even though her ensuing silence pained him, he felt a sense of release, even elation. Not because of a lack of consideration for her feelings but because there was nothing left to do. It was the truth: a *fait accompli*.

'We should prepare ourselves,' Angelika said eventually. She looked at Nate and wondered if he still wanted her with the fervour he had displayed in the boat the night before. 'Kirkbride has warned me that the paps are waiting for us by the truckload. None more than for you, Billie-Jo,' she added. 'We're famous now, international superstars by all accounts, whether we like it or not.' She supposed in a strange way they had all gotten what they wanted in the end: Billie-Jo would now have the fame she so desired; Mia and Nate had found each other; Joshua's band would attract huge attention on the back of the furore; and Rupert … she felt the pain burn inside her guts. Well, Rupert got to tell the truth about who he really was. So where did that leave her?

Nate suddenly seized her hand in his, in full view of everyone, though no one objected. This experience had pulled them all apart and thrown them back together in the strangest and most bizarre way. She took his hand gratefully and kissed it.

They didn't speak for the rest of the duration of the journey. There was no hate or animosity between them, just a collective sense of survival. The silent sense of comradery between them was almost palpable, each of them understanding the powerful connection they would have for life as a result of what they had experienced together. Angelika could not help but feel that even among the madness of it all – and the sadness – that somehow the wrongs had been righted and natural order restored. There had to be some good in that surely, because whatever else she understood in that moment as the plane finally began to make its descent onto home soil, she realised that wherever there was pleasure in life, there was always, inevitably, pain.

EPILOGUE

10 months later

'It's here,' Nate said smiling, handing her the envelope as he trotted out to join her on the patio where she'd been working and enjoying her favourite breakfast of fresh coffee, fruit and French toast.

'Wow, that really was quick,' she said, opening it, 'but then again I expected nothing less.'

He took a seat next to her, his hair still a little damp, his white T-shirt off-setting his suntanned skin. She loved him fresh from the shower; she loved him full stop.

Angelika looked at the decree absolute. The end of her marriage was right there: final, in black and white, stamped by someone deemed high enough to adjudicate such decisions. She wasn't sure how she really felt but it was something close to relief. There was no real bitterness, no anger, nothing but a sense of finality. She and Rupert had parted on the best terms as they could have, under the circumstances. In truth she had felt pity for him for having not been true to himself, or to her, for all of these years but it was hard to hate him; they had experienced so much of life together that she could not bring herself to regret, even if she struggled to forgive. Like her, being thrust into the public eye had been too much for Rupert to bear, the exposure just too intrusive, and as a result he had fled the UK for South

Africa with his son, Serg, for what he had called a 'life sabbatical'. She understood his need to escape the harsh glare of the media spotlight, to start over again. She would never forget him; a part of her would always love him in a strange way. But he was no longer the man she had married, perhaps he never really had been.

She stared at the official document for a few moments before folding it up and placing it back into the envelope. It was a glorious morning and the sun was high already as she gazed out across the patio at the tranquil setting, at the miles of spectacular Italian countryside below. She was happy here in Urbino; *they* were happy. The town, nestled on a high, sloping hillside, was as beautiful as it was historic, having been home to artistic greats such as Raphael, Botticelli and Piero della Francesca during the Renaissance period. It was peaceful and private and still retained much of its picturesque medieval charm. Their villa, perched atop a hill, was modest but stunning, with original wooden shutters that opened out onto the spectacular view and mosaic tiles on the walls. No one bothered them there; they were able to go about their day in relative obscurity, her with her writing and him with his photography. No one knew their story, and if they did then they certainly didn't remind them of it. It was the kind of town that was big enough for you disappear in, and remain anonymous – something with they were both content to be.

'How's the writing coming on?' he asked.

'It's getting there.' She smiled. 'I'll read you something if you like?'

'Yes, please.'

He studied her face, drinking in every part of her: her skin lightly sun-kissed; the faintest smattering of tiny freckles on the bridge of her nose which he was sure he'd never noticed until now; her long, wavy hair, which always looked as though she had just come back from the beach; and, of course, that snaggle tooth, the one at the front ... perfectly imperfect. She was a picture he would never tire of looking at, seeing something new in her every time.

'I have to say it's been quite cathartic so far,' she explained, 'and you never know, after this they might stop requesting interviews and finally leave us alone.'

The months following their return from Pleasure Island had passed in a blizzard of press attention of the like she had never seen, and that was some statement coming from a journalist. Nothing had prepared them for the media onslaught. The six of them had become an overnight sensation and the interest – particularly in her and Nate's budding romance – had been off the scale, eventually forcing them into hiding.

One small mercy was that the final act, as McKenzie had referred to it, had not been broadcast, thus sparing Nate and Mia from inadvertently sharing the revelation that she was his birth mother to the world. They had made a pact between them all to keep this information private, allow them to come to terms with the truth without the eyes of the world watching. Lord knows, everything else was out in the open, their tangled lives served up for scrutiny. It was a small victory perhaps, but a victory nonetheless.

Angelika sipped her coffee and gazed at Nate with loving eyes.

'Looks like Billie-Jo's having the time of her life,' she said, nodding to the newspaper on the table that contained his estranged wife's picture alongside the caption 'BillieJosh – the official on-tour pictures!' Angelika laughed. 'She's been on the front page pretty much every day since.'

Billie-Jo and Joshua – or 'Billiejosh' as they were now known in the press – in direct contrast to Nate and Angelika had positively relished the exposure in the wake of their ordeal, cashing in on their notoriety without regret. Billie-Jo's sex tape had jettisoned her into A-list territory, ranking her alongside the likes of Kim Kardashian, Paris Hilton and Pamela Anderson: a list she considered to be most illustrious indeed. Although at first Billie-Jo had been mortified by the fact the world had witnessed her sexual encounters on the island, not least because it had exposed her lack of moral compass, she had soon realised that there was a silver lining, *a platinum lining*, to such hideous intrusion.

The offers had subsequently flooded in: interviews; TV-show appearances; magazine spreads; modelling contracts … she'd been inundated. Even more sublime was the fact that she was, to all intents and purposes, largely perceived as a victim. After all she hadn't meant to make a sex tape, and certainly hadn't intended for it ever to be in the public domain. But it had been the biggest blessing in disguise, as now she and JJ were now the modern day Pammie and Tommy, a bona fide celebrity couple.

Her dreams had become reality: fame, money, notoriety, an agent and a rock-star boyfriend – perhaps she always would have realised her ambitions but Pleasure Island had certainly escalated the process for her and as much as she never wanted to relieve it, she could not regret it. She had even gone on record and finally spoken about the abuse she had suffered as a child and was working closely with a charity that helped survivors of similar backgrounds.

It had deeply saddened Nate to learn about Bee's suffering through the press; she had never opened up to him throughout their marriage but in a way her confession explained a lot. Nate supposed he was pleased for her of sorts; despite her infidelities he could not bring himself to hate her. Billie-Jo had got what she wanted, what she *needed*, at the end of the day. Then again, he supposed so had he.

'Any word from Mia?' Angelika asked.

'Actually, yes. I got a text. She and Richard are hoping to come and visit as soon as she's finished in the studio. She's been asked to act as one of the judges on the *Wow-Factor*.'

Angelika raised an eyebrow.

'Wow indeed! And …?'

'She says she's "considering her options, *darling*".'

The both laughed good-humouredly. Nate was beginning to come to terms with the knowledge that Mia was his mother, an idea that no longer seemed as shocking and preposterous as it initially had. He was happy for her that she had since been reunited with her ex-husband. Dickie had been waiting for Mia as she'd stepped off the plane.

'Good grief, woman,' he'd said as she had collapsed into his arms, 'no more drama, you said.'

'Where's your wife?' Mia had asked through her sobs.

'She ran off with someone … older,' he said. 'She couldn't bear being in your shadow any longer.'

'Oh, Richard.' Mia had held onto him so tightly he'd barely been able to draw breath comfortably.

'We're taking things slowly, darling … letting it happen organically,' Mia had told Nate in the text, though knowing Mia as he did, he doubted it. She'd had something of a career renaissance too, thanks to all the publicity, and had taken full advantage of the interest that surrounded her on the back of it by promptly bringing out a back catalogue of her music while promising a new album and tour.

'Strike while the iron's hot, my dear,' Bailey had advised her. Despite promising to, she had been unable to sack him in the end, silly old bastard; all those years counted for something, didn't they, even in the most uneasy of relationships?

In spite of how he had discovered the truth, Nate was now glad that he had. They were getting to know each other gently, establish a relationship and he was slowly, surely coming to accept Mia's explanations as to why she had given him up. It felt good to learn about his past, listen to the stories she had told him about family and relatives he'd never known, piece his life history together. He doubted he would ever call her 'mum' but he hadn't completely ruled the idea out; after all, above all people he knew that stranger things could, and did, happen.

'I think this is cause for celebration, what do you say?' He produced a bottle of Chateau d'Esclans Whispering Angel rose champagne from an ice bucket he'd deliberately hidden underneath the table earlier. It was the first time they'd drank champagne since they'd left the island.

'You planned this …' Angelika smiled at him through narrow eyes.

'Guilty as charged.' He grinned, popping the cork and messily filling two glasses.

'To being a free woman.' He touched her glass with his.

It sounded odd. She was no longer Mrs Angelika Deyton, no longer Rupert's wife. It felt good.

'No,' she said, 'let's not drink to my freedom. Let's drink to … Martin McKenzie.'

'McKenzie …?'

They had barely been able to bring themselves to say the man's name aloud in ten months, let alone raise a toast to him. The fact that Nate had discovered he was his biological father had been perhaps the most distressing of the whole sorry episode.

'What if I've got his twisted genes and just don't know it,' he'd said to Angelika earnestly one morning in bed together. 'What if his sickness is in my DNA?'

'Oh, Nate, darling.' Angelika had held him close, stroked his soft hair between her fingers. 'Remember what I said about nature, nurture that time on the island, down by the pool? No child is born evil.' She'd reassured him, though in truth she wasn't entirely convinced this was true; perhaps some people were born to develop into monsters, men like Martin McKenzie. Either way, she knew in her heart that the man lying next to her, whatever his biological provenance, was not one of them.

There had been no irony lost on the fact that McKenzie's fate had been to die in one of his own private jets, with the added bonus of a bullet to his brain. When the authorities had discovered the aircraft wreckage and the three bodies within it, part of Angelika couldn't help but feel cheated. By all accounts McKenzie's death had been mercifully swift, his suffering short-lived; he had died, somewhat ironically, in a plane crash and would never be held accountable, made to pay for his crimes or suffer the humiliation of his public fall from grace. Elaine's remains, a skull and some teeth, had been found washed up off the island of Santorini some months later. The coroner had recorded a verdict of suspicious death as it had been ascertained that she had received a large, blunt trauma to the side of her head prior to her death and was probably still alive when she'd hit the water. Poor Elaine; in a way she had been McKenzie's biggest victim of all.

'Why would you want to make a toast to *him*?'

She smiled at him, so handsome, so adoring and kind, so different to what she'd always known. Angelika opened her laptop and began to read.

'Chapter One: I suppose if nothing else it will make the ultimate story for the grandchildren one day when they ask, "how did you and granddad meet?" I'll admit I have pre-empted this question, given much thought as to how, when that times comes, to answer them, to make sense of the nonsensical, explain the unexplainable. It's usual for a writer to place their ac-knowledgments at the end of a book, but I no longer care much for protocol these days and so I would like to start by thanking Martin McKenzie. Now I know what you may be thinking, why on earth should I show a man like that any gratitude whatso-ever, so let me explain: without Martin McKenzie I would not be sitting here with the love of my life, on the balcony of our modest-yet-charming home, sipping on a glass of the local wine – just the one glass, mind, now that I'm in the family way... '

Nate's eyes widened and he almost spat out his champagne.

'You're kidding me … you're pregnant?'

His expression had been even more priceless than she'd imag-ined.

'Yes!' She giggled. 'We're having a baby.'

He scooped her up into his arms and she squealed.

'A baby … my God, I love you, Ange.' He kissed her lips and they tasted of French toast and champagne.

'I love you too, Nate,' she said as he carried her from the patio into the bedroom and laid her softly down onto the bed.

'Mmm,' she murmured as he gently untied her silky robe to expose her naked skin beneath and began to kiss her neck.

She thought once more about the pleasure/pain principle, how one could not seemingly exist without the other, the yin to its yang, only she had a suspicion that there would be far more of the former than the latter in her life now. She was done with pain; from now on it was going to be pleasure all the way.

LETTER FROM ANNA-LOU WEATHERLEY

I would like to take this opportunity to thank you, dear reader, for choosing *Pleasure Island*, I truly hope you gained as much pleasure reading it as I did writing it. In many ways, this book saved me as it was written during a difficult time in my life, but as the old adage says, where there's pleasure, there's pain!

One of my favourite things about being an author is receiving feedback and comments from you, the people who read my books. Your reactions are very important to me and I'd love to know what you thought about *Pleasure Island*. Who was your favourite character and why? Were you routing for Angelika and Nate and the sexual tension between them? Did McKenzie give you the chills, or did you love Billie-Jo's flawed naughtiness? Did you guess that Mia and Nate were linked and did you fall in love with the island itself? Did you expect the twists and turns that I so enjoyed creating for you?

These, among others, are things **I would love to know so if you enjoyed the story it would be fabulous if you could leave a review** and let me, and others know why. Your feedback means everything to me and if it encourages others to read one of my novels and share the pleasure (or pain) then that's wonderful and I thank you in advance.

If you want to keep up-to-date on my new releases, or view my past ones, just enter the link below to sign up for my special newsletter.

annalouweatherley.com/email

You'll need to give your email but I will never share it with anyone and only contact you when I have a new release, promise.

I'm busy writing my next novel, another dark, delectable tale filled with fabulously flawed characters, sinful secrets, deception, unexpected twists, drama and suspense. I hope you're going to love it! I will keep you posted.

Much love,

Anna-Lou x

 @annaloulondon

www. annalouweatherley.com

Printed in Great Britain
by Amazon

21584928R00224